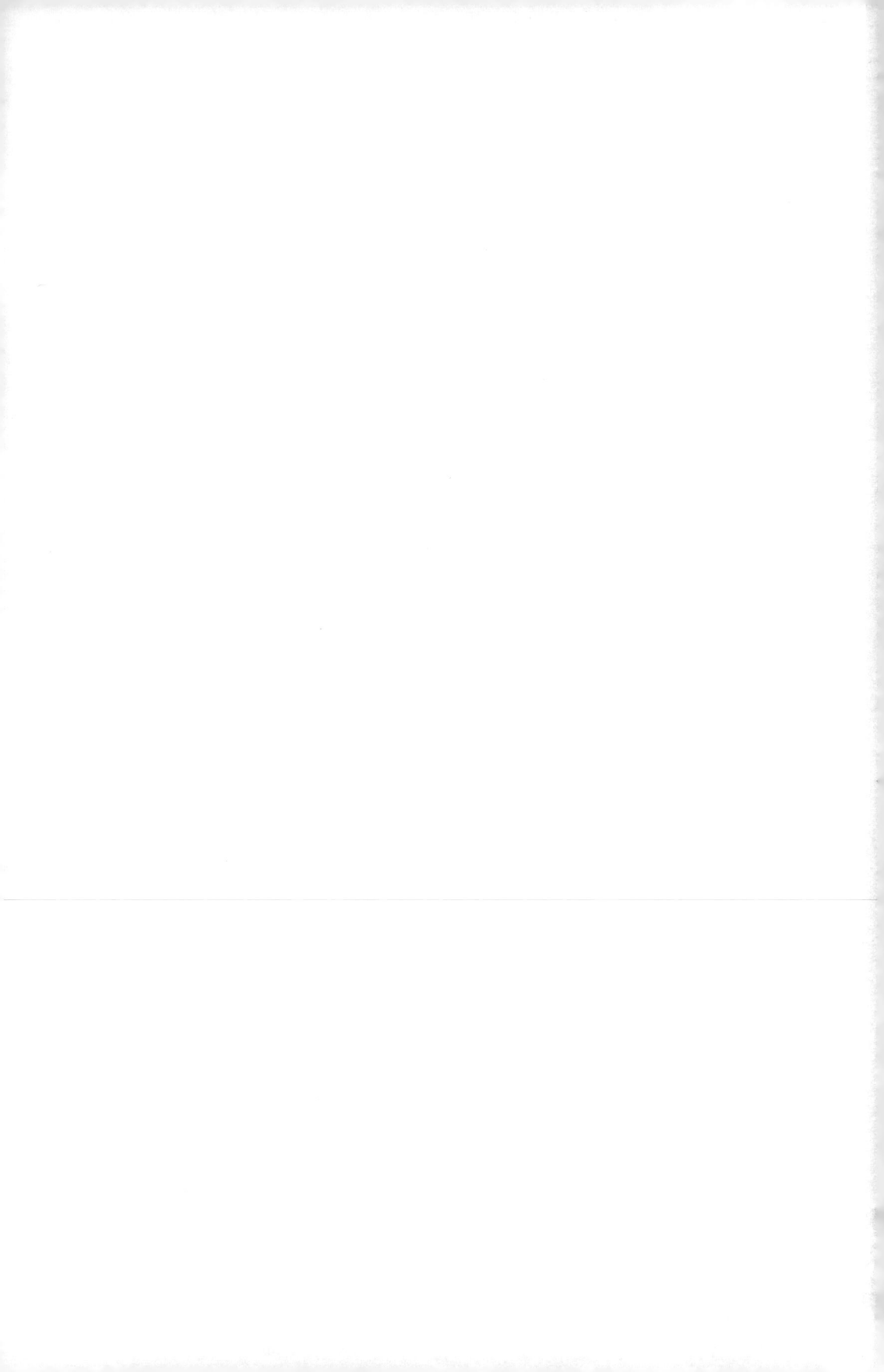

TOO MANY MURDERS

COLLEEN McCULLOUGH

Too Many Murders

HarperCollins*Publishers*

HarperCollins*Publishers*
77–85 Fulham Palace Road,
Hammersmith, London W6 8JB

www.harpercollins.co.uk

Published by HarperCollins*Publishers* 2010
1

A catalogue record for this book
is available from the British Library

ISBN (HB): 978 0 00 727185 6
ISBN (TPB): 978 0 00 731119 4

This novel is entirely a work of fiction.
The names, characters and incidents portrayed in it are
the work of the author's imagination, and, while
historical characters make appearances in the book,
this is a fictionalised account.

Set in Aldine by Palimpsest Book Production Limited,
Grangemouth, Stirlingshire

Printed and bound in Great Britain by
Clays Ltd, St Ives plc

Mixed Sources
Product group from well-managed
forests and other controlled sources
www.fsc.org Cert no. SW-COC-001806
© 1996 Forest Stewardship Council
FSC

FSC is a non-profit international organisation established
to promote the responsible management of the world's forests.
Products carrying the FSC label are independently certified
to assure consumers that they come from forests that are managed
to meet the social, economic and ecological needs
of present and future generations.

Find out more about HarperCollins and the environment at
www.harpercollins.co.uk/green

For WAYDE

loyal, loving, kind, generous

The best son a father was ever gifted with.

TOO MANY
MURDERS

April 1967

Mr. Evan Pugh   April 3, 1967
Paracelsus College
Chubb University
Holloman, Conn.

Dear Mr. Pugh,
    I concede defeat. Your $100,000 has been placed in your
room at college, as stipulated in your letter of March
29th. I will ensure that my presence in college seems
innocent if I am detected. Please do not attempt to obtain
more money from me. My pockets are empty.

                                    Yours sincerely,
                                    Motor Mouth

E van Pugh's hands were shaking as he read
this missive, put in his pigeonhole in a plain
white envelope bearing his name and ad-
dress typed with a carbon ribbon, like the letter. The dark square
aperture of his pigeonhole had been empty every time he looked between going downstairs for his breakfast and the end of lunch. Now,
at two thirty, he had his answer!
    The corridors were empty as he wended his way up one curving

set of open stairs at his end of the foyer; Paracelsus was a new college, of gloriously clean and sweeping lines, and had been designed by a world-famous architect who was a Chubb alumnus. It suffered the bleak austerity of his style too: Vermont marble floors and walls, glass-enclosed pebble gardens too small to enter, white lighting, minimal ornamentation. Upstairs, where Evan's dormitory was located, the white marble was replaced by grey-painted walls and a grey rubber floor—very practical, but airy and spacious. As were the rooms, for which reason Paracelsus's inmates loved their architect dearly. Of course, he himself had suffered the horrors of sharing a cubicle in a college built in 1788, so he had endowed Paracelsus with big rooms and plenty of bathrooms.

Upstairs was deserted too. Evan sidled along the corridor and let himself into his quarters with a swift glance around to make sure that his roommate, Tom Wilkinson, was in class with the rest of the sophomores in this wing of a pre-med oriented college. You had to be sure: even earnest types like pre-meds sometimes cut class. But he was alone. He was safe.

Amazingly, the room wasn't cluttered. Both young men owned cars, so no bicycles were in evidence, and the floor was free of the usual heaps of boxes students seemed to accumulate. A floor-to-ceiling bookcase separated their big desks, above which were the windows, and the oversized single beds stood one to either side of the entrance door. In each long wall was another door. Wilkinson, a joyous youth, had stuck posters of sexy movie stars on his walls, but Evan Pugh's were bare save for a corkboard on which were pinned notes and a few photographs.

He went straight to his desk; its surface was exactly as he had left it all day. None of its drawers was locked. Evan opened each one in turn and went through it, debating how large the bundle of cash might be. That depended upon the denomination of the notes, he concluded as he closed the last drawer. No cash, no bundle of any size. He looked across at his bed, a tangle of sheets and blankets, then went to it and rummaged fiercely from top to bottom—no bundle of cash on it, in it, or under it.

Next he checked the bookshelves with the same result, after which he stood wondering how he had been such a fool. How would his quarry know which side of the room was his? Or even that there were sides? Tom was untidy, but a careful ransacking of every part of his side revealed no bundle.

Remained only the closets. This time Evan went through Tom's first, without success. Then he opened the door to his own. In these walk-in closets the architect's true genius showed best, for he was one of those men who never forgot any aspect of his past, nor failed to understand how much junk young men—and women!—could accumulate during the course of a year occupying the same room. The walk-in closets ran the full length of the room and were three feet wide; at one end were racks of drawers, then came open shelves, then, for a full half of the area, vacant space. Only in the matter of lighting were they poorly equipped, as a result of the Dean's fear of fire in an enclosed area. Twenty-five-watt bulbs, no brighter! On springs, the doors closed after they were opened, yet another crotchet of the Dean's; he abhorred disorder and deemed open doors and drawers a danger as well as a legal liability.

Evan flicked the closet light on and stepped inside; the door swung shut behind him, but he was used to that. He saw the bundle at once, hanging from the ceiling on a cord. He rushed to it eagerly, not surprised that his victim had chosen to secrete it inside an inside, nor that it hung in an area where there were no drawers or shelves. He didn't look up at the ceiling; he looked no higher than the bundle, which even in the dim light he could see was bound tightly in Saran Wrap. The notes showed through clearly: hundred-dollar bills. They seemed new, their edges unswollen by the abuse of many fingers as they sat in a neat, flat brick.

Suddenly, his hands already grabbing at the brick, he stopped a moment to contemplate the magnitude of his coup, the triumph he couldn't confide to anyone else as long as he wanted to blackmail Motor Mouth. *Did* he want to continue the blackmail? After all, he didn't need the money; it was simply his choice of weapon. What he reveled in was the knowledge that he, Evan Pugh, a mere nineteen-year-old Chubb sophomore, had the power to torment another human being to the point of extreme mental torture. Oh, it was *sweet!* Of course he'd go on blackmailing Motor Mouth!

His movement resumed, he took hold of the plastic-wrapped packet. When it didn't budge he yanked at it sharply, an impatient jerk that saw it come away, drop downward to his hips. His hands followed, unwilling to give up their prize.

In the same instant there was a loud sound incorporating both a roar and a swish. As the terrible pain invaded his upper arms and chest, Evan genuinely thought he had been bitten by a *Tyrannosaurus rex.* He dropped the brick of money and clutched at whatever was engulfing him, his fingers closing on cold steel fixed in his flesh—not one, but a whole row of daggers, deep in his flesh, down past the bone.

The shock had been too sudden for a scream, but now he began to scream shrilly, hoarsely, wondering why his mouth was full of foam, but screaming, screaming, screaming . . .

The noise percolated out of the closet into the room, but there was no one present to hear it. That it didn't penetrate into the corridor was due to the architect, very much aware of soundproofing, and endowed besides with a bounteous budget. The Parsons wished something really first class if they had to part with a Rodin and some Henry Moores. Those couldn't possibly be housed in or near *rubbish.*

It took Evan Pugh two hours to die, his lifeblood leaking away, his legs refusing to work, his breathing one distressed gasp after another. His only consolation as consciousness left him was that the police would find the money and Motor Mouth's letter, still in his pocket.

*   *   *

"I don't believe it!" Captain Carmine Delmonico exclaimed. "And the day isn't even over yet. What time is it, for God's sake?"

"Getting on for six thirty," came Patrick O'Donnell's voice from inside the closet. "As you well know."

Carmine stepped through the door, with its spring now disconnected, and into a surreal scene that looked as if it had been posed for Major Minor's waxworks horror museum. Patsy had put two small klieg lights in the closet to replace the gloom of the Dean's twenty-five-watt bulb, and every part of the interior was ablaze. The body took his eye first, hanging limply from the low ceiling, its upper arms and chest cruelly gripped in the jaws of something akin to a great white shark's business end, but made of rusting steel.

"Jesus!" he breathed, carefully walking around as much of the body as he could. "Patsy, have you ever seen anything like this! And what the hell is it?"

"A king-sized bear trap, I think," said Patsy.

"A bear trap? In Connecticut? Except maybe for somewhere up in Canada or hillbilly country, there hasn't been a bear this side of the Rockies in a hundred years." He peered closely at the youth's upper chest, where the teeth had sunk in clear to the metal giving rise to them. "Though I guess," he added like an afterthought, "there might be a few people with one of these tucked away in a forgotten corner of a barn."

He stood back while Patrick finished his examination, then the two men looked at each other.

"I'm going to have to take the whole thing," Patrick said. "I don't dare pry him loose inside this closet—that thing must have a spring capable of taking a hand clean off if it gets away on us halfway through being forced open. This ceiling is much lower than the room's, but there's got to be a beam. What fun!"

"It's not screwed down, it's bolted," Carmine said, "so a beam there must be. Chain saw time? Collapse of building?" He saw the plastic-wrapped packet and bent to inspect it. "Hmm . . . Curiouser and curiouser, Patsy. Unless the interior is blank paper, this is a lot of money. Bait for the greedy. The kid saw it, made a grab for it, and literally sprung the trap."

Having ascertained that, Carmine's eyes took in the rest of the closet, which would have been a dream come true to a student, he reflected. Fifteen feet long, three feet wide, one end a bank of built-in drawers, next to them a series of open shelves, and the rest of the space given over to the storage of boxes, unwanted junk, the usual student impedimenta. The bear trap had been fixed over clear floor, not hard; the owner of the closet was neat and tidy.

"The guy who put the bear trap up knew his construction," he said. "The bolts must be fixed in a joist or beam. The thing didn't move a fraction of an inch when it was sprung."

"Well, at least it is sprung, Carmine. My guys will be able to detach it. Have you seen enough?"

"I guess so. But do you believe this, Patsy?"

"No. This one makes twelve inside eighteen hours."

"I'll see you in the morgue."

Carmine's cohorts, Abe Goldberg and Corey Marshall, were standing by Evan Pugh's desk looking dazed.

"Twelve, Carmine?" Corey asked as Carmine joined them.

"Twelve, and almost all different. Though this one takes the grand prize, guys—a bear trap. The victim's a skinny milquetoast, so it crushed him hard enough to kill him."

"Twelve!" said Abe in tones of wonder. "Carmine, in all the history of Holloman, there have never been twelve murders in one day. Four was tops when those biker gangs had a shoot-out in the Chubb Bowl parking lot, and that was simple, not even much of a surprise. You cleared it up in less than a week."

"Well, I doubt I'm going to do the same here," Carmine said, looking grim.

"No," said both his sergeants in chorus.

"Still," said Abe, trying to comfort his boss, "not all the cases are yours. I know Mickey McCosker and his team can't be spared from their drug investigation, but Larry Pisano is already working the shootings. That's three down, only nine to go with this one."

"They're all mine, Abe, you know that. I'm captain of detectives. What it's going to mean is that each of you gets one victim to work—you know my methods better than Larry's boys." He frowned. "But not tonight. Go home, have a decent home-cooked feed and a good sleep. The Commissioner's office at nine in the morning, okay?"

They nodded and left.

Carmine dallied, taking in the relatively spacious student room, and the rather glaring disparity between his murder victim's side and the side belonging to the young man who had found him.

Tom Wilkinson was waiting in a room set aside by the Dean as his temporary quarters; one of Patsy's technicians had escorted him into his own digs once a sheet was up over Evan's closet door, and supervised his selection of clothes, books, oddments. After a look at the technician's list, Carmine went back to examining the room. The two young men may as well have painted a line down its middle, so different were the two sides. Tom was haphazard and untidy, including the interior of his closet, whereas Evan Pugh was an obsessive. Even the notes pinned to his corkboard were squared off and neat. A quick perusal of them betrayed no hint as to why he had been murdered; they were just reminders to pick up his dry cleaning on such-and-such a date, shop for stamps, new socks, stationery. The photographs were all of a warmer place than Holloman—palm trees, brightly colored houses, beaches. And a mansion outside which a man and woman in their forties stood, clad in evening dress and looking prosperous.

When the desk yielded nothing further, Carmine went to see Tom Wilkinson, sitting miserably on the side of his new bed. He was very different from Evan Pugh, a single glance showed that: tall, handsome in a blond way, athletic, with wide blue eyes that stared at Carmine in a mixture of fear, horror and curiosity. Not the eyes of a bear trap killer, Carmine decided. The young fellow was cheaply dressed—no camelhair and cashmere here.

He tried not to babble his story of the blood leaking out of Evan's closet, his calling to Evan, the lack of an answer, his opening of the closet door. After that he found it harder to be logical, but Carmine gave him time to recover, then learned that Tom hadn't lingered to ascertain any details of the mess inside. Some pre-meds might have; a ghoulish tendency often went with the territory. If he had seen the money, he wasn't admitting it, and Carmine was inclined to believe that he hadn't. This pre-med student was scraping to find the money to stay at Paracelsus and would have been sorely tempted to filch the packet before anyone else knew it was there. He bore no blood on his clothes, and he had stepped around the puddle when he entered the closet. On his way out he hadn't been as careful, but the path guy who escorted him back into the room had taken his sneakers, he explained, wriggling his toes through the holes in his socks. The sneakers were new, he'd miss them, so—um—? Carmine found himself promising to have the shoes returned as soon as possible.

"Did you like your roommate?" Carmine asked.

"No," said Tom bluntly.

"Why?"

"Aw, gee, he was such a *weed!*"

"You don't look like a judgmental type, Tom."

"I'm not, and I could deal with a weed, Captain, if he was an ordinary weed. But Evan wasn't. He was so—full of himself! I mean, he weighed about ninety pounds soaking wet and had a face like Miss Prissy out of a Foghorn Leghorn cartoon. But he didn't believe he looked weird! To hear him talk, you'd get the impression that guys who weigh ninety pounds soaking wet and have faces like Miss Prissy are just what the doctor ordered. He had a hide so thick a naval shell couldn't dent it!"

"That's thick," said Carmine solemnly. "What was he like in class? Did he get good grades?"

"A-pluses in everything," said Tom despondently. "He headed the

10

class, even drew better than the rest of us. We got sick of seeing his drawing of a dogfish's cranial nerves or an ox's eyeball being held up as examples of what anatomical drawing ought to be like! Man, he was a pain! It would have been okay, except that he rubbed it in, especially to guys like me on scholarship. I mean, I'll probably have to go into the army or navy to get out from under debt, which gouges a hole in the years I'll have left to practice for myself."

"Did he socialize with his classmates?"

"Hell, no! Evan did weird things, like go to New York City to see an opera or some highbrow play. He never missed an avant-garde movie at the Chubb Film Society, bought tickets to charity banquets or those speech nights at country clubs when some kiss-ass politician was the speaker—weird! Then he'd bend our ears afterward as though the rest of us were peasants. I guess if anything surprises me, it's that no one here at Paracelsus has ever beat the shit out of him."

"Did he keep regular hours? Snore? Have unpleasant—er—personal habits of any kind?"

Tom Wilkinson looked blank. "No, but yes to the regular hours. Unless you call his conceit and bragging unpleasant."

"What time did you discover him?"

"About six. I have a car because it means I can get back to college for lunch and dinner. Cafeteria meals on Science Hill are expensive, and my sister gave me her old clunker when she bought a better car. Gas is dirt cheap, and my meals here are part of my room and board. The food's good too. I finished a physiology class in the Burke Biology Tower at five thirty, then drove home."

"Are most of your classes on Science Hill?"

"Sure, especially for a genuine pre-med. We have a couple of—um—dilettantes in our sophomore year who take art history and crap like that, but they go elsewhere for classes as well. The closest thing to a classroom Paracelsus has is a lecture theater that the Dean saves for sermons on untidiness and vandalism."

"Vandalism?"

"Oh, that's just the Dean. The freshmen get a bit restive and do things like chuck dirty old house bricks into Piero Conducci's pebble gardens; they have to use a cherry picker to get them out. I wouldn't call putting whore's underwear on a nude lady's statue vandalism, sir. Would you?"

"Probably not," said Carmine, straight-faced. "I take it that all the students in your wing are sophomores, Tom?"

"Yes, sir. Four wings, one for each year. Evan and I have an upstairs room, but down below us are more sophomores."

"So, given that the emphasis is on pre-med, that means the wing is deserted between lunch and around six in the evening?"

"Yeah, it is. If someone's too sick to go to classes, he's supposed to be in sick bay, where there's a nurse. Sometimes a guy cuts classes to catch up on an important assignment, but there's nothing like that on our schedule at the moment, sir."

"What about mornings?"

"The same, only shorter. I think the Dean tries to get the tradesmen in during the morning, so he can keep a better eye on them."

Carmine rose. "Thanks, Tom. I wish all my witnesses were half as candid. Go and have some dinner, even if you don't feel like eating."

From there it was off downstairs to see Dean Robert Highman. As Carmine descended the graceful but open staircase (he loathed stairs he could see through, like these), he stopped to take in the nucleus of Paracelsus College's broad, squat X. Each wing was devoted to student accommodation, but the center contained the offices and apartments of the college's senior faculty. The Dean and Bursar lived in commodious quarters here; though the four year Fellows each lived in a kitchenless apartment at the far end of the four wings, the four similar units adjacent to the nucleus were occupied by postdoctoral Fellows who had nothing to do with the college's administration.

The offices were downstairs, the Dean's and Bursar's apartments upstairs. The foyer was relatively large and quite deserted at this dinner hour; the open counter where a clerk worked during office hours was unmanned, and the offices clearly visible through glass walls were equally empty.

Resuming his descent, Carmine stopped short of the counter and debated how he was going to locate the Dean. A cheerful buzz emanated from the opposite side of the nucleus, where the dining room and common rooms were located. Sighing, Carmine girded his loins for a sortie into the midst of four hundred eating young men, but it never happened. A short, fussy man in a three-piece suit emerged from the dining side entrance, took Carmine in at a glance, and walked toward him. He had the gait of a duck, though he wasn't overweight. Just knock-kneed. His face was round and ruddy, his brown hair scant but assiduously brushed to hide as much scalp as possible, and his dark brown eyes held a flash that told Carmine he was capable of cowing most of Paracelsus's inmates. No one could have called him handsome.

"Dean Highman," said Carmine, shaking hands. Good, firm grip.

"Come upstairs to my apartment," the Dean said, lifting the flap of the counter and unlocking a glass door. Once through that, they ascended to the second floor in a tiny elevator, a smoother ride than tiny elevators usually gave.

"Dean Dawkins—Paracelsus's first dean and my predecessor— was a paraplegic," Highman explained as they floated upward, "but his qualifications outweighed both his handicap and the cost of in- stalling this." A soft chuckle. "Princeton thought it had him."

"Eat your heart out, Princeton," said Carmine, grinning.

"Are you a Chubber, Captain?"

"Yes, Class of Forty-eight."

"Ah! Then you were one of the young men who defended our beloved country. But you must have started before the war."

"Yes, in September of 1939. I enlisted straight after Pearl Harbor, so I lost my credits for the fall of 1941. Not that I cared. The Japs and the Nazis came first."

"Married?"

"Yes."

"Children?"

"A girl by a previous marriage, Sophia, now sixteen, and a son five months old," said Carmine, wondering who was conducting this interrogation.

"His name?"

"Still undecided."

"Oh, dear! Is that a serious marital contretemps?"

"No, more an ongoing, good-natured argument."

"She'll win, Captain, she'll win! They always do."

Dean Highman settled his guest in a leather chair and went to the bar cart. "Sherry? Scotch? Whiskey?"

"You didn't offer me gin, Dean."

"You don't look or act like a gin man."

"How right you are! Whiskey will do fine, thanks. Soda and ice, and drown it."

"Still on duty, eh?" The Dean sat down with his own generous glass of sherry. "Ask away, Captain."

"I gather from Mr. Pugh's roommate, Mr. Wilkinson, that the college is deserted during class hours?"

"Absolutely. Any student found wandering the corridors during class hours is certain to be queried. Not that it happens often. Paracelsus was built and endowed specifically for pre-med students by the Parson Foundation."

Carmine pulled a face. "Oh, that bunch!"

"You speak as one who knows them."

"I was involved in a case the year before last that had to do with one of their endowed facilities."

"Yes, the Hug," said Dean Highman, nodding wisely. "I do sincerely trust that the murder of Mr. Pugh does *not* embroil Paracelsus in that kind of disaster."

"I doubt it, Dean, beyond what leaks to the press and other media

14

about the circumstances of Mr. Pugh's death. Rest assured that we'll be trying to tone down our releases."

The Dean leaned forward, his sherry forgotten. "I am smitten with fear, Captain. How did Mr. Pugh die?"

"Between the teeth of a bear trap rigged in his closet."

The ruddy face paled, and the sherry stood in danger of slopping until the Dean lifted the glass to his lips and drank it off in a gulp. "Ye gods! Christ almighty! *Here?* In Paracelsus?"

"Yes, I'm afraid so."

"But—but—what can we do? I swear no one saw anything odd today! I've asked, I do assure you!" the Dean bleated.

"I understand that, but tomorrow there will be detectives back to ask a lot more questions on the subject, Dr. Highman. For which reason, I'd like to make sure that every single member of your staff, including janitors, trash collectors, gardeners, maids and other non-faculty be present all day. They'll all have to answer questions. No one will be treated harshly, but every last one will be seen individually," said Carmine, voice steely.

"I understand," said the Dean, sounding as if he did.

"How well did you know Evan Pugh, Dean?"

Highman frowned, licked his lips, and decided to pour himself another glass of sherry. "Evan Pugh was a difficult young man," he said, back in his chair and sipping gratefully. "I am afraid that no one either knew him—or, perhaps more important, liked him. I have dealt with youths and young men for many years, but the Evan Pughs of my acquaintance have been few. Very few. I am rather at a loss to describe his personality, except to say that it was—repugnant. I don't claim to be au fait with modern science, but I have read of substances called pheromones. They are emitted, as I understand it, to attract others, particularly of the opposite sex. The pheromones Evan Pugh emitted repelled." He shrugged, took a gulp of sherry. "More than that I cannot tell you, Captain. I didn't really know him at all."

Carmine lingered until he finished his drowned drink, chatting with the Dean about his college's endowment by the Parson clan, whose charities—amounting to millions upon millions—were always oriented toward something medical. Roger Parson Sr.'s choice of Piero Conducci as architect did not surprise him; had the younger members of the clan had their way, he was sure Paracelsus would have gone to a more conservative designer. It must have hurt them hugely to have to give up their edition of the *Burghers of Calais*, but yield it they had; it stood at the junior/senior end of the X nucleus, ensconced in one of Conducci's glass-walled, pebbled gardens, and it looked as stunning as a Rodin should.

"I imagine," said the captain of detectives gravely, "that any cherry pickers in the vicinity of Paracelsus are stringently policed."

"They would be, had any materialized, but I'm delighted to say that none ever has. There are many other works of art at Chubb far easier to steal than our Rodin."

"And there'll be still more, when the museum of Italian art goes up—lots of Canalettos and Titians will come out of the vaults. If, that is, the Thanassets can ever decide where their museum ought to go," said Carmine.

"A great university," said the Dean ponderously, "should *swim* in works of art! I thank God every night for Chubb."

Thus it was a little after eight when Carmine strolled into the Medical Examiner's segment of the County Services building on Cedar Street. The ME was his first cousin, though no observer would ever have picked up on the blood relationship from visual inspection. Patrick was blue-eyed and auburn-haired, with a fair, freckled skin; Carmine had dark amber eyes and black, waving hair that he kept disciplined by cutting it short. They were the children of the sisters Cerutti, one of whom had married an O'Donnell, the other a Delmonico. Though Patrick was ten years older than Carmine and the happily married father of six children, no difference could ever diminish the huge love that existed between them. An only son, Carmine had been rendered fatherless in his thirteenth year, the smothered darling of a widowed mother and four older sisters with no masculine leavening to help him survive until twenty-two-year-old Patsy stepped in to fill the breach. It was not a paternal relationship, however; they felt like brothers.

Coroner as well as Medical Examiner, Patrick had managed to pile most of his court duties on the back of his deputy coroner, Gustavus Fennel, who loved appearing in court and conducted a running feud with His Honor Douglas Thwaites, Holloman's cantankerous district judge. Patrick was completely enamored of the new science of forensics, and kept his department absolutely up to date on all advances made in that captious discipline, with its blood types, serums, hairs, fibers, anything that a criminal might leave behind as a signature. His perpetual headache was lack of funds to buy analytical equipment, but in the wake of the dissolution of the medical research center known as the Hug, the Parsons had given him an electron microscope, a Zeiss operating microscope, several other specialist microscopes, new spectrometers and a gas chromatograph. These, together with the latest centrifuges and other, more minor apparatus that found their way from the Hug to him, had enabled him to assemble the best criminal pathology lab in the state, and—a curious side effect—had predisposed Hartford to consent to demands for further equipment. To be dowered so lavishly by the Parsons obviously gained anyone brownie points with the Governor, was Patrick's explanation.

The morgue itself was stuffed with gurneys, something that happened only as a consequence of airline disasters or multivehicle road accidents. But not tonight. Each of these silent, still, draped figures was a murder victim. Added to them were the other bodies requiring a coroner's attention: inexplicable deaths, those whose doctor refused to sign a death certificate, and any death the police considered warranted autopsy.

There were a series of stainless steel doors in one wall, a total of sixteen altogether, and the room was a hushed hive of industry as two technicians worked to clear autopsied bodies out of the drawers while not confusing them with murder victims and others as yet un-inserted into drawers. Outside on the loading dock, Carmine knew, there would be vans or retired hearses sent from funeral homes to pick up released bodies, their crews grumbling at the ME's insistence that they come right now, at once, no delay!

He walked through into the autopsy suite, where Patrick stood at the side of a long stainless-steel table fitted with a huge sink at one end and drain channels along either side. A pair of ordinary whole-sale meat scales hung in a convenient spot, and several carts of covered instruments were arranged nearby.

Evan Pugh had been freed from the bear trap; it lay on a marble-topped bench some distance away, fenced off by carts. Carmine went to it first and stood staring at it, too wise to touch it. If Patsy had erected a fence around it, then it was highly dangerous. Spread out, as it was now, it was fully two feet wide at its hinged base, its stained, terrible teeth a good two inches long. Not barbed, not serrated, just knife-sharp. The base, which had been bolted to the closet ceiling, was wide enough for a man to put his feet on, one to either side of the hinge—the usual way, Carmine concluded, for its user to pull it apart and set it. There were six bolt holes, three in either side plate, marking the middle and each end. These had not been a part of the trap when it was made but had been added very recently. Every other surface was well rusted, whereas the holes gleamed with fresh metal. The killer had reamed them out himself.

"Don't even breathe on it, Carmine," Patrick said from the table. "It's on a hair trigger, and I'm not exaggerating. Whoever cleaned it up for this exercise used naval jelly on the spring to remove the rust and adjusted the pressure on the plate to trigger it with any old kind of tug, even from a weakling like our victim. What fascinates me is the size of the killer's balls, to handle his device so coolly that he was able to screw his bolts in all the way to their heads without setting it off. Jesus! I break out in a sweat just thinking about it."

Carmine moved to the table. "Any clues, Patsy?"

"A couple of doozies, actually. Here, read this. It was in his pants pocket."

"Well, it sure answers a lot," Carmine said, putting the clear plastic envelope back among Pugh's other possessions. "Among other things, it explains the money. Have you opened the package? Does it contain a hundred grand?"

"I don't know. I thought I'd save that treat for you. I did wash the blood off it and remove the first layer of wrap, though I doubt I'll find any prints on it apart from Pugh's."

Carmine took the brick and a pair of utility scissors and sliced the food wrap's many layers down to bedrock. Expecting blank paper beneath an outer layer of real notes, he was astonished to find that every note was a genuine hundred-dollar bill. There had been an outbreak of counterfeit hundred-dollar bills a year ago and he had been shown what to look for, but these were genuine. What kind of blackmail victim could afford to drop a thousand C-notes in the course of a murder?

"The money only complicates matters," he said, putting it in a steel dish and lidding it before peeling off his gloves. "There is a hundred thousand here, brand-new, but the numbers aren't fully consecutive. I'll have to hand it over to the Feds to find out its origins." He leaned his rump on a wall sink and contemplated the money dish sourly. "Motor Mouth . . . I wonder what Motor Mouth said to warrant not only murder but the sacrifice of so much money? Whoever he is, he knew he had no hope of retrieving his outlay—or his letter. Which says he's not worried, that he doesn't think we stand a chance of discovering his real name or what the subject of the blackmail was."

"Blackmail aside, Carmine, one motive is hate," said Patsy, inserting a probe inside one vicious chest wound. "The object here is physical agony, a slow death."

"But not a public lesson."

"No. A private vendetta. Motor Mouth isn't concerned about the details of his crime becoming public, but all his spleen was directed at Evan Pugh. Whoever he is, he's not an attention seeker."

"I'm guessing this was Pugh's first attempt at blackmail. Man, I'd love to get my hands on Pugh's letter of March twenty-ninth!" Carmine clenched his hands. "But Motor Mouth will have burned it. Say he got it on March twenty-ninth. That means he cooked up this incredible retaliation within four or five days. And he must know Pugh left no evidence of the blackmail behind. So it's not pictures, letters, memos, anything visual or auditory. Pugh had no safety deposit key, even one he'd think was cunningly hidden. No bus or train station locker key either. Of course he might have sent something to his parents, but I'm guessing he didn't."

"Oh, come on, Carmine!" Patsy objected. "Where blackmail is concerned, there's always physical evidence, even if it's no more than a written description of an incident."

"Not here," said Carmine, straightening. "I'm convinced that Motor Mouth acted with total security. Now that Pugh's dead, no threat remains. The blackmail evidence died with him."

"Cop instinct?" Patsy asked.

Halfway to the door, Carmine paused. "How are you coping with the chaos?"

"First off, no outside referrals for the moment. The last of our already autopsied cases will have gone to their funeral homes by ten tonight, and that will give us room to accommodate the murder victims plus whatever I couldn't deflect," Patrick said. "I'm sending Gus and his boys to the North Holloman labs to do outside cases there until my crisis evaporates."

"Poor Gus! North Holloman is a dump." Carmine resumed his progress. "Meeting in Silvestri's office nine tomorrow, okay?"

The lights of Holloman's east shore were twinkling in and out of the wealth of trees for which Holloman was famous as Carmine parked his Ford Fairlane on East Circle shortly before nine that night. Strictly speaking, the vehicle was a police unmarked, with a souped-up V-8 engine and cop springs and shocks, but it didn't look the part; since attaining captain's rank, Carmine got a last year's model every year, so it bore none of the stigmata of the usual cop unmarked. He took the sloping, curving flagged path down to his front door, tried the knob, and let himself in. Desdemona didn't bother locking doors, correctly reasoning that it would be a very rare criminal who entered Captain Delmonico's residence. Reasoning like that wouldn't have held water in a larger city, but everyone in Holloman knew where Carmine lived, which had its disadvantages but also its advantages.

His women were assembled in the kitchen, a large one permitting them to dine in it if they had no guests, thus saving the formal dining room and Carmine's exquisite Lalique table with matching chandelier for more festive occasions. The kitchen was pure white and clinically clean; in the matter of domestic decor Carmine's second wife had deferred to his taste as better than her own, and never rued that decision.

She stood at the extra-high counter putting the finishing touches on a dish of lasagna, while her stepdaughter tackled the salad enthusiastically. The counters needed to be forty-six inches high, for Desdemona Delmonico stood six foot three in bare feet; that they were not even higher was a concession to Sophia, a mere five foot seven, and to the economics of offering something usable if ever the family decided to sell. Desdemona's hair was a little tangled from running her hands through it, as she was a learner-cook who still suffered paroxysms of anxiety over her cuisine, though lasagna was fairly safe. Carmine's mother and sisters had taken her in hand, so what she learned tended to be southern Italian. Very alien to Desdemona, English to her fingertips, but she had her occasional victories too. A visiting friend from Lincoln had taught her to make a traditional roast dinner and a Lancashire hot pot, both devoured by her husband and his family with great pleasure. Fancy never eating potatoes peeled and roasted around the joint! To Desdemona, it was a terrible omission. Not to mention gravy made on pan drippings.

When she turned to greet Carmine it could be seen that she was rather plain of face, between the overlarge nose and the prominent chin, but when her face broke into smiles it lit up most attractively, and the eyes were truly beautiful, big, calm, the color of thick ice. Motherhood had endowed her with a bosom, all that had been lacking to render her figure splendid, if hugely tall. As her well-shaped legs were proportionately very long, men tended to think her rather dishy. Not a verdict they would have delivered during Desdemona's days managing the Hug; marriage had done wonders for her.

She went at once to Carmine and bent her face four inches to kiss him, while Sophia hopped from foot to foot, waiting her turn.

At sixteen going on seventeen, his daughter was undeniably lovely; she took after her mother, Sandra, who had aspired to a Hollywood career. Sophia was naturally blonde, blue-eyed, fine-featured, and her figure was everything a young girl could have hoped for. But while her mother was a cokehead still living on the West Coast, Sophia had a brain, considerable ambition, and more common sense than either her father or her stepfather, the famed producer Myron Mendel Mandelbaum, had ever hoped for in Sandra's child. She had moved from L.A. and the depressing influence of her mother when Carmine and Desdemona married nine months ago, and occupied a teenaged girl's idea of heaven: a square tower three floors high complete with a widow's walk. Shrewd enough to realize that its location made it nigh impossible for her to sneak people in or sneak out herself, Sophia had decided that its advantages far outweighed such minor stuff, for she was not by nature a rebel. Though her suite had a little kitchen, she was almost invariably to be found eating with her father and stepmother, with whom she got on very well.

Desdemona enfolded in one arm, Carmine stretched out the other for Sophia, who came into it and kissed him smackingly.

"Lasagna!" he said, pleased. "Are you sure you don't mind eating so late? I'd be happy with a plate warmed on top of the stove, honest."

"Sophia and I are sophisticated women of the world" was his wife's answer. "Eat too early, and one wakes up ravenous long before there's a chance of breakfast. We have afternoon tea at four, and that lasts us."

"How's What's-His-Name?" he asked, smiling tenderly.

"*Julian* is perfect," said his mother. "Asleep, of course."

"Give in, Daddy," said Sophia, contributing her mite. "Julian is a great name."

"It's sissy," Carmine said. "You can't expect a son of mine to go to St. Bernard's lumbered with a sissy name."

Sophia giggled. "Go on, Daddy! He's such a bruiser that he's more likely to get 'Big Julie from East Cicero, Illinois.' "

"Curse *Guys and Dolls*!" Carmine cried. "Sissy or gangstery, Julian isn't suitable. He needs to have an ordinary name! I like John, after my grandfather Cerutti. Or Robert, Anthony, James!"

The lasagna was being sliced; how did Desdemona know the hour he'd appear for dinner? Sophia had dished salad into bowls and was pouring the dressings of choice over them, then filling the wine glasses with a good Italian red, save for her own, which got a third of red on the bottom and then was topped up with sparkling mineral water. They sat down.

"How about Simon?" asked Sophia in a spirit of mischief.

Carmine reared back like a striking snake. "Sissy going on faggy!" he snapped. "Look, what passes for normal in England is one thing, but this isn't England!"

"You're prejudiced against homosexuals," said Desdemona, her sangfroid unruffled. "And don't say 'faggy'!"

"No, I'm not prejudiced! But neither have I forgotten how miserable his classmates can make a kid with a fancy name," said Carmine, still fighting valiantly. "It's not about whether I'm prejudiced, it's about the kids our son will associate with at school. Truly, Desdemona, the worst thing a parent can do to a child is lumber him or her with a stupid name, and by stupid I mean sissy or fancy or idiotic!"

"Then Julian is the best of a bad bunch," said Desdemona. "I like it! Listen to the sound of it, Carmine, please. Julian John Delmonico.

It has a nice ring to it, and when he's a famous man, think how good it will look on his letterhead."

"Pah!" snorted Carmine, and changed the subject. "This is a very good lasagna," he said. "It's better than my mother's, and getting up there with Grandmother Cerutti."

She flushed with pleasure, but whatever she was going to say never was said; Sophia got in first.

"Guess who's arriving tomorrow, Daddy?"

"When you speak in that tone, young lady, it can only be one person—Myron," said her father.

"Oh!" Sophia looked deflated, then cheered up. "He didn't say so, but I know he's visiting to keep me company. The Dormer is on midsemester break, and I did drop him a hint."

"Like a brick, huh? I'm kinda snowed under at work, so he couldn't have come at a better time," said Carmine, smiling.

"Bad?" Desdemona asked.

"Terrible."

"What's going on, Daddy?"

"You know the rules, kid. No police business at home."

On his way to bed an hour later Carmine visited the nursery, where his nameless offspring lay slumbering blissfully in his crib. Sophia had called him a bruiser, and it was an accurate description; big-boned and overly long, he had his father's muscular breadth too, though no one could have called him fat. Just a bruiser. His thick, curly hair was black, and his skin a rich tan like Carmine's. In fact, he resembled his father in all save his length. Feet and hands suggested way over six feet when mature.

It was then, with the Dean of Paracelsus's words about wives ringing in his ears, that Carmine Delmonico saw the light. This boy could bear any first name with impunity; no one was ever going to intimidate him or mock him. Maybe he needed the brake of a slightly sissy name to rein in his power, his size.

So when Carmine slid into bed alongside Desdemona, he turned to her and took her fully into his arms, body to body, legs around legs. He kissed her neck; she shivered, turned into him even closer, one hand in his cropped hair.

"Julian," he said. "Julian John Delmonico."

She emitted a squeak of joy and began kissing his eyelids. "Carmine, Carmine, thank you! You'll never regret it! Neither will our son. He can carry any name."

"I've just realized that," he said.

C ommissioner John Silvestri's office was large, though seldom called upon to accommodate as many men as gathered there at nine the next morning, April fourth.

Holloman, a city of 150,000 people, wasn't big enough to have a homicide division, but it did have three squads of detectives to investigate the full gamut of serious crime. Captain Carmine Delmonico headed the entire division, with two lieutenants who were nominally under him but who usually followed their own lines of enquiry. Lieutenant Mickey McCosker and his team weren't present; he was embroiled in a drug investigation the FBI was running, and couldn't be spared for other work, a point that rankled with Silvestri and the Staties, bypassed. So Carmine and his two sergeants, Abe Goldberg and Corey Marshall, were joined by Lieutenant Larry Pisano and *his* two sergeants, Morty Jones and Liam Connor. Also present was the Deputy Commissioner, Danny Marciano, due to retire at the end of 1968. Despite his impeccably Italian name, Marciano, of northern blood, was freckled, fair, and blue-eyed. Larry Pisano was due to retire at the end of this year, 1967, which had led to some difficulties for Carmine, both of whose sergeants had seniority over Pisano's men and were in line for the next lieutenancy. Since that meant a hefty raise in pay as well as greater autonomy, he couldn't blame Abe or Corey for wanting to move up.

Silvestri himself, a desk cop who had never fired his sidearm in the course of duty, much less a shotgun or a rifle, was never dismissed as a pantywaist; during World War II he had earned many decorations, including the Congressional Medal of Honor. But reinstalled in the Holloman Police Department, he had recognized his talents as administrative, and was one of the city's finest-ever police commissioners. He was a dark, smoothly handsome man who could still pull the women, reminded people of a big cat, and was intensely loyal to his department, for which he would go to bat with anyone from the Feds to Hartford. So good a politician that he was generally held to be politically inept, Silvestri had a brilliant media persona and only two weaknesses. The first was his protégé Carmine Delmonico. The second was his addiction to sucking and chewing on unlit cigars, whose slimy butts littered his wake like corks after a pleasure boat. Owning a streak of the diabolical, he had long ago realized that Danny Marciano loathed these cigars, and he always contrived to put the current one as close to Marciano as he could.

Under ordinary circumstances his striking face was rather expressionless during a conference, but this morning it was distinctly grim. As soon as Patrick O'Donnell came through the door and took the last vacant chair, Silvestri got straight down to business.

"Carmine, fill me in," he commanded, champing on a cigar.

"Yes, sir." Without referring to the sheaf of papers and folders on his lap, Carmine commenced. "The first call came at six a.m. yesterday, from the Chubb Rowing Club. Their premier eight had gone out for practice as soon as it was light enough—apparently conditions on the stretch of the Pequot River they use were perfect, so the coach dragged them all out of bed and put them on the river. They'd worked hard and were about to come in when two of the port oars struck an object just under the surface—the body of a small child. Patsy?"

Patrick took over almost in the same breath. "A toddler, about eighteen months old, dressed in top quality Dr. Denton's and a super-thick diaper of the kind certain institutions sell to families with handicapped kids. The body showed the stigmata of Down's syndrome. Cause of death—I prioritized the child—wasn't drowning, but asphyxiation due to smothering with a pillow. There were contusions indicating that the child had resisted. Death occurred about four a.m."

Carmine resumed. "The identity of the victim was a mystery. No one had lodged a Missing Persons for a Down's syndrome child. Corey?"

"At eight-oh-two we got a call from a Mr. Gerald Cartwright, whose house fronts onto the Pequot River near the Chubb Rowing Club," said Corey, striving mightily to keep his voice dispassionate and level. "He had just returned from an overnight trip out of state to find his wife dead in their bed and their youngest son, a Down's syndrome, missing from the house." He stopped.

Back to Carmine. "By this time several other things had happened. A prostitute we all know well—Dee-Dee Hall—was lying in an alley behind City Hall with her throat cut from ear to ear. That call came in four minutes before seven a.m., and was followed at seven-twelve by a call from the residence of Mr. Peter Norton, who died after drinking a glass of freshly squeezed orange juice. So I left Abe to deal with Dee-Dee's murder, Corey on the Cartwright affair, and went myself to the Norton house. I found the victim's wife and two children—a girl aged eight and a boy aged five—basket cases, especially the wife, who behaved like she was demented. What details I got were from the little girl, who swore it was the orange juice. The glass was on the breakfast table, about half drunk. The wife squeezed it every morning, then went upstairs to wake and dress the kids, during which time—about ten minutes—the glass sat unobserved and unattended on the table. So there was a window of opportunity for an outsider to add something to the juice."

"I have the remainder of the juice and the glass," Patsy said, one hand propping his chin; he looked tired. "Though I don't have any analytical results back yet, my guess is that Mr. Norton was poisoned by a large dose of strychnine." He grimaced. "Not a pleasant way to go."

"While I was at the Nortons'," Carmine went on, "I was called

28

to a rape and murder out on Sycamore. I sent Corey. Mrs. Norton needed a woman cop, and we're short on those. Report, Corey?"

"The body was discovered by the girl's landlord," said Corey, managing his voice better. "Her name is Bianca Tolano. She was on the floor, naked, hands bound behind her back. She'd been tortured, and there was a pair of pantyhose around her neck. But I don't think she died of strangulation, Carmine. I think she died from a broken bottle up the vagina."

"Quite right, Cor," said Patsy. "Autopsy is still pending, but I've made a preliminary examination. The pantyhose was an on-again, off-again form of torture."

"Jesus!" cried Silvestri. "Are we under siege?"

"It sure felt like it yesterday, sir," said Carmine. "I was still trying to get information out of Mrs. Norton when the call came about the shooting of a black cleaning woman and two black high school students—not gang related, according to the cop who phoned them in. They happened on his beat. I passed them to Larry here. Larry?"

A medium-brown man who had had an undistinguished but quite satisfactory career, Larry Pisano wiggled his brows ruefully. "Well, Carmine, it may have sounded ordinary enough, but believe me, it's not. Ludovica Bereson is a cleaning woman—she does five houses between Mondays and Fridays. She's well liked by her employers, doesn't shirk, never gives cause for complaint. Likes a good joke and something hot for her lunch. Her employers didn't mind the lunch because she was a good cook and always left enough for them to eat for dinner. She was shot in the head with a small-bore gun, and died instantly. No one saw it, but—and this is more interesting—no one heard it either. Cedric Ballantine was sixteen years old, a good student in line for a football scholarship to a top college. He works hard, has never been in trouble. He was shot in the back of the head by a medium-bore gun. Morris Brown was eighteen years old, an A student, no record of trouble. He was shot in the chest by a big old mother of a gun—a .45 or something like. No one saw or heard the boys gunned down either. All three victims had powder residue around the wounds, so they were shot at close range. Same beat cop, yeah, but Cedric and Morris occurred at opposite ends of his territory, and Ludovica in the middle. I had Morty and Liam hunt for casings, but *nada*—and not because they missed them! I tell you, Carmine, it was one helluva smooth operation! And the victims? Three totally harmless black people!"

"I doubt I'll get to them today," said Patrick with a sigh. "The poison cases take precedence."

"Poison *cases?*" Silvestri asked, eyes widening. "In the plural?"

"Oh, yes," said Carmine, nodding. "Mrs. Cathy Cartwright, the mother of the Down's syndrome child, didn't commit suicide. She was killed with an injection of something, and Patsy says she couldn't have maneuvered a needle herself into the vein that was used. Then we have Peter Norton, who ingested strychnine. And Dean John Kirkbride Denbigh, of Dante College at Chubb, who drank a lethal dose of potassium cyanide in his jasmine tea. Not to mention el supremo of Cornucopia, Desmond Skeps."

The Commissioner was gaping. "Sweet Jesus! *Skeps?* Desmond Skeps is dead?"

"Oh, yes. And don't think it didn't occur to me that all the other murders are simply a way of making Skeps's death look less like the object of the exercise," said Carmine, then scowled. "Had there been fewer, I might have inclined that way too, but not this many. Whatever way you look at it, twelve murders in one day are too many murders by far for a little city like Holloman."

"Let's see," said Silvestri, using his fingers. "The baby. The baby's mother. The strychnine-in-the-orange-juice guy. The rape murder. The prostitute—poor old Dee-Dee! She's been on the streets since I was a boy, it seems . . . Three blacks, shot. The Dean of Dante College with cyanide. The head honcho of Cornucopia . . . That's ten altogether. Who else, for pity's sake?"

"A seventy-one-year-old widow in very comfortable circumstances who lives on two acres just outside of town. She was discovered by her cleaning woman—no connection to the dead one—in a mussed-up bed with a pillow still over her face. And last, a Chubb pre-med sophomore who was blackmailing someone he called Motor Mouth," Carmine sighed, looked frustrated. "Four poisonings, a sex crime, three shootings, a whore's violent end, two pillow suffocations, and a bear trap."

"A bear trap?"

Carmine was just concluding his description of the murder of Evan Pugh when the coffee cart arrived, a special one for the Commissioner that held fresh Danish and raisin bagels from Silberstein's as well as distinctly better coffee. Everyone rose thankfully and stretched before descending on the cart like locusts targeting a lush green field after a season of burned stubble. Never having forgotten President Mawson MacIntosh's advice given at a Parson board meeting, Carmine chose an apple Danish. Yes, still delicious!

Carmine took Silvestri to one side as soon as he could.

"John," he began, voice low, "the press are going to wallow in this. How can we keep them off my back?"

"I'm not sure yet," Silvestri said in equally low tones. "I figure we've still got a few hours before I have to feed them something. I have a couple of ideas, but I want some time before I decide my best line of attack."

Carmine smiled. "Attack?"

The dark eyes opened ingenuously wide. "Damn straight, attack! The day I show them *my* belly is the day I retire."

After a much needed quarter hour spent discussing anything save murder, it was easier to return to the looming crisis.

"How do you want to run this, Carmine?" Silvestri asked.

"Apart from my supervisory role," Carmine answered, "there are several of the cases I want to reserve for myself. Namely, the poisonings and the bear trap. Larry, you and your guys concentrate on the shootings and Dee-Dee Hall. The old lady, Beatrice Egmont, goes to Abe because Corey's already on the rape victim."

No one demurred, though the division of labor had seen their captain keep almost half the cases for himself. Nor did anyone ask what Carmine intended to do about Jimmy Cartwright, the Down's syndrome toddler.

"How can I help?" Silvestri asked.

"Give us plenty of unmarked cars, and keep up the supply of drivers," Carmine said instantly. "We're going to generate scads of paperwork, and time in a car is paperwork time. So I want all of you in the backseat writing your reports."

"You'll get your unmarkeds and drivers," Silvestri promised. "Danny, you're liaison."

From Adams Street the Cartwright house looked only moderately prosperous; it was at the back, or by those in the real estate know, that it was revealed as prime property. The style of the building was traditional white clapboard finished with dark green shutters, and it spread sideways on its extremely long three-acre lot on the river side of a very tall hedge. What was seen from the street was the width of the master bedroom upstairs, and the short axis of a reception room downstairs. The front door was around the corner on the west, shielded from the backyard by that tall hedge, in which was a locked gate that looked formidable.

Carmine knocked, feeling oddly abandoned. Ordinarily Abe and Corey would be with him, two extra pairs of eyes to scan the scene as minutely as his own, yet with different perspective. Well, today that wasn't possible, he thought, waiting for someone to answer the firm tattoo he beat upon the door. A minute passed, then another. He was just about to repeat his demand to enter when the door opened a crack, and Gerald Cartwright peered around it.

"Mr. Cartwright?"

"Yes."

"I'm Captain Carmine Delmonico, Holloman Police. May I come in, sir?"

The door opened wide; Gerald Cartwright stepped back.

He looked exactly as a man should look who had just lost his wife and youngest child by murder: shrunken, grief-stricken, bewildered, in a great deal of pain. A man in his early forties, of medium build and coloring, under normal circumstances he would probably have given an impression of pleasant welcome and considerable charm, as was fitting in the proprietor of not one but two restaurants, both successful. Before leaving for this interview, Carmine had gone into Gerald Cartwright's background as closely as possible at such short notice; a desk sergeant back at County Services was continuing these enquiries, among others. Holloman's hoods and jealous husbands were on a temporary back burner while twelve murders occupied nine-tenths of everyone's time.

Interesting that Gerald Cartwright's two businesses were so dissimilar, and that he wasn't a chef. He owned a premier French restaurant, l'Escargot, in Beechmont, New York, and a diner, Joey's, on Cedar Street in Holloman, adjacent to the rearing towers of Chubb's Science Hill. Both did a thriving trade, the one catering for discriminating diners in search of new taste thrills, the other a highly successful pancake diner. Cartwright banked with the Second National, where he kept more than sufficient funds to cover his expenses; his real money was safely invested in a portfolio of stocks and shares with Merrill Lynch, Pierce, Fenner & Smith. Given the emergence of Motor Mouth, Carmine had looked for unusually large withdrawals, but none had been made.

He followed Cartwright into a sitting room furnished with good but not pretentious chairs and coffee tables, the kind of stuff prudent parents of four children would choose. Through double glass doors he could see into the huge reception room, far better furnished. Off limits to kids, he guessed.

Sitting down with a flop, Gerald Cartwright picked up a fat cushion and hugged it against his stomach.

"You weren't home the night before last, Mr. Cartwright?"

"No!" said Cartwright on a gasp. "I was in Beechmont."

"Where you have a restaurant."

"Yes."

"Do you stay overnight in Beechmont often?"

"Yes. I have family there, so does—did—my wife, and we keep a little apartment above the restaurant. I eat with my mother, usually. She lives two doors down."

"Apart from the presence of family in Beechmont, what makes l'Escargot special enough to occasion frequent nights away?"

Cartwright blinked at Carmine's use of the restaurant's name; his color faded visibly. "It's a French menu, Captain, and my chef, Michel Moreau, is very famous. He's also a prima donna who throws temper tantrums. For some reason, I'm the only person who can handle him, and if I lost him, my business would go down the drain. People drive eighty miles just to eat at l'Escargot, there's a three-month waiting list for reservations—it puts me in a terrible fix! So I stay twice or three times a week just to keep Michel happy. Cathy has always understood, even if it does make things hard for her. We have three kids at the Dormer Day School, and that costs a bundle."

"So must the mortgage on this property, Mr. Cartwright."

"Yes—and no." He gulped, swayed, hugged the cushion harder. "We bought at a good time, got our mortgage at four percent. We knew we couldn't lose. Given the size of the lot in this neighborhood as well as the river frontage, it's worth five or six times what we paid for it. The house was in good condition, we haven't had any massive repair bills." The tears started rolling down his cheeks; he fought for control.

"Take your time, Mr. Cartwright. Can I get you anything?"

"No," he said, sobbing. "Oh, it's so awful! The kids knew something was up, but I came in before any of them went to see why Mom hadn't come down yet. Or Jimmy. Before Jimmy they would have, but he—he kinda changed things."

"The Down's syndrome, you mean?"

"Yes. After he was born they told us she should have had an amniocentesis test, but no one suggested it when she found out she was pregnant. No one warned us of the dangers with parents in their forties! I mean, we'd had three healthy, normal kids."

His indignation was helping him overcome the shock and grief.

Carmine sat and listened, prepared to insert a prompting word if it proved necessary.

"Jimmy took up so much of Cathy's time, yet I couldn't be here any more often than always. I tried hiring a manager for l'Escargot, but it didn't work out. We didn't have any choice, it had to be me went to Beechmont." The tears kept falling.

"I take it that your wife's real problem was the three other kids," Carmine said gently.

Gerald Cartwright jumped, looked amazed. "How did you ever guess that?" he asked.

"It's a common reaction in any family suddenly endowed with a handicapped child. The new arrival consumes every scrap of the mother's time, yet the older kids aren't mature enough to understand the true nature of the problem," Carmine said dispassionately. "So they resent the new baby and, by logical progression, their mom. How old are yours?"

"Selma's sixteen, Gerald Junior is thirteen, and Grant is ten. I'd imagined Selma would be her mother's ally, but she was so . . . spiteful! Word got around school that she had a retarded baby brother, and she reacted badly. In fact, all three did."

"How exactly did they react, Mr. Cartwright?"

"Mostly by refusing to help Cathy, who didn't have time to make their lunches for school, or snacks when they got home. It wasn't so bad when Jimmy was a baby, but once he turned a year old, dinner-time often got delayed, and the menus became simpler, more monotonous. Cathy just didn't have the time to cook anymore. When she told Selma to take over laundry chores, Selma had a tantrum in Michel's league. Home life was a nightmare! The kids absolutely hated Jimmy, wouldn't be in the same room as him."

And you didn't have the guts to give them a kick in the ass, thought Carmine. You had Beechmont to retreat to, home-cooked dinners with your own mom, a peaceful bed to sleep in. Michel's temper tantrums must have seemed like manna from heaven, they got you out from under a situation you knew you shouldn't let continue but couldn't face dealing with. Your wife needed you home a hundred percent of the time. Okay, okay, there's much-needed income involved, but you're not in debt. Once you had your home predicament sorted out, you could have found another Michel and gotten l'Escargot up and running again.

He let Gerald Cartwright hug his pillow and weep, taking himself on a prowl through the big house to find those three older kids, see what they were like. But first, the master bedroom, fenced off with a police cordon.

It was charming, done in a beige the color of a potato's skin with various widths of black stripes breaking up the beige of curtains, bedspread, one papered wall. The carpet was black, the wood of the furniture lacquered that same potato-skin beige. The only jarring note was a large, heavy crib just to what he presumed was Cathy Cartwright's side of the bed. Its sides were overly tall, its thick posts close together; it looked like the cage of a dangerous animal. No one had disturbed its sheets and blankets, which were a tumbled tangle surmounted by a sheet. Nor had the king-sized bed been touched beyond forensic examination; it was neat by comparison with the crib, evidence that Cathy had not struggled. There was a postage-stamp-sized patch of browned blood on the bottom sheet about where her elbow would have rested.

Carmine knew that a glass of neat bourbon had sat on her bedside table, though it and what remained of its contents had gone to Patrick's labs. The results had come through just before he set out. This last nightcap she ever took had been laced with chloral hydrate, so when the massive dose of intravenous pentobarbital had been administered she was too deeply asleep to resist, even if she had felt the needle. Patrick had put the time of her death at about two in the morning, which meant she had died well before her baby. Someone had murdered her, but was this person the same individual who had murdered the child?

The en suite bathroom was clean and tidy. Burdened with a hand-

icapped child and three uncoöperative older children she might have
been, but Cathy Cartwright had still managed to keep her house in
reasonable condition. Poor woman! It must have seemed to her that
no one among those she loved had sympathy or time for her plight.

He found the three older Cartwright children in the den, a big
room that, together with an office/library, divided the children's
bedrooms from the master suite, thus completing the upstairs.

They were clustered around a big television set watching the
cartoon channel; cable had just come to town, and Pequot River, a
wealthy suburb, was first on the cable company's list. As the children
had cranked up the volume, they didn't hear Carmine enter, which
gave him ample opportunity to observe them with their guard down.
Selma, he decided, was a typical Dormer Day School princess. His
awareness of this creature had grown dramatically since Sophia had
started at the Dormer, especially given her previous school in L.A.,
where booze and drugs were easier to buy than candy and where the
students could write a check for the whole of Holloman without no-
ticing. So to Sophia the Dormer was a poor imitation, mercifully free
from booze and drugs, even if well populated by kids who considered
themselves far above the hoi polloi. Secretly chuckling, Sophia had
inserted herself into Dormer life as a glamorous West Coast import
who knew carloads of movie stars and dressed to the teenaged nines
when it came to fashion. What saved the Dormer was its fine academic record and some brilliant teachers, for most of the Chubb faculty sent their children here, and there were too many scholarly kids
for the cheerleader/jock faction to exert its usual control of school
and class activities. The Dormer was basically a nerdy place.

Selma must take after her mother, Carmine thought, watching
her. Tall, a good figure, streaky blonde hair, a tanned skin. The air
of hauteur, he decided, was hers alone. Gerald Junior was cast in the
same mold, though he probably played basketball, not football. Only
Grant, the youngest, took after his father—medium in size and coloring. While the other two maintained a lofty detachment from the

Tom and Jerry cartoons, Grant had buried himself in them, laughing a little too loudly.

Suddenly Carmine had a wish to go through their rooms before interviewing them; he slipped out of the den undetected and made his way to the four bedrooms at the far end of the upstairs.

One was clearly kept as a guest room, beautifully decorated, untouched. How lucky these children are! he thought, discovering that each bedroom had its own en suite bathroom. The three rooms belonging to the children were messes: unmade beds, gaping closets, all kinds of stuff spilling out of drawers or cluttering the carpets. Here at least Cathy Cartwright hadn't succeeded in the kind of good housekeeping she probably aimed for, though perhaps before the advent of Jimmy these rooms had been considerably tidier. They screamed of protest, of attention seeking, of adolescent misery. Each child had a television set as well as shelves of books and toys. How recently had the televisions been added?

Young Grant's room was the worst, and included such goodies as a slashed schoolbag, a Dormer placard ripped to tatters, some fifth-grade textbooks torn up. The eruption of this rage against his school had presumably happened on the day that news of Jimmy had gotten around there, which meant that months had gone by without anyone's trying to clean the room up. Cathy Cartwright had given up the fight then and there.

Grant's bathroom smelled sour. There were traces of vomitus, clumsily cleaned up, in the middle of the blue-tiled floor. When Carmine lifted the lid of the hamper he found a set of pajamas soiled and encrusted with vomitus; clearly they had been used to do the wiping up. There was probably a cleaning woman who did pretty much as she liked, and she hadn't gotten around to Grant's room yet, though when she did, her ministrations would be basic. Provided, that is, that she ever ventured in at all.

Time to go back to the den.

He knocked loudly. The three faces swung around, then all

three children got to their feet. A stranger! And a cop. Selma turned the volume right down.

"My name is Carmine Delmonico, and I'm a captain with the Holloman Police," Carmine said, pulling a straight chair to one side and sitting on it. "Swing your chairs around so you can see me, and sit."

They obeyed, but sulkily. Under the veneer of bravado were layers of fright, shock at the death of their mother, terror at what might happen to them, and a certain quiet satisfaction that Carmine put down to the death of Jimmy, who would not be mourned.

"Did you see or hear anything the night before last, Selma?" Carmine asked the girl, who, he noted, bit her nails right down to the quick.

"No," she said baldly.

"You're sure?"

"Yes!" she snapped. "Yes, yes, yes!"

"Greaser!" said Gerald Junior under his breath. Getting no reaction from Carmine, he spoke louder. "Damn greaser cop!"

So much anger! Carmine looked into Selma's eyes, which were the color of a sunny sky, then into Gerald Junior's identical orbs, and couldn't get past that all-consuming rage.

"What about you, Gerald?" he asked.

"I'm Junior," he said, suddenly less certain than his sister. "No, I didn't see or hear anything. You don't, at this end of upstairs, if the noise is down Jimmy's end."

Not down his mother's end, or his father's end. Down Jimmy's end, as if Jimmy owned it.

"Does Jimmy make a lot of noise, then?"

"Yes," Junior said abruptly, and shrugged. "Like a sheep or a goat. Maaaa!" He imitated an ovine animal, imbuing the sound with mockery. "He wakes up a lot, maaaa!"

One more kid to go. "What about you, Grant?" Carmine asked.

"I never heard nothin'."

Interesting that the Dormer hadn't yet managed to iron double negatives out of Grant's syntax. Carmine cleared his throat and leaned forward. "But you were awake at some time. You got sick."

Grant jumped, astonished. "How do you know that?"

"First, I could smell it. Secondly, I could see the remains of it. You used your peejays to clean it up, they're still in your hamper. Doesn't anyone ever do the laundry?"

"Hey!" cried Selma, stiffening. "You can't poke through our things, you East Shore greaser!"

"You senior Cartwright children are much addicted to that term," Carmine said gravely. "It's not general at the Dormer, or my daughter would have informed me. She's your age, Selma, she'd be in some of your classes—Sophia Mandelbaum." He watched the girl go crimson and understood a little more about the pecking order at the Dormer. Selma was a would-be, his daughter was establishment. How amazing that it started so early.

He went on. "You must know that your mother and your baby brother were both murdered the night before last, so why are you so obstructive? You watch enough television, you must be aware of police procedure. In a murder investigation nothing is sacred, including laundry hampers. Just settle down and answer my questions in the comfort of your own home. Otherwise I'll have to take you downtown and ask you the same questions in a police interrogation room. Is that clear?"

Resistance collapsed; the three children nodded.

"So, Grant, you got sick?"

"Yeah," he said in a whisper.

Some instinct stirred; Carmine looked at Selma and Junior. "Thank you, the pair of you can go. But the lady policeman should have arrived, so ask her to come here at once. I can't harm Grant if she's here, can I?"

Obviously Selma wanted to stay, but she wasn't quite game to say so. After a suggestive pause that Carmine ignored, she sighed and followed Junior out. The woman cop came in quickly.

"Sit down over there, Gina. You're chaperone," Carmine said, then turned to Grant. "Okay, Grant, tell me what happened."

"I pigged out on Twinkies—dinner was so late!" The boy looked indignant. "Mom gets carried away with Jimmy all the time—we don't get dinner regular anymore. Then it was"—he pulled a face—"spaghetti! *Again!* I filled up on Twinkies, and when they ran out, I found a Boston cream pie."

How long was it going to be before these children realized their mother really was dead? That if dinner had been irregular over the past eighteen months, it was going to become far more so in the future? They were so wrapped up in themselves, in what they perceived to be intolerable injuries. Keeping his face impassive, Carmine pressed on.

"Did you sleep at all, Grant?"

"Oh, sure! I watched some stupid movie on WOR—black-and-white, yet!—and I must have gone to sleep around midnight with it still on. Then I woke up feeling sick, but I figured it would go away. It didn't, it got worse. I raced to my bathroom, but I didn't make it. Splat! All over the floor. I felt better after that, so I went back to bed and went to sleep."

The boy's demeanor had changed, become uneasy. All truculence had fled, and the brown eyes that had been fixed on Carmine moved suddenly away, refused to return. The truth had come out, but not all of it. And now, while a fraught silence persisted and Gina endeavored to melt into the wallpaper, Grant was trying to manufacture a story that a police captain might swallow. Unfortunately he'd had scant experience confabulating, which indicated a life spent out of real trouble; his lies to date had been simple ones, his parents trusting fools who believed him. Only, what was he hiding? What could he possibly have to hide that required a properly constructed fairy tale?

"Crap!" said Carmine, barking it. "You didn't go back to bed and you didn't go back to sleep. What did you do? The truth!"

All color leached out of the boy's healthy skin; he gave a gulp, his throat working convulsively. "I am telling the truth! Honest! I went to bed and I went to sleep."

"No, you didn't. What did you really do, Grant?"

It came out in a despairing rush; people didn't usually set themselves against him, and he couldn't—he *couldn't*—dream up a story that convinced even himself. "I went to Mom's bedroom to tell her I'd been sick on my bathroom floor."

Ah! "What happened then?"

"The light was on—not a night light, the lamp on her table. Jimmy'd never settle down with a night light. The place stank of shit—I mean, it stank, really stank!"

Carmine waited for him to go on, but he didn't. "You can't stop now, Grant. I want it all."

"Jimmy was standing in his crib, yelling his head off. I saw Mom asleep in bed, so I went to wake her. But I couldn't, sir! I shook her and yelled in her ear, but she went right on sleeping. Then I saw the glass on her table, and I knew she'd knocked herself out. She often did. Great, just great! Jimmy was screeching fit to bust, these real animal noises. I yelled at him to shut up, but the little creep didn't even notice. *Gross!* He must have dumped tons of shit in his diaper, the stink was so bad."

Carmine's eyes encountered Gina's; she looked a query, but was answered by a tiny shake of the head. A cold and nauseating presentiment had taken hold of Carmine, who drew in a long breath and forced himself to remain detached. "Go on, Grant, you may as well tell me the rest—I'll find it out anyway. It will be better if it comes from you."

The brown eyes turned back to him at last, resigned, full of tears. Grant lifted his shoulders as if to shed a burden. "I went to the crib and let down the side. I figured that if Jimmy was loaded with shit, it would maybe teach Mom a lesson not to knock herself out if she woke up in the same bed as shitty Jimmy. But the little creep hollered even louder. Then he swung a punch at me! Spat in my face! I punched him back. He fell over in the crib, and I don't know what happened next. Honest, sir, I don't! All I remember are the screeches and howls, the spits—I mean, he spit on me! I put the pillow over his face to shut him up, but it didn't. Even through it the noise hurt, but he couldn't spit on me. I kept pushing the pillow against his face until he did stop yelling. Then I kept it there to make sure. Man, it felt good! The little creep spit on me!"

Oh, sweet Jesus! "Tell me the rest, Grant."

The boy looked better, relieved of a frightful burden. Did his siblings know? Probably not, or Selma at least wouldn't have left him. Carmine thought she had an inkling but hadn't had time to follow up. Just as well. The death of Jimmy Cartwright would otherwise have masked the death of his mother.

"I switched on the central light," said Grant, "and I saw that Jimmy was blue. Blue all over. No matter how I pinched him, he wouldn't move. Then I realized he was dead. At first I was real glad, then I figured out that if I told, I'd go to jail—I will go to jail, won't I?"

"Just keep on telling it the way it happened, Grant, and things will go better for you. Jail is for grown-ups," said Carmine. "What did you do then?"

"I wrapped him in a sheet off his crib and took him down the stairs," said Grant more easily. "I went out the back door and carried him down to the Pequot, then pushed him in. He sank right away, so I walked back home and put the sheet back in his crib, and checked up on Mom. She was still asleep. Only she wasn't, was she, sir? She was dead too."

"Yes, since before your first visit," Carmine said. "What did you do when you reached your own bedroom?"

"Tried to clean up the bathroom floor, then got into bed and went to sleep. I was whacked."

No qualms of conscience, thought Carmine. Nor may there ever be. Though he's a smart kid. If his father finds him the right lawyer, he'll prove a good student. By the time the social workers get to him, he'll be oozing penitence, and by the time the courts get to him, he'll have developed all the necessary memory lapses.

But what fools indeed these parents were! Which one was so frugal that no housekeeper was hired after Jimmy was born? If ever a woman had needed a full-time housekeeper, it was Mrs. Cathy Cartwright. They could afford the expense, in spite of three sets of Dormer Day School fees.

"It would never have happened if the mother hadn't been overwhelmed," Carmine said to Patrick. "Why do I feel the parsimonious one is Gerald Cartwright? Though Cathy must have been spineless where he was concerned, not to insist on help."

"It also would never have happened if the mother hadn't been dead," said Patrick, arranging instruments on a cart.

"True. What set the kid off was the smell of shit—an indication that Cathy had already been dead for several hours when Grant went to find her, probably sometime after four. I knew he was concealing something when he didn't admit to going in search of his mother, because all kids go in search of Mom if they've thrown up, especially if they've missed the toilet. I didn't expect a confession of murder, but that fits too. The father is selfish and career-oriented, which has led to his spending a great deal of his time away from home, and the mother had suddenly been inflicted with a super-demanding child after waiting hand and foot on her first three. Poor little Jimmy was the inadvertent cause of much hatred and resentment."

"Well, Jimmy's murder at least might have been averted if the parents had been more aware of how their older children felt, but what about the mother's murder?" Patrick asked.

"A different horse entirely. Thus far, no leads whatsoever. Gerald Cartwright may be unpardonably selfish, but he's not an unfaithful husband or a bad provider. When he's staying at the French restaurant in upstate New York, he's surrounded by family—hers as well as his. He's regarded as a model husband, an image he took some pains to reinforce. As for Cathy herself—ask me where she'd find the time for extramarital affairs with four kids, and the youngest with Down's syndrome?" Carmine scowled.

"Did she get out at all?"

"Very occasionally, according to Gerald, who likes a social life. They'd go to plays trying out at the Schumann, to movies that got good reviews, charity dinners, country club events. If the chef threw a tantrum and Gerald was called away, he insisted that Cathy go on her own. Probably not as bad as it sounds—they're well known, she'd meet up with friends. The last time she got out was a solo expedition to a Maxwell Foundation charity banquet, something she didn't want to miss because the Maxwells give generously to handicapped children's research. I got all that at great length from Gerald, who managed to keep his act together if he could hug a cushion." Carmine poured himself fresh coffee. "Any other news on the pathology front, Patsy?"

"The poisoning cases are all in," Patrick said, but not in triumphant tones. "Peter Norton was dispatched with enough strychnine to kill a horse. It was in the orange juice. His blood revealed no other toxic tampering over a longer period of time, which tends to support Mrs. Norton's likely innocence, as does the choice of poison. It's a strong-stomached poisoner who can administer something as horrible as strychnine and then stick around to witness the dying."

"I agree, Patsy. It's a good thing for her that she did go upstairs to get the kids ready for school."

"You've only got her word for it."

"I have the kids' words as well. They're a little young to be coached as accomplices. What brought them all downstairs was the noise their father made, and though Mrs. Norton did try to shoo the kids away, they both witnessed the death. I'm inclined to believe Mrs. Norton's story that she squeezed the juice before going upstairs, and that she was up there for ten minutes before she heard her husband go down to breakfast, which he ate running."

"Poison is a woman's weapon," said Patrick.

"Usually, yes, but not always. What makes you think this is not a female poisoner?"

"That window of opportunity. Literally, as the juice could only be seen through the kitchen window, but not reached through it. Seizing an opportunity on the spur of the moment isn't very female, yet that's what this killer had to do. See the juice, go in the back door, add a hefty dose of strychnine to the glass, then leave. What if someone had come downstairs? He'd have been discovered, so he must have had a convincing story ready. No, this poisoner is a man."

"Chauvinist," Carmine said slyly. "What about Dean Denbigh?"

"Oh, that one's up for grabs—and you know it! Potassium cyanide crystals mixed with jasmine tea leaves inside a perfect bag in turn enclosed inside a hermetically sealed paper packet that my technicians are willing to swear in court was opened only once— by Dean Denbigh himself. And the tea bag is machine stitched, not stapled—stitched only once, those swearing technicians again. All four of the students invited to his klatch were men."

"While Dr. Pauline Denbigh the wife held her own klatch around the corner in her study," Carmine said with a grin. "Her guests were all women."

" 'Klatch' is disrespectful," Patrick said solemnly. "Granted, you can't very well call morning coffee a soiree, yet I gather the function operated rather like one—poetry read out, and so forth."

"It should really be matinee, but that's taken. How about a matutinal recitation?"

"Spot on, Carruthers! Your Limey wife is showing."

"But you like her better now, Patsy, don't you?" Carmine asked anxiously.

"Of course I do! She's ideal for you, and that alone makes me love her. I guess it was being towered over that set me against her, and that snooty Limey thing. But now I know she's brave, and gallant, and very smart. She's also sexy," Patrick said, still trying to mend his fences. Carmine's doubts were receding, but it was still a conversation they had from time to time. The trouble was, Patrick hadn't read the signals correctly, hadn't known just how deep Carmine's feelings for the lady were. If he had, he would never have breathed a disparaging word about her. And Sandra she wasn't, thank God.

"Anything else in Denbigh's blood?" Carmine asked.

"Nothing."

"What about Desmond Skeps?"

Patrick's face lit up. "Oh, he's a doozy, Carmine! He had no long-term drugs or toxins in his blood, but he got a cocktail the day he died."

"Day?" Carmine asked, frowning.

"Yes, I think the process started well before the sun went down— maybe as early as four in the afternoon, when he took a glass of single-malt Scotch laced with chloral hydrate. While he was out, the killer put a Luer-Lok IV needle in his left intercubital fossa and taped it down. It stayed until he was dead."

"The same technique as Mrs. Cartwright?"

"Superficially. The similarity ended with the introduction of the IV. Mrs. Cartwright was killed as soon as the needle was in the vein, but that wasn't Skeps's fate. He was intubated and given a medical curare that enabled the killer to inflict painful bodily harm on the poor bastard, too immobilized to fight back. He was bag-breathed, but if it was attached to a respirator I don't know. The torture was burns, mostly, but never severe enough to interrupt pain pathways to the brain—he felt it all, believe me! That says the killer must have some medical knowledge. Third-degree burns aren't felt; the pain pathways have been destroyed too."

"The instrument of torture?"

"Some kind of soldering iron is my guess—a red-hot tip that could be manipulated. He even wrote Skeps's name on his belly, after a sloppy dry shave of the body hair that left the skin grazed and raw. I photographed it extensively. Wouldn't it be interesting to nail the sucker on a handwriting analysis?"

"Pipe dreams, Patsy."

"While the curare was still concentrated enough to sustain the paralysis, the killer injected Skeps with a small amount of something dilute but caustic. The pain must have been terrible."

"Jesus, Patsy," Carmine said, "whoever murdered Skeps hated him! The only other victim of outright torture was the rape case, Bianca Tolano."

"At some stage," Patrick went on, "the killer brought Skeps out of his curare paralysis. The airway was removed and Skeps was bound at the wrists and ankles with single-strand steel wire about an eighth of an inch in diameter, tight enough that it would have hurt atrociously to struggle. Yet he struggled! The wire ate into his flesh, though the areas are too bony for deep penetration." Patrick ceased, and looked enquiring.

"The killer needed to interrogate Skeps, I'm guessing. Or, failing that, needed to hear the mighty tycoon beg and plead like some peon at the bottom of the Cornucopia hierarchy. Under curare, he was mute, especially around an airway. That's the most important thing you've told me, Patsy. A vocal Desmond Skeps was necessary to round out the killer's purposes."

"The vocal period can't have lasted more than an hour, if that long, Carmine. Then Skeps was re-intubated and got more curare— a stronger one. He would have been immobilized when he was finally killed with a solution of common drain caustic. Jesus! All in all, I estimate that from the Scotch to the Drano took twelve hours."

"And Cornucopia is without its owner-director," Carmine said. "That alone is of national importance. One of the biggest engineering conglomerates in the world, leaderless overnight." He huffed. "Any other information I should have?"

"Nothing calculated to make your task easier, at any rate. The bullet boys have reported back on the three shootings, and I've managed to do the autopsies. Ludovica Bereson was killed with a .38, but we thought at first it was a smaller caliber because the bullet didn't exit. It lodged in the mass of bone at the base of her cranium. Cedric Ballantine was killed KGB style, with a .22 bullet into the back of his head just below the inion. The bullet was inside. Morris Brown took a bigger caliber—a .45 to the chest. It exited his back but hit the spinal column squarely on its way out, so it didn't travel as far as Pisano's men assumed. I sent them back to the crime scene and they found the bullet where Morris fell. It was too mangled for markings, but intact enough to gauge the caliber. That means three different handguns."

"That no one heard," said Carmine, growling. "The gunmen used silencers. But the guy who commissioned the hits must have asked for different calibers, otherwise I think the weapons would all have been .22s, everybody's favorite for close-up work."

"Larry thinks the shootings are way out of Holloman's league."

"He's right. And the old lady out in the Valley?"

"Smothered with her own pillow. She was a congestive cardiac failure who didn't let it stop her, but her heart gave out very quickly under the pillow. The bedclothes were a little mussed, but she probably didn't last long enough to suffer much."

"What about Dee-Dee Hall?"

"Throat cut with a cutthroat razor. No sign of it at the scene. She was cut twice—very cunning! The first slash went from ear to ear, just deep enough to sever the jugulars. No sign of a fight—no defensive wounds. She seems to have stood there pouring blood while her killer watched, then she fell to her knees and collapsed. When he figured she'd lost too much blood for her arteries to spurt, the killer moved in again cool as you please and cut her throat a second time, way deeper than the carotids. About all holding her head on was the spinal column."

"A cool killer indeed. Abe's got it, right?"

"No, you passed it to Larry Pisano and his boys. Abe's got the old lady, Beatrice Egmont, and Corey's got the rape girl, Bianca Tolano."

When Patrick frowned, Carmine stared at him in surprise. "What gives, Patsy? What did I say?"

"Both your guys are applying for Larry Pisano's lieutenancy when he retires at the end of the year. They've worked together a helluva long time, and they get along together fine, but they're two very different men," said Patrick in apologetic tones. "And I know you know all this, so I must sound as if I'm teaching my dear old granny to suck eggs, but sometimes it takes someone on the outside to see things clearly." He paused to see how this was going down.

"I'm listening," Carmine said.

"I think it has to be kid gloves for you between now and when the decision about who replaces Larry is made. Are you a member of the job panel, Carmine?"

"Uh—yeah," said Carmine, feeling the stirrings of unease.

"Then get yourself removed from it, that's first off. Only one of your guys can succeed, and to bring in an outsider for no better reason than to keep the status quo between them would be grossly unfair. Either of them would make a better lieutenant than Larry, as I'm sure you understand. But the rivalry has begun, and they're looking sideways at each other. Every task you set them is judged in the light of how it measures up. So when you gave Abe his first case, you gave him a little old lady smothered with a pillow. Not much time has elapsed, but it's sufficient to tell Abe that *his* murder isn't going to be glamorous or juicy. Whereas you give Corey a sex murder! He's got clues to work, an interesting crime scene, a list of possible suspects in the men who've dated the girl. As far as Abe is concerned, your scales are balanced in Corey's favor. And, into the bargain, Abe is a Jew. Yeah, yeah, Carmine, I know you don't have an anti-semitic bone in your body, and under normal circumstances Abe knows that too. But this is an Italian-Irish police department, and Corey's roots are Irish. The fact that, of the two of them, it's Corey *looks* like the Jew is suddenly irrelevant to Abe. He thinks you're on Corey's side."

Carmine gave a groan. "Shit!"

"It's not too late, but watch your step in the future, and make sure you display a keen interest in Beatrice Egmont's murder—without treading on Abe's toes. Don't forget both men have wives at home to keep up the pressure and exaggerate the slights. There's a big difference between a senior sergeant's and a lieutenant's pay and perks. You don't have two people vying for the promotion, Carmine, you have four."

"Thanks, Patsy," he said, and left.

When Carmine phoned Beatrice Egmont's home, Abe answered. He sounded down, didn't have the usual note of optimism in his voice.

"Are you very busy with your case, Abe?"

"Anything but, Carmine. I've done the neighbors and her two sons, who live in Georgia but took the first plane north. So far it's bleak," said Abe. "Nothing's gone from the house, not even a cheap ornament, and no one, including me, can find a motive for the poor old thing's murder. She wouldn't harm a fly."

"There seems to have been a lot of that among the deaths—harmless people. But one or two stick out, and I could use some help, Abe. I can't move on Desmond Skeps yet, but I need someone with your people skills to start ferreting out a list of possible suspects. A man that powerful has to have plenty of enemies, and he wasn't famous for his tact and diplomacy either. If you're satisfied that you can't proceed with Beatrice Egmont unless you catch a break, would you mind looking into Skeps's friends and acquaintances for me?"

The voice when it came was eager, enthusiastic. "I'd be glad to, Carmine. Is the file at Cedar Street?"

"I'm looking at it as I speak. But before you start, go talk to Patsy, who can fill you in on the way Skeps died. Diabolical!"

There. A little mending of fences had been done, but he'd have to hope that Dean Denbigh and Mr. Peter Norton didn't mire him down. It was vital that he insert himself personally into Skeps's murder as soon as possible, and Carmine had his own way of working, which did not include flitting between several cases. The two that stuck out were Evan Pugh and Desmond Skeps—theirs were cruel, detached killers.

Now to get Dean Denbigh out of the way.

*   *   *

Two Chubb colleges, he thought as he drove up the north side of Holloman Green. The huge park, bisected by Maple Street, was still populated by skeletal trees, but even bare, they were magnificent, for they were venerable copper beeches planted in clusters that ensured plenty of sun-drenched grass. Garden beds already planted out promised a wonderful showing in May, and daffodil shoots were poking above the grass blades, not long off their profligate blooming. Dogwood trees indicated that there would be a breathtaking, curiously oriental wealth of flowers at the end of the first week in May, when the Green would be thronged with visitors photographing madly. Holloman Green was a "must" for spring tourists.

The other side of North Green Street belonged exclusively to Chubb University, whose campus was Princeton's only rival. In between gardens and grassy knolls stood the colleges, with the gothic cathedral bulk of the Skeffington Library dominating the far end. Most of the oldest colleges were at the top end of the Green, an orderly array of eighteenth-century buildings smothered in Virginia creeper. Here, along this side, were the frat houses and secret societies as well as the later colleges, some Victorian gothic, some the imitation Georgian so popular as the nineteenth century turned into the twentieth, and some the modern wonders belonging to the twentieth century. He passed the sprawling X of Paracelsus College with a grimace, quite forgetting that two months ago he and Desdemona had stood admiring its austere marble façade and the Henry Moore bronzes flanking its entrance.

Dante College was old, its anonymous architect unconcerned with the prospect of immortality; he had built gables and a profusion of dormered windows, absolutely dying to have his work buried under Virginia creeper. However, it had been modernized with ruthless skill and now boasted a plethora of bathrooms, an adequate kitchen and in-college laundry facilities way above the usual. Its student rooms were not as large as Paracelsus's, but they didn't need to be; Dante's rooms were all singles. As it was coeducational (the first of Chubb's colleges to take the plunge into mixed bathing), Dean John Kirkbride Denbigh had decided to divide his accommodation by floor, and put the women undergrads in the attic.

"We have a hundred boys and only twenty-five girls," said Dr. Marcus Ceruski, deputed to receive Captain Delmonico. "Next year we'll have fifty girls and only seventy-five boys, but we'll cross that bridge when we come to it. There has been a huge reaction against women students among the alumni, as you can imagine, and what frightens us is a significant diminution in alumnus funding. Many just cannot stomach a coeducational Chubb after two hundred and fifty years of men only."

Carmine listened as if he had never heard any of this before, wondering how Holloman's Gown segment could be so divorced from Town that they automatically assumed no townies would be interested in this new social convulsion—or be aware of it.

"Paracelsus is due to take women next year," Dr. Ceruski went on, "but they'll find it easier, as they're able to put half of the students upstairs and half downstairs."

An arrangement that wouldn't please the feminists, Carmine reflected; they wanted real integration, men and women on the same floor. Quite why, he hadn't worked out, though he suspected the object of the exercise was to make life as uncomfortable for men as possible.

"I believe that Cornucopia has endowed the building of an all-women's college," he said, straight-faced.

"Correct, though it won't be finished until 1970," said Marcus Ceruski, whose doctorate was probably in medieval manuscripts or something equally esoteric; Dante had a reputation for scholars of unusual bent. He opened a door, and they entered a large room paneled in some dark wood, most of its walls occupied by books in custom-made shelves—no higgledy-piggledy sizes in here! "This is Dean Denbigh's study."

"Where it happened," said Carmine, gazing around.

"Correct, Captain."

"Are the four students who were present here today?"

"Yes."

"And the wife, Dr. Pauline Denbigh?"

"Waiting in her study."

Carmine consulted a small notebook. "Would you send in Mr. Terence Arrowsmith, please?"

Dr. Ceruski disappeared with a nod, while Carmine prowled. The big leather host's chair closest to the desk was clearly where Dean Denbigh had sat; the Persian rug around it was ominously stained, as was the chair seat and one arm. When the door sounded, he looked toward it in time to see the entrance of a genuine scholar-in-the-making: round-shouldered and stooped, thick-lensed glasses over pale eyes, a full-lipped crimson mouth, an otherwise nondescript face. His breath was coming fast, the hand on the door trembling.

"Mr. Terence Arrowsmith?"

"Yes."

"I'm Captain Carmine Delmonico. Would you please sit down in the chair you occupied when Dr. Denbigh died?"

Terence Arrowsmith went to it dumbly, sat gingerly on its edge, and stared up at Carmine like a rabbit at a snake.

"Tell me everything as if I'm in complete ignorance of what happened. The whole story, including why you were here."

For a moment the young man said nothing, then he licked his impossibly red lips and began. "The Dean calls them Monday Fortnight Coffee—we all drank coffee except for him. He drank jasmine tea from some shop in Manhattan, and he never invited us to share it, even if someone said they liked jasmine tea. The Dean said his was very expensive and we shouldn't acquire a taste for it until we were at the very least senior fellows."

Interesting, thought Carmine. The Dean rubbed his preference in as exclusive, and his student guests didn't appreciate it. Though Terence Arrowsmith had scarcely begun his story, Carmine was getting an impression that the Dean hadn't been liked.

"You have to be a junior or a senior to be invited," the young man went on. "I'm a senior, and a fairly regular guest, which isn't unusual. It was more like a coffee klatch for favored people. The Dean was an authority on Dante himself, and those of us doing Italian Renaissance literature were his pets. If you were studying Goethe or moderns like Pirandello, you didn't get invited."

He's meticulous, thought Carmine. He'll give me the lot.

"I'm writing a paper on Boccaccio," said Terence Arrowsmith, "and Dr. Denbigh liked my work. He held his sessions on a Monday, every second week. The worst of it was that he ignored the time, so those of us who had a class straight after coffee break were sometimes so late we weren't let in. If the lecture was important, it was terribly frustrating, but he'd never let any of us leave until he was finished with whatever he was talking about. He expected give and take, so we knew it was useless to try to speed him up by letting him have the floor."

"Was there anything different about yesterday's session?"

"No, Captain, not that any of us noticed. In fact, the Dean was in a really good mood—he even told a joke! The routine was strict. We'd come in on the dot of ten and go straight to the cart, pour ourselves coffee and take one pastry. While we did that, the Dean went to a cupboard and got out the little box that held his jasmine tea packets. I remember that he was annoyed to find only one packet in the box—he said there should have been three. But I guess we all looked blank enough to pass inspection, because he didn't blame one of us. As we were sitting down, he took his packet across to the cart, where there's a special carafe of boiling water for him." Arrowsmith shivered, started trembling again. "I was watching him—after the business about the missing tea, I think we all were. He tore the packet open, dropped it on the cart, and put the tea bag in his mug."

"Is there any mistaking his mug?" Carmine asked.

"Not a chance. For one thing, it's made of fine china—the rest are ordinary thick pottery mugs. And for another, it's got 'The Dean' on both sides in German Gothic script. I guess the writing of fifteenth-century Italy wasn't florid enough, but his story was that his wife gave him the mug. He poured boiling water into the mug, carried it to his chair, and sat down. His smile was so—self-satisfied! We knew we were in for a long morning, that he'd found something fresh to discuss.

"Sure enough, 'I've found out something extremely interesting I wish to share with you, gentlemen,' he said, and stopped to blow on the surface of his tea. Funny, how vividly I remember that! He snorted and said something none of us really heard—about the tea, we all think in retrospect. Then he lifted the mug to his mouth and took a series of little sips—it had to have been scalding hot, but he made a real production of those sips, as if he was telling us we didn't have the intestinal fortitude to drink such hot liquid. Next I think was the noise, though Bill Partridge says the change in his face came first. I don't honestly think it matters much either way. He started to make a strangling, gurgling kind of noise, and his face went a bright red. He seemed to stretch out from the top of his head to his toes, stiff and straight as a board. Foam gushed out of his mouth, but he didn't retch like a vomit. His hands flailed about, his feet drummed on the floor, the foam flew around as his movements grew wilder, and we—we just sat there paralyzed and looked! It must have been close to a minute before Bill Partridge—he's the most scientific of us—suddenly jumped up and shouted that the Dean had had a seizure. Bill ran to the door and yelled for someone to call an ambulance, while the rest of us backed away. Bill came back and checked the Dean's pulse, looked at the pupils of his eyes, put his ear on the Dean's chest. Then he said the Dean was dead! And he wouldn't let any of us leave!"

"A sensible young man," said Carmine.

"Maybe so," said Terence Arrowsmith grimly, "but it sure destroyed a day of classes! The ambulance guys called the cops, and the next thing we knew, everybody was talking poison. Bill Partridge said it was cyanide."

"Did he, indeed? Upon what did he base that assumption, Mr. Arrowsmith?"

"A smell of almonds. But I didn't smell any almonds, and neither did Charlie Tindale. Two did, two didn't. Not good enough," said Mr. Arrowsmith.

"Did Dean Denbigh say anything from the moment he began sipping his tea until he died?"

"He *said* nothing, he just made obscene noises."

"What about the paper packet enclosing the tea bag? You said the Dean dropped it on the cart. Did anyone go near it?"

"Not while I was in the study, sir, and I didn't leave until the criminal pathology technicians came in."

"Did he simply drop it, or did he crumple it up?"

"He ripped it open to get the tea bag, then dropped it."

Which marked the end of Terence Arrowsmith's useful information. And, as it turned out, of the usefulness of all four students. Even Mr. William Partridge, the scientific one, could add nothing to Terence Arrowsmith's admirably sedate description of events. All Partridge was concerned about was cyanide. So when Carmine was done with them, he breathed a sigh of relief and headed around the corner to the Dean's wife's study.

She too was senior in the college; he had found that much out sitting at his desk in County Services. What he wasn't prepared for was her absolute detachment. A tall woman whom a great many men would call extremely attractive, she had a mass of red-gold hair pulled into a soft bun on her neck, a creamily flawless skin that didn't show her age, chiseled features that reminded Carmine of a Grace Kelly without the vulnerability, and a pair of yellow eyes. A lioness, if ever he had seen one.

Her handclasp was firm and dry; she put Carmine into a comfortable chair and seated herself in what he assumed was "her" chair when she wasn't behind her desk.

"My condolences for your loss, Dr. Denbigh," he said.

She blinked slowly, considering his statement. "Yes, I suppose it is a loss," she said in a light, clipped voice, "but luckily I have tenure, so John's death doesn't affect my career. Of course I'll have to move out of the Dean's apartment, but until Lysistrata College is finished in 1970—I'm in the running for Dean—I'll live in a room upstairs among the girls."

"Won't you find that confining?" Carmine asked, fascinated at where she was leading their conversation.

"Not really," she answered, composure unruffled. "John took up four-fifths of the space in our apartment. Most of my living is done here, in this room."

A twin of the Dean's, and no less spacious. He gazed at the rows of books, which seemed to be mostly in German. "I believe you're a great authority on the poetry of Rainer Maria Rilke, Dr. Denbigh," he said.

She looked surprised, as if policemen townies were not supposed to know that name. "Yes, as a matter of fact, I am."

"Under different circumstances it would be a pleasure to have a chat with you, as I'm a Rilke fan, but I'm afraid it's the death of your husband that concerns me today." He frowned. "From your manner, Dr. Denbigh, I might be pardoned for thinking that your marriage was a rather distant one?"

"Yes, it was," said she. "I see no point in dissimulation. If you talk to any of the faculty attached to Dante, they'll tell you the same. John and I had a marriage of convenience. To be dean, a man has to be married, and the possession of a scholar for a wife is an advantage. Put plainly, I am frigid. John was prepared to overlook that. His own sexual tastes ran to young girls, though he was always very careful. He had to be! His ambition was to be president of an Ivy League university, and he had all the prerequisites, including an ancestor off the *Mayflower*. My own aspirations didn't conflict with his in any way." She let her thick, perfectly painted lids fall over those remarkable eyes. "We got on together extremely well, and I worried for him."

"Was there anything different about him yesterday morning?"

"No, not really. If anything, his mood was somewhat sunnier than usual. I remarked on it to him over breakfast—we ate in the dining hall—and he laughed, said he'd had good news."

"Did he tell you what this good news was?"

The yellow eyes widened. "*John?* Pigs would fly first, Captain. Frankly, I thought he was tormenting me."

"How did you feel when you were told what had happened?"

"Stunned. Yes, I think that's the most accurate word to describe my feelings. John just wasn't the kind of man to be murdered—at least, not in this way, and inside his own study. Nor by such a subtle method, if one may call a brief agony subtle."

"What kind of murder wouldn't have left you so stunned?"

"Oh, something violent. Shot—beaten to death—stabbed. No matter how careful one might be, it's dangerous to philander with young girls. They have fathers, big brothers, boyfriends. I never re-member his being afraid of the consequences, because of his special genius, and it was genius! Any one affair lasted from three to six months, depending upon the girl's sexuality allied to her intellectual stupidity—he didn't choose them for their brains. But the moment he began to tire of a girl, he became carping, critical, unpleasant. It usually took two weeks for her to break off the relationship, con-vinced that the grievances were all hers."

"He satisfied her self-esteem, you mean."

"Precisely. And he did have a genius for it, Captain! He played those silly young things like a virtuoso plays a violin. And when she broke it off, the girl would be terrified of being found out, since she was leaving it behind her."

"Did he foul his own nest, Dr. Denbigh?"

"Never. A Dante girl—this is the first year we've had girls, of course—was absolutely safe. He picked up his prey in Joey's Pan-cake Diner on Cedar Street. I gather that's a haunt for kids from East Holloman State College and the Beckworth Secretarial College. He rented a little apartment in Mulvery Street, just a walk from the diner, and went by the name of Gary Hopkins, which he said had a plebeian ring. To the best of my knowledge, he was never found out."

"Sooner or later he would have been."

"Then I'm profoundly glad about whoever put the cyanide in his tea, Captain."

Wow! thought Carmine, leaving Dante College some time later. Dean John Kirkbride Denbigh was quite a guy. Until his murder, luck had smiled on him. With a patricianly beautiful wife whose scholarship matched his own and whose frigidity allowed him to indulge a perilous penchant for undergraduate girls, he couldn't lose. That is, if what his wife said was accurate. And there was no reason for her to lie; dead or alive, Dean Denbigh had ensured that her career would prosper. Still, rarely had he encountered such a cold fish. Had her husband been equally detached? No, probably not. He at least had appetites above and beyond scholarship. How old was he? Thirty-six. Plenty of time left to scramble up the academic ladder, not toward a full professorship in his field, but toward university administration. M.M., who was President of Chubb, still had a full ten years in the job, but the Secretary of Chubb, Henry Howard, was due to retire in four years. Odd that Mawson MacIntosh was always known as M.M., whereas Hank Howard had never managed to become H.H.

Midafternoon: time to return to County Services and see what his men had learned.

Abe and Corey shared an office, but when Carmine walked in, only Abe was there, head bent over sheaves of paper.

"How goes it, Abe?" he asked.

"Skeps's murder is one not short on suspects," Abe said. "By tomorrow I ought to have a paper trail a mile long for you."

"Fantastic," said Carmine, going out the opposite door.

A quick visit to Patrick revealed no further progress, so he went down to the basement parking lot, climbed back into his Ford Fairlane while its engine was still cooling down, and drove out to the Cartwright residence, himself behind the wheel. He just wasn't in the mood to hang around waiting for a driver, and he had Delia for his paperwork anyway.

The mood at the Cartwrights' had changed, and drastically; with Grant in custody for the murder of Jimmy, a pall of gloom had descended over the three remaining Cartwrights, suddenly horribly aware of Cathy's death. The haughty princess Selma was in the kitchen trying to prepare dinner, her tears running unchecked into a bowl of cooked elbow macaroni. Several different kinds of cheese stood on the counter together with a carton of milk. Carmine took pity on her.

"Grate a cup each of cheddar, Romano and Parmesan," he said, tearing off a sheet of paper towel and handing it to her. "Wipe your face and blow your nose, then you'll be able to see." He took a piece of macaroni, popped it in his mouth, and made a face. "No salt in the cooking water."

The girl had obeyed him and was now gazing into a cupboard. "What does a grater look like?" she asked, sniffling.

"This," said Carmine, producing it from a cabinet. "Hold the block of cheese against it and shove it downward—onto a plate, not the counter. Find the measuring set and keep each cheese separate. While you do that, I'll find your father. When you're finished, wait for me, okay? We'll get there."

Gerald Cartwright was in his office upstairs, weeping quite as hard as his daughter.

"I don't know what to do, what would work out for the best," he said helplessly when Carmine came in.

"Get your mother down here, first off. And a sister, yours or hers. You can't bring up your daughter in ignorance of domestic routines and then expect her to pitch in like a trained housekeeper—which you should have employed when Jimmy was born, then at least the Grant half of this mess wouldn't have happened. Can't you afford a housekeeper, Mr. Cartwright?"

"Not right now, Captain," Cartwright said, too dejected to defend himself. "Michel just quit—he's gone to a restaurant in Albany.

Now I have to decide what to do with l'Escargot—close it, or change the cuisine along with the name."

"I can't help you there, sir, but I do suggest that you think a little less about your businesses and a little more about your children!" Carmine said tartly. He sat down and glared fiercely at Gerald Cartwright. "However, right at this moment I want to know about your wife. You've had time to think, and I hope you've used it. Did she have any enemies?"

"No!" Cartwright said on a gasp. "No!"

"Did you engage in pillow talk when you were home?"

"I guess so, insofar as Jimmy let us."

"Which one of you did the talking?"

"Both of us. She was always interested in what Michel was doing. She thought I was too soft on him." Cartwright stopped to mop his eyes. "She talked about Jimmy, how unhappy the other kids were—and you're right, she kept asking for a full-time housekeeper. But I thought she was exaggerating, honest! We've always had Mrs. Williams once a week for the heavy cleaning."

"Did Mrs. Cartwright ever mention anyone stalking her, or otherwise annoying her? What about her friends? Did she get on with them?"

"It's like I told you before, Captain, Cathy didn't have time for a social life. Maybe other wives complain about catty friends or the bargains they picked up in Filene's Basement, but not Cathy. And she never once mentioned a man."

"So you have no idea why she was murdered?"

"No, none at all."

Carmine got up. "Make your business decision quickly, Mr. Cartwright, and bring some family in. Otherwise you might have Junior in trouble with the law too."

Gerald Cartwright went sheet-white, and bent his head over his books defensively.

Junior was glued to the giant television in the den next door; on his way past, Carmine beckoned imperiously.

"Come on, kid, turn it off. Until she gets some help, your sister needs a hand in the kitchen."

The boy did as he was told, but sulkily, and followed Carmine downstairs with dragging steps.

The cheese was grated, but the recalcitrant block of Parmesan had bitten back. Its crumbling tendrils were stained, and Selma was sucking her knuckles.

"Junior, get a Band-Aid," Carmine commanded, inspecting the graze. "Lesson number one when grating: watch your hands when the cheese wears down."

He sprinkled salt into the macaroni, teaching as he went, showed Selma how to make a tolerable cheese sauce, then made her mix half the Parmesan with breadcrumbs and sprinkle it on top of the macaroni and cheese. Into the oven it went, then, perched on a kitchen stool, Carmine found Cathy Cartwright's copy of *The Joy of Cooking* and picked out half a dozen easy recipes for Selma to follow. She was displaying some enthusiasm, having just (with Carmine's help) produced an edible meal on her first try. The princess was only skin deep.

"Did your mom have any enemies that you know of, Selma?" he asked, thumbing the pages of the cookbook.

"*Mom?*" The girl looked incredulous. "No!" The first sadness entered her eyes, and she blinked rapidly. "What time did she have for enemies, Captain?"

He put the cookbook down, slid off the stool and pressed her shoulder briefly. Then his gaze fell on Junior, about to disappear through the inside door; his lips tightened.

"And you," Carmine said to her brother as he opened the back door, "are going to do your share of the chores in future. If Selma is the cook, you're in charge of the laundry."

Snap! The door closed on Junior's outraged protests.

As he walked to his car, Carmine was grinning. It was rare for him to involve himself so personally in a family's tragedy, but the

Cartwrights were a special case. Not one but two murders, each by a different killer. They would survive, but thanks to Selma rather than to either Gerald. Though she hadn't known how, she had already been trying to cook when he arrived. The tragedy had thrown her in at life's deep end, but she was paddling bravely.

Carmine went back to County Services and a desk piled high, sat himself down and thanked his lucky stars for his secretary, Delia Carstairs, who happened to be Commissioner John Silvestri's niece. One incidence of nepotism actually working, he thought as his gaze traveled over the neat piles. Delia was a treasure he had inherited along with his captaincy; mere lieutenants didn't have secretaries, they availed themselves of the typing pool or their own typing skills, and they did their own filing. The odd thing was that she had belonged to Danny Marciano, his senior still, yet Danny had given her up with no more than a loud wail of anguish—and two secretaries to replace her.

She walked in from her tiny office, tiny only because all four of its walls were taken up by monstrous filing cabinets.

"About time," she said, distributing another sheaf of papers on various stacks.

She was thirty years old, short, and dressed in a manner that she called smart but that Carmine privately called appalling. Today she wore a fussy suit of some multicolored, knobby fabric whose skirt barely reached her knees. Two utterly shapeless legs of the kind seen on grand pianos supported a tubby body and the weight of far too much massive costume jewelry. Her face was caked with makeup, her frizzy hair was an improbable shade of strawberry blonde, and her shrewd, twinkling, light brown eyes were surrounded by enough paint to satisfy a Cleopatra. The only product of a union between

Commissioner Silvestri's sister and an Oxford don, Delia had been born and raised in England.

Both parents despaired of her. But Delia required no parental guidance of any kind; she knew exactly what she was going to do and where she was going to do it. A course at a top London secretarial college saw her graduate at the head of her class; as soon as her papers and certificate were in her hands, she packed her bags and climbed on a plane for New York. There she went to work in the NYPD headquarters typists' pool, and soon found herself the private secretary of a deputy commissioner. Unfortunately, the bulk of his work concerned social misfits, and it quickly dawned on Delia that she was actually too desirable to wind up where she wanted to be—in Homicide. The NYPD was just too vast, and she was too good at her job.

So she took a train to Holloman and asked Uncle John for a job. Since his phone had been ringing off the hook about her all the previous day, Silvestri ignored his dictum about nepotism and grabbed her. Not for himself, but for Danny Marciano, whose administrative duties were far heavier. What Delia didn't know about police work could have been written on the head of a pin, but it didn't occur to Uncle John that his niece craved blood and gore until Carmine was promoted to captain. Please, begged Delia, could she work for Captain Delmonico, the murder expert?

"There's hours of reading here," said Carmine to her.

"I know, but it's all absolutely riveting," said Delia in her polished Oxford accent. "Twelve murders in one day!"

"Don't rub it in, you horrible woman!"

She laughed and tittupped out on very high heels, leaving her boss to stare at the surface of his desk. Where to begin?

With Larry Pisano's cases, that was logical, the three shootings and the prostitute.

Three different handguns, all silenced. Now why had it been done that way? What about the victims dictated the use of three different firearms? The answer kept coming back to nothing, which didn't make sense. Silencers indicated professional killers, not the style of shooting common in the Hollow and in the Argyle Avenue district. And that spoke of big money to take out three harmless blacks. . . . What on earth could they possibly know to warrant such an outlay? Pisano and his team had burrowed assiduously, without results. The woman was elderly and inoffensive, both the youths fine types. Blood analysis on all three had found its way into the pile, to reveal no trace of any illicit substance either over time or on the morning of their deaths. They were just what they appeared to be, the kind of people who didn't get killed by a deliberate act, by selection. Yet these three had been selected, had been deliberately killed, by men taking no chances, men who were professional assassins. The whole thing screamed of out-of-state to Carmine. Though Connecticut had its share of black militants, gangsters, and hoods, it didn't run to hired assassins using silencers, men competent enough to pick their moment on the street when the victim wouldn't be noticed going down in a heap until the getaway had been invisibly made.

Okay, thought Carmine, setting the shootings aside, I am going to presume that the perpetrators are out-of-state, and bring Larry and his boys onto fresh fields as soon as I make up my mind where the exhaustive investigations are going to yield fruit.

Next he went to Larry's last case, the prostitute. Everybody knew Dee-Dee Hall, and not because she was always in trouble: far from it. Though she worked the street, she had her beat and never strayed from it. Her pimp was Marty Fane, part of the reason why she stayed out of trouble; he was easygoing for a pimp, and he valued Dee-Dee too highly to ill-treat her. Though she was now thirty-two years old, she had weathered her eighteen years on the street better than most and kept her striking good looks. The pity of it was that, had she only been a few years younger, Carmine reflected, she would have become a call girl rather than a streetwalker, but by the time call girls were a common phenomenon, Dee-Dee's gloss was gone. At six feet, her height was in her shapely legs, and she still had a voluptuous body. Her hair was brassy, her eyes green, her skin the color of café au lait. All of which procured her plenty of johns, but was not the basis of her popularity. That lay in her ability to give a great blow job; it was said she had more suck than Eskimo Nell. This particular speciality also meant no unwanted pregnancies, hence her good health and the preservation of her figure. Her pimp, Marty Fane, pampered her by feeding her heroin habit and making sure her room with bath and kitchenette on the fringes of the Argyle Avenue ghetto had cleaning and laundry service. Dee-Dee was his top earner.

According to Larry, who had taken on Dee-Dee's case personally, Marty Fane was devastated at his loss. No matter how intensively Larry questioned the denizens of that seedy world in which Marty and Dee-Dee lived, he could find no evidence of a falling out between pimp and prostitute. The two had been seen giggling together as they took a break somewhere around two a.m. Which made Marty the last person known to have seen her alive. Her beat lay behind the Holloman City Hall, where the neighborhood was far less salubrious than in front. It was an area of parking lots, workshops, warehouses and blue-collar offices, deserted after dark save for those who cruised looking for a little sexual action, like Chubb students, commercial travelers and night workers.

Bitter at her murder, even grief-stricken, Marty Fane was quick to yield up the names of her regular johns insofar as he knew them, which had led to some embarrassing interviews with men foolish enough to deny their connection. The young Chubbers tended to be rather thrilled until it dawned upon them that they were suspects in a murder, whereupon those with powerful daddies suddenly demanded to see their lawyers and tried to say nothing. Once the lawyers were persuaded that their clients were more a source of information than suspects, they coöperated, but to no avail. Dee-Dee's death remained shrouded in mystery.

Zilch, said Carmine to himself, adding the prostitute to the three shootings. Whoever had done it was as cool as Dr. Pauline Denbigh, though he doubted it was her. Not an out-of-stater either; the killer knew exactly where to find the hapless victim. Maybe someone to whom she'd given one of her fabled blow jobs in the past? Weep your heart out, Marty Fane! It will be a very long time before you find another Dee-Dee Hall.

Cathy Cartwright, killed before her handicapped child made a mess in his diaper. Like Desmond Skeps, yet unlike him. The drugged glass of bourbon—sad, to think that the poor woman had to go to bed in order to have a civilized drink. When she felt the effects of the chloral hydrate she probably didn't try to fight them, deeming herself bone-weary and looking forward to a few hours of peaceful sleep, wondering when Jimmy would wake her demanding to be changed. Patrick thought the pentobarbital had been injected immediately; she was perhaps the first of the night's victims to die, very quickly and without any pain. The vital centers in her brain stem had gently ceased to function, and she slipped away. What about her had prompted mercy? It said the killer felt kindly about her, regretted the necessity.

Carmine, Carmine! He sat up straight, conscious of the sweat trickling down the back of his neck, running between his shoulder blades. You're thinking as if there's only one murderer! But there can't be. Too many crimes in too many different places at close enough to the same time. Unless some of the murders were commissioned? But that calls for huge amounts of money, and a mastermind. Look at it dispassionately, and you'll see how wrong you are. . . . About the only reason for such an orgy of killing at more or less the same moment is a spirit of mischief, which is ridiculous. Manifestly ridiculous! Think of the risks! Anyone intelligent enough to hatch a plot like that would be too intelligent to contemplate its hatching.

Confess it, Carmine, the idea only entered your mind after you learned that Desmond Skeps was among the dead. How brilliant, to conceal the importance of his murder under a landslide of other murders! An idea that might have held water, had there been fewer murders. But *ten* others? Jimmy Cartwright was a red herring, but the rest looked planned. Four other murders would have been ideal, and feasible. Ten others? Insanity!

Unless . . . unless, Carmine, all those people had to die. Unless between March twenty-ninth and April third something happened that forced this particular solution. Only, what? Oh, Carmine, Carmine, don't complicate your job so crazily! And don't you dare voice this suspicion to anyone, even John Silvestri.

Aware that the worm, having been born, was wriggling inside his brain and lighting every hidden, darkened cranny, Carmine put Cathy Cartwright on the "seen" pile and took Corey's file on Bianca Tolano.

Bianca, twenty-two years old, had come to Holloman from Pennsylvania ten months ago. A graduate in economics from Penn State, she wanted to get an MBA at Harvard Business School, Corey had deduced from her correspondence and other papers in her apartment. But at present she lacked the money, so she had secured a job as an executive assistant at Carrington Machine Parts, one of the many Cornucopia companies dotted around Holloman. It paid well and she was a success at it; her savings account with the Holloman National Bank was growing fast. The top floor of a three-family house on Sycamore Street, her apartment was less than a block from his wife's old apartment, Carmine discovered with a shudder. Back came the memories of Desdemona's ordeal there, and the garotted cop supposed to be guarding her front door. A respectable neighborhood. Then Desdemona. And now this.

Her landlord had noticed her open front door, called out, and, receiving no reply, entered to find her naked body on the living room floor. According to Patsy, she had been tortured, including with a pair of pantyhose tightened and loosened around her neck a number of times; she had been burned with a cigarette, cut with scissors, pinched with cruelly wielded tweezers, and killed with a broken bottle rammed into her vagina. Apart from the temporary asphyxiations, she was conscious throughout; there were no drugs in her bloodstream.

Interviews with her colleagues had revealed that she kept to herself but was not shy. Her relationship with her boss, James Dorley, was pleasant and friendly in a professional way. As she was attractive, she had had offers of dinner or a movie, and had accepted several without any romantic consequences. The men were at pains to explain that Bianca had proven aloof, didn't offer a guy any encouragement. Her landlord, an inquisitive old man, said he'd swear on a stack of Bibles that she hadn't had any male visitors. Quiet, that was Miss Tolano. The women she worked with gave Corey no leads either. She'd participate in a coffee klatch, do her share of giggling, but gave the other girls the impression that nothing was going to come between Bianca and that MBA from Harvard. They did tell Corey that her home in Scranton had not been a happy one, that she didn't keep in touch with her family, and was very glad to be somewhere else. Did she ever go out? asked Corey. Sometimes, the women answered, usually because Mr. Dorley gave her tickets to the theater or to events he couldn't manage to attend. The only one she didn't take him up on was a charity ball—she didn't have a stylish enough dress, she said.

Another big fat zero, thought Carmine, adding Bianca Tolano to the "seen" pile. If Corey hoped Bianca Tolano would make him shine for the selection panel, he was wrong. His case was as bare as Abe's.

Abe had done his best with Beatrice Egmont: no stone was unturned, from the trash collectors to the sons to the neighbors. What stood up high above the level plain of her existence was her personality; everyone who knew Beatrice Egmont loved her. She didn't intrude herself into other people's lives or doings, but she was always there with some appropriate gesture, suggestion, gift. Nor did she live the life of a recluse just because she had been a widow for many years; she was invited to all the local parties, loved busing into Manhattan for dinner and a show, bought Girl Scout cookies and raffle tickets, was never missing from the guest list of Holloman charity affairs. She knew the Mayor well, which had led to enquiries from City Hall about her murder. As far as Abe could ascertain, nothing was missing from her house; her Ming vases and Flemish tapestries were untouched, and her Baume & Mercier watch was still on her wrist when she was found. She had not been drugged prior to retiring for the night, but her heart had given out too quickly for her to struggle. "I can find no reason whatsoever for her death," wrote Abe.

Goodbye, Beatrice Egmont, you poor old thing. Carmine put her file on top of the growing heap he had tabled. There remained his own cases: Dean Denbigh, Peter Norton, Desmond Skeps, Cathy Cartwright and Evan Pugh.

Undoubtedly Dean Denbigh had courted disaster, but his wife was quite right: why a subtle death like cyanide administered in his study? He should have been shot, stabbed, beaten to death somewhere in the vicinity of Joey's Pancake Diner—was the diner a link between him and Gerald Cartwright, who owned it? According to Patrick's report, the packet enclosing the tea bag bore only one tear, that made by the Dean, and powerful microscopy hadn't revealed oversewn stitch holes on the tea bag. The theft of two tea packets had forced the Dean to use the last one in his box; clearly he was destined to die on this day and no other, making his poisoning different from ordinary cases of poisoning. Some killers accepted a certain randomness, but not his killer. Thou shalt die today, the third day of April, and on no other day. . . . And why cyanide? To make absolutely sure that the Dean of Dante College would not survive.

Peter Charles Norton was different. Though Carmine had managed to visit the Norton house only once, what he found there disposed him to dismiss the wife as a suspect, despite the fact that she had squeezed the glass of orange juice. He'd left them alone because the only adult witness, the wife, had been madly hysterical. Tomorrow he'd send Abe or Corey back expecting answers to his questions. However, he had made deductions, the first being that Peter Norton was the sole drinker of orange juice; a jar of cranberry juice in the refrigerator suggested that the wife and children drank that. All she squeezed was one glass, for a man who gulped it down and ate his toast going through the door. Carmine had a private bet that Norton had a second breakfast at Joey's Pancake Diner. The toast and juice were sops to Mrs. Norton.

On April third he had died, but only after long, excruciating agony. This said that the killer thought Norton should die with maximum visual effect. Was he punishing the husband, or the wife? That depended upon how soon into his dying Norton lost consciousness. There were no traces of any other substances in his blood, though his sugar was significantly elevated and his arteries were already showing signs of the burger-and-fries diet a cop on door-knock queries had noted he loved. Patsy had raced back and tested the sugar in a bowl and a larger container, since the blood evidence suggested Mrs. Norton sweetened the juice, and what if the kids put it on their cereal? But no poison of any kind was found in it. Good thinking, Patsy!

Delia had left bank statements with the Norton papers—what a gem she was! The manager of the Fourth National Bank, Norton clearly had no financial worries. He lived within his means and had made no large withdrawals over the past year, which was as far back as Delia had gone for the moment. His Ohio family was a wealthy one, whereas Mrs. Norton came from a blue-collar family in Waterbury.

He tossed the file in the direction of the rejects and stared down at Evan Pugh with a heavy frown. His instincts said this was the extraordinary murder, the one that differed from all the others. Who was Motor Mouth? And what had prompted such a bizarre method of killing? A bear trap! Not one of the dinky specimens designed to keep the bear in one spot until pleasure could be taken in shooting it; this was the man-trap kind, big enough to maim the bear, ensure it bled to death. A weapon of survival for man, extinction for the bear.

Evan Pugh's parents were on their way from Florida, where they lived in one of those grandiose mansions fronting on an artificial waterway; having made a bundle in retail electronics, Evan Pugh's father had retired to enjoy the life of a lotus eater in a place where it never really got cold, let alone snowed. Evan was their only child, so life for the police investigating his murder was about to become a great deal less comfortable; the Pughs were bringing their lawyer with them.

Which left the one crime whose scene Carmine hadn't yet had time to visit. There was no hurry, he knew. Desmond Skeps's penthouse was sealed, its private elevator locked, the two sets of fire stairs barred and padlocked. Abe hadn't wasted time going there; he'd worked from Skeps's office as he gathered information about the tycoon's subordinates and acquaintances. The grisly details of his murder Carmine knew from talking to Patsy. Like Bianca Tolano, Skeps had been tortured, though his was no sex crime, and like Cathy Cartwright and Peter Norton and Dean Denbigh, he had been poisoned. Yet which had true significance, the similarities or the dissimilarities?

There you go again, Carmine, assuming this is a single killer! You haven't a shred of evidence to prove that—but then, you haven't a shred of evidence about multiple killers either. In fact, the commissioned out-of-state killer feels right for maybe half of the victims, and that *does* suggest a mastermind, at least for those murders. Why not hired assassins for all of them? Is there anything to suggest a hands-on murderer? Yes, but only in two deaths—Desmond Skeps and Evan Pugh. These smack of personal enjoyment. And if Pugh's blackmail concerned the killings, it makes sense, even to why there was no written legacy of its subject matter. All Pugh had to do was speak, and the brilliant eye of police investigation would be refocused in a direction the killer couldn't afford to have illuminated. Which brings it back to Skeps himself as the main target. But why did the others have to die at all?

Time will tell, thought Carmine, more comfortable now with his theory. I've only just begun to start unpicking the pattern; then I have to knit it together again. Tomorrow I go back to my customary way: working each crime myself, with Abe and Corey in tow. Too bad if they don't get any cases to work on their own! I'm like an amputee without Abe and Corey. I need three pairs of eyes, three pairs of ears, and three brains.

He glanced at the big clock above Delia's door. Six thirty! Where did the time go? Her light was on, so he poked his head around the open door.

"Go home, otherwise some lustful cop will hit on you."

"In a minute," she answered absently, missing the joking compliment entirely. "I just want to collate these bank records. It took me all day to get them."

"Okay, but don't stay forever. And gather everyone for a conference in Silvestri's room at nine tomorrow morning, please."

Now, with Myron Mendel Mandelbaum in residence on East Circle, he'd better go home.

There were few men Carmine loved deeply. Pride of place was held by Patrick O'Donnell, but next on the list was his ex-wife's second husband. Neither man had ended up loving the wife in common, Sandra, but both were completely devoted to Carmine's and Sandra's daughter, Sophia. Though Myron missed her with that awful hollowness of an empty house and absent laughter, he hadn't even hesitated to send her east after Carmine married Desdemona, knowing her life in the relatively modest house on East Circle would be far better for her than to continue in his own replica of Hampton Court Palace, where her mother displayed no interest in her and Myron himself had calls on his time he couldn't avoid without running the risk of losing everything he owned. A prenuptial agreement, uncommon in 1952, had ensured that Sandra would get no more than a few millions upon his death, but Sophia was his heir, and he wanted the girl to inherit a massive estate. Not for one moment did he think Sophia would fritter it away; his rooted conviction was that this beloved stepdaughter would do very well by it. Though she had been educated in all the acceptable disciplines from mathematics to English literature, he had also made Sophia privy to one of his business activities, the raising of funds to produce motion pictures and the overseeing of the picture's finances from preproduction to in the can and theater distribution. By the time she was twenty-one, Myron had resolved, Sophia would be fit to wear the hat of a Hollywood producer, if such was her inclination, or else be well on her way to managing all of his many business activities.

Myron knew Carmine guessed at his plans for Sophia, but they had never spoken of them; Carmine was too sensitive of Sophia's position to make the first overtures, and Myron was too cagey. If his dear friend Carmine had any real idea of the extent of his business empire, Myron knew he wouldn't want Sophia burdened with a tenth so much. But the Sophia Carmine knew was a shadowy figure; it was Myron who had been to all intents and purposes her permanent father between her second and her sixteenth birthday, so it was Myron who knew her far better.

Besides, Myron was still hale and hearty, and blithely expected to live for many years to come. Therefore he failed to see why he should take Carmine into his confidence while the girl herself happily pursued the life of a sixteen-year-old in a loving home and at a good school. What didn't occur to him was that, newly deprived of his beloved child and inexpressibly lonely, he was ripe for someone enterprising to pluck him.

Knowing himself always welcome at Carmine's, he took a few days off every time he visited New York City and appeared at the house on East Circle. This visit, however, was a surprise; the latest film, featuring no fewer than three top stars, was still in a state of flux. His excuse was that the money for it was in New York, but to Carmine it rang false; the money was always in New York. No, Myron was here because the death of Desmond Skeps was making headlines.

When Carmine walked in, Myron was seated in a large chair in the living room with a glass of Kentucky straight bourbon and soda near at hand, reading a copy of this week's *News* magazine.

At fifty, he was older than Carmine, and his famed ability to attract beautiful women was a by-product of the power he wielded rather than any remarkable good looks. He was bald enough to keep what hair he still owned cut very close to his scalp; his long and clever face had a firm mouth and greenish-grey eyes that, Sophia insisted, saw clear through to the soul. When he stood to give Carmine a hug, he was revealed as a short man with a slender body that bore no sign of the fleshpots he adored.

The hug over, he brandished the magazine at Carmine. "Have you seen this?" he demanded.

"Only in passing," Carmine said, kissing his wife, who came to join them carrying her own tipple, gin and tonic. Sophia was on her heels and gave him a glass of bourbon made exactly how he liked it, diluted with soda but not drowned.

"You must read Karnowski's article on the Reds," Myron said, subsiding into his chair. "It's been years since I've seen anything this good, especially on the historical side. He's given detailed sketches of every member of the Central Committee who's ever aspired to the secretaryship since Stalin died, and his portrait of Stalin himself is riveting. I'd love to know his sources—there's material in here I've never seen at all."

"Under ordinary circumstances I'd be buried in it," Carmine said ruefully, "but not at the moment. Too much on my plate."

"So I hear."

"Little pitchers," warned Carmine, rolling his eyes at Sophia. "Which New York banker is holding you to ransom, Myron?"

"No one you'd know." Myron looked uneasy, then shrugged. "I guess I'd better get it off my chest right now," he said, his tone defensive. "I'm divorcing Sandra."

"*Myron!*" Desdemona gave a gasp. "What on earth has the poor creature done after so many years?"

"Nothing, really. I just got tired of her shenanigans," said Myron, still sounding defensive.

"What will Sandra do?" Desdemona asked, looking sideways at Sophia, who sat with an expressionless face and a glass of Tab she wasn't drinking.

"She'll be fine, honest! I've settled twenty million on her, but in a way that means no money-hungry guy can grab it, even by marriage and community property. She gets to take the housekeeper and the maids, so her habit's safe."

Sophia found her voice. "Daddy, *why?*" she asked.

Carmine didn't make the mistake of thinking the question was directed at him; Sophia called both men "Daddy."

"I told you, honey. I just got tired of her."

"I don't believe that! You got tired of Sandra years ago! What's changed?"

Here it comes, thought Carmine, sipping his drink.

Myron coughed, looked shy. "Um—well . . . I met a lady. A real lady."

"Ohhh!" Sophia's eyes went round, then something fierce and intensely proprietary flashed into them; by the time she gazed at Myron it was gone, replaced by a limpid curiosity. "Tell us more, Daddy, please!"

"Her name is Dr. Erica Davenport, and she's the chief legal officer attached to Cornucopia. She lives right here in Holloman! It's early days yet, but I figured with the death of her boss, Desmond Skeps, she can probably do with some moral support. When I called her from L.A. she sounded harassed. She didn't ask me to come, but I have anyway."

Carmine swallowed. "Myron, this could be a conflict. You should have stayed on the West Coast," he said.

"But Erica's my friend!" Myron protested.

"And a possible suspect in her boss's death. I can't stop your seeing her, Myron, but she can't come anywhere near my home, surely you see *that!*"

"Oh, potties!" said Myron, using an expletive he had picked up somewhere and thought innocuous enough for Sophia's ears.

"You're in love, that's why you want a divorce," Desdemona said, gathering empty glasses.

"Do you think so?"

"I do. One more drink, then we eat. Roast leg of New Zealand lamb with all the trimmings."

She and Sophia left for the kitchen. Carmine stared at his beloved friend sternly. "Myron, I don't need this complication."

"I'm sorry, Carmine. I didn't think! I just wanted to be at Erica's side."

"As long as you understand the limitations."

"I do, now that you've spelled them out. I'll take Erica to lunch tomorrow and explain."

"No, you won't. Like all the other suspects, she has to be in the Cornucopia building tomorrow, all day. Maybe into the night as well. I suggest you explain matters on the phone, and hope that I'm done with her in time to take her to dinner."

"Shit!"

"Be it on your own head, Myron. And don't expect to get much sympathy from Sophia."

"Fuck!"

"Your vocabulary's going downhill, old friend. So what's so exciting about this *News* magazine article?"

"Weren't you listening? Just that it's the best article on the Reds in years, especially about the Central Committee members. In case you've forgotten, Carmine, this country is in the middle of a cold war with the USSR."

"No, I hadn't forgotten that. But at the moment my city seems in the middle of a hot war against persons unknown. And here come our second drinks, so let's go back to *News* magazine."

Since everybody present at the meeting knew how little progress had been made, the only man in attendance who wasn't surprised at its being called was Carmine. The only woman, Delia Carstairs, had a very good idea what was going down, but her function was to take minutes, not make comments.

"We're going about this the wrong way," Carmine said after John Silvestri opened the proceedings. "From today on, the department goes back to normal insofar as it can. Larry, you and your guys will take over Holloman's routine crimes—by which I mean crimes unconnected to the twelve deaths of April third. If we don't pay them any attention, we'll be swamped by robberies and domestic violence as well as biker and militant and other gang feuds. Get out there and let the local hoods know we haven't overlooked them. You did great work on the three shootings and the prostitute, Larry, but that's ground to a halt, and I'm not wasting our manpower chasing leads that go nowhere. So thanks very much, guys, but I won't need you anymore."

Significantly, Larry Pisano and his men didn't look at all indignant. Rather, they looked relieved. In being sent back to Holloman's routine crimes, their success rate had just soared. In fact, so eager was Larry to get onto his new task that he rose to his feet without being dismissed.

"Then you don't need me here, Carmine, right?"

"Right."

Carmine waited until the three men left the room. "What I say now goes no farther, understood?"

"Eminently," said Commissioner Silvestri. "You've formed some conclusions?"

"Yes, sir, I have. I don't claim that they're the correct ones, but for the moment they suit my purposes. Some of the eleven murders—from now on we ignore Jimmy Cartwright—I believe were commissioned from out of state. The three shootings, definitely. Possibly also Peter Norton's poisoning, Bianca Tolano's rape, Cathy Cartwright's killing, and the smothering of Beatrice Egmont. Each was done professionally, and I include the sex murder in that because it was so—*textbook*."

"You're talking seven crimes, Carmine," said Patsy, frowning.

"Yes."

"What about Dee-Dee Hall?"

"No, I think she was a personal kill. And so were Evan Pugh and Desmond Skeps."

"You're forgetting Dean Denbigh. Where does he fit in?"

"I'm not sure yet, Patsy. My instincts say a commission, but if it is, why go to such tortuous lengths with the tea packet and tea bag? Why shouldn't they show evidence of tampering? Maybe he's a stray."

"That I refuse to believe!" said Danny Marciano. "On any other day, there's a chance, but not on April third. You've used up your stray with Jimmy Cartwright, Carmine."

"I know, I know!"

A silence fell, suddenly so profound that the susurration of Silvestri's state-of-the-art air conditioner was a roar.

Silvestri broke it. "You're proposing one murderer, Carmine."

"Yes. And if I'm right, he made a terrible mistake in dispatching all his victims on the same day. That meant he had to farm most of them out. But this isn't a dodo, this is a mastermind. Therefore he *knew* he was making a mistake, and that says he had no choice. For some reason they all had to die on the same day, which suggests that the threat they posed is very recent and had to be acted on at once." Carmine's face looked both grim and elated, an expression everyone there knew: he was looking forward to—yet dreading—the hunt.

Silvestri shook his head. "I don't know how you manage that, Carmine, conning us into thinking your way before we really know what you're driving at. One murderer? It's crazy!"

"I agree, sir, but let's go with it! Is it any crazier than twelve murders in one day in a city the size of Holloman? In fact, to me it's the only answer that makes any sense. If eleven people have died in such disparate ways, doesn't it scream one killer? Mass murder happens, but it's some psycho with a machine gun in a crowded place, or a hijacker bringing down a plane because he didn't understand the thing he was holding. This is different."

"I get your drift," the Commissioner said. "Go on."

"To hire professional killers says the mastermind—that's not a word I like—has unlimited money. Why don't I like the word 'mastermind'? Because on at least one occasion he was very indiscreet and earned himself the nickname of Motor Mouth from Evan Pugh. That's why we've found no trace of anything Pugh could have used

for blackmail. The subject of the blackmail is simply something Motor Mouth said and everybody except Evan Pugh forgot. The hardest
kind of blackmail to prove."

"It's too far-fetched," said Danny Marciano.

"I agree, it is far-fetched, but not *too* far-fetched. Give me a better reason for three out-of-state shootings, Danny! Those harmless
people were handpicked for execution by men using silencers and accustomed to fast getaways. Far too sophisticated for Holloman! One
incident, yes, but three, all at the same time? Never happen. I get the
feeling that the guy who commissioned these killings is laughing at
us as provincial dunderheads."

"Then he doesn't know you, Carmine," said Abe loyally.

"Oh, I think he does, Abe, if only socially. This is a small city, and
I get around."

"How do you intend to proceed?" Silvestri asked.

"My usual way, sir. I'm taking all eleven cases back, and Abe and
Corey as well. Sorry, guys, but I can't do without you. If I send either of you to question people, I can be sure it'll be done as if I did it
myself. That goes for looking at evidence too. Today we concentrate
on Desmond Skeps. Abe's done the workup, but now we tighten the
noose at Cornucopia."

Carmine looked directly at his boss. "You may get some pressure
from Hartford on this if we ask too many awkward questions. Or
even from Washington. I also have to inform you that my fool friend,
Myron Mandelbaum, is smitten with Cornucopia's legal officer, a
woman named Erica Davenport. I've warned him off and he knows
he can't invite her to my home, but I don't want any flak coming your
way because of him."

Silvestri remained unruffled. "What's a bit more flak from Hartford and Washington, when I have a press conference in a few minutes? The sharks are in a feeding frenzy over Skeps's death, so I intend
to throw them chunks of Skeps. Keep them chomping at his carcass.
Twelve murders? *What* twelve murders? I'll be firm that we have no
local suspects for Skeps's murder, of course. That's why the FBI is

here. We're looking in New York and other financial capitals. That's the way I'm going to play it, one press conference after another. Keep the sharks way away from Holloman." He waved a hand. "Go away! I have to think."

Carmine went, frowning. FBI? What did Silvestri mean?

The Cornucopia building stood on the corner of Maple and Cromwell, downtown in the shopping and business district, and was only a year old; at forty storeys it was the tallest structure in Holloman. The penthouse was Desmond Skeps's residence, while the lower thirty-nine storeys housed the head offices of all of Cornucopia's many companies, with Desmond Skeps's own offices located on the thirty-ninth floor. Curiously, he had provided no direct access between his working and living quarters; in order to enter the penthouse, he had to leave his offices and travel back down to the first floor and his private elevator to the penthouse. I suppose, thought Carmine, it keeps business truly separated from pleasure.

The downstairs foyer was sheathed in multicolored marble and adorned with lush palms in handmade marble pots; a closer inspection revealed that the palms could be lifted out holus-bolus in smaller, plastic pots. There was an enquiry desk and a visitor's desk whose lone attendant's job was to pin a tag on each visitor. Those who worked inside the building took no notice of anyone on their way in or out. One bank of elevators served floors two to nineteen, the other floors twenty to thirty-nine; the penthouse elevator stood alone at the blind end and had NO ADMITTANCE painted on a wooden stand in front of its shiny copper doors.

Armed with a key, Carmine triggered the doors, which opened onto an interior plush with squabbed tannish-pink leather, a rosso antico marble floor, and carved and gilded trims. The panel bore only two buttons: UP and DOWN. How arrogant, he thought, amused. At the top it opened directly into the apartment, which was huge. First was a foyer the size of most living rooms, then a living room the size of most houses, with glass walls on two sides; one overlooked North Holloman, and one Long Island Sound and the Harbor. Carmine could see his own home's jetty clearly, and his square tower with the widow's walk. A low-powered telescope on a tripod made him wonder what else Desmond Skeps had seen, and in more homes than Carmine's. Mr. Skeps, he thought, I do not like you. Privacy is our last defense against the barbarian, and you are as big a barbarian as federal governments.

The decor was interior decorator beige, conservative and safe, nor were there any precious objects scattered around to suggest that Skeps collected art or even kitsch. The pictures on the walls were second-rate watercolors the decorator had probably passed off as first-rate, though in the bedroom this individual had gone for etchings torn out of over-sized Victorian books and framed. The bill had undoubtedly been astronomical, but Carmine spared no pity for a man who didn't know second-rate when he saw it.

Skeps had been murdered not in his bed but on his massage couch, a taller, narrower item of furniture that would have suited his murderer's intentions admirably. Either he had climbed onto it voluntarily, or the murderer was strong enough to lift him there bodily after his glass of single malt Glenlivet and chloral hydrate. Certainly he wouldn't have consumed the Scotch lying flat out on what was to become his deathbed. A strong killer, Carmine said to himself, thinking of the bear trap. These two killings were done personally, and they argued great physical strength. Look for someone rolling in money and built like Mr. Universe and you won't go far wrong. But what if no one was both? What if no one was either?

Patsy's boys had been over the crime scene meticulously, so he didn't bother going over it again. What he wanted was to get an idea of Desmond Skeps from his living arrangements.

He knew what the rest of the world knew already, and from the same sources: gossip magazines, columnists, an occasional serious article in the *Wall Street Journal* or the *New York Times*. Skeps's father, a successful manufacturer of automobile parts, had seen the war clouds gathering over Europe in 1938, and had not overlooked Southeast Asia either. He had founded Cornucopia (the name, he said, simply meant a horn of plenty) to manufacture artillery, then branched into airplane engines and machines of war. After Pearl Harbor his empire mushroomed, and it never ceased to grow. Now, in 1967, it manufactured surgical instruments and equipment, guns and howitzers, turbine engines, generators, atomic reactors, missiles, and small arms, and had branched into plastics, particularly those with military importance. Cornucopia had a huge research facility and was on the cutting edge of all it manufactured; it also held a large number of defense contracts for the armed services.

Skeps's job was enormous, but not hands-on in any way. He had about fifty managing directors, and they didn't lay their hands on much either; about three or four down the pecking order saw the first such men, Carmine guessed. Well, that was what happened in any conglomerate, and Cornucopia was a modest conglomerate. The physical description he had of Skeps was of a tall, thin, dark and ungainly man who was magnetically attractive to women. That was the power operating, of course, the same as with Myron Mendel Mandelbaum. Once married to a very beautiful woman, he had driven her away with his jealousy, and he had not married again. There was one child, a boy, now aged thirteen, who went to the Trinity Grey School. His name—no surprise—was Desmond Skeps III. His mother had full custody, which indicated Skeps had done something pretty bad to blot his copybook.

What Skeps thought of his son or the boy's mother was hard to tell, as no photograph or portrait of either hung in the apartment. He would have to see the mother, of course, but that necessitated a trip to Orleans, on Cape Cod, where Philomena Skeps lived. So, at the moment, according to his information, did the boy, convalescing from some serious illness. He had been out of school already for five weeks and wasn't expected back at school before Trinity Grey closed for the academic year. Which probably meant he would have to repeat. No fun, that.

"What do you think?" he asked Abe and Corey after their tour.

"That someone beat the ME's boys here," said Corey.

"I agree," said Abe, pointing to a vase that had been dusted twice for prints, only the color of the powder giving it away.

Carmine scowled. "My mistake," he said. "I figured we'd do better to get the smaller fry out of the way before tackling Mr. Skeps, a real whale. I'm scared he won't give us latitude for the rest. The question is, was anything removed, and if it was, what, why, and by whom?"

"An arm of the Justice Department," Abe said.

"FBI—the Commissioner has heard something, he dropped a hint. But he didn't get it from an official source, nor long before our arrival. Jeez, I hate that!" Carmine cried. "Why not come to us and tell us they're interested instead of floundering around like cockroaches on a wedding cake?"

"They'll be downstairs in the offices," Corey said, looking aggressive.

"We play it cool, guys," said Carmine.

The agency, they learned as they ducked under the police rope at the entrance to Desmond Skeps's offices, was indeed the FBI. He was standing, all six foot five and two-fifty pounds of him, in the middle of the main office supervising two Cornucopia janitors removing a four-drawer filing cabinet precariously perched on a dolly. He was a good-looking man with thick dark hair and dark eyes, but how he got to be an agent in the field was a puzzle to the three Holloman cops; his sheer size made him far too memorable for most investigative purposes.

"At your size, Mister, why don't you just pick it up and carry it? Or is that beneath your dignity?" Carmine asked affably.

The giant jumped, tried to look commandingly superior, and

failed. "I hope you're not going to be obstructive," he said, flashing his credentials. "I'm Special Agent Ted Kelly of the FBI, and this is vital evidence."

"Have you got a warrant?" Carmine asked.

"No, but I can get one faster than your cat can lick her ear," he said, "so don't even think of it."

"My cat's ear is squeaky-clean, Special Agent Kelly. I have a warrant right here, so I'm taking the vital evidence by the power vested in me by the State of Connecticut, County of Holloman. The name's Carmine Delmonico. This is Abe Goldberg, and that's Corey Marshall. Guys, wheel my evidence out. And you, Special Agent Kelly, are contaminating my crime scene. Why don't you go get your pieces of paper, then come back and make your seizures legal?"

"I would get you, wouldn't I?" Kelly asked, his face flushed. "I can't say I wasn't warned."

Carmine lifted the rope. "Goodbye, Mr. Kelly. And don't come back until you're willing to share everything you've got with the Holloman Police Department."

Shit! he thought as he was left victor on the field. That filing cabinet means I won't be home early tonight, no matter what tricks Myron is up to; by tomorrow the Feds will have pulled enough strings to get their evidence back. No other filing cabinet has been targeted, so whatever Special Agent Kelly hopes to find lies within this one alone. And why do I think there's more to this than a routine FBI presence? He went to the nearest phone and dialed.

"Delia? Dig out our security clearances, there's a good girl. Keep yours with you, and send mine over here right now. I'd rather not get arrested on a federal warrant, it's too hard to find a Get Out of Jail card."

He hung up on the squawks, grinning, then dialed again. "Danny? The Feds are here, and I smell something rotten in the state of Cornucopia. Tell Silvestri he might have a harder fight on his hands than we expected. Now put me back to Delia."

She had stopped squawking. "Your credentials are on their way," she said briskly, "and mine are in my handbag right next to my Saturday night special. What else, Captain?"

"Corey and Abe should be wheeling a filing cabinet into County Services any minute. It's a big bone of contention, Delia, and we may not win the fight to keep it. The moment it arrives, I want it put in my office and as many photocopiers as our power supply will stand put in there too. Get all the girls out of the typing pool and put them to photocopying the contents"—he grinned—"faster than your cat can lick her ear. Said contents, I add, are for your and my eyes only."

"What about the girls?" she asked anxiously.

"I don't think we need to worry about them. They'll be working too fast to notice what they're copying."

"And," she said, catching on, "they're dear girls, but they wouldn't know a polymer chain from a chain reaction."

"Exactly."

And that should do it, he thought, putting the receiver down again. Just get the filing cabinet back to County Services, guys! It's a myth that big men are slow, but here's hoping I caught Mr. Ted Kelly on the wrong size-seventeen. By the time he remembers that he could snatch it en route, he'll be too late. I hope the cabinet doesn't do my Fairlane's backseat much harm.

They looked like ordinary offices. Carmine walked from room to room noting the usual paraphernalia: desks, chairs, typewriters, telex and Xerox machines, calculators. Then, fascinated, he found two small rooms whose desks were filled by massive consoles he recognized only because sometimes he was called upon to visit Chubb's computers, rented out to firms and institutions when Chubb didn't need them. These were just such computer terminals, so somewhere in the bowels of the building there existed an arctically air-conditioned vault occupied by the computers themselves. It made sense that Cornucopia would have its own computer banks.

The police rope was confined to Desmond Skeps's properly walled domain only, about half the space the floor offered. On the far side of his wall were more offices that continued to function, and in less salubrious surroundings. Grey panels fenced people off into cubicles about chest-high, obliging each denizen to stand up to see out and about. Today there was a lot of standing up; nerves, probably. In the far corner he found a larger office, fully enclosed, that bore a sign saying it was the lair of one M. D. Sykes. When he opened the door he discovered a small, middle-aged man behind a desk that dwarfed him.

"Captain Carmine Delmonico, Holloman Police. What does the M.D. stand for, sir, and what's your function?"

Terrified, the little fellow rose to his feet, fell back again, gulped and swallowed. "Michael Donald Sykes," he said, squeaking. "I'm the general manager of Cornucopia Central."

"Which is?"

"The central firm, Captain. The one that oversees all the other Cornucopia firms. They are its subsidiaries," said Mr. Sykes, finding courage.

"I see. Does that mean that, for example, Landmark Machines doesn't own itself? That Cornucopia owns it?"

"Yes, it does. No Cornucopia firm has much autonomy."

"So you're in charge, now that Mr. Skeps is dead?"

The round face screwed up as if about to burst into tears. "Oh, no, Captain, no! I occupy a limbo somewhere between middle and top management. Mr. Philip Smith is senior vice-president and a nominal managing director. I imagine that he will assume command."

"Then where do I find Mr. Philip Smith?"

"One floor down. His office is directly under Mr. Skeps's—the view, you understand."

"Plus the key to the executive washroom?"

"Mr. Smith has his own washroom."

Wow! said Carmine, but silently. He took the elevator down a floor, followed the signs and was intercepted by an elderly, beautifully dressed woman who looked him up and down as if he'd come about the janitor's job before she reluctantly agreed that he could see Mr. Smith.

His office had that same wonderful two-sided view, but no telescope. Philip Smith himself was tall and suave, immaculately tailored in grey silk, and sported a tie Carmine had heard about but never seen: the pure silk, handmade version of the Chubb produced by an Italian designer. His shirt was French cuffed, his links understated solid gold, and his shoes handmade in St. James's, London. He was fair and handsome, spoke with a Philadelphia Main Line drawl, and had grey eyes that perpetually hunted for a mirror in which to see himself.

"Terrible, just awful!" he said to Carmine, offering him a cigar. When Carmine declined, he offered coffee and was accepted.

"How much of a real difference does the death of Mr. Skeps make to the operation of Cornucopia?" Carmine asked.

It wasn't a question Smith had expected; he blinked, had to stop to formulate his answer. "Actually, not a lot," he said finally. "The day-to-day functioning of the various Cornucopia companies is left to their own management teams. Cornucopia Central is a little like the father of a large brood of children—it does all the things kids can't do for themselves."

You condescending prick, thought Carmine, face politely interested. I should pay you back for that with a couple of hours in a County Services interrogation room, but you're small potatoes in spite of the wardrobe, Mr. Smith.

The coffee arrived, and gave Smith a breathing space while the snooty secretary poured—heaven forbid he should pour a cup for himself!

"Why is there an FBI special agent sniffing around your nether parts, Mr. Smith?" Carmine asked as soon as they were alone again.

But the nominal managing director was ready for that one. "Inevitable, given the number of our defense contracts," he said smoothly. "I imagine D.C. and the Pentagon automatically take an interest in the violent death of an important man."

"How violent do you think the death of Mr. Skeps was?"

"Well, er—I don't know, exactly. One presumes murder to be violent by definition."

"When did Mr. Kelly arrive?"

"Yesterday, midday. Grotesque, isn't he?"

"No, Mr. Smith, not grotesque, which implies an unpleasant element. Special Agent Kelly is a particularly fine specimen of man. What did he do after he arrived?"

"Asked to see Desmond's penthouse and offices. Naturally we coöperated fully."

"Did it not occur to anyone to call Commissioner Silvestri and notify him of an FBI presence in a local murder scene?"

"No."

"That's a pity."

"I don't see why. You're all on the same side."

"Are we? That's comforting to know. However, if Mr. Kelly took something from either place, the Holloman Police should be told, and were not. If you're personally aware that anything has gone missing, I suggest you tell me right now."

"Uh—apart from Desmond's personal filing cabinet, nothing," said Smith uneasily. "He kept it in his walk-in safe, but Mr. Kelly had a key and the combination. There's nothing in it would interest the Holloman police—too esoteric. The files were all sensitive aspects of our defense contracts. You would not have the necessary security clearances, Captain Delmonico."

"You might be surprised, Mr. Smith."

Smith laughed derisively. "Oh, come, Captain! You're a big fish in a very small puddle. Don't let it go to your head."

"Thank you for the reminder. In the meantime, I'd be grateful if you issued a Board directive to all Cornucopia Central staff to coöperate with me and mine." Carmine rose to his feet. "My thanks for the coffee." He went across to the Long Island Sound window and looked at his house, frowning. "Now if you seat yourself behind your desk, sir, we can get down to our real business."

Smith obeyed, seeming uncomfortable; the suavity had gone.

"Tell me what you know about Desmond Skeps."

"He was detestable," Smith answered, both hands on the desk palms downward. "I doubt you'll obtain a different opinion from anyone who knows him—knew him. Though Cornucopia is listed on the stock exchange, Desmond owned a clear majority of the shares, so he could do pretty much as he liked. And he did."

"Can you give me an example of his doing as he liked?"

"Certainly. Cornucopia Research. We all opposed his setting up our own research laboratories, chiefly because our companies span such a gamut of industries, but he insisted. It meant a massive facility with a bill in the hundreds of millions. He was right in one way—we don't have to go hat in hand to outside labs anymore. The research stays here in Holloman with us. When he stole Duncan MacDougall from PetroBrit, Cornucopia Research was complete. MacDougall is one of the three men in the world who can administer a unit that size. Why am I complaining? Because we'll never recoup the outlay. Dividends plunged."

"Did you associate personally with Mr. Skeps?"

"Naturally! Far more, however, when he was married to Philomena. Now there was an ideal tycoon's wife! Educated, beautiful, charming, modest as women should be but rarely are. These days they're trollops, all of them. Desmond was obsessed with Philomena, especially after Desmond Three was born, but he couldn't overcome his completely unfounded jealousy. The pool man was her lover, the gardener, the phone technician, even the paperboy. In the end, no man who wanted to keep his job would go near her, and the poor woman had a breakdown. When she came out of it, she left Desmond for good, even though she didn't have a bean. I respected her, Captain, truly respected her."

Carmine glanced briefly at his papers. "I have Mrs. Skeps listed as living in Orleans, Massachusetts, sir. That doesn't suggest she's on the breadline. You're going to have to explain why she didn't—er—have a bean."

"Desmond overstepped the mark when she sued for divorce," said

Philip Smith. "He persecuted her—hired seedy private detectives to hound her, even kidnapped Desmond Three, though she hadn't denied him access to the child. By the time the case got into court, she had an attorney worth his weight in gold, Anthony Bera. Expressed briefly, she was awarded astronomical alimony and sole custody of Desmond Three. She bought a property in Orleans and sent the boy to the Trinity Grey School last year. Despite her retaining Mr. Bera to watch over her interests, she isn't a vengeful woman, Captain. Desmond continued to have access to the boy, who hasn't been poisoned against his father."

"I see. How long ago was the divorce?"

"Five years ago last November."

"And has Mr. Skeps had intimate congress with other women since then? Has he a mistress? Girlfriends?"

Philip Smith looked irritated. "How would I know?"

"You had plenty of contact with the man."

"Not when it came to whom he philandered with, Captain! I am known to disapprove of such activities." He drew a breath. "Go ask Erica Davenport!"

Myron's inamorata! "Why? Is she the likely one?"

"No, definitely not. That woman's an iceberg. But she may know the more prurient aspects of Desmond's life."

"Fill me in on the iceberg, Mr. Smith."

"This is like being the class tattletale!"

"Tattle away, Mr. Smith."

"Erica is the head of Cornucopia Legal, which oversees the activities, contractual and otherwise, of all Cornucopia."

"Define 'otherwise,' sir."

"Oh, how would I know? Things like verbal indiscretions, potential libels and slanders, compromising behavior in senior personnel."

"Wow! Mr. Skeps ran a tight ship."

"He had to. We do a lot of business with the Pentagon."

"So it would be fair to say that Miss Davenport heads up Cornucopia's private KGB?"

"Oh, *unkind!* She's a 'doctor,' actually. Dr. Erica Davenport. She's been with us for ten years. Her undergraduate studies were at Smith, in economics, then she went on to Harvard Law. After which she did the customary dreary apprenticeship all lawyers do—at a firm in Boston. When she came to us, we funded her doctorate in corporate law at Chubb. A terrifyingly intelligent woman! She took over Cornucopia Legal from Walter Symonds ten years ago. Those years in Boston were not wasted, Captain. We got a fully polished gem."

"Her childhood background, Mr. Smith?"

"WASP, from Massachusetts—plenty of money in the family." Smith examined his buffed nails. "She knows all the right people—I was told she was the most beautiful debutante of her year."

Where did she fit it all in? Carmine wondered. Debutantes don't usually end up working for dreary Boston law firms.

"Thank you for your time, Mr. Smith. Please remember that, no matter what the federal interest in Cornucopia might be, this is first and foremost a murder investigation." On his way to the door he paused. "Where will I find Cornucopia Legal?"

"Right below here."

That pecking order again! Clearly Dr. Davenport rated a two-viewed set of windows—unless, of course, the size of her office was considerably reduced.

It was not. Here there were definite signs of feminine occupancy: vases of spring flowers, delicately pastel paper on the two solid walls, woodwork painted pale green to match the leather upholstery, a pink-hued oriental rug on the blond wood floor. A room that gave an impression of a soft, nice, intensely feminine occupant. Horseshit, thought Carmine. The woman Philip Smith had described ought by rights to be flaunting black leather and chains. Women just didn't rise to head a segment of Cornucopia without more than their share of cunning, ruthlessness and utter heartlessness. The only person she'd cry for was herself. Poor Myron!

She was coming to meet him, which gave him a good opportunity to assess her. Yes, the private school princess brought to full bloom. He knew she was born on February 15, 1927, which made her forty years old, but she could have passed for thirty. Of medium-tall height, she moved very gracefully and had a whipcord-slim body atop a pair of extremely shapely legs. The clothes could not be faulted, from the cobalt blue dress with a floating, longish miniskirt to the French shoes with very high heels. The studs in her ears were two-carat diamonds, and the single diamond on a chain around her neck added another four carats. Her streaky blonde hair was cut almost as short as a man's and combed forward to frame a face of sculpted bones under thick tanned skin; her mouth was red-lipped and full, her nose had a slightly aquiline curve, and her large, open eyes were a cobalt blue reflection of her dress. Here was the queen bee; how had Desmond Skeps managed to dominate her?

He held his hand out. "Captain Carmine Delmonico, Holloman Police," he said. At first glance he had begun to revise his opinion of how she had risen to head Cornucopia Legal; a woman this beautiful could do it on her back. Then he encountered her eyes, and dismissed the idea of a horizontal promotion. The ruthlessness, cunning and heartlessness were all there, and well used. She would have despised woman's wiles, taken on her adversaries with their own weapons.

Her grip was like a man's, but brief; she indicated that he should take the client's chair, and seated herself behind her desk. Erica Davenport would never consciously place herself in any situation where she might lose one iota of her hard-won authority.

"I believe we have a friend in common," he said.

"Myron Mandelbaum? Yes. What a pity I'm barred from meeting him on his own turf, but of course I understand. Who could ever have predicted Desmond's death?"

"Who, indeed? Not you, I take it, Dr. Davenport?"

"No. It came as a terrific shock."

"Do you think it's linked to his business activities?"

"I have no idea, honestly."

"What happens now—on the business front, I mean?"

"We wait to see what Desmond's will contains, as he's the majority shareholder and the virtual owner of Cornucopia." Like Smith, she studied her nails, which she kept long and lacquered pale pink. Probably not a lesbian, he thought.

"How long before the will is read?"

"That depends on his personal lawyers, who are situated in New York City. I believe someone is coming up with all his testamentary papers tomorrow. His son is bound to inherit, and whoever is named as little Des's guardian at law won't be in a position to tamper with Desmond's dispositions."

"Even so, I'd appreciate a copy of the will as soon as it's been read," Carmine said. He changed tack. "Has anything been different over the past few days, Dr. Davenport? His mood, for example?"

She frowned, concentrating. "No, I don't think so."

"Do you have any idea who the woman in his life is?"

A laugh. "Oh, that! I don't believe there was one."

"You're beautiful. It wasn't you?"

"No, it certainly wasn't me," she said, her tone even. "He didn't go for blondes, as you'll find out when you see Mrs. Skeps."

"Neither of them married again."

"No. Or looked at anyone else, is my theory."

"Why is the FBI here?"

"Our Pentagon contracts, I imagine."

"Has it caused trepidation at Cornucopia Legal?"

Her thin, plucked brows rose. "Why should it? Cornucopia has done nothing wrong. I'm assured the FBI presence is routine."

"You don't strike me as a trusting person."

She stiffened. "What do you mean?"

"Just a hunch. Have you anything else to tell me?"

"No," she said curtly, then summoned up a charming smile that suggested she was remembering that Myron, whom she liked very much, was tied to Carmine Delmonico by the strings that laced his heart.

"Then I'll leave you to your work."

Out in the foyer, he found Abe and Corey.

"Did you get it home safely?" he asked.

"As a baby, Carmine. We left Delia in charge."

"Good."

"Who's the looker?" Corey asked.

"Dr. Erica Davenport. Lovely but lethal."

"Isn't she Myron's new girlfriend?"

"Yes, unfortunately."

"Come on, Carmine, Myron's not impressionable," said Abe.

"I wouldn't worry if she were another gold-digging bimbo, but she's not. Her face might not have the power to launch a thousand ships, but her job combined with her intelligence just might. Still, it's not my business. How's Special Agent Kelly doing?"

Corey and Abe laughed. "Not pleased when he found his filing cabinet on untouchable territory without that warrant, and he'll have to go to Hartford to find a federal judge. So we sent him to see Doubting Doug Thwaites."

Carmine joined their mirth. "Brilliant! He'll be hours."

Carmine, Corey and Abe decided to eat in the Cornucopia cafeteria, where, to Abe and Corey's surprise, Carmine led the way to a roomy table where Michael Donald Sykes was eating a lonely lunch. Carmine's prey—for such he clearly was—looked uneasy at first, then rather pleased.

"Don't you have a ticket to the executive dining room?" Carmine asked, unloading his New England clam chowder, chicken-and-rice, and lime Jell-O with pears and cream.

"If I want it," Sykes said defensively.

"Isn't the food upscale from this?"

"That's the trouble, it is. Also more expensive. I like eating plain. Besides, you've met Philip Smith—would you want to listen to him discussing which wine to have with his escaloppes de veau? What a pain that guy is!"

"Not a wine buff, Mr. Sykes?" Corey asked.

"I'm not an anything buff when it comes to food or drink," said Mr. Sykes. "Model soldiers, now, that's different!"

"Shiloh spread out in the basement, huh?" Abe asked.

Sykes looked scornful. "No! I'm a Napoleonic era man! Austerlitz and Marengo."

"And Waterloo?" Carmine enquired.

"Waterloo is like the Civil War—common."

"How common is wealth among the Cornucopia executives?" Carmine asked, wondering if Mr. Sykes's war games extended to military takeovers of industrial giants. That would certainly lift his basement activities out of the common way.

"Apart from me and Erica Davenport, they're all as rich as Croesus." Michael Donald Sykes carefully cut his Jell-O into cubes and topped each one with a dollop of cream. "It's an old-boy network—*Mayflower* families, fancy prep schools, Chubb University. It wouldn't surprise me if they were all related. Desmond Skeps's father was well heeled, you know, otherwise he would never have found the capital to establish Cornucopia. Up until 1938 he'd manufactured parts for automobiles, but it was chickenfeed, couldn't have funded Cornucopia. Yet he had the clout to call on enough private loans among his friends from family and school to do it. But he was too smart to part with shares. As soon as the Second World War was raking in the money, he paid his loans back with interest and sat on the company like a dog with a dinosaur bone."

Well, well, thought Carmine, leaning back. Mr. Sykes might dwell in a limbo between middle and top management, but he sure knows all the dirt. A wonderful thing, the soul of a gossip.

"So where does Philip Smith fit in?" he asked.

"A Skeps connection by blood or marriage, certainly. *Hugely* rich! You always know how rich they are by the size of their salaries and perks. Like a vast fortune automatically entitles you to more. Take Gus Purvey, managing director of Landmark Machines—that's a polite term for field and naval guns. Not one of the biggest or most profitable subsidiaries, but Gus Purvey earns almost as much as Phil Smith. On a par with Fred Collins of Polycorn Plastics, and Wallace Grierson of Dormus—turbine engines. Their take-home pay would stagger you, Captain. It would stagger the President of the United States of America, for that matter. Whatever they work for, it isn't the money. Every last one of them could live the life of a playboy until he died, and still not have dented what he's got."

"The Puritan work ethic?" suggested Abe.

"Or the impulse to make even more?" asked Corey.

"Huh!" Michael Donald Sykes sucked up the last cube of Jell-O. "I don't believe it's any of those reasons. I believe that the life of a playboy would bore them, but they can't stand being at home all day with their wives. They're avoiding their wives without the grief of philandering. I mean, can you see *Philip Smith* working up a sweat fucking? Nah! Never happen."

"Sykes is a cuckoo," said Corey as they departed.

"Maybe, but we know more about the men at the top of the Cornucopia heap," said Carmine, very satisfied. "Philip Smith, Gus Purvey, Fred Collins and Wallace Grierson. Fine old WASP names, apparently accompanied by fortunes in the league of Scrooge McDuck. I know I have to dig deep into the contents of Special Agent Kelly's filing cabinet, but I also have to dig into those four gentlemen, all of whom have the money to hire assassins."

"Speak of the devil," Carmine said not a minute later, when Special Agent Kelly appeared out of the elevator. "How goes it?" he asked amiably. "Get your warrant?"

"Tell me something, Captain, is everyone in this pint-sized state a total eccentric? My bosses are convinced Commissioner Silvestri is ready for the men in white coats, and the judge who finally issued me a warrant is like someone out of Longfellow!"

"Longfellow is a poet," said Carmine, "who didn't versify about eccentrics. But I'm glad you got your warrant."

"Yes, and my filing cabinet," Kelly said triumphantly. "Too soon for you to bust into it, lucky for you. But one thing—how did you wind up with Delia Carstairs? When the Director heard that she'd finally left the NYPD, he tried to get her, but she'd fallen down a crack somewhere."

"A crack named Holloman. She's a total eccentric, you see," Carmine said gravely. He jerked his head at a vacant table in the cafeteria, rapidly emptying. "In here, Special Agent, only that's the last time I'm calling you something so clumsy. From now on, it's Ted. I'm Carmine, no diminutive. Corey and Abe here are going back to Desmond Skeps's offices while you and I have a little chat."

They sat down.

"Okay, espionage," Carmine said. "To me, the word means the selling of official secrets to an enemy power or nation, and I daresay it could be extrapolated to include enemy individuals. If Cornucopia is involved, then I presume the espionage isn't of a place nature—plans, routines, locations. I would guess the secrets are tangible—advances in atomic reactors, analytical apparatus, plastics—a whole slew of stuff. Am I right?"

Kelly was staring at him, stunned. "How did you work that out?" he asked.

"I would have thought it was obvious to anyone with half a brain, Ted. I know you—know of you, rather. It was only a question of time before I remembered that you're an espionage agent. And why else would the FBI be here? A murder? No, no matter how important the victim. The sensitive nature of Cornucopia's contracts? Not unless the firm was already under scrutiny and Skeps's murder confirmed federal suspicions. I'm right, aren't I?"

"Oh, yes," Kelly said grimly. "Someone here has been giving secrets to the Communists for two years."

"How did you find out?"

"When a top-secret missile fuel governor was stolen from the Russians with great pain and some loss of life. It turned out that the governor was ours, invented by Cornucopia Research. The Reds hadn't even bothered to modify it."

"Someone at Cornucopia Research is the villain?"

"If he is, we can't find a trace of him. It's not Duncan MacDougall. He had the same kind of job at PetroBrit, and they've never lost the schematics of a pencil sharpener. The trouble is the same trouble we always have with private industry—people come and go anywhere they want if they've got the rank. Security? It's a piece of paper you put in a safety deposit box."

"You're talking about the fat cats at the top?"

"Sure."

"Why would they steal for the Reds? They don't need money, and it's hard to doubt their patriotism."

"It's hard to doubt anyone's patriotism, Carmine, but treason happens. It's ideological when money's not the object of the game. I say 'game' because I've encountered two spies who did it to show how clever they were."

"But they slipped up in the end. What else has gone?"

"It's hard to know, but once you know there's a leak, you look for any Russian or Chinese device that takes a sudden leap ahead. Other firms have lost secrets too, but in things they share with Cornucopia."

"I'm surprised you continue to use Cornucopia."

"Oh, come, Captain, you're nobody's fool! Industries that produce esoteric items are thin on the ground! And whoever the traitor is—our code name for him is Ulysses—he takes fine care to confine his thefts to articles or parts that Defense can't obtain elsewhere. There's also the onus of proof. Cornucopia Legal has argued most persuasively that the leaks happen in Washington elsewhere than at the Pentagon, like consultants, and they're hard to refute. The most telling point against Cornucopia is that they can be connected to everything we know or suspect has been stolen."

"And do you think that Desmond Skeps's filing cabinet will reveal the answers, Ted?"

"No, I don't. Skeps's murder suggests to me that he found out who Ulysses is."

"Well, under ordinary circumstances I'd tell you to stick around and watch a murder expert in action, but you probably know that Holloman is snowed under with murders, and you've got your work cut out finding a spy. I'm not helpless, but Skeps is just one of eleven corpses, and I can't be sure any of the deaths are related to Ulysses. Including Skeps's."

"You can keep your murders," Ted Kelly said with a grin. "How about we meet again for coffee here tomorrow, ten-ish?"

"Suits me," said Carmine.

And down seven floors, to Polycorn Plastics and Frederick H. Collins, its managing director.

Who was like Philip Smith, yet unlike him. The suit was wool from Savile Row, the tie that same silk Chubb edition, the links on his French-cuffed shirt platinum-and-enamel replicas of his old college coat of arms, the shoes custom-made in London. He looked fiftyish too, impeccably shaved and manicured, but he lacked Smith's air of the weary aristocrat. In fact, thought Carmine, his face would have suited a butcher, and his black eyes found it hard to settle, not because they hunted for a mirror, but because they had things to hide.

"Terrible, awful!" he said, squirming in his chair.

"Were you and Mr. Skeps friends, sir?"

"Oh, yes. Very close. All of us on the Board are. We're a trifle older than Des—there was no one in his graduating class with whom he formed a close attachment, you see."

"Why do you think that was?"

"I have no idea, though I *heard* his classmates didn't like him. He drank heavily back then, and when he was drunk he could be—er—abrasive. Desmond Skeps Senior died a week after Des graduated, so Des stepped into Cornucopia as Chairman of the Board and owner of the majority of the shares. No experience whatsoever! Three of us already worked here as junior executives—Gus Purvey, Wal Grierson and me. Chubbers all! Phil Smith was thrust on us by Des as his cousin. I think he admired how Phil looked and talked. Since the word 'work' is as alien to Phil as the word 'fuck,' we got used to his being around as decoration. He's sixty if he's a day, so he knew Des's dad well. Chubb, but before us."

"How many are on the Board, Mr. Collins?"

"Phil Smith, Gus Purvey, Wal Grierson, Erica Davenport and yours truly, with Des in the chair and Phil as his deputy."

"That's a very small board, surely?"

"There's no law regulating a board's size, Captain."

"What about the external shareholders?"

"They're the four of us and hundreds of thousands of strays. Erica represents the strays."

"Does that mean she's at loggerheads with the rest of you?"

Collins laughed. "Lord, no! Think of us as like IBM—to own twenty shares is a small fortune, but peanuts all the same."

"How much top-secret work do you discuss?"

"The lot," said Frederick H. Collins, looking surprised.

"You're the head of Polycorn Plastics. Where do you make your cutting-edge advances, sir? At your factory?"

The big butcher's face crumpled into another bout of mirth. "No, sir! All I do is manufacture tried and true plastics. The research is where it should be—at Cornucopia Research."

"So you have no top-secret formulae lying around?"

"No, I do not! By the time I see a new plastic, it's been thoroughly tested and looks to anyone at Polycorn to be no different from every-thing else. I don't broadcast advances."

"What makes a new plastic so desirable to the Reds?"

"Do you have security clearances, Captain?" Collins demanded.

Carmine handed over the typed contents of a wallet.

After a thorough inspection, Collins shrugged. "Super-hard plas-tics that will prove suitable for the manufacture of hand and shoulder weapons," he said. "Also different super-hard plastics for armor plat-ing, engine blocks. Enough?"

"Thank you, more than enough. Has any of your research been leaked to the Communists?"

Collins gasped, pressed his hands against his eyes. "Oh, Jesus! Not as far as I'm aware. The first breakthrough since we knew about Ulysses came not much more than a month ago, and I refused to accept the formulae. In fact, I ordered Dr. MacDougall to put them and every last vestige of the test pieces including the shavings into his vault under seal. The Reds aren't dumb, Captain, they do research too. But I will not see the Communists profit from *my* research! No new plastics will go into production until Ulysses is caught."

Okay, thought Carmine, I believe he's sincere. Not a very likeable guy, but I pick him as a genuine patriot.

"What does Special Agent Kelly say?" he asked.

"Not a fucking thing," said Frederick H. Collins bitterly.

Time to change horses. "Are you married, sir?"

"Yes," said Collins, looking blank.

"For how long?"

"Two years, this time. I've had three previous wives."

"Any of them last longer than two years?"

"My first, Aki. We were married twenty-one years."

"Do you have a family?"

"Two boys by Aki, a boy by Michelle, a boy by Debbie, and another boy by Candy, my present wife."

"Lots of alimony."

"I can afford it."

He's into bimbos, thought Carmine, wondering what had sent him off the rails after twenty-one years. Man, won't there be a squabble after he dies, with all those boys! Obviously he had the money to hire professional killers, but it wouldn't be in the service of Uncle Joe Stalin's heirs. With nothing to suggest the espionage and the murder were connected, Frederick H. Collins's name would remain written on the list stored inside Carmine's mind.

Then it was down two more floors to the offices of Landmark Machines, whose managing director was Mr. Augustus Barraclough Purvey. Not like the other pair, Smith and Collins. Purvey was Brooks Brothers from head to foot, wore a polka-dot bow tie and very expensive loafers. His thick, waving hair was greying, his smooth-skinned face was attractive, and his dark blue eyes looked directly into those seeking his. Carmine liked him much better than he had Smith or Collins.

The only top-secret modification Landmark had lost to the Communists was a new gunsight, Purvey said.

"Our real aim," he went on, "is years away—namely, to link artillery fire to computers able to calculate the target precisely. It's colossally complicated, and will require our sending up satellites whose function is to plot the globe. So it's not exclusively Cornucopia. In fact, we only have a little corner of it. Everyone's involved, from NASA on down."

"What effect would concrete knowledge of the project have on Russian or Chinese defense plans?" Carmine asked.

"Serious, very serious. They smell *something*, but there are just too many cheeses on the board."

"What if Ulysses knows?"

"Knows what? The thing I've just outlined to you, Captain, is so speculative and—and—*ephemeral* that I for one have no faith in our ability to do it."

"I thank you for your candor, Mr. Purvey. Now to other things. Are you married?"

"I was, but not for the last ten years." Purvey grinned. "In my opinion, women aren't worth the pain. I'd want a quiet meal at home, she'd want to go to a party or a reception, get her picture in the society pages. My fault! I should have married one of my own kind. Instead I married a cocktail waitress. I mean, I don't mind a party or a reception, but not every goddamn night!"

"Any children?"

"No. They would have slowed her down."

"Do you date?"

"Oh, sure."

"Anyone I know?"

"Erica Davenport. She's my regular. Socially acceptable, a good blind for a guy who's still a sucker for cocktail waitresses. Erica's a good sport."

"What do you spend your money on, Mr. Purvey?"

"Donzi motorboats. I've got a cabin on Moosehead Lake in Maine—Connecticut's lakes are too crowded."

"How do you make it way up to Maine for a weekend?"

"Fly my Sikorsky helicopter—I'm loyal to the locals."

"Do you travel regularly to anywhere else?"

"New York City. I have an apartment on East Seventy-eighth."

"Do you have a favorite cocktail waitress?"

"No, sir! I learned my lesson. Nowadays I cruise."

"Thank you, Mr. Purvey."

Carmine descended six more floors to Dormus, apparently so successful that it occupied three of them.

Here he met blue jeans, Caterpillar boots, a faded shirt and no tie at all. Mr. Wallace Grierson dressed the part of a turbine engineer, and carried it off convincingly. He was not unlike Ted Kelly in build—very tall and muscularly heavy—but he had fair and freckled skin, a mop of sandy curls, and shrewd grey eyes. Carmine liked him on sight.

"I'm only here, Captain, because I was ordered to be here," he announced across the acreage of his boots, up on the desk. "By rights I should be at my factory."

"Sorry about that, Mr. Grierson," Carmine said, sitting down. "I didn't think there were any hands-on executives, at least on a board level. What's so different about Dormus?"

"Nothing. I'm the difference. Unlike those tailor's dummies, I actually qualified as an engineer, and nobody else is going to run Dormus, including on the shop floor."

"Have you lost any top-secret items to the Reds?"

The question didn't faze him in the least. "In two separate divisions, Captain. The first, development of the ramjet, which pushes standard-wing planes up over Mach two. The second, our rocket division, where the leaks have been hot and heavy. It was the discovery of my governor on a Russian rocket that opened this whole can of worms, and I am fit to be tied! If Ulysses isn't put out of business soon, Cornucopia is dead."

"Are defense contracts so vital to Cornucopia?"

"Hell, yes! Des Skeps wanted it that way—he got a charge out of manufacturing America's defense. Even if we go into new areas outside defense, Captain, we're just as vulnerable to the spy. Industrial espionage is actually more serious than the treasonous kind to any manufacturer who goes into new territory. It's a dog-eat-dog world, in case you haven't noticed."

"But the treasonous kind benefits America's *real* enemies." Carmine changed tack. "You don't look like a man with millions."

"Whereas the tailor's dummies do. I could buy and sell Phil Smith or Fred Collins, and I'm neck-and-neck with Gus Purvey."

"Are you married?"

"Sure! We had our silver anniversary five months ago. We met at CalTech, both doing engineering."

"Interests in common, huh?"

"The double whammy, Captain. Margaret's gorgeous too."

"Any children?"

"Four. Two girls, two boys. The two oldest are at Brown."

"What do you spend your money on, sir?"

"Not much. We have a nice home out Sleeping Giant way, but it's not a mansion. Ever try to have a mansion *and* four kids? We have a hunting cabin in Maine, but we don't hunt. We hike. Mustang cars— all the kids drive, so we have a fleet of the things. And a ranch at the foot of the Grand Tetons in Wyoming. We usually go there for the summer."

"What matters most in life to you, Mr. Grierson?"

"My family," he answered without hesitation.

"And after them?"

"Dormus. If Cornucopia goes under, I'll buy it and keep right on making turbine engines for boats and planes."

"Funny," Carmine said as he got to his feet, "I always forget that ships are powered by turbines these days."

"Have been since 1906 and the dreadnaughts, Captain."

There remained only another interview with Erica Davenport. On his way into Cornucopia Legal, he met Phil Smith coming out.

"A moment, Mr. Smith. Are you married?" he asked.

Smith looked offended. "Of course I am!"

"Once? Twice? Thrice? More?"

"Natalie is my only wife, of thirty-four years. I do not believe in divorce or infidelity, you impertinent dolt! Nor does she! Would it serve your prurient interest to see our sleeping arrangements? Paddle your greasy hands through our night attire?"

"That won't be necessary, sir. Any children?"

"Yes, three! My daughter did not go to university. My two sons went to Harvard and MIT."

"Not Chubb, huh? That's interesting."

"What business is it of yours where my children went to school? Your questions, Captain Delmonico, go beyond the limits of acceptable behavior! I intend to report you to everyone in a position to discipline you, is that understood?" He was beginning to splutter. "You're a—a—Gestapo inquisitor!"

"Mr. Smith," Carmine said gently, "a policeman investigating murder uses many techniques to obtain information, but more than that, he also uses them to learn in the small amount of time at his disposal what kind of person he's questioning. During our first interview you were rude and overbearing, which leaves me free to tread heavily on your toes, even though your toes are sheathed in handmade shoes. You imply that you have the power to see me—er—'disciplined,' but I must tell you that no one in authority will take any notice of your complaints, because those in authority all know me. I have earned my status, not bought it. Murder means that everything in your life is my business until I remove you from my list of suspects. Is that clear?"

Two Philip Smiths suddenly looked out of one pair of eyes. One was the haughty aristocrat; the other was watchful, careful, hard, and highly intelligent. Carmine pretended not to notice.

Smith brushed past him without answering. Carmine went on into Erica Davenport's outer sanctum, staffed, he was intrigued to see, by a thin young man of nondescript appearance.

"You have a male secretary," he said, going to her window.

"It seemed a nice conceit for a woman executive. How may I help you further, Captain?"

"You didn't tell me you're on the Cornucopia Board."

"Is it relevant? If it is, I fail to see why."

"Everything is relevant in a murder enquiry, Dr. Davenport. And did you really think I wouldn't find out why the FBI is so interested in Cornucopia? Both you and Mr. Smith passed it off as—irrelevant. I've also learned that your regular date is Mr. Gus Purvey, whose penchant for cocktail waitresses you're happy to conceal from his fellows."

Her lips thinned. "Then I had better tell you, Captain, that Mr. Purvey's cocktail waitresses are men in drag. He likes them about eighteen or nineteen years old, with their own hair grown out and their body hair depilated."

"It's nice to have one's suspicions confirmed," he said, smiling. "Now what about Mr. Kelly?"

A scarlet spot had appeared in each cheek and the lips were a straight line. She answered obliquely. "For two people who may end in seeing a lot of each other, Captain, we're not getting on too well. Though of my own volition I would never have made a friend of you—you're too much the male chauvinist pig."

He laughed, understanding her. "It's a lot of years since a man has ever been in a position to throw uncomfortable questions at you outside your legal province, and now here he is, and you don't like it. Or him. We're not having a social encounter, Dr. Davenport. You're being interviewed as a possible suspect in a murder. When we do finally meet socially, this has to be forgotten, not toted like extra baggage."

The cobalt eyes flew to his, astonished. Some internal struggle took place, then she sighed and nodded. "Yes, I see, Captain. I apologize. Yes, I am a member of the Board, purely because Desmond Skeps felt he needed Board representation from his legal department. And my dates with Gus Purvey aren't regular. They're limited to functions the Board considers obligatory. As for Mr. Kelly—I presume you've learned that he's here to investigate espionage. However, that knowledge is surplus to your requirements, surely. You're simply an insatiably curious man, Captain Delmonico, one of those irritating guys who can't bear not knowing every prurient detail of everyone's life."

"What a great reading of my character! Insatiably curious! Right on target, Dr. Davenport. However, it's my insatiable curiosity that's responsible for my ability to get solutions."

"You are, the Governor tells us, formidable."

Carmine left the window with a resolution that, for the duration of this investigation, every blind in his house would be drawn. There were too many barbarians.

"I'll see you tomorrow, ma'am."

And off he went, leaving his quarry still standing in front of her desk, full lips thin.

The filing cabinet contained all of Cornucopia's data pertaining to any item Desmond Skeps had reason to think had either definitely or possibly been passed to the Communists.

Delia, whose security clearances were quite as high as Carmine's, had already waded into the document fray. When Carmine joined her it was four in the afternoon, and she had dealt with the two top drawers, the definite thefts.

"Jesus!" he exclaimed. "Has Uncle Sam got *any* secrets left?"

"Cheer up, Carmine, it's not as bad as it looks," she said. "What you see is the paperwork attached to eight items, from the rocket fuel governor to the gunsight. In addition there are two separate and distinct improvements to something called a ramjet, another rocket part, the blueprints of an experimental aviation cannon, a new atmospheric analyzer, and the formula for some sort of steel—this last, it seems, highly experimental. Bad enough, but at first I thought it was going to be far worse. Mr. Skeps stuffed everything in the drawers, including letters and memos. I think he intended to go through every sheet himself—or perhaps he even had, if his murder is related to the espionage."

"Which it may or may not be. What's in the bottom two drawers?" Carmine asked.

"Things that Mr. Skeps may have considered more terrifying than the confirmed thefts. They concern items that passed into production as long ago as a decade."

Carmine whistled. "That *is* scary! If Skeps was right, it means Ulysses has been active inside Cornucopia for the last ten years."

Delia sat down on a wheeled stool with a flop that sent it whizzing away until Carmine caught it, by which time they had both found a laugh, soon dead. "If the FBI doesn't know, they will as soon as they open the bottom drawers. Every company engaged in defense work has lost something," Delia said.

"The most maddening part is that I don't need the extra work involved in looking for Cornucopia's spy. I'm tempted to call Ulysses a red herring, except that he's the size of a blue whale, and I don't know enough to be certain that Skeps's murder has nothing to do with Ulysses. I feel as if I'm stuck up to my chin in quicksand, Delia."

"I believe that in films quicksand is actually just a bath of water with sawdust on top," said Delia, who was an inveterate moviegoer. "Perhaps this is the same."

"Then the bath's too deep for my feet to reach the bottom."

"Why do they need to? Tread water, Carmine, and spit out the sawdust."

"How right you are! Kelly's the espionage expert, not me. I'll go after the murderer, and if he happens to be the spy, that's gravy." He grinned. "Or sawdust."

When he let himself in his front door shortly after seven that evening, Carmine expected to hear the joyous sounds that always followed in the wake of Myron Mendel Mandelbaum. Instead, his ears found silence. When he walked into the little sitting room where they usually gathered before dinner, three of the five people he loved most in all the world were there, mute. Desdemona's face was downcast, Sophia's tear-stained, and Myron's a mixture of frustration and anguish.

"Carmine, tell them I'm not deliberately hurting them!" Myron cried, jumping up.

"I would, if I knew what you were talking about."

"Daddy, he's leaving!" Sophia said, weeping afresh.

"Leaving?" Carmine asked, astonished. "You only just got here, Myron!"

"He's not leaving Holloman," Desdemona said, getting up to pour Carmine a drink. "He's moving to the Cleveland Hotel."

"You're joking!"

"No, Carmine, I'm not joking. The thing is, I want to be free to see Erica, have her come and go as she pleases and as I please. I understand why you can't have her as a guest in your house, I really do, but much as I love Sophia, she's not the reason why I made this trip east. I came to be with Erica, who's going through a rough time . . ." Myron faltered, ran down, and stood staring at Carmine helplessly, one man to another.

God, he must be head over heels in love with the woman, Carmine thought. *Myron* so thrown off balance that he wounded Sophia with ill-chosen words? It must be the first time ever. And Sophia was howling like a five-year-old, Desdemona was furious at such lack of tact, Myron was shaking as if he was about to keel over—what to do? One thing at a time, Carmine. Get rid of Myron first.

He threw an arm around Myron's shoulders and propelled him out of the room. "Are your things packed?" he asked.

"Yes!" A gasp. "Carmine, I'm so sorry! I didn't know how to tell them, then I fucked it up—Sophia, my Sophia!"

"Don't worry about her, she'll forgive you. Are you sure you want to do this?"

"Yes."

"Then I'll call a cab." He picked up the hall phone. "Get your bags out of the house up to the road and wait for your cab there. I'll stay with Sophia and Desdemona."

"Thanks, Carmine. I'm in your debt forever. Once all of you get to know Erica, you'll love her. She's—wonderful!"

Hah, thought Carmine, returning to the sitting room. Your Erica is devious, a man-hater, everything you loathe in women, only you can't see it. What's her magic, and why don't I feel it?

It took a long time to calm Sophia, who was devastated. What else had Myron said to her, between his arrival and now, to provoke the kind of grief that feels like the end of the world? He had made no secret of his reason for coming, and Sophia had seemed to take the news well. But not now, face covered in snot, howls loud enough for the neighbors to hear, and they were way away. Nor could he get through to her, as if she had transferred some of Myron's crime to him. Because he was another man, or because he was another Daddy? Carmine didn't know, but his child's grief cut at him like a blunt knife.

He had never seen Desdemona so upset either, though a part of him rejoiced at that; it said she loved Sophia with heart and soul, would go to bat for her no matter what.

"But a hotel!" she said between clenched teeth. "How dare he? The Cleveland is close to a hundred years old!"

"If he doesn't like the way the toilet flushes, he can afford to call a plumber. Besides, they refurbished their suites last year, and you know Myron—no poky single room looking at the back of Macy's. He's sleeping with her, Desdemona."

Finally, Sophia put dinnerless to bed and Desdemona a little mollified, he got his drink.

"I wonder where he met her?" Desdemona asked.

"Given the effluxion of time, my love, we'll find out."

"Do politicians really use that phrase? It's so pompous."

"I'm led to believe they do. But, far more important, how's Julian? That kid could sleep through the San Francisco earthquake—the noise element, anyway. I'd forgotten how loudly Sophia can howl. Poor little runt."

"Erica or no Erica, Myron can jolly well take Sophia out to lunch and buy her that set of peridot jewelry she's been lusting after for weeks."

"It's not too valuable, is it?" Carmine asked anxiously.

"No, dear heart. A semiprecious, apple green stone, medium on the Mohr scale, and set in fourteen karat gold."

"Can he really buy her?"

"Oh, no! Because she loves him as her father, she'll forgive him, but she has to make him understand that forgiveness comes at a price. Today she crossed a narrow arch across the abyss, and the last vestiges of childhood are gone. We've witnessed the tragedy of life— that even the strongest ties begin to fray. Myron is *hers* in a way you've never been, Carmine. In future she'll love Myron quite as much, but never with complete trust. He betrayed her by showing her that this new woman is more important to him than she is."

"But that's like trying to have your cake and eat it too," Carmine protested. "If she hadn't come to us, Myron wouldn't have gotten so lonely. He was a sitting duck."

"Yes, we both know that—and so does she. But there was enough child left in her to think she *could* have her cake and eat it too. Now she knows differently, and a part of her sorrow is because she left him," Desdemona said.

"My children are very lucky," he said, pulling her into the chair and kissing her tenderly. "They have a wise mother."

"No, just a rather elderly one." She gave him a kiss of her own and draped her long body across his lap. "Our dinner is ruined, and we daren't get Emilia in to babysit, with Sophia feeling mildly suicidal—no, no, she won't do anything silly, but she'll think about it, and I'd rather be here. Therefore you have your choice between bologna and cheese on your sandwiches. Or you could have both."

The murder of Desmond Skeps continued to preoccupy Carmine, who met Ted Kelly in a quiet corner of the Cornucopia cafeteria unaccompanied by Abe and Corey.

"The contents of the filing cabinet were disappointing," he said, eating scrambled eggs on toast, a dozen rashers of crisp bacon and a mess of baked beans; bologna sandwiches did not a dinner make, and Julian had decided to go colicky just as Desdemona got out the frying pan.

"How do you know what was in the filing cabinet?" Kelly demanded. "I got it back before you had time to go through it!"

"Uh . . . photocopiers?"

He gaped. "You can't photocopy top-secret information! That's a hanging offense!"

"I've never been clear on federal death penalties—do you hang them, shoot them, or fry them? It's been a while since a treason case hit the newspapers. But to counter your statement, Ted, no one has seen my photocopies since they came off the Xerox machine except Delia Carstairs and me, and we've got the clearances. Besides, can you see Ulysses sneaking into the Holloman County Services building in search of secrets? Our copies are locked in the evidence cage along with everything from bloody axes to counterfeit plates and a few keys of heroin. It's a small department, which means the evidence cage sergeants know every cop face that comes through the door. The fact of the matter is that Holloman PD security is infinitely better than Cornucopia security, and you know it. Those dipshits you rubber-stamped as security personnel at Cornucopia couldn't find their ass with both hands inside their shorts. The real linchpin of good security is knowing the faces that go through the door, and writing every single one of them down in a log. If that happened, you'd know who Ulysses is, even if he'd been Desmond Skeps himself, because not every visit would be bona fide. People are *lazy*, Ted! They cut corners. And unfortunately employers like Cornucopia save the high salaries for their board members. But you pay peanuts, you get monkeys. If there are log books, how often are they used? Yeah, yeah, I know it's not under your direct control, but it should be. You're built like Hercules, but these Augean stables fill up with shit far faster than you can shovel."

He had eaten his way through this speech while Ted Kelly watched, fascinated; anyone would think the guy hadn't had any dinner! But, being a just servant of Justice, he nodded.

"I concede all your contentions, Carmine. What we need are stiffer laws and penalties, and in that respect Ulysses is a good thing." He smiled ruefully. "And I'm glad you looked into the filing cabinet. At least now I know it's disappointing."

"Why? Where is it?"

"Under armed guard en route to D.C. When it gets there, it will take weeks for news of the contents to get back to me."

"Well, the FBI is like the rest of our national capital—full of paper pushers who have to justify their existence."

The plate was absolutely clean. Carmine drank coffee and stared contentedly at Ted Kelly. "I want to know what you pinched out of Desmond Skeps's penthouse."

"I didn't pinch anything!"

"Horseshit! You did, and before my Medical Examiner and his team reached the crime scene."

"You have no basis for saying that."

"I do. Otherwise, my friend, you wouldn't have disturbed my crime scene ahead of the coroner. You know the rules as well as I do, and you know who has jurisdiction in a murder that doesn't cross state borders or have concrete ties to juicy stuff like espionage. There was something inside Skeps's penthouse that you didn't want us provincial turkeys seeing, and I intend to find out what it was."

"I didn't take so much as a paperclip! I just had a look at the body and walked around."

"Did you touch the body?"

"No!"

"Describe it."

"After more than twenty-four hours? Give me a break!"

"Crap! You're a trained observer. Describe it."

Special Agent Ted Kelly closed his eyes. "Skeps was lying on his back on his massage couch, the mark of an IV needle in his arm. It had dribbled a tiny drop of clear pink fluid, no blood. And yes, I used a swab to take a sample, which dried it up. Skeps was naked. Someone had done a rough shave of his body hair down to the base of his penis, but no farther, and his name was written in a burn. There were other burns as well. His nipples had been cut off with something blunt and heavy. There were ligature marks on his wrists and ankles. That's all."

"God, you're a liar, Kelly! Never touched the body, eh?"

"I didn't touch it! The swab did!"

"How long was it between your leaving the penthouse and the arrival of Dr. O'Donnell?"

"Half an hour."

"Did you remain in the vicinity?"

"No, I went downstairs to Skeps's offices."

"And you refuse to tell me what you pinched?"

"I didn't pinch anything."

"Well, as far as I'm concerned, Ted, the espionage is a goddamn nuisance. If you'd left things alone, we would have shared with you. It's a pity that the pendulum only swings one way. I won't be giving you any professional courtesies, be warned."

"Skeps was murdered by Ulysses, this is a federal case."

"Offer me some tangible evidence."

"I can't."

"Or won't, more like."

"Honestly, Carmine, my hands are tied!"

"Luckily mine aren't." Carmine got up. "Comforting to know that all cafeteria coffee is lousy, isn't it? If you want a good meal and good coffee while you're in a pint-sized state full of eccentrics, Ted, eat at Malvolio's Diner. It's right next to County Services." He stopped. "Are you married?" It seemed the question people hated answering.

"Used to be," said Kelly, looking sour. "She hated the fact that I was away from home so often, thought there was another woman."

"Did they ever put you undercover?"

"At my size?"

Carmine grinned and resumed his progress out. "Good to know that someone at the FBI has a brain. See you around."

"The IV wound shouldn't have had a droplet of any kind," Patsy said when Carmine told him what Ted Kelly had done. "I know we were late, but Skeps had been dead too long by the time he was discovered to be oozing liquid Kelly could soak up on a swab. Incidentally, it means he came armed with specimen jars, tubes, swabs, the whole nine yards. He must have swabbed every orifice, put a magnifying light over what he could see of the body. I bet no one there even noticed if he had equipment."

"I'm going to subpoena the FBI for their analytical results, especially the droplet," Carmine said. "Judge Thwaites will love it! A Longfellow eccentric indeed! Kelly didn't even know Longfellow was a poet, the ignorant shit. Though sometimes I wonder how much of his act is an act."

"I'm still fretting about the liquidity," Patsy said.

"Heparin?"

"Why, for God's sake? Skeps was immobilized. If the IV came out, there were other veins. Unless our murderer isn't an expert jabber. Maybe he got lucky on his first vein and decided not to risk failure later on. Hence, heparin. I'll swab the area myself." He looked unhappy. "What this does show me beyond a shadow of a doubt is that I need to go back to Skeps's body for a second look. I wasn't thorough enough."

"Patsy, Skeps was one of twelve cases."

"I know, and that's what really scares me. How many of them got my best shot? The baby and his mother . . . I'm going back to nine out of the eleven, Carmine, and this time every last one of them will get my best shot."

There was no point in arguing; Patrick's mind was made up. "Then start with Evan Pugh," Carmine said.

"The most important, you think?"

"Not think. Know."

"Evan Pugh it is. By the way," Patsy said a little too casually, "I hear that Myron's moved out of East Circle?"

"How the hell does the word get around?"

"The East Holloman grapevine, which has a particularly large tendril wound around the cops. Aunt Emilia is livid."

As Aunt Emilia was Carmine's mother, he gave a very Italian shrug. "Then you know as much as I do."

"More, probably. He's taken the entire top floor of the Cleveland Hotel and is planning to introduce his darling Erica to all of Holloman who matter."

"Wow! He *is* serious."

"I just hope she is."

"My hope is she's innocent of murder."

"Is she high on your list?"

"No. Just about halfway up."

Carmine left Patrick assembling his forces for another attack on Evan Pugh and went to his office, where a small stack of single sheets of paper awaited him. Most were memos, some more formal letters, but they had leaped out at Delia because they were neatly typed, neither signed nor initialed, and gave no hint of their origins.

"Sir," said the top one, a memo, "this is to remind you that you agreed to meet me to discuss the suggested improvements to our atomic reactor design. The usual place and time, please."

All fifteen—four letters, eleven memos—had the same fishy smell to them, Delia said.

"They look as if they've all been typed on the same machine, but that's a lot harder to establish if your firm uses IBM golfball machines whose letters haven't worn or warped, and it seems to me that all the executive secretaries have new or nearly new typewriters. The carbon ribbon is used only once and there are no mistakes, which suggests a very good typist. I hate to say it, Carmine, but I think Mr. Kelly should look at the executive secretaries, not the executives. I don't know of a managerial sort who can type for tuppence."

"What about a woman executive?" Carmine asked.

"Unless she started as a secretary, I'd say the same applied to her. And Dr. Davenport has never been a secretary. In college she paid a typist to do her papers and theses."

"I suppose that's a relief." Carmine thought of Myron.

"Have you had your invitation yet?"

"Invitation to what?"

"Mr. Mandelbaum is giving a reception and buffet dinner at the Cleveland Hotel on Saturday night. Uncle John's been asked, so has Danny, and so have I," said Delia.

"Then I daresay Desdemona, Sophia and I will see you there. In the meantime, is there anything else from the filing cabinet I should tackle, or can I leave it with you?"

"I think I can safely burn the rest of the contents."

"Then let's not do Ted Kelly's work for him, the lying son of a bitch. We're going back to our murders. Today is Thursday, but it's too late to drive to Orleans and get back again by dinnertime, so Mrs. Skeps can wait until tomorrow. Let her know I'll be coming, would you? Where are Abe and Corey?"

"In the newspaper morgue, reading. Shall I phone them?"

"No need. I'll pick them up on my way through."

The public library had its own premises farther down Cedar

Street, but the newspaper morgue was inside County Services, where it was handier for everyone from the police to the fire departments. The public used it too, and there were several habitual browsers in residence, dreamily turning the vast broadsheet pages of ancient copies of the *Holloman Post*, always full of interesting local news. It was slowly being converted to microfiche, and Carmine wondered how the browsers would like peering at a screen, white on black. They'll hate it, he concluded, wiggling his brows at Abe and Corey.

"Progress," he said apropos of nothing to his bewildered henchmen as they left, "can kill a lot of the fun." Then, as they left the building, "Find anything?"

"A fair amount on the Denbighs, who are into good causes. Mrs. Dr. Denbigh is a literacy nut. The Dean was into anything about the Renaissance. They both supported children's disease charities. Mrs. Dr. Denbigh is also a women's libber, big time. Desmond Skeps got a lot of press, we expected that. We noted articles that mentioned him and photocopied the ones that featured him. There wasn't a lot about the divorce, a bit strange."

"Well, it was out of state, and Cornucopia would have tried to play it down." Carmine smiled at Corey, who had given the report, but made sure to include Abe—that lieutenancy was a pain, and when he'd tried to get off the panel, Silvestri said he stayed on it.

"Where are we going?" Abe asked as they headed up South Green Street toward Maple.

"The Cleveland Hotel, where we have to meet the Pughs. They're here to identify the body, but they don't intend to go home until they can take the body home too. Their lawyer is with them."

"Trouble, Carmine?"

"I don't think so. Danny Marciano took the call, and he says they sounded like decent people."

The Pughs had been placed in a suite on the floor below the top, overlooking the red stone outcrop of North Rock. With the trees just coming into leaf, the forest that spread around Holloman looked as if a wispy, translucent chartreuse veil had been thrown over it, but Carmine knew that David and Enid Pugh would not notice.

They were in their mid-forties, tanned and fit, dressed in the bright colors that betrayed the climate they lived in, and they were far handsomer than their son. If ever there was evidence for a changeling, it was in the form of Evan Pugh, so conceited, self-absorbed and amoral. The Pugh parents were none of those things, five minutes in their company showed that, and the lawyer was there only to help them with any legal formalities they might encounter. Their grief was private, enclosed, yet unmistakable. How had they produced Evan? They insisted upon being told the entire story of his murder, a painful business for Carmine, who hated to shatter their illusions.

But, "Yes, he would do that," said Mrs. Pugh sadly. "Evan liked to pull the wings off butterflies. We tried every remedy known to man, Captain Delmonico, but none of us could do a thing to humanize him. The psychiatrists called him a psychopath and said there was no treatment. Davy and I just hoped and prayed that when he became a grown man, he would humanize himself. He was so brilliant! A perfect SAT score . . . When he chose Chubb, we had to let him go—we wanted him somewhere closer, but he was set on Chubb. The best pre-med and medical school. Medicine was the only choice as far as he was concerned." She sighed. "Davy and I have been waiting for something like this to happen for a long time."

"I am so very sorry, Mrs. Pugh, Mr. Pugh," Carmine said.

He didn't speak again until he and his sergeants were safely in the elevator. "I suppose some of them have to have model parents."

"The Pughs are my first," said Corey.

"And mine," said Abe.

So when they encountered Myron escorting Erica Davenport through the Cleveland's foyer, Carmine felt caught. Dr. Davenport was wearing a purple suit today that turned her eyes violet and, he was amused to note, shoes with lower heels; Myron wasn't tall. Wait until she meets Desdemona! he thought, nodding to his team to go ahead.

"How is Sophia?" was the first thing Myron said.

"Desdemona seems to think that if you take her to lunch—solo— and buy her the peridots she's been hankering for, you stand a chance of getting back in her good books," said Carmine.

"It will be done tomorrow, since school's out."

"That's another thing, Myron. In spite of what you said to her about Erica, Sophia got it into her head that you were really coming to entertain her while I worked a heavy case. She adores her baby brother, but he takes up most of Desdemona's time."

Myron groaned. "Oh, Carmine, I'm really, really sorry!"

"Tell her, not me."

"I'll buy her diamonds!"

"You will not! Desdemona says the peridots are suitable for a sixteen-year-old, and I trust her judgment a hundred percent."

He nodded again to Erica Davenport, who hadn't said a word, then followed Abe and Corey out.

"Who is Desdemona?" came her light, crisp voice.

Whatever Myron answered was lost, but Carmine had a fair idea that he would laugh, look mysterious, and tell her to wait and see.

"They're all talking about her and Myron," said Abe.

"No wonder she's wearing diamonds," said Corey.

Yes, no wonder, thought Carmine. How long has Myron known her, and how can we continue to be friends when I detest the woman? She's a harpy, feasting on living men.

The rest of the day passed fruitlessly, so when Friday dawned bright and clear, Carmine breathed a sigh of relief. He needed a break from routine. Driving himself, he headed out on I-95 for Cape Cod, a difficult destination because of the huge bites some geophysical monster had taken out of the coastline, Buzzard's Bay being the biggest. Whichever way he went, it was a long way, so while he was in Connecticut he put his light on the Fairlane's roof and used his siren to barrel along at well over the speed limit of 70 mph.

Orleans occupied the first part of the Cape's forearm after Chatham's elbow, and was commonly held to be the prettiest of many very pretty villages, though at this time of year most of the compounds and cottages would be untenanted. The Cape was a summer resort. Its houses were usually made of cedar boards and shingles left unpainted for the sea to weather them silver, and in July were festooned in pink or white rambling roses. The arm-shaped peninsula, bent like a man displaying his biceps, hugged the placid waters of Cape Cod Bay, glassy smooth in summer, while its outer edge saw the full force of the Atlantic, on the forearm a spume-soaked mass of wave-pounded sand dunes.

Carmine loved the Cape, and if he had an unfulfilled wish, it was to own a summer cottage anywhere on Cape Cod between Hyannis and Provincetown, the first place the Pilgrims made landfall.

Philomena Skeps's residence was at the end of a lane whose post-and-rail fences would be smothered in rambling roses by July. It was a traditional Cape Cod colonial in silvered cedar, with its share of rose trellises and enough land to say that the property was extremely valuable. It went down to the placid water of the sheltered side and had its own jetty and boathouse; someone liked messing around in boats. On the side wall of the house toward the front was a fuel oil outlet that said the tenant lived here all year round. Gazing about in delight, Carmine trod up the crunchy pebbled path to the front door.

Mrs. Skeps answered it herself. Hers was a dusky beauty, of thick black hair that curled, dark skin, black brows and lashes, dark green eyes.

"Come in, Captain," she said, leading him down a long hall to the back of the house, where an English-style conservatory had been added, all glass joined by graceful Art Nouveau iron struts painted white. It was stuffed with plants, some of them touching the transparent roof, but space enough had been left for a white-painted table and chairs and, in a different spot, two small white-padded settees. The pots, he noticed, were all painted white; Mrs. Skeps was a perfectionist. Green shall be the color of the room's glory, white shall all else be.

She had provided him with pastries. As he hadn't stopped on the road for breakfast, he made short work of the dainty goodies along with several cups (no mugs!) of coffee. Only when he was done did he lead the conversation away from pleasantries.

"You never remarried, did you?" he asked.

"No. Desmond was my only love," she said, giving Skeps his full name as if she never did otherwise. Then she dropped her bombshell, voice tranquil. "We were reconciling."

His startled eyes rested on her face, which remained smooth and impassive. "You were? After so long?"

"Yes, for young Desmond's sake. I contacted Desmond over four months ago, and we've been having a series of discussions ever since. There is another woman, you know."

"If there is, Mrs. Skeps, we haven't found a trace of her."

"It's Erica Davenport, of course."

"She denied it emphatically, ma'am."

"Naturally! It wasn't a great love affair, to be sure. On either side. Nevertheless, Captain, that Desmond should dispense with her services was one of my conditions."

"And did he dispense with her services?"

"Yes, shortly after I first contacted him."

"Did he give her a farewell gift of diamond earrings and a diamond pendant?" Carmine asked, curious. Well, according to the selfsame Erica Davenport, curiosity *was* his besetting sin.

Mrs. Skeps laughed, genuinely amused. "Who, Desmond? No! He may be one of America's richest men, but he's a miser." Her eyes filled with tears. "Oh, dear, it's so hard to speak—or think!—of Desmond in the past tense. No, what Desmond gave Erica was infinitely more valuable than diamonds, though it cost him nothing."

"A seat on the Board, among other things."

"Quite so. I didn't mind her at all. While she was with Desmond, he didn't plague me."

"You're well educated."

"Yes, mostly from reading."

"The sheepskin's fine, but it's the extracurricular reading that really educates. But why, Mrs. Skeps, did you make your overtures of reconciliation? Your husband's jealousy ruined your marriage."

"I told you, because of young Desmond."

"Isn't he better off without the horrors his father used to put you through? I've had to read all the divorce material, so I know."

"I made him give me his word that he'd never repeat that kind of conduct," said Mrs. Skeps. "His word was sacred to Desmond. You see, young Desmond is moving into his teens, and a boy of that age needs a father, no matter how inadequate. I would die for my child, Captain! I also believe that, having given his word, Desmond would have kept it."

"And now all your plans have collapsed."

"Yes, but at least I tried, and young Desmond knows that I tried. With his father gone, my own brothers can step in—they didn't dare while Desmond was alive. He threatened them with hired killers, and he meant the threat. He said anyone could buy a killer if they knew where to go."

I wonder, who else knows where to buy a hired killer? Dr. Erica Davenport, maybe? Philip Smith? Frederick Collins? Gus Purvey, even if I do like the man? Carmine thought. Aloud he asked, "How is your son?"

"Recovering slowly. He had such a terrible bout of what I'd always dismissed as a benign children's complaint—chicken pox. He had the sores right down inside his throat—everywhere! The worst is that he's going to have to repeat his school year."

"Not if you hire coaches and he goes to summer school," said Carmine, whose own health had always been rude.

"Only if he feels up to it," Philomena said, tone steely.

Uh-oh! An overprotective mom! Carmine changed the subject. "Tell me about Erica Davenport, Mrs. Skeps."

"I detest her as a person, but she deserved her seat on the Board, which is more than I can say for those other slugs. Oh, not Wally Grierson! That man's a treasure. When old Walter Symonds headed the legal division, it was pathetic. Cornucopia was forever making contractual errors and settling out of court for big sums on damage lawsuits. But after Erica took control, all that gradually stopped. Desmond adored her because she saved the company so much money."

At that moment someone shouted from the front regions of the house, answered by the hoarse, light voice of a boy. Quick talk passed, but when the newcomer entered, Desmond Skeps III was not with him. The fellow might have passed for Carmine's brother, cast in the same muscularly tall mold, with the same olive skin, broad facial bones, and extremely intelligent eyes; the differences lay in the hair, his worn fashionably long, and the color of the eyes—in his case, dark brown. He wore bell-bottomed jeans, a white sweater and denim jacket, but contrived to make the clothes look formal, and with him he brought an air of ownership that wasn't lost on Carmine.

"Tony Bera," he said, extending his hand.

"Carmine Delmonico."

"You all right, Philomena?" Bera asked Mrs. Skeps.

"Perfectly, thank you." She turned to Carmine. "Tony seems to think the whole world is out to get me."

"Don't decry a good watchdog, Mrs. Skeps. I wouldn't be visiting you if there weren't a murderer on the loose. Not that I think you're in danger—I don't. Just the same, I'm happy to see Mr. Bera. Do you live hereabouts, sir?"

"Yes, just down the lane."

"Good. According to Desmond Skeps's will, Desmond Skeps the Third inherits everything. I was supposed to get a full copy of the document, but so far it hasn't materialized. Dr. Davenport called

Captain Marciano and said your son was the full heir, but gave no further details. Maybe you can fill me in, Mr. Bera?"

"I wish I could," the lawyer said, frowning, "but so far, we haven't even heard that much."

"I thought there had to be a reading, especially in the presence of the heir," Carmine said.

"Not necessarily. It all depends what the will itself directs be done. Mr. Skeps's lawyers in New York City will have known the contents. If young Desmond is the heir, I'm entitled to see the will in its entirety because I act for his mother, and therefore for him."

"Is that ironclad, sir?"

"Well, no, but she'll be his guardian!"

"Yes, of course." He looked at Philomena Skeps. "There are still a few things I need to know, ma'am. Can you give me an actual date for your first overture to your ex-husband about the possibility of reconciliation?"

"We talked about it on the phone on the Monday of the third week of last November."

"And when did Mr. Skeps hand Dr. Davenport her marching orders?"

"Very soon afterward. That same week, certainly."

So Erica Davenport had known of the reconciliation for four months, give or take a few days. Not much reason for murder now. A woman scorned with murder in mind wouldn't have waited this long. It looked more as if, the Skeps fish having slipped her hook, she baited it again and caught Myron. The diamonds were a gift from Myron, the most generous of men. Given that they totaled about eight carats, the price tag must have been somewhere between a quarter and a half million dollars. No chunks of Coke bottle for Myron Mendel Mandelbaum! And he was *serious*. The last time he threw gems like that around was for Sophia's mom.

"Now tell me about the—er—slugs, Mrs. Skeps."

She sneered, an expression that didn't suit her face. "Oh, them! Desmond called them his yes-men, with good reason. Phil Smith admits it freely—he can't even be bothered heading up a specific company, which I guess means he's landed on his feet as usual. He'll step into Desmond's shoes, chair the Board, you name it. Hypocrite! Anyone would think he was royalty."

"What about their past histories? Shady activities? Shady deals? Shady women?"

"Not that I know of, apart from Gus Purvey, who pretends to be a man's man—and is, in the one respect men's men don't aspire to. Namely, that he is a homosexual with a penchant for youths dolled up as women."

Carmine looked at Anthony Bera. "Anything to add, sir?"

"No. I'm not a part of the Cornucopia world."

Maybe not, thought Carmine, getting to his feet, but I am going to be investigating your whereabouts on April third, Mister Fat Cat Lawyer. A winterized house in Orleans says your legal practice must pull in a healthy income. You're in love with Mrs. Skeps, but she doesn't even see you except as her friend. That's a very frustrating situation to be in.

He repeated his trick with flashing light and siren on the journey home; from Providence back to Holloman was a well-worn beat. Maybe the visit to Orleans had done his soul some good, but it hadn't advanced his investigation. Time to get tough. If no copy of the will had appeared at County Services, he had every intention of invading Erica Davenport's lair and demanding one immediately. But the document was waiting. Accustomed to legalese, he read its many pages swiftly, then sat back, winded. Someone had blabbed that he was seeing Philomena Skeps today, and Erica Davenport had deliberately withheld knowledge of the will from him and Philomena Skeps until the meeting was in the past. No wonder! The fur would have flown like wildcats locked in mortal combat. What a blow for Philomena Skeps and Anthony Bera! What might they have said in the throes of rage?

Desmond Skeps III was indeed the sole heir, but guardianship belonged to Erica Davenport. Not in a maternal sense: Philomena was still free to house the boy, feed him, dress him, nurture him. Be his mother in his home. But she was stripped of all ability to control his destiny, his fortune, the fate of Cornucopia. When it came to the power and the money, Erica Davenport stood *in loco parentis*. And in the years between now and the boy's twenty-first birthday, Erica Davenport was the head of Cornucopia. Nor could Carmine see how Anthony Bera had a hope of overturning the will in court. Philomena Skeps had no business experience, nothing to offer a judicial panel. No, the only way Philomena Skeps could win anything was to stay on the right side of Dr. Erica Davenport, chief of Cornucopia. Whom she detested.

Poor Myron! This lightning bolt meant that Erica didn't need to find a rich husband, if that was what had prompted her assault on the affections of Carmine's friend. She could set her own salary and perks, with no one to gainsay her—Van Cleef's, here I come! No, thought Carmine, the gold-digger image felt wrong. This woman was after power, not money, which suggested a side to Myron he hadn't suspected. Myron had come into Carmine's life nearly fifteen years ago and been taken at face value as a very wealthy film producer; it hadn't occurred to Carmine to burrow into the dear man's commercial affairs. Now, far too late for it to matter, he was beginning to think he should have.

And what of the woman given her marching orders by Desmond Skeps over four months ago? She'd probably interpreted her lover's action as the beginning of her absolute end. Instead she had succeeded him as ruler of the Cornucopia kingdom. So the big question was: did Erica Davenport know the contents of Desmond Skeps's will? A colossal motive for murder if she did. But how could she have discovered what lay inside a document held in a vault in New York City guarded by a firm she didn't know? The only way would have been if Skeps told her, but would he? No, he would not, was Carmine's instinctive conclusion; Skeps wasn't that kind of man. Rather, he would have relished tormenting her as the weeks and then the months went by; beneath the obvious differences, he was not unlike Evan Pugh. I bet they both pulled the wings off butterflies, Carmine thought.

When had the will been made? Carmine looked again, just to make sure he hadn't mistaken the date. But no, he hadn't. It was made two months ago, well after Skeps had dispensed with the lady's services as his mistress. That meant Skeps had coldly considered her merits for the job, and liked them.

He looked at his watch: still time to pay Dr. Davenport a visit before Cornucopia closed its offices for the day. Nor did he call her to make sure she was there; with this new job draped around her shoulders, she'd be there.

Having made a useless trip to Skeps's offices, he found her upstairs in the penthouse. Which, Abe had discovered, had a small internal staircase hidden inside a guest lavatory. The back wall opened inward when the second in a row of fancy knobs was pressed, revealing a very tight set of iron spiral steps. So Carmine used them, and emerged as if he'd availed himself of the facilities. His appearance didn't alarm her, just annoyed her.

Today she was wearing dull red, and the eyes she turned on him had gone khaki. Chameleon's eyes, he thought. They reflect the color around her, but they can't achieve dull red. The pigment for it isn't there.

"I must be your prime suspect now," she said.

"No, if anything you've gone down a few notches. Unless he told you what was in his will?"

"Desmond Skeps, so indiscreet? The only thing that ever loosened Desmond's tongue was alcohol, and by the time I met him, he'd limited his intake severely. One single-malt Scotch a day, that was it, and he never, never deviated. He headed one of the country's biggest companies, and he knew the damage a loose tongue could wreak. When he first took over the firm, he compromised Cornucopia's tender for one of the earliest atomic reactors, which enabled a rival company to undercut him using Cornucopia's own design. It all but killed him. Grierson was the one pulled him out of the fire—if Des loved anyone, it was Wal Grierson. His board was brand-new then. He should have fired all of them except Grierson, but he decided yes-men had their uses—provided, that is, that the boss didn't get drunk."

"Obviously you indulged in pillow talk, Dr. Davenport."

"Oh, she told you, did she? She would!"

"Did Mr. Skeps like women? Get on with them?"

"Oh, come now, Captain, you know full well he hated women! That's why his will really staggered me. It never occurred to me that Des valued my business sense. Now look at me! I'm Chairman of the Board and I have complete control of young Des's shares, interests, money." She gave a breathy laugh. "I, Erica Davenport, am cock of the walk!"

"So you're going to rub Mrs. Skeps's nose in it."

"Not at all." The eyes were so earnest they were struggling to be blue. "I have no intention of interfering with Philomena Skeps or with her duties as a mother."

"I have a different question for you, Dr. Davenport. What would happen if Desmond Skeps the Third died?"

Her skin lost its color. "Don't! Oh, don't!"

"You're a lawyer, the eventuality must have occurred to you. So what happens?"

"There are other members of the Skeps family. I daresay the closest agnate relative would inherit."

Carmine's heart sank. "Mr. Philip Smith?"

"No, definitely not. Mr. Smith *claims* blood relationship, but the degree has never been investigated. There is a male nephew and a male first cousin. They would come first, with the first cousin ahead. The nephew is the child of Desmond Skeps's sister. The first cousin is the child of Desmond Skeps Senior's younger brother. However, the will was drawn up under New York State law, and I am no expert on that."

"And it's irrelevant besides, since Young Des is very much alive. Thank you." He looked around. "Are you planning to live here?"

"I don't see why not, though I'll have to gut the place. Poor Desmond had no taste."

"You do?"

"I'd rather say that my taste is quite, quite different. I'll be buying paintings for my pension plan, and hanging them in here. I'll also be getting rid of that monstrosity." She flapped a hand at the telescope. "He used to love to play Peeping Tom."

"So I realized. Did he have a camera attached to it?"

She jumped. "Yes, he did! He did! But it's not here now."

"It wasn't here when his body was still on his massage couch," said Carmine grimly. "Well, at least I know what Ted Kelly removed."

"Or perhaps the murderer removed it," she said.

"Possibly."

He moved toward the elevator.

"Captain? Will you and your family be at Myron's party tomorrow?"

"If we've been invited, yes."

"Good! I'm anxious to meet your wife."

"Why, in particular?"

"She's brave. Myron told me. It's not a quality usually associated with women."

"Hogwash!" Carmine snapped, goaded. "Women are incredibly brave, every day of their lives. To a cop like me, they're prey. There's always someone out there watching, stalking, snooping, and no one knows which woman will be a target. Though that's not what I was driving at, ma'am. Women are brave because they bear the babies and hold the home together—and, man, that can be hard!"

"You're a romantic!" she said, clinically surprised.

"No, I'm a realist. Good night, Dr. Davenport."

And what would you know about *real* women, you attenuated society princess living in an executive washroom world? He seethed, thinking of the thousands of women he had met in the course of his work, tiny memories flashing in and out of his rage, understanding himself no more than a witness to their troubles, pain, hideous predicaments. Cooling, he began to think of the upside, and was able to go home with the worst memories returned to his subconscious.

"You are so too a romantic," said Desdemona, handing him his bourbon and soda.

He had actually made it in time to receive a wide-awake Julian, who jigged up and down on Daddy's lap because he wasn't old enough yet to do much else. Opened, his eyes were revealed as a pale topaz color with a thin outer ring of jet; their lashes were thick, black, and so long they curled, and he had a thatch of black curls atop his big head that would have done credit to any girl. In spite of which no one mistook his sex; there was too much Carmine about him, determined, dogged.

His genesis was a source of perpetual wonder to Carmine, who had never imagined himself fathering a son, and couldn't think of enough ways to show Desdemona what a gift she had given him so far into his life.

"Squeeze Daddy's hand," he commanded.

Julian squeezed; Carmine went through a histrionic performance of ow's and flinches that had the baby squealing with delight. After that father and son indulged in an orgy of kisses that ended only when Desdemona swooped on the child and bore him off.

"He never tries to fight it," Carmine said when she returned and sat down to sip her gin and tonic. "I always expect him to try on a power play, or at least start bawling. We were having real fun, then— wham! Mommy cut it short."

"He's clever enough to know already that there's no escaping the fell hour of bedtime. Julian saves his energies for more attainable objectives," she said, smiling and lifting her glass in a toast.

"Where's Sophia?"

"Having dinner at the Cleveland with Myron and his Erica."

"No kidding?"

"No kidding. Myron took her to lunch and gave her the set of peridots, though of course he wouldn't be Myron if he didn't exceed orders. She got a very pretty set of garnets too."

"I presume the breach was healed?"

"Oh, yes. Then the little minx smarmed up to Myron until he agreed to this dinner with Erica. I let her go because if she takes against the woman, it's better that she should do so in private, not in front of a million people at this wretched bash Myron's throwing tomorrow night. I've accepted on our behalf, of course." She glanced at her watch. "I imagine she'd have come home by now if things weren't going well."

"Erica Davenport is a puzzle, Desdemona."

"And a murderer?"

"I don't think so, though Skeps's death has given her great power. According to his will, she's the head honcho."

"My goodness! A signal victory for women," Desdemona said, gazing at Carmine through the eyes of total love. It was fine to be an independent woman answering to no one; she had been one of those well into her thirties, and perhaps it was better to get the independence urge out of the system early. But there could be no doubt that life with Carmine, at the very center of a large Italian-American family, was infinitely preferable.

"What's for dinner?" he asked, secretly craving Italian.

"Spaghetti and meatballs a la Emilia Delmonico."

What a night! He'd gotten to cuddle a wakeful Julian, his dinner wish had been granted—maybe later on he and Desdemona would make a brother or a sister for their son. Though he felt it was too soon, Desdemona didn't.

He drained his glass. "Then let's eat," he said. "Tomorrow night we'll have to eat all the things that give us indigestion—lobster, soft-shell crab, Iranian caviar, raw this and raw that. Myron's importing the chef, I hear."

* * *

Carmine may not have been looking forward to Myron's party, but he seemed to be the only one. After Erica's promotion it had changed from lounge suit to black tie, whether at Myron's whim or Erica's no one knew, and sent the female guests into conniption fits—*what to wear?*

Much to her father's relief, Sophia decided not to go. No reason was tendered, but Desdemona suspected the girl was thoroughly intimidated by Myron's new girlfriend. After her dinner with them she had come home enthusiastic, all "Erica this" and "Erica that," but it rang hollow. So much patrician beauty, sophistication, intelligence and aloofness were just too formidable when met in the same person. Sophia had understood herself checkmated.

Since at her size Desdemona couldn't buy off the rack, Carmine was spared the what-to-wear dilemma; though it wasn't vast, his wife had a wardrobe for every emergency. Privately he thought she looked stunning in an ice-blue gown she had embroidered herself in the manner of a dress Audrey Hepburn had worn in a film called *Sabrina*. In the days when she had managed the Hug, Desdemona had earned large fees for her embroidery, so skilled that she had made vestments for Roman Catholic priests. And, Carmine was delighted to see, she hadn't minimized her height. Her size thirteen silver sandals (*so* handy to have drag queens in New York City!) sported three-inch heels.

The first couple Carmine and Desdemona encountered, in the elevator, were Mawson MacIntosh and his wafty wife, Angela. She left Chubb politics to her husband while she explored other planes of existence from yoga to astrology. Theirs was a good partnership, for under the waftiness Angela had a memory that never forgot a face, a name or a conversation. Handy for the President of Chubb! Carmine had long given up wondering how Myron, a West Coaster born, bred, educated and domiciled, knew so many of the East Coast establishment; he just did.

"So tonight we meet the new head of Cornucopia," said M.M.

"Indeed we do," said Carmine, refraining from telling M.M. that she was one of his suspects. M.M. probably knew anyway.

"Darling, we've already met her," said Angela. "Surely you remember? At a charity banquet four months ago. She was with Gus Purvey. I remember her because she's so beautiful—an Aquarius with Scorpio rising and her Jupiter in Capricorn."

"Huh!" M.M. grunted and stood back for the ladies to go out first. "You look delicious, Desdemona."

They plunged straight into the fray, headed by Myron and Erica. Their hostess was in silver-grey taffeta and silver tissue, which turned her eyes pale grey; the heels were down under two inches, Carmine noted. Whatever kind of feminist she was—and she had to be one—her technique was subtle, didn't include intimidation of the male on any tangible level. Myron was so proud of her, so anxious to introduce her to everyone who mattered, apparently oblivious to the fact that she was a major player of the power game in her own right. What was going to happen when they clashed in a board room, as inevitably they would? Or had she factored that in too?

Myron introduced her to Desdemona while Carmine watched. As she was obliged to tilt her head far back to look up into Desdemona's face, she could only see it from beneath, not its most flattering aspect. So her eyes, seeking a more comfortable level, fixed on Desdemona's rings.

"Lovely," she said, forcing a smile. How could a grotesquely tall woman possibly feel at home with her grotesqueness? To wear high heels! Carmine Delmonico was a tall man, but she dwarfed him, and he didn't seem to mind! How could she catalogue them?

"The diamond is my engagement ring," Desdemona was saying, "and the sapphire is for the birth of our son."

"You're English?"

"Yes, but an American citizen these days."

Desdemona smiled and moved away; the crowd was building up.

"What do you think of the snow queen?" Carmine asked.

"Not snow, love. Snow's soft and yielding. Ice queen."

"Good point. Does her age show?"

"To me it does. She's very hard, in a way you can't be at twenty or even thirty. I imagine that soon she'll avail herself of face lifts—the grooves between the sides of her nose and the corners of her mouth are beginning to show."

"Is she capable of murder?"

"Corporate murder, certainly. But in the manner of a shark. She'd bite you in half before you so much as noticed her in your vicinity. But I can't see her getting herself into any situation that would re-quire physical murder. Unless, of course, something pushed her into making a terrible slip."

"While you stood with her she read you as a freak, but now we're half the room away, she can't take her eyes off you."

"No, I think she was more interested in you, Carmine. She had hopes of seducing you, I think, but after seeing me, they died. She can't cope with people outside her experience, which is actually quite limited. To her, men are such poor, insecure creatures that they couldn't bear to be towered over, for example. Now she doesn't know what to think."

"That's what I read on her face, though not the seduction. What does that mean, my oracle?"

"That she's attracted to you, silly!"

Delia came up, extraordinary in pink frills; Carmine left his wife and his secretary to chat while he started to prowl. No one was ab-sent, as far as he could see.

He stopped by Mr. Philip Smith, whose wife was elsewhere.

"How do you know Myron, Mr. Smith?" he asked.

The cat showed at once. "It's Phil at social functions, Carmine. Myron is the head of a New York bank with which we do a great deal of business, Hardinge's. A merchant bank only, no depositors in the First National sense."

Condescending prick! "Is that how Myron met Dr. Davenport?"

"Erica, Carmine, Erica! Yes, of course. She's Cornucopia Legal, always involved in our banking business."

"When did this meeting occur?"

Smith shrugged. "I have no idea. Ask them. In fact, if you're so intimate with Myron, I'm absolutely astonished that you don't know. Or is the intimacy just a Myron exaggeration? He's such a dreadful leg-puller sometimes."

"Ask him," said Carmine affably.

And eat shit, you stuck-up clotheshorse! said Carmine to himself as he walked away. Your speech is as stiff as your back.

Next, he encountered Dr. Pauline Denbigh and the acting Dean of Dante College, Dr. Marcus Ceruski. They were busy devouring lobster patties, ecstasy written on their faces.

"Not in mourning, Dr. Denbigh?" Carmine asked, Smith's snaky gibes still smarting.

She snorted, unabashed. "I look like a terminal cirrhosis in black, Captain, so no. Besides, I was dying to meet the new head of Cornucopia. What a victory for women!"

"Yes, it is, particularly as the decision was made purely on merit. Why don't you try for Dean of Dante? That would be just as great a victory."

"Chubb would give the job to someone from Mars first—*if* he had a penis and was a Chubb alumnus. I'm trying for Lysistrata when it's built."

"Isn't it weird to build a college exclusively for women when all-male colleges are being held discriminatory?"

"Of course. We'll have our share of men students, I'm sure. The real victory will be a woman-dominated administration. Chubb owes us that at least," said Dr. Denbigh.

"What if your husband hadn't been murdered? Or perhaps I should say, what would happen if your husband were alive at the time Lysistrata is finished?" Carmine asked.

"I would still have applied for the deanship. If John had refused to go with me, I would have divorced him. Lysistrata, I am assured, will not be hidebound in the matter of a married couple. Such rubbish!"

"How do you feel about the crumbling of time-honored customs and practices, Dr. Ceruski?"

He flushed, looked confused. "Ah—it's really none of my business, Captain. Especially given that it's hypothetical."

Bestowing a smile on them, Carmine moved on. *Could* she have done it? An idea was stirring in his head, but it would have to wait until Monday . . . And this isn't bad fun, his unruly mind was telling him as his eyes fed it information. Thank God my wife can look after herself and knows exactly why I'm here. Good Lord, a woman in a *hat!*

The next fish he caught in his net were actually two fish, according to M.M.'s astrologically inclined wife: joined at the hip, one swimming upstream, the other down. Dean Robert and Mrs. Nancy Highman. She was charming and in the Dean's own age group. Their children were grown and gone from the nest, which made living in college at Paracelsus ideal.

"I hope you find out who killed that poor, unfortunate young man," Mrs. Highman said, sipping a glass of white wine. "I had his parents to lunch—such lovely people! What can one *do* to ease their pain? Try to give them back the body soon, Captain! As for Bob—he just isn't himself. Well, how can he be? I don't know how word gets around, but every parent of every student in college knows about the bear trap. Trying to persuade people that none of the other young men is in danger takes up so much of Bob's time! I don't suppose you'd let us tell the parents about Evan's blackmail?"

Who the hell told the Highmans about that? The Pughs? "I'm afraid not, Mrs. Highman," he said gently. "That's what we call sequestered evidence. If it became general knowledge, it would muddy the waters."

She sighed. "Yes, I see." Then she brightened. "Well, I do have some information that might help," she said.

"What?" he asked warily, not sure how far she was prepared to go to ease the weight off Dean Highman's shoulders.

"I was in that afternoon. Usually I'm not—I have a life class in drawing at the Taft Institute. But our instructor got sick, and it was canceled. I came down late for lunch, about a quarter after one. The foyer was deserted, but there was a fellow in a brown uniform going up the sophomore stairs. I only remembered him tonight after I got here because of that woman over there in the brown tabard with the glittery tapestry tunic underneath it—see? See her? It's that huge pancake of a brown hat! The fellow was carrying something on his head, brown and circular—the brown cloth made me think of the cover on an instrument. It was bigger than the hat by far, but the hat jogged my memory. Isn't she a fright? Why's she wearing a hat to a formal affair? The fellow in brown had a tool belt and pouch like a carpenter, which is why I never thought to notice him."

Suppressing what he felt was an excusable exasperation, Carmine leaned a little into Nancy Highman's face. "Madam, you have been questioned twice. Each time you swore you'd seen no one—in fact, you didn't even tell my men that you were in college last Monday!"

"Oh, dear! *Please* don't be annoyed, Captain! I'm just not a remembering kind of person unless something jogs me, truly! Like that hat over there. It's so ugly! And then—bang! There was the workman in brown, with the brown pancake on his head. He— he rose to the surface!"

"Was he a big man?"

"No, he was very small, like a child. Thin . . . And he had a limp, though which was the bad leg I can't remember. If his boots had made a black mark on the marble floor I would have called him down and rebuked him, but they didn't have those icky rubber soles that drive Bob crazy. So I went on into the dining room and forgot him."

"Did you see his face?"

"No, I was looking at his back."

"His hair?"

"Hidden by the brown pancake."

"What about his hands? Was he a white man or a black man?"

"I think he wore workmen's gloves."

Jesus, the guy had balls! Here we've been assuming he picked an hour when the college was deserted, when all the time he was there while the dining room was serving lunch. At any moment a sophomore student might have taken it into his head to visit his upstairs room, and run into this limping, diminutive murderer. Who would have—done what? Nothing beyond what was expected of a carpenter, even if the youth who encountered him was Evan Pugh. But it hadn't happened. The killer had a sublime faith in his luck, apparently substantiated. How many more surprises would Myron's reception yield? And, wondered Carmine, who is the woman in the brown pancake hat?

Gus Purvey, Wallace Grierson and Fred Collins had circled their wagons, but Carmine had no trouble breaking their formation. Now he had Desdemona with him, and they were awed into submission. Purvey, deprived of Erica, had come alone. Collins was squiring his twenty-year-old wife, Candy. Grierson's wife, Margaret, another tall woman, was looking indescribably bored when the Delmonicos arrived, and seized upon Desdemona with glee. They moved away a little and commenced animated talk.

"Your wife's loaded with class," said Grierson to Carmine. "Was she—or is she still, maybe—a detective?"

"No, she was a hospital administrator, one of the new kind that couldn't castrate a tomcat," said Carmine. "Hospitals are run as businesses now, more concerned about ledgers than the quality of nursing."

"Pity, that. Health isn't a commodity, it's a state of being."

"We'll have to get you on the Chubb-Holloman Hospital board."

"I wouldn't mind that."

"I envy any woman with a career," said Candy with a sigh.

"Then go get a career, Candy," Grierson said, not unkindly.

"You've got your career!" Collins snapped. "Wife and mother."

Purvey laughed. "You're just sour at being pipped at the post by the old grey mare," he said through the guffaws. "It's a good color for our Erica, grey. But cheer up, Fred! Maybe the race isn't over yet."

"It is for me. And for you. And for Phil. Not for good old Wallace here, of course. He'll survive," said Collins.

"You mean you could find yourselves out in the cold, cold snow?" Carmine asked.

"Bound to be," Purvey answered.

"I guess it was a big shock" was Carmine's next comment.

"What?" Collins asked.

"The will."

"It was an insult! Disgusting!" Collins hissed.

"Did any of you expect it?"

Grierson chose to answer. "Not even Phil Smith, and he was closest to Desmond. I'd say it was a forgery, except that Tombs, Hillyard, Spender and Hunter drafted it, kept it, saw Desmond sign it, and then put it in their vault. It came up to Holloman in a top-secrets briefcase chained to the courier's arm, and Bernard Spender opened it in our presence. It's the genuine article, for sure. I'd hoped that somewhere it would say why Desmond decided on Erica, but it doesn't. There's not one personal reference in it, even as a footnote. Just pages and pages designed to foil Anthony Bera if he sues on Philomena's behalf."

"Don't you think Dr. Davenport will make a good chief, sir?"

"I think she'll run Cornucopia into the ground. That's why I'm going to get an agreement out of her that I get first refusal of Dormus when the crash happens," Grierson said.

"How many of you knew that Dr. Davenport was Mr. Skeps's mistress?" Carmine asked.

That flabbergasted them; there could be no mistaking their reaction. None of them had known. And here am I, Carmine the mischief maker, inserting that barb under their skins, yet another poison. "Oh, come!" he said, sounding mocking. "You must have wondered the moment you heard the contents of the will, even if you hadn't believed anything amorous existed between them before that."

"I for one genuinely believed Desmond chose her for her ability," Grierson said. "In fact, I don't see how their being lovers changes that. Desmond wasn't the kind of man to be influenced by emotions. He was wrong to judge her so capable, but it wasn't a judgment he made because she was his mistress."

"Thank you, Mr. Grierson. As a matter of fact, Mr. Skeps dispensed with Dr. Davenport's services as a mistress four months ago, and didn't make his will for two more months. Whatever his emotions were, they clearly didn't enter into his decision, just as you contend. What fascinates me is that you go against the general direction of opinion in saying Dr. Davenport isn't up to the job. Have you any reason?"

"My gut," Wallace Grierson said. "Erica's all smoke and mirrors, a con merchant. You're a clever man, Captain Delmonico—also an enormously experienced one. There's always a kid at the top of the class with near-perfect scores and a brilliant future. But there's always another kid who hangs around the top without ever getting there because her—we'll use the feminine—her work is too individual, too unorthodox. And guess what? At the twenty-year reunion, she's the one with the brilliant career. Erica is the perfect kid with the perfect scores. But she's never been the head of anything apart from Legal, so she has tunnel vision and a calculator for a mind. She leaned heavily on Desmond, who didn't realize it." He frowned. "My gut also says that her heart isn't in running a business empire. She burns for something else, but what it is, I don't know."

"A gut, Mr. Grierson, is a splendid thing," said Carmine solemnly, walking off without collecting Desdemona.

Parties, he thought, can be better sources of information than formal police interviews. If Myron hadn't thrown this one, the woman in the brown pancake hat wouldn't have jogged Mrs. Highman's memory, and the old Cornucopia Board would not have been the worse for booze.

And our hostess is flagging, he realized as he wandered in her direction. Of course she's flagging, because she isn't a party person. Whereas Myron, West Coast to the core, is utterly enamored of parties—no, put that another way, Carmine! He has to be perpetually surrounded by glitz and bustle, beautiful people strutting their stuff, the tinkle of tinsel, the chatter of people making deals all around him. Parties are just one aspect of it. Equally important are things like lunch at the Polo Lounge and dinner at whichever restaurant is in vogue this week. When Myron visits us, he's doing penance. No, Jews don't do penance. He's like one of those guys who get flogged with a bunch of switches before taking the cold plunge or the steam or whatever. We are Myron's bunch of switches so he can appreciate the deliciousness of his own world. Why do I love him? Because he's a total gentleman, Sophia's true father, kindness and generosity personified, and an all-round great guy. What kills me is *my* gut feeling that Myron is in for a rocky ride through the tunnel of love. First Sandra, now Erica. He's a bad picker.

"Had enough?" he asked Erica, reaching her.

She looked startled. "Does it show?"

"Not really. But you don't have the gift of small talk, and you're not motivated to acquire it."

"Are you suggesting that I find the motivation?"

"That depends. If you're serious about Myron, then yes. He lives in a world of small talk, banter, double-talk and the patois of wheeling and dealing. Where did you meet?"

"In New York, at a board meeting of Hardinge's, the bank. I thought Myron was tremendously attractive."

"You and half the feminine world. No doubt he's told you that he's married to my ex-wife?"

"Yes. I confess I can't understand how he and you would ever have eyes for the same woman."

"Oh, that's because you'll never know what Sandra was like at twenty! Very much in your mold, though without the brains. What she did have was an adorable waifish quality that made a man want to shelter her from every wind that blew. Sophia is very like her physically, but her intelligence masks that."

"Just as well, in my opinion. I loathe stupid women!" said Erica tartly.

"Stupidity doesn't mean a woman's unlikeable, surely."

"It does to me!"

"So you're glad Sophia is smart."

"Yes. She doesn't despise her face, but she's not going to let it decide her destiny."

"You think of Sophia's beauty the way you think of your own—as a tool if your back's against the wall, but otherwise as a nuisance. Whereas Sophia is very different. She thinks of her face as part and parcel of what's behind it. Sophia doesn't live in compartments."

"You always manage to put me in the wrong!" she snapped, turned, and spotted two latecomers. "Philomena, Tony!"

Carmine retired to a good vantage point and watched Erica take Philomena Skeps and Anthony Bera to meet Myron, who, as ever delighted to see new faces, welcomed them with all the verve of a host greeting his first guests rather than his last.

Philomena, Carmine decided, was probably at least five years younger than Erica, and quite cast the ice queen in the shade. Like Delia, she was wearing a tight-waisted dress of pink frills, but there the comparison ended. Despite what she had said to Carmine about Skeps's miserly tendencies, she was wearing a suite of amazing pink diamonds. Paired with Bera, she looked complete.

Some talk passed between Philomena and Erica, then Myron took Bera away to meet the Mayor while Philomena and Erica continued their discussion. Their manner seemed pleasant, their smiles genuine, but Carmine still felt that whatever they were saying was not all sweetness and light. A glass of champagne was refused, but one of a Chilean red wine accepted; Erica fluttered around Desmond Skeps's ex-wife like a nervous bride around a fierce mother-in-law. Lobster? No? Chicken vol-au-vent? No? This wonderful country terrine? Oh, good!

Finally Bera extricated himself from Myron's clutches and rescued Philomena, escorting her to a chair, finding a little table, then giving her the glass of Chilean wine and putting a piled plate down on the table where she could pick at it. Having settled her, he took up his station behind her and let his gaze follow Erica Davenport wherever she went. There were undercurrents here, but Carmine wasn't sure of their origin or their nature. Phil Smith arrived, with his wife, who—ye Gods!—was saying hello to Philomena in all the glory of her brown pancake hat.

Smith's visit with Philomena was brief. His wife, poor soul, was unhappy to be dragged away willy-nilly, and tried to stay, but Smith hustled her off as if afraid of what she might say. Recognizing a kindred sartorial being, Delia grabbed her out from under her husband's grasp, and the two worst-dressed women in the room went off together. Gus Purvey and Fred Collins paid court next, Collins without Candy. Anthony Bera greeted them stiffly, then fell silent and listened to Philomena talk. When Collins, drunk enough now to stagger, began to get agitated, Bera moved quickly in front of Philomena's chair and obviously told Purvey to remove him. Purvey obeyed, but not a minute later Philomena gave Bera orders to leave her. He protested, but she lifted her chin in a gesture so imperious that Carmine was intrigued. Biting his lip, Bera stalked off, leaving her alone on her chair. Who did she want to see?

Then Myron joined her, and that meant the excellent host had just ruined the lady's plans. How exactly she got rid of him the watching Carmine couldn't know, but she did, and so charmingly that he gave her a worshipping smile as he went away. Philomena Skeps was alone again.

Several more people approached her and were dismissed with the same charm she had used on Myron: Dr. Pauline Denbigh (interesting, that one!) and Mawson and Angela MacIntosh. Carmine inched closer, wishing that the room wasn't beginning to empty; he would never be able to overhear what Philomena Skeps said.

And finally came the desired one; the body language was unmistakable. Erica Davenport.

A waiter passed by; Philomena detained him, and the little table was stripped bare instantly. Erica perched herself on it, turning sideways to see Skeps's ex-wife, who slewed sideways as well. Frustrated, Carmine stared at their profiles as they talked; he could lip-read dialogue if it was well enunciated and its speakers face-on, but side-on it was impossible.

They talked with such a determined air of isolation that several people, heading their way, backed off. Possibly too the news of Erica's guardianship had spread party-wide, and no one wanted to be the inadvertent destroyer of a pact. It certainly seemed as if negotiations were going on, and it solved the riddle of why Philomena Skeps had come to the party at all. Neutral ground. Where else could she plead her case without the specter of Cornucopia looming? At Orleans? Erica would never come.

Anthony Bera watched the two women with painful intensity, absently answering the questions Wallace Grierson was throwing at him. Then Phil Smith and the brown pancake came up, blocking Bera's view of Philomena's chair, and he gave up.

Treaty negotiations must have lasted a good half hour, at the end of which Erica Davenport looked very tired and Philomena Skeps more beautiful than ever. Then Erica slapped her hands on her knees and got up from her perch. She leaned down to drop a kiss on Philomena's brow, and walked off toward Myron.

"I'm pooped," Desdemona said, kicking off her sandals as soon as she was in the car.

"Me too, my lovely lady. You looked fantastic tonight."

"Did I?"

"Yes, you did. Your figure is as good as any Hollywood movie star's, and that dress set it off just fine."

"Isn't it funny? Women are always moaning that babies ruin their figures, but Julian did mine the world of good."

"How do you think Myron is feeling right now?"

She frowned. "Good question. He's fathoms deep in love—did you notice the diamond bracelet?—but it must be dawning on him by now that his darling Erica doesn't relish a party. Sandra would have suited him better, I imagine."

"I did find out that he hasn't filed divorce papers yet."

Desdemona sat up as the Fairlane eased out onto a deserted South Green Street. "Oho! He hasn't removed his last defense."

"That's how I read it."

She slid across the wide seat and snuggled into his side. "Did you notice the woman in that terrible brown hat?"

Judge Douglas Wilfred Thwaites presided over the Holloman District Court, and was an institution. He had taken both his undergraduate and law degrees from Chubb, and was a Chubber to his bootstraps. Imbued with no ambition to move on to greater jurisdictions, he was a Connecticut Yankee who couldn't conceive of living or practicing anywhere else. He had a delightful house on Busquash Point from which he could mess around in boats, a devoted wife who thought him deliriously funny, and two children in their early twenties who had escaped his tyranny by seeking higher education on the West Coast, a place he equated with the planet Mercury.

It was probably a fanciful childhood memory of Ichabod Crane that had prompted Special Agent Ted Kelly of the FBI to call him an eccentric, a term that wasn't fair either to Washington Irving or to Doug Thwaites. His Honor prided himself upon his detachment, which was real enough—provided, that is, that he hadn't previously formed his own conclusions about a person. Though Carmine knew all this—and a great deal more besides—about the Judge, he was prepared to do fierce battle when he appeared in chambers at ten on Monday morning, April tenth. He needed a warrant to search the premises of Dr. Pauline Denbigh before Dante College politely asked her to vacate the Dean's apartment, and he was sure he was going to be opposed.

"Granted!" barked Judge Thwaites halfway through Carmine's preamble. "That woman is capable of anything!"

Oh! Myron's party! Of course Judge and Mrs. Thwaites were there, and so was Dr. Pauline Denbigh. Their paths must have crossed. How was she to know that Doug loathed all women's libbers with a passion? He believed ardently in righting their wrongs, but not in the antics of the visible, vociferous segment of the movement. Bra burnings and the invasion of hallowed male portals, not to mention psychic emasculation, were anathema. To him, it was a legislative struggle, and such shenanigans degraded it.

Carmine went away with his head spinning, and kicking himself that he hadn't been witness to the clash of that particular pair of titans. He'd have to phone Dorothy Thwaites and ask her for the gory details. In the meantime, he had his warrant.

He took four uniformed cops to keep the rubberneckers at bay, and knocked on Dr. Denbigh's study door.

"Come," said her languid voice.

"Dr. Pauline Denbigh?" he asked, paper in hand.

"Well, you know that!" she said tartly.

"Please vacate these premises and the Dean's apartment at once. I have a warrant to search both," he said.

The color drained out of her face instantaneously, leaving it as yellow as old parchment. She rocked on her feet, then righted herself and stood straight. "This is an outrage," she said in a whisper. "I challenge your warrant."

"You are at liberty to do so, but it will be after the fact. Have you someplace you can go, Dr. Denbigh?"

"The small common room. I want my cigarettes, my lighter, my papers, book and pen."

"Provided you permit us to examine them first, of course."

"Pigs!" she snapped, her color returning in a rush.

Her goods vetted, she was escorted to the common room and settled there under the eye of a cop, while Carmine, Corey and Abe tackled her own study.

Every book had to be opened and its leaves shaken, a huge task in itself. The walls backing the bookshelves were tapped, while Abe, who had an instinct for concealed doors, went over every inch of the dark paneling and knocked on the floorboards listening for a drummy one. The room yielded nothing; two hours later Carmine declared it clean.

"But she's hiding something," he said as they moved to the Dean's apartment, "so it must be in here."

A storage closet in the bedroom produced a small electric sewing machine. "We're getting warmer," said Carmine, smiling. "Where's the workbasket?"

Handy to have an embroidering wife!

But the workbasket when found was innocuous: the cut-out pieces of a blouse, a skirt with darts. Dr. Denbigh liked to sew, and made some of her own clothes.

Abe found the cupboard in a vacant section of kitchen wall. It opened on a spring mechanism that responded to pressure from a hand laid flat on the door. Inside was a thick pipe with a U-bend and a grease trap outlet at its base.

"Dante's old enough to have been replumbed," Abe said. "I don't think this pipe's connected."

Corey got the camera out and started taking photographs while Carmine found Dr. Marcus Ceruski.

"You're our witness, sir," Carmine said.

"I know nothing about this!" Ceruski protested.

"That's the whole idea. You're here to watch us remove whatever is in that secret cupboard, okay?"

Resting in the elbow of the pipe was a black drawstring bag, now well photographed. Gloved, Carmine lifted it out and put it on the counter, where the camera recorded its angular bulk before Carmine loosened its mouth and with a rapid movement turned the bag inside out. Abe and Corey fielded in case any item rolled, but nothing did; even the spool of thread that fit the sewing machine lay where it fell. The blue flashes went on for some time as Carmine moved the contents around.

"If her prints are on any of this, she's a done dinner," Corey said, grinning.

"They will be," said Carmine tranquilly. "Go get the evidence bags, Corey."

There was a box of Dean Denbigh's jasmine tea from his special shop, a roll of glossy pink paper printed in black with Art Nouveau lettering and detail, a roll of filmy gauze of the kind used to make tea bags, lengths of thin twine each ending in a jasmine tea label, the spool of thread, and a glass jar of potassium cyanide bearing a commercial label.

"Not a word, Dr. Ceruski," said Carmine, ushering him out. "If the defense alleges this evidence was planted by the Holloman Police, you will be called to the stand, not otherwise."

"She made her own tea bags and the paper jackets wrapping the tea bags," Corey said in tones of wonder. "Where the hell did she get the pink printed paper and the gauze? The strings with the labels on the end?"

"From the supplier," said Abe. "Label says, in Queens."

"Where else? Abe, find out from the supplier if she got her bits and pieces openly or by stealth. I'm picking she stole them. It wouldn't be hard, just a trip to Queens late at night. Security wouldn't consist of more than a night watchman. The cyanide would have been more difficult."

"She's a resourceful woman," Abe said. "A chem lab?"

"No way! Cyanide's on any lab's poison register, it has to be kept in a safe, you know that," said Carmine.

"Huh!" Corey grunted. "Nerds are nerds, Carmine. They go round in a daze, leave the safe open, probably use it to keep their lucky rabbit's foot from sticky fingers."

"That's bigotry! I know nerds as sharp as tacks!" said Abe.

They were happy, thought Carmine, only half listening. We just solved another one, we're down to ten unsolved.

And, he admitted to himself, he was happy too. Won't Doug Thwaites be pleased? What a nose for a villain!

*   *   *

He didn't see her again until he walked into an interview room late that afternoon.

"You are aware of your constitutional rights?" he asked.

"Yes, perfectly." She looked composed and better groomed; one of their three woman cops had found the clothes she wanted, and brought them to her together with a full selection of makeup. So the glorious red-gold hair puffed softer around her face, and the yellow lion's eyes had been emphasized with mascara and pencil. Her dress was severely cut, but its flattering tawny shade needed no embellishments. Carmine knew she was frigid because she had told him, but no man would have believed that, looking at her.

"Would you like a lawyer present?" he asked, nodding to the woman cop to move her chair into the far corner.

"Not yet," she answered, then gestured irritably at the cop. "Must that poor girl be here? I'd rather talk to you in private."

"I'm sorry, ma'am, she has to stay. She's a chaperone, she ensures that I do nothing untoward."

"You're a puzzle, Captain. One moment speech larded with colloquialisms, the next the speech of a well-educated man."

"But colloquialisms are wonderful, Dr. Denbigh! They prove that English is a living language, always moving on." He sat down and turned the tape recorder on, gave it the details.

"We found your cache inside a concealed cupboard in the Dean's apartment kitchen, Dr. Denbigh."

The yellow eyes went wide. "Cache? Cupboard? I know nothing of either."

"Your fingerprints say differently, ma'am. They're all over every printable item in the bag, as well as on the pipe and the door. We have you, Dr. Denbigh," Carmine said.

She didn't cease to fight; rather, she changed her tactics. "After they hear my story, Captain, I don't think there's a jury alive would condemn my actions."

"You want a jury trial? That means pleading not guilty, but you've virtually confessed. Confession means no jury trial."

"I haven't confessed to *murder!* I acted in self-defense."

Carmine leaned forward. "Dr. Denbigh, this was a premeditated crime! Carefully planned and executed. Premeditation negates self-defense."

"Nonsense!" she said with a snort of contempt for his density. "Fear for one's life, sir, engenders different reactions in people because all people are different. Were I some battered housewife, I would have used a hammer or a hatchet. But I am an associate professor at Chubb University, and my husband, the source of my terror, was a dean of that same institution. Naturally I hoped that my participation in his death would not be discovered, but the mere fact that it was does not make me a cold-blooded murderer. I lived in fear for my life through every day of it because I was the only person who knew of John's sexual activities. If I was plotting to save my life, Captain, he was plotting to end it! The story I told you just after John's death was true, but it merely touched the peaks of mountains of sordid details and six—yes, six!—attempts my husband had made to kill me. A car crash, a skiing accident, three attacks of food poisoning, and a shotgun accident while we were in Maine. John liked to shoot hapless deer, then actually *eat* them!"

Carmine stared at her, rapt, and thanked God that not many murderers were this smart, or this good-looking. At thirty-two years of age, she was in her prime. "I hope you can produce proof of these attempts on your life," he said.

"Witnesses, certainly," she said coolly.

"What made you decide on saving your life with a dose of cyanide in a tea bag?" he asked.

"The cyanide, actually. I found it sitting on a shelf in the freshman common room. I'd gone hunting for one of my books I knew a freshman had borrowed—most irregular! He didn't ask my permission, of course, but I suspected him because few in their first year are interested in Rilke. I removed the cyanide, of course—so dangerous! Then it occurred to me that I had found the ideal way to get John out of my life forever, provided I could find a way of administering it that did not imperil any other person. And that led to the jasmine tea at his idiotic Monday fortnight sessions. After that"—she shrugged—"it was easy. The shop was in Manhattan, but the place where the tea bags were made was in Queens."

"You haven't made a satisfactory case against the Dean, Dr. Denbigh," Carmine said.

"Here? Now? Why should I even bother? I will plead my case in court. Mr. Anthony Bera will conduct my defense," said the lioness, licking her chops. "And that is all I have to say before Mr. Bera arrives. I think it is very fair of me to—er—show my hand, so to speak. You know how I will plead, and what my defense will be."

Carmine stopped the tape recorder. "I thank you for your frankness, Dr. Denbigh, but I warn you, the prosecution will prove murder, and ask for the maximum penalty."

"Any bets she slips the net?" he asked Silvestri a few minutes later. "That's one helluva smart woman, sir."

"Depends how well Bera picks his jury," Silvestri said, his cigar rolling from one side of his mouth to the other. "He'll ask that the case be heard in a different jurisdiction, and that's in the lap of the gods. But it's always been hard to get a conviction when the defendant is a looker. You'd think the women jurors would take against them, but they don't, and the men are putty. So yeah, Carmine, you could be right." His sleek cat face bore an expression of content despite the uncertain outcome of Pauline Denbigh's trial. "Ask me, do I care? Not much. The important thing is that Dean Denbigh's murder is one hundred percent solved."

"I don't think the other ten are going to be that easy."

"Do you still go for the idea of one killer?"

"More than ever. There's no one else outside the pattern, chief," Carmine said. He frowned. "And damn that woman! She threw me off with this self-defense nonsense so badly that I didn't ask her the one question I intended to."

"Then go back and ask."

"With Bera present? He'll direct her not to answer."

"Bail hearing is in an hour, Captain, so Dr. Denbigh can't give you much time," Bera said the next morning.

"I am aware of that, Mr. Bera." Carmine sat down and turned on the tape recorder. "Dr. Denbigh, how are you?"

"Well, thank you," she said, unaware that Judge Thwaites, who would be on the bench, thought her capable of anything.

"There is one question I would like you to answer, ma'am. It doesn't directly pertain to your own case or its defense, but it's very important to the investigation of ten other murders."

"My client did not do murder," said Bera.

"Ten murders," Carmine amended, swallowing his ire.

"Ask your question, Captain Delmonico," said Bera.

"Was there any reason that you decided to preserve your life by terminating your husband's life on Monday, April third?"

His head to one side, Bera considered the implications, while Pauline Denbigh sat side-on, staring into his face.

"Dr. Denbigh had a reason," Bera said.

Exasperated, Carmine shook his head. "That's not the kind of answer I want," he said. "I need specifics."

"You're not going to get them, Captain."

"Let me try again. Whatever your reason might have been, Dr. Denbigh, was it in any way connected to—say, a rumor you'd heard that other deaths might occur?"

"Claptrap," Bera said disdainfully.

"Was it to do with a pact, or an agreement, that other people should die? Or was it sheer coincidence that your decision to act on Monday, April third, happened to be the same day eleven murders happened in Holloman?"

"Ohhh!" she exclaimed, ignoring Bera's fierce grimaces. "I see what you mean! My reason for choosing that day will come out in court, Captain, but it had nothing to do with ten—or eleven—murders. It was sheer coincidence."

Carmine's sigh of relief was audible. "Thank you, ma'am! I can't do anything to help you, but you've just helped me." He decided to press his luck. "Who knew you were afraid of your husband? That you feared for your life?"

"If you answer that, Dr. Denbigh, I can't help you," Bera said ominously.

She lifted her shoulders and smiled at Carmine ruefully. "I am in Mr. Bera's hands, Captain. To answer you would damage my defense, I can see that for myself."

Which was, Carmine reflected as he left, a brilliant way of saying that yes, she had confided in at least one other woman. Now he had to find her best friend.

Erica Davenport? Philomena Skeps? Or some unknown, unmet proponent of women's liberation?

He lurked outside until Anthony Bera left the interview room and detained him. "You shouldn't have any trouble getting her acquitted," he said affably.

"So I believe."

"How can she afford your fees, Mr. Bera? Chubb isn't famous for overpaying women faculty."

"I'm acting pro bono," Bera said shortly.

Are you indeed? said Carmine to himself. Now why? I think I have to go back to the Cape and talk to Philomena Skeps again. She becomes more and more like the lady spider at the center of the web.

He called a little conference in his office: Abe and Corey, Delia and Patrick.

"Okay, we're down to ten," he said, not trying to conceal his pleasure. "We can forget the three shootings, that's an absolute. But I'm putting them down as solved when we catch our mastermind, because they were definitely commissioned. That leaves us with six cases—Beatrice Egmont, Bianca Tolano, Peter Norton, Cathy Cartwright, Evan Pugh and Desmond Skeps. For the moment we shelve Beatrice Egmont as unsolvable. Okay, *five* dead people, and that's where we begin. Everything we have we throw at the textbook rape murder of Bianca Tolano. Commissioned, yes, but after a bit of thinking I've realized you don't shop for a sex killer. Money doesn't interest them. Therefore he's a local. Our mastermind found out about his fantasies, took him in hand and educated him. If we don't get him, he'll kill again, now that he's had a taste of it. If the Ghost taught me nothing else, he taught me that sex killers can't stop."

"How do we know what to look for?" Patsy asked. "That was our trouble with the Ghost—anonymity. How is this any different in that respect?" He glowered. "I thought you weren't going to call the murderer a mastermind?"

"I hate it, yes," said Carmine patiently, "but it's both accurate and convenient. Unless you want to go all FBI and give the guy a code name? How about Einstein or Pauling? Moriarty? No? Let's just stick with what we've got. As to how this one is different, Patsy, it is because someone else—the mastermind—evicted the killer from his fantasy home, and our hermit crab isn't comfortable yet in his new shell. Walking sideways still terrifies him, and he's no Ghost. I have an idea where to look for him—the Ghost was fantastic training. Refresh us on Bianca, Patsy, please."

"She was found naked," Patsy began, "wrists and ankles tied with single-strand steel wire. She was conscious throughout, except for brief periods of asphyxiation induced by a pair of pantyhose around her neck. Burned in twenty-nine places by a cigarette, cut in seventeen places by something like a Sheetrock knife. Particular attention was paid to the breasts and pubes. Multiple rape, but no semen was found in any orifice. Death was caused by a broken bottle shoved into the vagina; she bled out. There's a case exactly like it in a book about sexual deviance that's well thumbed by psych students."

"How old is the book?" Delia asked.

"Published ten years ago to an outcry. It was felt to be too accessible to thrill seekers." He looked wry. "Not like wading through Krafft-Ebing and wondering what frottage was—dictionaries didn't give definitions of words like that in my day. I think the author was German and the book was translated from the German. Kaiserine Germans invented the sex vocabulary."

"Thank you, Patsy," said Carmine firmly. "We know this guy. By that, I mean we must have seen his face several times, maybe even interviewed him. He's undersized and unattractive, but I'm not sure of his age group."

"We go to Cornucopia," said Abe instantly, "and we start with Dr. Davenport's male secretary."

"What makes you say that?" Corey demanded, looking jealous and frustrated. Larry Pisano's lieutenancy was never far from the forefront of his mind.

"I remember the secretary," Abe said. "He fits."

"When you said you weren't sure of his age group, Carmine," asked Delia, "did you mean very young, young, and older young?"

"No, Delia, I meant young, middle, or elderly."

"What about his job?" she pursued, not having been there during the frantic days of the Ghost.

"With sex killers, that's a mystery, but in this case I'd say he was more used to taking orders than giving them. Otherwise the mastermind couldn't have brainwashed him."

"That's an interesting choice of verb," Patsy said. "It's to do with ideological conversion, I thought."

"Brainwashing? Don't forget the FBI is sniffing for espionage on the perimeter of this case," Carmine said. "But seriously, I think the term can be applied to any kind of conversion process that digs deep into the psyche."

"Especially," said Abe, "if there's a tendency already."

*　　*　　*

Back they went to Cornucopia to begin with Richard Oakes, secretary to Dr. Erica Davenport, Chairman of the Board and now managing director of Cornucopia Central. She was outraged, but she couldn't prevent Abe and Corey from subjecting the young man to an inquisition that lasted two hours. When he emerged he was in tears, shaking uncontrollably, and suffering the onset of a migraine aura that had his boss put him in an ambulance and ship him to Chubb-Holloman Hospital.

"I'll sue you for this!" she shouted at Carmine.

"Rubbish," he said scornfully. "He's as nervous as a filly at a starting gate, is all. It wouldn't matter who interrogated him for a suspected wrong, he'd react the same. Importantly for me, he's cleared of the Tolano murder."

"What grounds have you got for believing him guilty?" she asked, stiff with anger.

"They're none of your business, Dr. Davenport, but I will inform you that I'll be questioning some other men at Cornucopia, as well as in other places around Holloman, including Chubb."

She gave a mew of frustration, and flounced into her office.

Hmm, thought Carmine. I begin to see why Wallace Grierson thinks she'll run the Cornucopia ship aground.

As if determined to produce an opposite reaction to Richard Oakes's, Michael Donald Sykes entered into his interrogation with glee, aplomb, and faultless good humor. He was entranced with the idea that anyone could suspect him of sexual murder, and made Abe's and Corey's lives a misery interrogating them.

"I believe you have fixated on me," he said solemnly, "due to the fact that I do not have Gettysburg laid out in my basement. How can I, an American, prefer to lay out Austerlitz? And what, you ask, is Marengo, if not a recipe for chicken? Napoleon Bonaparte, sirs, as a military genius put Sherman and Grant and Lee in the shade! By blood he was an Italian, not a Frenchman, and in him the old Italian genius flowered again."

"Shut up, Mr. Sykes," said Corey.

"Yes, Mr. Sykes, shut up," said Abe.

But of course he didn't. In the end they evicted him from their commandeered office, and he skipped off very pleased with himself. Passing Carmine, he stopped.

"There's a fellow in Accounting you should question," he said, wreathed in smiles. "That was so refreshing! And to think that when you first appeared here a week or so ago, I was scared out of my wits. But no more, no more! Your devoted followers are gentlemen who accepted my dismissal of the Civil War generals as if they heard it every day. Very kind of them!"

"Who in Accounting?" Carmine asked sharply.

"I don't believe I've ever heard his name, but you can't mistake him, Captain. No more than five feet tall, very thin, and walks with a heavy limp," said Mr. Sykes.

Shit! Carmine grabbed Abe with one hand and Corey with the other, hustling them to the elevator. "What floors are Cornucopia General's accounting?" he asked.

"Nineteenth, twentieth, twenty-first," said Corey.

Which, which, which? "Twenty-one," he said, diving into the elevator. "We'll work our way down."

"Jesus!" said Abe as they emerged on the twenty-first floor. "Mrs. Highman's carpenter!"

But he wasn't there, and the few people they encountered knew they'd seen him but had no idea where.

"Conceited idiots!" said Corey as they went down a floor. "The peons are beneath notice."

How did I know it was too good to be true? Carmine asked himself as they emerged into a scene of controlled panic. Two ambulance medics came out of another elevator wheeling a gurney and were pounced on by half a dozen anxious people, escorted into a huge room divided into chest-high cells. Using their badges, Carmine and his team followed.

Too late, of course. The small, slight body was slumped over a desk, quite dead. It was Carmine who checked for signs of life, Abe and Corey who kept everyone else away.

"You can go, guys," Carmine said to the medics as he picked up a phone. "He goes to the Medical Examiner."

Within minutes the area was cordoned off. Patrick O'Donnell and his team walked in a little later. Patrick's fair face was grim, but he didn't speak until he had done his preliminary examination of the body.

"Cyanide, I'm betting," he said then to Carmine. "It seems to be the poison of choice, doesn't it? I wonder how many hands that jar you found in Dr. Denbigh's drawstring bag has passed through? Or how full it was? The lethal dose is very small."

"Could this have been Mrs. Dean Highman's workman?"

"Undoubtedly, unless there are two five-foot-nothings with the left leg three inches shorter than the right in Holloman," Patsy said. "He wore boots with the left one built up, but the limp never really disappears. The knees are out of synch, and so are the ankles. The built-up boot keeps the hips level, helps ease lumbar pain. I won't know until I get him on my table if it's congenital or acquired."

"Well," said Abe as they returned to County Services, "I guess Erica Davenport is our mastermind."

"I agree," said Corey positively.

"Not necessarily," said a gloomy Carmine from the backseat. "Once we moved to interview undersized and unattractive males, the word could have gotten around faster than a fire in tinder. Mrs. Highman is a doll, but discreet she ain't. Nor is Dotty Thwaites, Simonetta Marciano—sssh!—or Angela MacIntosh. Haven't you noticed that this is a case full of women? I sure have. Suspects, victims, onlookers, witnesses—women, women, women! I hate cases like this! I'm out of my depth! I know two women with zippers on their mouths—one is my wife, the other is my secretary. Grr!"

The two in the front seat took the hint and said no more.

At County Services they split up. Armed with details supplied by the head accountant, horrified at violence in the world of numbers, Abe and Corey went to the dead man's apartment. Carmine, a ferocious look on his face, walked up to the autopsy room, unaware that people who saw him scattered.

"Joshua Butler, single, aged thirty-five," said Patsy, who had the stripped body on his table already. "He's one of those poor souls with a congenital pituitary syndrome that prevented hormonal maturity. His testes are undescended, he has no body hair, and he has the penis of a prepubescent boy. I doubt he could sustain an erection, let alone ejaculate motile sperm. So if he's Bianca Tolano's murderer, the rape was all done with an object, probably the bottle before he broke it. He didn't act in a frenzy, as you remember—he cleaned up too well. The short leg is due to a break that was disgracefully treated at some time during childhood. I doubt a doctor saw it at all. I'll find what I'm looking for inside the cranium, when I see the base of the brain and the pituitary. Histology will be very important. He might be a situs inversus as well—heart on the right side, some other organs reversed too. Cause of death? I've not changed my mind. It's cyanide."

Carmine sighed. "He could never have installed that bear trap in Evan Pugh's closet," he said. "I know strength can't always be equated with size or even muscularity, but this guy is definitely a ninety-pound weakling. I'm right, aren't I?"

"Yes," said Patsy, itching to get on with his examination. It wasn't every day that he saw a body like this.

So somewhere, Carmine thought, leaving Patsy to it, there is an exceedingly artful dodger capable of impersonating a runt like Joshua Butler. And capable of igniting a fire inside Joshua Butler hot enough to drive him to murder.

Not five minutes later Patsy called him.

"Carmine, the cause of death is definitely cyanide, but I don't think it was murder. I found a capsule inside his mouth made of very thin plastic, and shreds of the plastic around his teeth. He committed suicide."

"That makes sense," said Carmine, beyond amazement. "Just like Dr. Goebbels, except that he wouldn't have any kids."

"Be of good cheer!" said Delia, trying comfort. "At least you're chipping away at them. Bianca Tolano is sorted out."

"Huh!" Carmine grunted. "All it goes to show is that if you turn over enough stones, you're bound to find something horrible. We're down to four that have real answers to our questions."

"Go home," Delia said sternly. "You need a dose of Julian."

A dose of Julian did help, but then Myron ruined Carmine's well-being by turning up on his doorstep angry enough to adopt a fighting stance. Carmine took one look and broke into fits of laughter.

"Myron, you dodo!" he said, throwing an arm around his friend's shoulder and forcing him inside. "You look like a whippet squaring off against a Great Dane!"

Myron's umbrage lasted a few more seconds, then he gave in. "At least you called me a whippet," he said then. "I can count myself lucky I guess that you didn't call me a chihuahua."

"No," said Carmine, rolling his eyes at Desdemona, "you're not yappy. On the other hand, you're not big enough to be a greyhound, though you do have a lot of the breed in you. Have a drink and tell me what's bothering you."

"Your—your *persecution* of Erica, that's what's bothering me! Why are you picking on her?"

"I am not picking on her, Myron." Some women! he thought to himself. Why do some women always sweet-talk a poor, hapless schmo into fighting their battles for them? "She can't have her cake and eat it too. Cornucopia is in a lot of trouble, and she is now el supremo—or la suprema. You're a businessman, you know that kind of power has a price tag. If Erica can't stand the heat, she'd better get out of the kitchen."

The mood had utterly vanished; Myron could never sustain rage against a beloved friend, especially when his position was untenable. "Oh, Carmine," he wailed, "how did I wind up in the middle? I love the girl and I hate to see her badgered, but she made me promise I'd try to get you to ease up on her." He looked doleful. "But I can't, can I? You're not a Great Dane, you're a bulldog."

"This conversation's gotten far too doggy." Carmine handed him a Scotch. "Has it occurred to you that Erica is petrified at being handed Cornucopia? I don't think she expected it, and I do think she's afraid she won't make the grade."

The Scotch was going down smoothly. Carmine kept good liquor, though it was not a boozy house. "There's that to it," Myron admitted.

"She'd believe you way sooner than me, so why don't you tell her to cool her jets? It's my experience of mighty undertakings like corporations and governments that they tend to run themselves. The problems start when people interfere with the running, you must know that. Cornucopia has rolled along for years and years, just like the river in the song. She should just let it keep on rolling."

"You'd run it better than any of us," Myron said.

"Me? No! According to the girl you love, I'm too insatiably curious, and she's right. I'd spend all my time poking and prying into what shouldn't concern me."

"Are you eating with us, Myron?" Desdemona asked. "It's a rib roast, and there's plenty."

He groaned. "I wish I could, but I have to get back to Erica." The last of the Scotch disappeared. Myron rose to his feet and stood looking at them a little disconsolately. "I wish things could go on the way they used to," he said wistfully, "but they can't, can they?"

"That's life," said Desdemona, and laughed. "How's that for corny? Never you mind, Myron dear. Things will settle down."

"But they won't," she said to Carmine later, when some of the rib roast had been devoured. "If only I could like her! I can't, you know. She's so brittle, though brittle I could manage if it weren't for the coldness. She'll break poor Myron's heart."

"Maybe not," said Carmine, feeling the optimism that went with a full stomach of good food. "I think he's fascinated by all the things in her we dislike. He's fifty years old, lovely lady, and ready for a bitch. Erica's a phase."

"Do you think so? Truly?"

"Yes, I do."

"Is shepherd's pie all right for the leftover roast?" she asked. "I got a big one because Sophia said she'd be in, and have two friends sleeping over."

That irritation flared up again. Carmine scowled. "It may be high time to have a word with my daughter," he said.

"No, Carmine, don't! There will be a good reason, I'm sure of it," said Desdemona.

As if on cue, Sophia burst through the front door wide-eyed and white. "Daddy!" she cried, going straight to him. "Someone locked me in the physics lab closet!"

See, what did I tell you? Desdemona's eyes were saying, but Carmine held Sophia off and looked at her closely. She was a little disheveled, and her fright was genuine. "Do you know how it happened, honey?" he asked.

"No, that's just it! It shouldn't have! No one ever locks that closet!" She shivered, shrank against him. "I could hear someone on the other side walking up and down, and something thumping on the floor. Daddy, I don't know why, but I was sure he was after *me!* I was on tidy-up duty, everyone saw me going back and forth to the closet. At first I thought it was a joke, then I heard the walking and I got this awful feeling!"

"Did he go away?" Carmine asked, conscious of a sinking in his belly. "How long were you in there?"

"About five minutes. I *knew* he was going to open the door and attack me as soon as the school quietened down, so I got out through a manhole in the roof. It led to the main fume duct, so I crawled for ages and came out in the fume cabinet at the other end of the lab. The lights were off, but it was still daylight outside, and I could see him—a little guy with a limp. I tried not to make any noise and kind of wriggled out of the cabinet onto the floor. Then I crawled for the door at my end and waited until he was walking the opposite way before I opened it a crack and wriggled through. Then I got to my feet and ran!"

Amazing, thought Carmine. She's my girl, for sure. Gives a good report even if she is scared stiff. "Then you made it to your car and drove home," he said.

She stared at him scornfully. "*Daddy!* If I'd done that, I would have been home ages ago! No, he must have opened the closet door and found nobody there. I ran and dived into the forsythia just in time—he was heading for my car. That's how I know he was after me—not just anybody, *me!* So I hunkered down and waited until it was dark, then I sneaked up to Route 133 and hailed a cab. But I wouldn't get in until I got a good look at the driver. He was black, so I knew I was safe. He's up on the Circle now, Daddy. I didn't have my pocketbook, and the fare's humongous!"

Desdemona slipped out, money purse in hand, while Carmine led his doughty daughter into the sitting room and gave her a red wine spritzer.

"To use a phrase of the Mayor of New Britain's, you done good, kid," he said, bursting with pride.

That, plus gratitude to whatever power had looked after Sophia, carried him through giving her dinner—she was starving—and getting her to bed sedated with one of Desdemona's "bombs." Once the girl's elation at escaping by her own efforts died down, she would sleep a sleep of nightmares unless her busy, clever brain was damped.

Then the reaction set in. He sat and shook as if in a rigor, twisting his hands together.

"The bastard! The fucking bastard!" he said to Desdemona, his teeth clenched. "Why couldn't he come after me? Why a sixteen-year-old innocent, for crying out loud? The sweetest, nicest, kindest kid imaginable! I'll rip his head from his neck!"

She cuddled in close and stroked his face. "You don't mean that, Carmine. You mean a life sentence, marked never to be released. Are you sure it's your murderer?"

"A little guy with a limp? It's got to be. But why Sophia? He chose her deliberately—targeted her at school, had it worked out down to the last *t* crossed and the last *i* dotted. By rights her body should have been found tomorrow in the physics lab closet, maybe beaten to death if what he thumped on the floor was a baseball bat. The best club ever invented. What he didn't count on was Sophia's presence of mind in a crisis."

"And the fact that she's inherited your gut instinct, dear heart. Where any other victim would have assumed she was locked in by mistake, Sophia knew almost at once that she was in danger. So she concentrated on escape rather than waiting to be let out."

He managed to find a smile. "Resourceful, isn't she?"

"Yes, very. I don't think you ever need worry about Sophia being one of life's victims," said Desdemona. "She's going to pick life up and wring it dry."

He got up feeling like an old man. "I don't think I'll be making a little brother or sister for Julian tonight, Desdemona."

"There's always tomorrow night," she said cheerfully. "Now let's break the rules and have a drink before bed. I can bomb Sophia and keep her out of school tomorrow, but I can't do that to you. An X-O cognac is the answer for Daddy."

"I'll have to put a cop at the Dormer to keep an eye on our daughter," he said, taking the snifter and warming it in his hand. "Concealed surveillance, but Seth Gaylord will have to know in case the duty sergeant puts a dodo on watch. Then tomorrow you'll have to talk to Sophia and persuade her not to mention the incident to anyone, including Myron."

Desdemona blinked. "Including Myron?"

"We can't trust his tongue these days because I don't know how discreet his lady love is. Tell Sophia it's not a good idea to be marooned on her own at school or anywhere else right now. She's to stick with a group and leave school along with everyone else. And that goddamn red Mercedes that Myron gave her goes into the garage! She can drive my mother's Mercury clunker."

Desdemona shivered. "It's like the Ghost," she said.

"Yes. That's why I'm convinced our best weapon is Sophia's in-genuity. If you talk to her frankly and don't pull your punches, she won't buck."

The news about Sophia hit no one quite the way it did John Silvestri, whose daughter Maria had been savagely beaten some years ago. It had been a revenge aimed at Silvestri, who took it very hard. But Maria healed, married happily and moved on with her life; the per-petrator got a thirty-year sentence, twenty before parole. Knowing all this, Carmine told him in private of the attempt on Sophia; to see Silvestri weep was an ordeal and not for other eyes.

"Terrible, just terrible!" the Commissioner said, mopping his face. "We have to catch this bastard, Carmine. Anything you want, you got. Such a beautiful child!"

"I know it doesn't really look that way," Carmine said, sitting down, "but somehow I feel as if we've rattled his cage. It's nine days since the twelve murders, and we've actually managed to solve some of them—Jimmy Cartwright, Dean Denbigh, Bianca Tolano—and catalogued the assassination of the three blacks as commissioned. There's been a thirteenth death—the suicide of Bianca Tolano's killer."

"I think it's impressive," Silvestri said, composure restored. "Where to now?"

"Peter Norton, the banker who drank strychnine in his orange juice. An agonizing death."

"So's cyanide," Silvestri pointed out.

"Yes, but cyanide is quick. As soon as enough of the blood's hemo-globin is stripped of its oxygen, death ensues. Whereas, John, strych-nine takes twenty, thirty minutes, depending on the dose. Norton got a huge dose, but drank only half of it. He was a dead man, but not for some time. Vomiting, purging, strong convulsions—I don't know how much consciousness remains, but his wife and two little kids witnessed it. That's disgusting."

"Are you implying that the killer wanted that?"

"I don't know. Maybe I am," Carmine said, sounding surprised.

"If choosing a method that tortured Norton's wife and kids was a part of the crime, it opens up new territory, Carmine," the Commissioner said thoughtfully. "Maybe we should be looking harder at the victims' families."

"Every stone will be turned over again," Carmine promised.

Mrs. Barbara Norton had had more than a week to recover from her screaming hysterics, though Carmine suspected her doctor had her on some pretty powerful tranquilizers. Her eyes were vacant, and she moved as if pushing her way through a sea of molasses.

However, she spoke logically. "It's some nutter he refused a loan to," she said, giving him a cup of coffee. "You have no idea, Captain! People seem to expect a bank to lend them money without any collateral at all! Most people eventually give up, but the nutters never do. I can remember at least half a dozen crazies who filled our mailbox with dog do, put caustic soda in our pool, even wee'd in our milk! Peter reported all of them to the North Holloman police, so look there for the names."

She was fairly plump, Carmine noted, but her rotundity had a certain seductiveness for some men, and she had a pretty face—dimples, rosy cheeks, flawless skin. When her children came in, he stifled another sigh at this second sight of them: this was a fat family, the genes predisposed to obesity. Peter Norton, he remembered from the autopsy, had been very overweight in the manner of one always so: fat arms and legs, puffy hands and feet, the adiposity packed on from shoulders to hips rather than just around his middle. According to police notes taken in the neighborhood, Mrs. Norton had tried to limit the family's food intake, but her husband would have none of it. He was always taking the kids to Friendly's for parfaits and shakes.

"Were your friends your husband's friends as well, Mrs. Norton?" Carmine asked.

"Oh, definitely. We did everything together. Peter liked me to have the same friends."

"What kind of things did you do?"

"We went bowling on Tuesday nights. Thursday nights were canasta at someone's home. Saturday nights we went out to dinner and took in a movie or a play."

"Did you use a babysitter, ma'am?"

"Yes, always the same girl, Imelda Gonzalez. Peter picked her up and drove her home."

"You never went out on your own?"

"Oh, no!"

"Who are your friends?"

"Grace and Chuck Simmons, Hetty and Hank Sugarman, Mary and Ernie Tripodi. Chuck's with the Holloman National, Hank's an accountant with a tax practice, and Ernie owns a bed and bath store. None of us girls work."

Middle management types, thought Carmine, sipping coffee. It was flavored with cardamom, a pet hate. In his opinion coffee was coffee, never to be adulterated with alien tastes.

"Did you ever go anyplace else, Mrs. Norton?"

Her bright curls bounced in time to her nods, robotic. "Oh, sure! Charity functions, mostly, but they aren't regular. Cornucopia functions Peter and I went to on our own—the Fourth National is owned by Cornucopia. Otherwise the eight of us went together." Her face fell, her chin wobbled. "Of course from now on I can't go to anything much. Our friends are real kind, but I'm a drag without Peter. He was the joker, full of tricks!"

"Things will sort themselves out, Mrs. Norton," Carmine comforted. "You'll make plenty of new friends."

Especially, he thought privately, with the size of Peter Norton's pension and insurance payouts. Beneath the dominated housewife lurked someone determined to save herself. Maybe she'd go on a luxury cruise looking for someone she could dominate? Were it not for that inescapable date, April third, he might have suspected her of putting paid to domination by a person few seemed to like. Despite the horror of his death, a certain kind of poisoner would have relished witnessing his suffering. But Mrs. Norton had not relished it. She had gone into hysterics so strong that the neighbors had heard and come running. By the time that he, Carmine, had arrived, the children were emerging from their shock, whereas Mrs. Norton had needed two medics, her doctor, and a shot of something so potent she had slept for hours.

He turned to the children, seeking some idea what kind of family theirs was. The little girl, Marlene, was aggressive and intelligent—probably not popular at school, he thought. The little boy, Tommy, apparently lived for food; when he grabbed at the cookies put out for Carmine, his mother slapped his hand away viciously, with a look on her face the child retreated from.

"You have no outside interests of your own at all?" Carmine asked.

"No, none—Tommy, leave the cookies *alone!*"

He plucked it out of thin air. "Women's liberation?"

"I should think not!" she snapped, bridling. "Of all the stupid, *embarrassing* things—! Do you know they actually tried to proselytize me? I don't remember her name, but I sure sent her packing with a flea in her ear!"

"When was this?"

"I don't remember," said Mrs. Norton, fighting the drugs and losing. "Some function or other, a long time ago."

"What did the woman look like?"

"That's just it! She looked *normal!* Shaved her legs, wore makeup and nice clothes. For a while I was quite taken in, then she—she stood forth in all her evil panoply! I learned that at school, and it fit, Captain, it fit. When I told her what I thought of women's libbers, she got nasty, and I got nasty right back! I must've frightened her—she gave up and left."

"Was she a blonde? A brunette? A redhead?"

"I don't remember," said Mrs. Norton, yawning. "I'm tired."

*   *   *

"I told you," said Carmine to Abe and Corey, "this is a case full of women. Now where the hell does feminism enter into it? Because I believe it does, at least in the death of Peter Norton. Someone or something influenced our killer to punish Mrs. Norton by making her watch him die. It worked—she's still under a lot of sedation—but she had a lucid moment when she talked of the feminist who looked 'normal.' I wish I knew more about the Nortons! Something is escaping me, but what it is, I have no idea. Maybe it's not knowing for sure what kind of woman Mrs. Norton is. Like a psychiatrist inheriting a patient so doped up he can't get to square one on a diagnosis."

"You couldn't get any more out of her?" Corey asked.

Carmine looked at him sympathetically; Corey's wife wouldn't let him rest, nagged nonstop. "She only remembers what suits her," he said. "Corey, you're on the Norton background. I want to know the name and the date of every function Mrs. Norton ever attended— well, modify that. Make it five years." He turned to Abe. "Abe, you're on the feminist angle. Use the good Dr. Denbigh as your starting point. She's in the thick of the movement, and she fits Mrs. Norton's description—no hairy legs or armpits for our Pauline. Incidentally, she told me she was frigid, but I doubt that very much. I know we've got her for the Dean's murder, but her past still bears looking into. What was her reason for picking April third for the deed, huh?"

"You didn't believe it had nothing to do with the other murders?" Corey asked, fretting that he wasn't chalking up enough points.

"She's a congenital liar. When she does tell the truth, it's obliquely."

He watched them leave his office, then put his chin on his hands and prepared for a think session.

"Carmine?"

He lifted his head, surprised; it wasn't like Delia to interrupt a thinking boss. "Yes?"

"I have an idea," she said, not sitting down.

"Coming from you, that's encouraging. Explain."

"The filing's all up to date and you haven't exactly snowed me under with letters lately," she said delicately, looking at him with eyes that always reminded him of a kewpie doll—wide, ingenuous, impossibly painted.

"That's true, Delia, I'm the first one to admit it."

"Well—ah—would you mind if I followed a hunch of my own? That is the right word, isn't it?"

"For a gut feeling, yes. Sit down, Delia, please! I can't bear watching a woman stand while I'm on my butt."

She sat, pink with pleasure. "You see, most of these deaths have to be connected, don't they? You've always felt that, but nothing has come to light to support it. What I'm wondering is, where could they all have been present at one and the same time? The only answer, I believe, is at either a public meeting or a function of some sort. You know what I mean—you sit in a row waiting ages for the curtain to rise or whatever, and you start talking to those around you. Or you sit at a table with strangers and strive to chum up—if you don't, you have an awful evening. Most people are naturally gregarious, so they achieve this end. You do see what I mean, don't you?"

"I love the English habit of ending every sentence with a question," said Carmine, smiling. "But yes, Delia, I do see."

"Then if I may, I'd like to use my spare time to find out how many public meetings and functions have been held within the city of Holloman itself over the past six months."

"Just six months?"

"Oh, I think so. More time than that, and I believe the murderer's crisis would not have occurred at all. Something happened that didn't present as a threat at the time, but by the third of April, it did. If I can find an affair which all of our dead people attended, then we have one side of the equation."

"Delia, it's a huge undertaking," Carmine said. "Sooner or later it might have had to be done anyway, but I was saving it for Corey and Abe and total investigative inertia."

"I am aware of that, and I do not pretend to claim it as my own idea," she said with dignity.

"Oh, Delia, don't go all huffy on me!" he said, looking hangdog. "I didn't mean to steal your thunder, honest!"

She softened at once. "Well, I know that, Carmine dear. But may I do it?"

He shook his head, defeated. "You won't listen when I warn you. What else can I say except, go to it?"

She hopped up, beaming. "Oh, thank you, thank you! I have a protocol worked out," she chattered on her way to the door. "I intend to concentrate on the affairs themselves first. Then, if I find one or more that fits, I'll go to phase two."

"Goodbye, Delia!"

A glance up at the railroad clock told him it was almost noon. He picked up the phone, and after several false starts was finally connected to Special Agent Ted Kelly of the FBI.

"Eaten yet?" Carmine demanded.

"No."

"See you in Malvolio's in a quarter of an hour."

Though Kelly had to drive and find parking in the County Services underground facility, he was sitting defending a booth when Carmine walked in.

"You'd swear they knew who I was," he said as Carmine slid in opposite him, "yet there's not one cop in here I've ever set eyes on."

Carmine grinned. "They can smell you, Ted. No, seriously, what do you expect in a place the size of Holloman? The whole department knows there's a giant from the FBI in town." He consulted the menu as if he didn't already know what he was having. "A Luigi Special salad with Thousand Island dressing. Then I don't need to waste space on vegetables tonight."

Merele the waitress had filled their coffee mugs and stood poised. Kelly ordered a hot roast beef sandwich, then leaned back with a sigh. "You were right about Malvolio's," he said. "It's the best thing about this fucking awful town."

Kelly spoke sincerely, seriously. Carmine's anger stirred at such rudeness. Sit on it, Carmine, don't say a word! "How's the search for the elusive Ulysses going?"

"Nowhere. Tell me about Joshua Butler."

Carmine looked surprised. "I sent you my report, Ted, but if you want it verbally, okay. He raped and murdered Bianca Tolano, then chewed a cyanide capsule rather than be taken in for it. The crime lacked spontaneity—by which I mean that Butler followed a rape out of a textbook to the letter."

The FBI man gave a loud Bronx cheer. "Don't be stupid, Delmonico! I want to know the other details." He leered. "A little bird told me that he had peanuts for balls."

"Which little bird?" Carmine asked, looking at Kelly through a thick red haze.

"You don't need to know," Kelly said smugly.

"Don't fuck with me, you FBI cunt!"

Jaw dropped, the FBI man stared at Carmine incredulously. Then his outrage conquered his amazement and he stiffened in his seat. "Them's fightin' words," he said, not joking.

"Then let's step outside."

The diner had grown absolutely quiet. Luigi flicked his fingers at Merele and Minnie, who scuttled behind the counter, and thirty assorted cops looked enthralled.

"You *mean* it? You actually mean it?"

"I'm fed up with being pissed on by a Fed!" Temper roaring in his ears, Carmine snarled. "Let's step outside."

"You gotta take that back! We fight, there'll be rumbles from Portland, Oregon, to Portland, Maine!"

"You're still being clever, you big-city, know-it-all cunt! You piss on my town, you piss on my department—Eat shit!"

"We step outside," Kelly said, scrambling to his feet.

It was very brief. The two men squared off, fists clenched, and Kelly swung a haymaker that didn't connect. The next thing, he was sitting on the ground wondering if he'd ever be able to breathe again.

All he could see when he looked up were cops' faces in Malvolio's windows, and Carmine's hand reaching down.

"I never so much as saw that coming," he said after he got his breath back—a painful business. "But I refuse to be called a cunt. Forget lunch!"

"Refuse to eat with me after I put your ass on the ground and the rumbles will turn into real tremors," Carmine said, his mood rejoicing. "It's high time guys like you realized that you can't shit on the locals."

They walked inside and sat down again.

"Thanks for doing me no visible damage," Kelly said sourly.

"Oh, I couldn't reach your face, so it had to be your bread basket," Carmine said, still enjoying the sweet victory. "Now who told you about Joshua Butler's testicular endowments?"

"Lancelot Sterling, the head of Butler's section."

"What a lovely boss! Remind me not to apply to Cornucopia for a job. Why wasn't I supposed to know *that*?"

"No reason, honest! I was—I was just being smart. But I never thought I'd hear you sticking up for a piece of shit like Joshua Butler."

It was Carmine's turn to display incredulity. "Jesus, Mr. Kelly, you are thick! It's true that I abominate the kind of conduct in law enforcement that elevates gratuitous gossip to the status of need-to-know information, but I didn't deck you on behalf of Joshua Butler. I did it for me and, man, it felt good! A kind of one-man Holloman Tea Party."

But that Kelly couldn't believe. In fact, Carmine wondered if he knew even now what the fight had really been about.

"You're just evading the issue," he said. "You stuck up for Joshua Butler, Delmonico."

"If that's going to be your written reason when you make your report to J. Edgar or whoever, you'll probably avoid a rap on the knuckles, but luckily for me, my word is good enough for my boss." Carmine pushed away his empty bowl. "That was one fine salad.

Goodness gracious me, Mr. Kelly, you've hardly eaten a thing! Tummy sore, huh?"

"You're a sanctimonious prick!" the FBI man snarled.

Carmine laughed. "Since I may as well be hung for a sheep as a lamb, can I have the FBI's file on Erica Davenport?"

Ted Kelly looked suspicious, but after some thought he shrugged. "I don't see why not. She's one of your suspects in the death of Desmond Skeps, and it suits us. The more hands on the pumps, the better."

"If you knew about boats, you'd know that the best pump of all is a frightened man with a bucket," Carmine said.

"I'll send the file over," said Kelly, feeling his midriff.

"Tell me," Carmine ventured in a conversational tone, "have your Cornucopia informants—or should I say, gossips?—mentioned anything about an attempt on the life of my daughter?"

Kelly stared. "N-no," he stammered.

"Even Erica Davenport?"

"No." Kelly regained his composure and looked genuinely concerned. "Jesus, Carmine! When did this happen?"

"It doesn't matter," said Carmine shortly. "I can look after Sophia, but more important, she can look after herself. Good! Word of it hasn't leaked, and I don't want it leaking from you, understood? I asked because I needed to know, and you are the only one attached to Cornucopia whose discretion is even remotely reliable. Don't prove my trust misplaced, Mr. Kelly."

He was too intrigued to be insulted. "Intimidation?"

"I would think so, but he wasn't just futzing around. I was supposed to find my daughter dead, and if she were an ordinary kid, she would be. Lucky for me and unlucky for him, she's far from ordinary. She escaped. I didn't know anything about it until it was all over."

"She must be a nervous wreck!"

"Sophia? No! She missed a day of school, but as far as my wife and I can ascertain, she bears no mental scars. It helps to have gotten yourself out. She feels a victor, not a victim."

"I'll keep my ear to the ground."

"Good, as long as your mouth stays shut."

Erica Davenport's file was modestly thick, chiefly a series of statements taken from people who had known her at some time during her forty years. Phil Smith had—implied?—said?—that she came from a wealthy Massachusetts family, but nothing in her early history bore that out. If the Davenports had a Pilgrim ancestor, knowledge of it had disappeared by the time Erica was born in 1927. Her father was a foreman in a shoe factory, and the family lived in a neighborhood of mixed white- and blue-collar workers. Her straight As had been achieved in public schools, wherein, Carmine was interested to learn, she was never cheerleader material. The Great Depression had wrought havoc on the family; the father had lost his job when the shoe factory folded and became as depressed as the economy. He didn't drink or otherwise fritter away what money there was, but he was no help either. The mother worked cleaning houses, was paid a pittance, and put her head inside the gas oven when Erica was seven. Care of Erica and two young brothers devolved upon an older sister, who preferred servicing men to cleaning houses.

Sordid, thought Carmine, staring into space; however, it was a typical Thirties story, a decade of horror for people of all classes and all walks of life. Until then, men had found a job, a trade or a profession in their teens and expected to fill it until retirement. The Thirties destroyed permanency, for the Davenports among millions of others.

How the hell did she get to Smith? The answer to that lay in a statement from the widow of the principal of Erica's last high school. It was barbed, bitter and biased, yes, but it also rang true. Lawrence Shawcross had seen beyond the painfully thin and immature body of Erica Davenport, seen beyond the sharp features of her face, seen beyond the cramped inexperience of her mind, and taken this child of brilliant promise in hand to see if he could breathe life into her. Though Marjorie Shawcross fought her coming with tooth and nail, Erica Davenport moved into the Shawcross house in September of 1942, when she was fifteen years old. The battle that ensued was a secret one, for if it became known that Shawcross's wife was an unwilling participant, he would have lost his job, his reputation and his pension. So Mrs. Shawcross, caught, pretended she was delighted to do what she could for this child of brilliant promise. Erica had new clothes, was taught how to care for herself, eat daintily, use a napkin and all the right cutlery, speak clearly with good diction, and all the other things Lawrence Shawcross deemed vital if his Erica were to make her deserved mark on the world.

Teacher and pupil became lovers in 1944, when Erica was seventeen, according to Marjorie Shawcross. Frowning, Carmine considered it, and decided that while it was likely Erica had found a lover, he was not Lawrence Shawcross. One of the things this would-be Professor Higgins would have taught her was never to foul her own nest. And she, seizing on everything he said as gospel, would have seen the good sense of that advice immediately.

The straight As became A-pluses, but with the war ending and millions of servicemen coming home, Erica didn't stand a chance of getting a place in a top university; it would have to be a women's college. Despite a partial scholarship to Smith, things looked grim for Erica: extremely gifted students were a dime a dozen in 1945. And then, out of the blue, Lawrence Shawcross died. The cause of death was put down as a cerebral catastrophe by his doctor, treating him for high blood pressure. Mrs. Shawcross's allegations of murder by Erica Davenport were dismissed as the ravings of a grief-stricken woman, though his will gave her some grounds—just not enough. The bulk of his estate went to his widow, but the sum of $50,000 went to Erica Davenport for her education and concomitant expenses.

Erica went to Smith and chose economics as her major, with

high grades in mathematics, English literature, and . . . *Russian?* Did Smith even teach Russian?

Back he went to her childhood, cursing himself for skimming some of the statements. But no, he couldn't find a single thing. Davenport had never been Davenski, so much seemed sure. On he waded through the various schools she had attended—no luck there either. What about the mysterious lover during her last year in high school? Papers went flying. Then he thought of Delia and called her in.

"You have a better eye for the written word than I do," he said, handing her the years Erica had spent living with the Shawcrosses. "See if you can find any reference to a Russian or the Russian language."

Off she trotted, while Carmine sat with mind buzzing. The FBI knew this particular quarry had learned Russian, which surely put her at the top of their Ulysses suspect list. So why hadn't they told him? "Because," he muttered to the empty room, "you are a provincial nonentity, a dumb dago cop in a pint-sized place full of eccentrics! Next time I'll punch the cunt's lights out, even if I have to grow wings!"

"No, no," said Delia when she returned, "you do the man an injustice, Carmine. He *did* give you the file."

"He thinks I'm too stupid to read."

"Then that's his mistake, isn't it?" Having tidied the mess on his desk, she sat down and handed him the sheaf he had given her. "It's a glancing reference only, by"—she giggled—"who else, the milkman. Now he's genuinely stupid, and I'm sure you gained the impression that he had rather a crush on Erica. In amongst his ramblings about her boyfriends—I must digress and say that they seem without foundation, which may be why no one put a note beside the reference. Why do they ink out some words or phrases? Anyone can fill them in from imagination!"

"Get on with it, Delia!"

"Oh! Oh, yes, of course. One of her boyfriends talks gibberish, and she gibbers back. Here it is, and I quote: 'He jabbers at her like he does with his pals, real quick.' It could mean a fast talker, but if he jabbers at Erica, then she must understand the jabber and, by extrapolation, jabber back."

"A Russian boyfriend in 1944, huh? An immigrant?"

"Why not? From what I know and have seen of Dr. Davenport, she likes secretiveness. Conversing in a foreign language would have been just her ticket."

"According to the milkman, he had pals."

"That's not uncommon, Carmine. Immigrants with poor command of English tend to clump together. Where is this place?"

"An outer suburb of Boston."

"Then presumably there would have been work."

"In 1944? Scads of it."

Okay, so she spoke Russian, Carmine decided, going back to the Smith years. Shawcross's money must have come in handy. The formal exchange program hadn't yet found its feet, but the students were encouraged to broaden their experience as well as their education by going elsewhere for two semesters, fall and spring, in their junior year. In 1947 the twenty-year-old Erica asked if she could attend the London School of Economics, provided her courses there were accredited toward her degree. And so off to London she went. Her brilliance and dedication at the L.S.E. never faltered; while other students stumbled at the strangeness of different routines, attitudes and customs, Erica Davenport fitted into her new environment faultlessly. She managed to acquire a few friends, go to parties, even have several love affairs with men generally held unattainable.

Having concluded her studies at the close of the academic year, she spent the summer of 1948 exploring the Continent; her canceled passport showed entry and exit stamps for France, the Netherlands, Scandinavia, Spain, Portugal, Italy and Greece. She traveled second-class and unaccompanied, explaining to those who asked that the solitude was good for her soul. When she touched base in London between trips, she inflicted color slide shows on her L.S.E. circle, one of whom complained that the scenery was gorgeous, but where were the people?

"I am not insensitive enough to photograph people going about their usual existence as if they were freaks!" she had said, annoyed. "If their costumes are alien to us, to them they are what everyone wears."

"Then pay them to have their pictures taken," someone said. "You're a rich American, you can afford the dollar."

"What, and drag them down to our level? That's disgusting!"

Well, well! Carmine fingered this statement as if the paper were coated in gold. Once upon a time you had passions, Erica! Strong, ineradicable passions. Ideals too.

The law degree from Harvard and the doctorate from Chubb produced nothing new; the only thing about Erica Davenport's second twenty years that he found intriguing was how immobile they were. After that three-month orgy of sampling Europe's charms, she never went back, and that was strange. In his experience people always tried to recapture the joys and flings of youth, especially when they involved junkets to Europe. She hadn't gone to West Germany and she had steered clear of Cyprus and Trieste; she had caught a ferry from Brindisi to Patras, thus avoiding any chance of encountering Yugoslavia. Was the visa situation that bad in 1948, before the cold war heated up?

"Delia!" he hollered. "I'm going to Cornucopia!"

"How good's your Russian?" he asked Dr. Erica Davenport bluntly. "The Russian boyfriend hone your grammar too?"

"Oh, you are a busy boy!" she said, tapping the end of a gold pencil on her desk.

"It can't be a secret. It's in your FBI file."

"Am I to infer that you believe the FBI have cleared me of suspicion in their espionage investigation?" she asked coolly.

"The FBI is the FBI, a law unto itself. In my eyes it does not clear you of suspicion," Carmine said.

"I had a Russian boyfriend in my teens, I admit, and I happen to pick up languages very easily. A Smith professor gave me a special course in Russian grammar and literature out of sheer gratification at finding someone interested. I also toyed with the idea of going into the State Department as a diplomat. Satisfied?"

"How much of this does the FBI know?"

"Clever Captain Delmonico! You know I didn't mention the boyfriend, yet you knew about him. Someone in the FBI slipped."

"Bigger organization, more chance of slips." He tilted his head and considered her. "What happened to the passion?"

"Excuse me?"

"The passion. At twenty you were full of it."

Her smile resembled a sneer. "I don't think so."

"I do, and you'll never convince me otherwise. Your aspirations for humanity burned your brain like red-hot pokers. You were going to change the world. Instead, you joined it."

The face had gone pinched, pale. "I think . . ." she said slowly, "I think I found new outlets for my passions, if by that you mean youthful dreams. I discovered that women are not equipped to change the world, because the power resides with men. They assert it both physically and psychically. First things first, Captain. We must acquire power, that is our primary objective at this time."

"We? Our?"

"The monstrous regiment of women."

"Knox was a woman hater as well as a dirty old man."

"But think of the power he wielded! Then name me a female equivalent. You can't. Old men can deflower young girls with impunity when they control and direct the thoughts of others."

"Are you tied to Dr. Pauline Denbigh and the feminists?"

"No."

"Is Philomena Skeps?"

She laughed. "No."

Carmine got up. "I'd like to meet Dr. Duncan MacDougall."

"Why? To badger him the way you did my secretary?"

"I hardly think so. He's director of Cornucopia Research."

"I see. Power again. Underlings can be badgered, chiefs are sacrosanct." She picked up a file. "Do your worst," she said, sounding bored. "He makes his own appointments."

The hardest aspect of having a conversation with Dr. Duncan Mac-Dougall lay not in lack of coöperation but in understanding what he said. Carmine got a taste of it in the parking lot, his prearranged meeting spot. He watched the slight, sinewy little man walk toward him, stop, gaze at the array of chimneys dotting the vast hangarlike roof, then finish his approach at a run, face terrified.

"Coom on, mon, the lamp's reekin'!" he cried, and hustled Carmine along like a teacher to a tardy child.

At least, that was what Carmine thought he said. Inside, the director hollered down a phone, then looked relieved.

"The lamp shoodna reek," he said to Carmine.

"Excuse me?"

"There was smoke coming out of Peabody's chimney."

And so it went, though Carmine managed to translate most of what Dr. MacDougall said into plain English. It was impossible to fault his security measures, or see how he could improve them. Inside his time vault were a number of smaller safes, their size depending upon what they had to contain; blueprints went into big, flat safes with drawers inside, whereas papers went into the more usual kind of repository. There were guards, and they were as competent as well trained, and getting a document out of the vault was the most public of undertakings.

"I don't think the thefts happen here, Dr. MacDougall," he said at the end of a very comprehensive breakdown of procedures. "For instance, the new formulae for Polycorn Plastics and all the experimental scraps have never left this vault since Mr. Collins refused to take delivery. And I'd bet my bottom dollar Ulysses hasn't gotten a whiff of them. I had some hard things to say about security in Cornucopia headquarters, but I don't include this facility, sir. Keep it going like this, and you'll always be squeaky-clean."

"Yes, but that's not good enough!" MacDougall said angrily. "So much great work comes out of Cornucopia Research, and no one who works here can stomach the thought that his or her ideas, energies and labor end up in Moscow or Peking."

"Then we have to catch Ulysses, sir. You can do your share by making careful logs of exactly who handles sensitive material once it leaves you. You must have some notion of who the people in each division are as well as in Cornucopia Central. I'd really like to see what names you come up with."

"As distinct from the FBI," said Dr. MacDougall.

"Definitely," said Carmine. "They don't share much."

"Och, aye, ye shall hae it!" the director said. Or something like that, anyway.

"No one understands a Scot except another Scot," Desdemona said, dishing up veal scallops in a cream and white wine sauce made with mushrooms; she was getting very gastronomically adventurous now that Julian was turning into a human being.

"He might as well have spoken a foreign language." Carmine eyed his plate with almost lascivious pleasure. Rice—ideal for sopping up sauce—and asparagus. This was definitely one of those occasions when he could thank his lucky stars he had amnesia of the stomach—after two hours it forgot it had eaten, so Luigi's salad wasn't even a memory.

He didn't speak again until the scallopini were all gone. Then he grabbed his wife's hand and kissed it reverently.

"Superb!" he said. "Better than my mother by far. Better even than my grandmother Cerutti, and that's saying something. How did you get the veal so tender?"

"Beat the blazes out of it," said Desdemona, delighted. "I am not a five-foot-nothing old lady from Sicily, Carmine, I'm a six-foot-three

Boadicea. I can actually reach the back burner of a stove without stretching."

"Sophia missed a feast, serve her right. Pizza, yet!"

"She's entertaining in her eyrie, my love. Much as I adore her, it's nice to have you all to myself sometimes."

"I agree. It's just that someone should have been here to bear witness to your skill."

"Enough about my skill. I won't be able to get my head through the door. You look pleased about more than mere food tonight, so pray enlighten me."

"I called FBI Kelly a totally unprintable word, he insisted we step outside—we were in Malvolio's—and we had a fight."

"Oh, dear," she said, sighing. "Is he still alive?"

"Walking wounded. It wasn't much of a fight—he's no boxer. A Primo Carnera, trips over his own feet, they're so big. It was nice, I enjoyed it. Saw the usual suspects. Felt sorry for poor old Corey— the wife's on his back big-time. Stirred up a hornet's nest or two, and set Delia the human bloodhound on a new scent. I wish I could give her the lieutenancy!"

He frets more about that wretched promotion than he does about his murders, Desdemona thought, watching him. One of them has to lose. I could kill John Silvestri for keeping him on the panel! It's a sort of death knell, and Carmine knows it. The loser will seek promotion in another police department, and the old team will be gone forever. Maybe the state legislature will raise the retirement age and the crisis will disappear. No, it won't. If anything, retirement age will go down, not up. I love him so much, and I know he loves me equally. We have a life together, even when we're apart. We look forward to each other.

"Poor Erica Davenport!" she said suddenly.

"Huh?"

"The brains, the beauty, the bank balance. Her life is so terribly empty."

"She doesn't think so," Carmine said, grinning. "In fact, she preached me a sermon about it this afternoon. Power, that's the well-spring of her existence."

"Pooh! Power over what? People's jobs? People's lives? It's an illusion, it has the same substance as chessmen on a chessboard—very bright men play a game with inanimate pieces. Only one thing grants genuine power—the loss of personal liberty. That awful certainty that if one's papers are not properly stamped or one is in a place one shouldn't be, one will be put against a wall and shot. That one can be shipped off to a concentration camp without a word of explanation, and that there is no process of appeal. That where one lives, works, even goes for a holiday, is decided by someone faceless without consultation. Power turns human beings into beasts—tell *that* to your precious Dr. Davenport next time you see her!"

Whatever else she might have had to say on the subject was not said. Desdemona found herself flat on her back on the dining room floor, looking up into a pair of fiery eyes.

"Carmine! You can't! What if Sophia . . . ?"

"Then you have ten seconds to hit the bedroom."

"How far can the long arm of coincidence go?" Carmine asked Abe and Corey early the next morning.

Neither man had any idea what he meant, but both hesitated to say so: was this some kind of test?

Corey swallowed. "How do you mean, boss?"

"April third. Jimmy Cartwright was coincidental. So, we're being led to believe, was Dean Denbigh. The thing is, could our fat banker also have been coincidental to April third?"

"That's stretching it," Corey said, relieved that he'd been frank. With Carmine, you never knew whereabouts his mind might go. Last night Corey'd had a bitter fight with Maureen that almost became knock-down, drag-out, but it had cleared the air, and this morning he felt as if the nagging and the whining might actually stop. She'd smiled at him and cooked him breakfast, and said not a word about the promotion.

"What makes you wonder, Carmine?" Abe asked.

"That window of opportunity. It's so—convenient. I'd spend more time on Mrs. Norton, except for the date. April third! How can it possibly be her?"

"Is there anything else significant about April third?" Corey asked. "It's a Monday. It's the first working day of the month, which is the last month of quite a few financial years—"

"It's a frustration because April Fool's Day fell on a Saturday," said Abe, grinning. "No pranks this year."

"A source for the strychnine never turned up," said Carmine.

"No," said his team in chorus.

"Let's look at things a different way, even if it does make us seem macabre."

Carmine didn't like using a blackboard, but occasionally it became necessary to tabulate things, and then a board was handy.

"There are gentle deaths and agonizing deaths." He drew a line up the center, forming two columns. "On the gentle side are Beatrice Egmont, Cathy Cartwright, and the three black victims. I call them gentle because none of them saw it coming and all of them died very quickly. Okay, five gentle."

He entered the left-hand side of his board. "Agonizing has to include Dean Denbigh, but we exclude him here because he falls outside our scope. Which leaves us with five agonizing deaths: Peter Norton, Dee-Dee Hall, Bianca Tolano, Evan Pugh, and Desmond Skeps. However, I want to write them down in order of magnitude—easiest to worst. Who had the easiest death?"

"Peter Norton," Corey said. Man, he was flying today!

"Why?"

"Because he probably lost consciousness the moment the convulsions began. I know we can't say that for sure, but I'm betting Patrick would say generalized convulsions interrupt the brain's conscious pathways."

"I agree, Corey. So we write Peter Norton down as easiest. Who next in this grisly catalogue?"

"Dee-Dee Hall," said Abe. "She didn't fight. She just stood and exsanguinated. A slow bleed from both jugulars, but slow is relative—the blood would have poured out like any liquid under pressure from a pump, and the heart's a perfect pump. Her suffering would have been as much mental as physical, except that she didn't move a muscle to defend herself or run. That might suggest that Dee-Dee wasn't sorry her life was ending."

Carmine wrote her name on the blackboard. "So we equate her as more or less equal with Peter Norton."

"Evan Pugh next," said Abe.

"You really think so, Abe?"

"I do too," Corey said. "He died of trauma to the spinal cord and internal organs. It was slow, but it was *clean*. The worst of it would have been inside his mind, and that we can't speculate about. Everybody's different."

"Evan Pugh," said Carmine, writing. "Next to last?"

"Desmond Skeps," said Abe. "His death was diabolical, but most of the torture wasn't half as bad—in my view, anyway—as what Bianca Tolano went through."

"Abe's right, Carmine," said Corey firmly. "Skeps was a famous man, he knew he'd made a lot of enemies, and he must have known there was always a chance one of them would hate him enough to kill him. His torture was superficial, even the cut-off nipples. Whereas Bianca Tolano was an innocent who suffered the ultimate degradation. Skeps could only have equaled her if he'd been raped, and he wasn't. His murderer—um—"

"Preserved his integrity as a man," Carmine finished. "Yes, that's important. None of the male victims was sexually tampered with, and only one female: Bianca Tolano."

He wrote her name at the bottom of the right-hand column, and stared at the board. "We have to presume that the killer knew them all, so what was it about each one that decided their particular death?"

"Beatrice Egmont was a real nice old lady," Abe said.

"Cathy Cartwright was a nice woman having a helluva bad time with her family and Jimmy," Abe said.

"And the three black victims were so totally harmless," Carmine said. "What about the agonizing ones?"

"The banker was a bully who sometimes abused his power," Abe said. "And Dee-Dee was a hooker—a crime in itself to some people."

"Evan Pugh was a blackmailer who picked the wrong victim," Corey said, "and Skeps was probably responsible for the ruination of tens of thousands of lives in one way or another."

"Yet the worst death of all was reserved for an innocent." Carmine stood frowning heavily. "What about her made the killer white-hot hate her?" He looked at Corey from under his brows. "You did the preliminary work, Corey. Did anything ever surface that suggested Bianca wasn't an innocent?"

"No, absolutely nothing," Corey said steadily. "She's exactly who she seems, I'd stake my life on it." He went red. "I was on the ball, even if I was having a few personal problems."

"I never doubted that you were." Carmine sat down and waved a hand at chairs. "So here we have a killer of nine or ten people who is capable of pitying some of his intended victims, yet simultaneously capable of implacable hatred for some others. In one case only, the hatred went from ice-cold to white-hot—Bianca Tolano. A twenty-two-year-old economics graduate aiming for a Harvard MBA. Very pretty, a great figure, but on the shy side. Not man-hungry. At second autopsy Patsy decided she was probably a virgin."

"She reminds me of Erica Davenport," said Abe thoughtfully.

"What?"

"Well, she does!" Abe prepared to defend an untenable position. "I can see Dr. Davenport at that age, with her summa cum laude degree and the whole world in front of her. She's an icicle now, but I bet she wasn't back then. I bet she wasn't man-hungry either. Too ambitious. Just like Bianca."

"Now why didn't I see that?" Carmine asked slowly. "I spent half of yesterday afternoon looking at Erica Davenport's FBI file, and failed to see it. Bianca was a surrogate Erica."

"Jesus, this case gets screwier by the minute!" Abe cried.

"Think about it!" Carmine said eagerly. "If Bianca is a surrogate Erica, it puts her murder in perspective. The random element is disappearing. They *are* all related somehow! We can rule out Erica Davenport. The biggest question I have about her now is whether Bianca's murder removes her from danger."

"There haven't been any more murders," Corey said.

"Where do we go from here?" Abe asked.

"You guys concentrate on Peter Norton," Carmine said, tone

brisk. "I'm finding it harder and harder to believe that window-of-opportunity garbage. What if Mrs. Norton had been meaning to kill her husband for some time, and was manipulated into doing the deed on April third? If she's guilty, then she had to get the strychnine somewhere, and maybe that's the connection to our mastermind. I want both of you lifting up the flagstones on Mrs. Norton's buried past. A boyfriend? I doubt it, but it has to be excluded. Is she in debt? Jewels? Furs? Clothes? Gambling? Is she bored with her life as Mrs. Small City Banker? She's plump, but not unattractive. Look behind every blade of grass, guys. I want to know where this murder belongs."

Which left him time for lunch at Malvolio's with Myron, who looked careworn.

"Is she leaning too hard?" Carmine asked, sliding into the booth, his smile disarming the question's intrusive side.

"Not as much since I advised her to let S.S. Cornucopia sail under its own steam. I should have seen that for myself."

"You're the ham in the sandwich." Carmine turned to the waitress. "I'll have a lettuce, tomato, cucumber and celery salad with oil-and-vinegar dressing, Minnie, and crackers on the side." He looked from Minnie to Myron suspiciously. "So what's the big deal about that?"

Minnie melted away; Myron shrugged. "For you, Carmine, it's horrific. What happened to the Thousand Island dressing? The hard rolls? The butter?"

"If you'd been eating dinner at my place, Myron, you'd know." Carmine sipped black, sugarless coffee. "My wife has turned into one of the world's great chefs, so either I eat rabbit food for lunch, or no lunch at all. Otherwise I'll turn into the Goodyear blimp."

"Holy Moses! What gives with the murders?"

"We're making progress. How much has Erica told you about her childhood and young womanhood?"

"More than she told Desmond Skeps, I think. She conned all the

Cornucopia executives out of self-preservation, but she came clean to me when I asked her. Depression children had a hard time, Carmine."

"Don't tell me, I was one. My father was lucky, he kept his job, but his wages had to be spread around the family some. East Holloman was one of the first districts to improve, so by 1935 things were looking up again. St. Bernard's high school was underpopulated. We got a lot of teacher time."

"I never felt it," Myron confessed. "The movie industry did well, so did my pop."

"It was a crazy decade." Carmine munched through his salad as if he was enjoying it. "How do you think Erica wound up the person she is now, Myron?"

"I have no idea, and she won't tell me."

"Has she ever mentioned what she did in Europe while she tripped around there in the summer of 1948?"

"I didn't even know she went to Europe, just about London."

"It's in her FBI file, and it might answer a lot."

"I won't spy for you, Carmine."

"Nor would I ask you, but spying is already a part of this case. Someone at Cornucopia is selling secrets to the Reds, and Erica is a strong suspect."

Myron had gone chalk white. His fork fell onto his plate with a clatter. "Oh, God, that's awful!"

"It's also classified information. You can't tell anyone, Myron, though you can tell Erica. She knows all about Ulysses."

"Ulysses is the spy?"

"It's his FBI code name. I don't think Erica is Ulysses, but I do think she knows who Ulysses is. Your security clearance is probably much higher than mine, so I don't have any qualms about telling you. If you don't know, then your businesses and your associates are not involved. But it might be that Erica would welcome a true friend."

Myron's wide grey eyes filled with tears. He nodded quickly, speechless. When he did speak, his voice sounded normal.

"I seem to have lost my appetite," he said. "This superb meatloaf is virtually untouched. I don't suppose . . . ? "

"Sorry, no, rabbit food only."

"My God! Desdemona must rank with Escoffier!"

"I don't know about that, but she certainly outranks my grand-mother Cerutti, and that's saying something."

The next day brought another trek to see Philomena Skeps. Why, he asked himself, does she have to live in Orleans? A three-hour drive even with the siren on in Connecticut, and this time he doubted she'd give him brunch. It wasn't a hospitable kind of day; the sky was overcast, the wind was blowing, and the Atlantic was trying to demolish the sand dunes, or maybe pile them up higher.

He was right about brunch. Mrs. Skeps met him at the door ac-companied by Anthony Bera, who directed Carmine into a small parlor poorly lit by a window covered in rambling rose canes. The lawyer had gone fully formal in a three-piece suit with a Harvard tie, and Philomena wore a mossy green wool dress that showed off her voluptuous figure. Why was such a gorgeous woman wasting her fragrance on the Cape's salty air? Bera he could understand; Bera was the mastiff hoping to be tossed a bone.

"Do you have any contact with the women's liberation move-ment, Mrs. Skeps?" he asked.

"Not really, Captain. I have given small donations for any projects dear to my heart, but I don't call myself a feminist."

"Have these projects been drawn to your attention by Dr. Pauline Denbigh?"

"I know her slightly, but she has never solicited me for either membership or money."

"Do you sympathize with feminist causes?"

"Don't you, Captain?" she countered.

"Yes, of course."

"Then there we have it."

"What did you and Dr. Erica Davenport discuss so earnestly at Mr. Mandelbaum's party?"

"You don't need to answer that, Philomena," Bera said. "In fact, I advise you not to."

"No, I'll answer," she said in that sweet, patient voice that never lost its cadence. "We discussed my son's future, as Dr. Davenport is now the arbiter of his fate. I went to Mr. Mandelbaum's party for no other reason than to see Erica, and I can't imagine she had any other reason for asking him to invite me. Erica is not welcome in my home. I am not welcome in any Cornucopia premises. Therefore we chose neutral ground."

"I suspected that much," Carmine said. "But you haven't really answered me. What aspects of your son's future did you discuss, and what was the outcome of your—negotiations?"

"My son must endure almost eight years of Dr. Davenport's authority, and the last three or four of those years will be quite insufferable for him. He doesn't like her, he never has. What I hoped was to persuade her to agree to having another—a second—person involved in his future. It worries me terribly that this woman could ruin his inheritance. Not intentionally, but through incompetence."

"But anyone left in charge during an heir's long minority might ruin a business empire," Carmine objected. "I take it you have no faith in a woman at the Cornucopia helm?"

"No, it's not that, it's *her!* I asked her to bring Tony—Mr. Bera— in as the second person. She refused. And that was the end of our conversation."

"You must have been mighty thick with Dr. Davenport to have fallen out so badly," Carmine said. "Why does your son dislike her? When and where have they met?"

Her head slewed to Anthony Bera. Help, help, rescue me! What do I say? What do I do?

"I advise you not to answer, Philomena," said the mastiff, earning his bone.

Carmine extricated himself from his extremely uncomfortable chair. "Thank you for your time, Mrs. Skeps."

I feel like Michelangelo chipping away at a hunk of marble, he thought, commencing the interminable drive home. Today I have bared an elbow, a forearm, and a hand. But is it the right one, or the left? And where *does* Ulysses fit in?

On his return he discovered that Delia had usurped half of his office, where a trestle table and a wheeled chair now stood.

"I'm too cramped," she explained. "Uncle John really has not been fair about space! The captain of detectives must have a secretary, and said secretary must have a suitable office. I occupy a cupboard!"

"Then why don't you go complain to Uncle John? Where are Abe and Corey going to put their chairs if I call a conference? And much as I love you, Delia, I do not need your ears flapping in time with your mouth. A work space is only useful to one person. How can I think if every time I look up, I'm looking at you?"

She took this in the spirit it had been tendered, but she had no intention of moving the acres of paper she had spread around, huge sheets with smaller ones clipped to them. Now I have to go fight Delia's battles, he thought, moving to the door as soundlessly as always. Any other man, thought Delia, would have stomped, but not Carmine. By next Monday I will have a bigger office.

She waited until a certain emptiness invaded the air, her way of telling whether Carmine was in the building. Good, gone!

"Have you worked out how to do it, Uncle John?" she cooed, sidling around the Commissioner's door.

"No, Delia, I have not. I figured I'd just sit here and wait for you to come tell me how to do it," Silvestri said.

"How very perspicacious, Uncle John. It's Mickey McCosker is the trouble. He has twice as much room as Carmine or Larry, but he's never here. What I propose is that you give Carmine his two rooms, and put Mickey where Carmine is. Shall I have Plant Physical do it tomorrow?"

He nodded wordlessly. Why is she always right?

"Tell me that," he said to Carmine in Malvolio's five minutes later, "and I'll give you Danny's job. Or mine, if you want it."

"Cheers, chief." Carmine raised his glass. "I'm happy to be a captain of detectives, especially if I can have Mickey's office—or am I supposed to move into his second room?"

"No, you get his office. The second room, Delia informs me, is twice as big." Somehow he managed to turn his face into a passable imitation of his niece's, and said in a shrill falsetto, " 'Bags I the second room, Uncle John!' I said yes. Easier in the long run." He sipped his bourbon reflectively.

"As I remember Mickey's second room," said Carmine, "even at the rate Delia acquires filing cabinets, it should shut her up for two-three years." He grinned. "Then you'll have to run for mayor, John, and build her a new County Services."

"In a pig's eye!" The Commissioner downed the last of his drink and waved for another. "What's Delia doing?"

"Some crazy project only she could understand or want to do. It's about public meetings and functions and it's germane to the case, so I guess I'm using her as a detective." Carmine waved for another bourbon, then looked hopeful. "I don't suppose you'd give her the lieutenancy?"

"No, I would not! Bad enough that she's got me drinking at four-thirty in the afternoon. Delia and her paper chases!"

Of chaos there was none; by Monday midday Carmine was well ensconced in his new office, which was at the back of County Services and consequently suffered little traffic noise. Light came in through a series of high windows that faced Holloman's prevailing winds, giving him an occasional cool gust during the dog days of August. The proximity of Abe and Corey's office was an additional bonus; it lay two doors down the hall. Carmine's old office was up two flights of stairs on the same floor as the Commissioner's.

"We need a coat of paint and new furniture," said Delia.

"When I go on vacation," said Carmine in his no-arguments tone as he inspected her quarters, strewn with broadsheet-sized papers. "What are these? Plans?"

"Of a kind. With more floor space, I can really spread them out. I should be able to give you my report on Friday."

Corey walked in. "Carmine, a domestic in the Hollow," he said. "Woman battered to death, lover nowhere to be found."

And this, said Carmine to himself as he left, means we've hit a stone wall with the mastermind. For now, it's business as usual. There has to be a loose thread somewhere! I am not giving up, I am not pulling these nine files out of my current load and shelving them at Caterby Street!

"There's been a development at the Norton house," Abe said quietly on Tuesday morning. He looked drawn, horrified.

Carmine was up and around his desk in seconds. "What?"

"The little boy is dead."

His step faltered. "Oh, Jesus! How? Why?"

"Drank or ate something, I was told."

"But the strychnine was never found!"

"I don't know if it is strychnine, Carmine."

"What else could it be?"

"Let's wait until we know for sure, okay?"

He could walk again. Carmine began to hurry, then wondered why. Poor little Tommy was dead. "Is Patsy on his way?"

"I told him first. Corey went with him." Abe's voice shook.

"What's the little guy's proper name?"

"Thomas Peter. Five a few days ago in April, so he doesn't go to school until September. Never will now."

They climbed into the Fairlane; Abe put the light on the roof automatically. Carmine sat in the front seat, hands over his face.

A nightmare, it was a nightmare! The noise of the siren was oddly comforting: a lonely, desolate sound. They were approaching North Holloman before he took his hands away.

"Has she confessed? Who's seen her?"

"Only Dave O'Brien—he's sergeant on duty at North Holloman this week. She called him calm as you like, didn't call anyone else. Dave went right on over to the house and then called me. That's all I know."

"How could that stupid doctor of hers not know what she was hiding? She was so doped up both times I saw her, I didn't stand a chance of getting anywhere! I should have pushed her, Abe, but she fooled me!"

"Carmine, none of us could have known. If she did kill her husband, the reality was so far from what she imagined that she flipped out—she *wasn't* acting! But we don't know if she did it yet, and that's the only fact that matters."

"What else could it be except the strychnine?"

"I don't know and you don't know. Shit happens, Carmine, but we don't know what kind of shit it is, so cool it!"

A few neighbors had collected, the other two North Holloman cops had cordoned off the path to the house, and Patsy was on the porch waiting for them. He came to meet them.

"Not strychnine," he said shortly, keeping his voice low. "He choked to death on a pencil eraser that looked like a strawberry."

The relief flooded through Carmine and Abe like a break in a dam wall, too overwhelming not to be felt before the shame of feeling it succeeded it. Not their negligence! But it might have been, it might have been. The poor little guy was still dead, though a merciful God had spared them the ultimate grief.

"How is she?" Carmine asked, aware that he felt faint.

"Sit down, cuz. You too, Abe."

They sat on the steps leading up to the porch.

"She's in there," Patsy said, sounding savage, jerking his head at the living room windows. "Thank God he's not. I don't want to set eyes on that woman ever again!"

Carmine got up at once, astonished. "Patsy! What did she do? Feed the thing to him?"

"She may as well have, but she'll tell you all about it." He led them through the front door and up the stairs to Thomas Peter's bedroom.

Abe and Carmine watched Patrick gather the little boy up tenderly, put him into the towel-lined cavity of a bag, then hurry him away on what looked to the curious like a flat, empty gurney; it had a troughlike bottom that did not betray the presence of a small body.

Mrs. Barbara Norton was sitting with Corey and Sergeant Dave O'Brien. Her calm was unimpaired, and it was only as her story unfolded that the layers of insanity peeled away to ever deeper ones. She seemed to have no idea that her son was dead, though she had known it when she spoke on the phone to Dave O'Brien, had told him that Tommy was black in the face and not breathing; but more, she had said she killed him.

"Now that Peter is gone," she told the men, "I can do what I want at last." She leaned forward and spoke in a whisper. "Peter was a glutton. He insisted we had to eat whatever he ate—the children swelled up like balloons! I never tried to argue, it wasn't worth it. I just bided my time. I bided my time." She nodded seriously, then sat back and smiled.

"No one really likes fat people, you know," she began once more, "so after Peter died, I put us on a diet. Marlene and Tommy drink water. I drink black coffee. We can eat all the raw vegetables we like, but no bread, no cookies, no cake, nothing with sugar in it. No milk, no cream, no desserts. I let Tommy and Marlene have crackers at breakfast and lunch. We eat broiled skinless chicken or fish, and steamed vegetables. Rice. The weight just falls off! By the time Tommy goes to school this September, he'll be as trim as our hedge!"

When a silence fell, Carmine decided to risk a question. "How did you stay so trim, Barbara?"

"Stuck my finger down my throat."

It's clear why the poor little guy choked trying to eat an eraser, Carmine thought, but how long has the madness been there? What brought it out? Peter Norton's death? Or did he die as a consequence of it? Tommy's death has tipped her right over the edge, but I have to try to get some answers.

"What did you do with the strychnine, Barbara?"

"Threw the bottle in the Pequot."

"Did you take the cap off first?"

She looked indignant. "Sure I did! I'm not stupid!"

"Why did you pick April third as the day to put strychnine in Peter's orange juice?"

"Oh, silly, you know that!" she said, eyes widening.

"I forget. Tell me again."

"Because it only worked on April third! Any other day, and the potion lost its magic. He was very firm about that."

"Who was?"

"Silly, you know who!"

"It's my memory again. I forget his name."

"Reuben."

"I've forgotten his last name too, Barbara."

"How can you forget what he didn't have?"

"Where did you meet Reuben?"

"At the bowling alley, silly!"

"What magic worked the potion on April third?"

She was getting bored and tired, or perhaps it was both; her eyelids drooped, then she made an effort and lifted them. "Magic only lives for a single day, Reuben told me." She began to stir in her chair, agitation growing. "He lied! He lied! He told me that Peter would just go to sleep! I did not get it wrong! April third was the day!"

"Yes, Barbara, you got it right," Carmine said. "He was the liar. Sit a while and think of happy things."

The four men endured the silence, too afraid to catch any other pair of eyes, trying not to look at her.

She spoke. "Where's Tommy?"

Not Marlene, the girl. Just Tommy.

"He's asleep," Carmine said.

"I don't imagine she'll ever come to trial," he said later to Commissioner Silvestri, "and the poor little boy solved the case. Can you credit it, John? A starvation diet inflicted overnight on a fat five-year-old who's been eating nonstop since he started to walk. The girl is three years older, and cunning. She stole from Mommy's purse to buy food, but she couldn't steal enough to feed her own appetite, let alone her kid brother's as well. She was scared stiff of the day Mommy counted her change, but she would have gone on stealing until Mommy did find out."

Silvestri shook his sleek dark head, blinked rapidly. "Is the girl okay? Are there any relatives willing to take her? The system would turn her into another master criminal."

"Norton's parents are taking her—they live in Cleveland. She's sole heir to his estate, which I imagine will go into a trust until she's of age." Carmine found a smile. "Maybe she stands a better chance this way. At least, I have to hope so."

"A rubber strawberry!" Silvestri exclaimed. "Was it that lifelike?"

"Only to a ravenously hungry little boy," Carmine said, "though I didn't see it before he tried to eat it. It wasn't his, it belonged to the little girl, old enough to know it for what it was. He'd combed the house looking for edibles."

"I guess it means that if you don't want fat kids, you have to start 'em off right," Silvestri said. "That stupid diet turned one child into a thief and killed the other." His black eyes gleamed at the godless Carmine. "I hope you're going to have some masses said for little Tommy's soul—St. Bernard's can do with a new roof. Otherwise Mrs. Tesoriero will see Our Lady's face wet next time it rains, and claim a miracle."

"We've all had wet faces today, John. Yes, I'll see you ten masses and raise you one."

*   *   *

"I don't suppose I have any choice," said Desdemona that evening as they shared their before-dinner drink.

"Choice?"

"I've married into a Catholic family, so my children will be raised Catholics."

Carmine stared at her in surprise. "I didn't think you minded, Desdemona. You've never mentioned it."

"I suppose that's because until Julian's advent I hadn't thought it important to you. You're not at all religious."

"True. That's my work, it gets God out of the system. But I want a Catholic education for my kids—my old school for the boys, St. Mary's for the girls," said Carmine, preparing to do battle. "They should be exposed to a Christian God, and what better one than the original?"

"If we were in England," said his wife thoughtfully, "I'd plump for Church of England, but there's really no equivalent here. I like the close-knit East Holloman family network, and I don't want our children on an outer orbit because their parents failed to agree. I'm the one married into the circle, and the advantages outweigh the disadvantages. But I refuse to convert or go to mass, and I won't make our children go to mass."

"Sounds fair," he said, enormously relieved that there would be no battle. "I only go to mass at Christmas and Easter, though I will go for Tommy Norton. I made a pact with Silvestri."

"That man is brilliant," she said, smiling.

"What's for dinner?"

"Roast loin of pork with crackling."

"I am putty in your hands, lovely lady." He looked at her over the rim of his glass. "Why didn't you fight harder? I expected you to. You did insist on a civil wedding."

"I was pregnant at the time, and in no mood to fiddle with the bride business. I just wanted to be Mrs. Carmine Delmonico as quickly as I could."

"It doesn't answer your attitude tonight," he persisted.

"Very simple," she said, draining her glass. "I abominate coeducation, and East Holloman's Catholic schools are not coeducational. The last thing teenaged children need as they suffer the onslaught of hormones is the presence of the opposite sex in a classroom. Oh, most children survive it, but the cost is dearer. Look at Sophia, tarting herself up every day just to go to school. A dose of uniforms would do her good."

"There are no limits to your surprises," he said, following her into the kitchen. "Did you wear a uniform?"

"We mostly all do. I went to a Church of England day school and wore a hideous navy blue tunic over a shirt and tie. My hat was held on by elastic under my chin to keep it from blowing off in a wind—hats were expensive. And I think," she went on reflectively, bending to lift the roasting pan out of the oven, "that of all the indignities a uniform meant, that elastic under the chin was the worst." Out came the roast onto a board. "Now it has to rest." She rapped the beautifully bubbled skin. "Ah! Perfect! All-male schooling is very important for Julian," she went on without pausing.

"Why him in particular?"

"Because he's going to be tall, dark, and terribly handsome. If there were girls in the classroom and schoolyard, he'd never have any peace. It would also swell his ego. The St. Mary's girls can worship from afar."

"The St. Mary's girls will find a way."

Desdemona looked curious. "Is that the voice of experience?"

"What else?"

"You mean I married a high school heartthrob?"

"No, you married a man in his forties with arthritis."

"Peter Norton's death proves the existence of a mastermind," Carmine said to the Commissioner, Danny Marciano, Patrick O'Donnell and his own men. Delia, pleading work, had declined to come.

"We now have four cases closed—Jimmy Cartwright, John Denbigh, Bianca Tolano and Peter Norton—with the three shootings a given. Though we suspected the existence of a mastermind, he hadn't shown his hand directly until Barbara Norton explained why she chose April third to kill her husband. We'll never get a description out of her, and the name Reuben is a fiction. My guess is that Pauline Denbigh was conned with some highly sophisticated ploy; again, we may never get anywhere by questioning her. She's aiming for an acquittal. Barbara Norton needed to be reassured that her husband would just go to sleep, whereas Pauline Denbigh didn't care what her husband suffered as long as she didn't have to watch. The cyanide evidence ceases with the murder of the Dean—we have the bottle. If there are to be more cyanide deaths, then the salts have already been taken out of the bottle. How much do you think is gone, Patsy?"

"If the bottle was full, about sixty grams—two rounded tablespoons," Patrick said.

"You were right, Carmine," Silvestri said. "One killer."

"An adroit and ingenious killer. He used whatever tools were available to him—usually frustrated people. Barbara Norton and Pauline Denbigh both wanted to be free of domineering men without messy divorces and visualized persecution. Joshua Butler wanted to live his fantasies in the real world, but needed to be shown how."

"What about the rest, Carmine?" Corey asked.

"More direct, if by 'rest' you mean Evan Pugh and Desmond Skeps. We can forget solving Beatrice Egmont, Cathy Cartwright, and the three shootings. An insurance company would call them collateral damage."

"You don't think that of Dee-Dee Hall?" Marciano asked.

"No, I think he killed her in person—why, I don't know."

"Okay, next phase?" Silvestri asked, parking his ashtray and its cigar under Danny's nose.

"A general regrouping," Carmine said, and sighed. "Oh, how I hate Cornucopia! But it's back into the fray, guys."

"Erica Davenport?" Corey asked hopefully.

"She's involved, but she's not the mastermind. I put her down as—" He broke off, frowning. No, he couldn't mention Ulysses. "I put her down as a red herring."

"That wasn't what you were going to say," Silvestri said as everyone filed out of his office.

"Well, I couldn't say it! That's why I hate Cornucopia—too many secrets."

Myron was waiting in his office, eyeing it appreciatively.

"You could do with a coat of paint and some new furniture" was his opening remark. "But it sure beats the previous premises."

His friend was turning into an old man almost overnight; the eyes were red-rimmed, the cheeks sunken, the mouth slack, and his perky, straight-backed posture had sagged.

"No one touches it until I'm on vacation," Carmine said, seating himself behind his desk. "A mug of cop coffee?"

"No, thanks! I'd like to live to see a lunch menu."

"What can I do you for, Myron?"

"I'm flying west this afternoon."

"Not before due time, I would have said in the old days. Now"—Carmine shrugged—"that's debatable. Does Erica know?"

"Yes."

"Have you proposed to her yet?"

"No," Myron said unhappily.

"Why not, if you love her?"

"That's just it—I do love her! But I don't think she loves me. At least, not the way Desdemona loves you."

Carmine sighed. "Myron, you have to remember that Desdemona and I are a special case. We shared a common danger, and that tends to forge a special bond. We started out disliking each other—Jesus, you can't look at us and wish for the same relationship! That's sophomoric."

Myron went scarlet, compressed his lips. "Well, okay, I admit that. But how do I get inside the defenses of a woman I *know* isn't the cold WASP princess she pretends to be?"

"I can't help you," said Carmine, bewildered. "What makes you think I could?"

"Because when she speaks of you, she has strong feelings! If it weren't for you, I'd genuinely believe she doesn't own any." He waved his hands about wildly. "No, she doesn't have the hots for you, so don't start looking for the fire escape! I thought that maybe you had a cop technique . . ." He trailed off miserably.

"And that wasn't what you meant," Carmine comforted. "All you really mean is that something about me gets under her defenses, and you're hoping I know what it is. But I don't, Myron. Even if I did, I wouldn't pass it on. You can pull women effortlessly. You pulled her. And actually you've gotten under her defenses enough for her to have confided in you. No one at Cornucopia knows she's not a cold WASP princess, whereas you do. I'd call that major progress."

"It's chickenfeed," Myron said despondently. "She lets me make love to her—she initiated our first time, I didn't—but she goes away somewhere, Carmine. 'Lie on your back and think of England' might have been written just for her, except it's not England she thinks of."

"That's not you, Myron. That's her," said Carmine, dying for the conversation to be over. "If I were you, I'd go talk to Desdemona."

But Myron shook his head emphatically. "No, it was hard enough talking to you." He got to his feet. "Give my undying love to our daughter."

"You should do that yourself."

"I can't. I need to get away from here as fast as I can."

And he was gone. Carmine stood listening to the sound of his footsteps retreating down the hall, and prayed that his most beloved friend would chance upon a greener feminine field in his own purlieu.

"But I think you can rest easy about your mother," he said to Sophia that evening. "Divorce is not in the cards."

"Then I forgive him for going," Sophia said magnanimously. "That icy bitch would kill him."

W hen Carmine came in on that Friday, April twenty-first, at eight in the morning, Delia was waiting for him. It was clearly some kind of red-letter day for her; she had dressed in her smartest outfit, a combination of purple and orange that hurt the eyes unless, like Carmine's, they were inured to her palette.

"If you don't mind," she said, sitting on a chair across from his at the desk, "I would rather speak to you privately in the first instance. Is that permissible?"

"Sure. Go ahead."

A rolled-up sheet of paper was laid reverently on the desk, together with several sheets of ordinary size. Carmine looked at them and then back at her, brows raised.

"I have found a function at which all eleven of the dead people were present," she said, carefully excluding triumph from her voice. "It was held on Saturday, December third of last year, in the Holloman City Hall, and was given by the Maxwell Foundation in aid of research funding for long-term children's disorders." She stopped, beaming.

"Wow!" Carmine breathed, a better vocabulary knocked out of him. "And they were *all* present? Including the three black victims?"

"Yes. It was a dinner-dance for five hundred people, who were seated at round tables for ten people or five couples. Most of the tables were 'bought' by a company or institution of some kind— undoubtedly you and Desdemona would have been there at Uncle

John's table if you hadn't been new parents. It cost a hundred dollars a plate, which brought in a thousand per table. Most of the sponsoring companies and institutions donated a matched thousand per table. Cornucopia and its subsidiaries sponsored twenty of the fifty tables. Chubb sponsored ten tables, the Mayor had one, Police and Fire ended up sharing one, and so forth." She paused again, eyes bright.

"Amazing," said Carmine slowly, feeling some comment was called for, but having no idea what, beyond marveling.

"I am floored, Carmine, at how much planning goes into a function of this sort," she said in tones of awe. "It's worked out like a battle, though I strongly suspect that if most battles were worked out so scrupulously, the results would be different. Where a table sponsored by an organization should go, its relationship to other tables belonging to that organization, placement of tables to left, right, up, down, and sideways—I doubt Lord Kitchener ever devoted the same time to planning his bloodbaths! When the table master plan was finished, each table was given a number. Then came the business of seating the guests! Due attention had to be paid to those who came as a group of five couples, or wanted to sit at X or Y table, or asked to be seated with anything from one to three other couples. There were also guests who came alone or with a companion, who did not have any preferences, such as Beatrice Egmont. A small group of Maxwell volunteers dealt with all these logistics, and they did it truly magnificently. They even abolished that dreadful crush in the foyer when hundreds of people simultaneously try to see their names listed on a board. Six volunteers with lists sat at a reception desk to give each enquirer his or her table number." She stopped.

"I get your drift, Delia. Don't tease, just go on!"

"One of the many Cornucopia tables was sponsored by the Fourth National Bank under the aegis of Mr. Peter Norton. Due to the vagaries of fate, it was far thinner of company than Mr. Norton could have expected. His wife, for instance, had the gastric flu that was going around at the time—I had it myself—and was too ill to attend. Dean Denbigh's wife also had this flu and didn't come. Beatrice Egmont came on a single ticket, no companion. Mrs. Cathy Cartwright's husband was in Beechmont with the temperamental chef. Bianca Tolano came on one of the tickets given to her by her boss, Mr. Dorley, when he and his wife couldn't go. It seems Bianca made no effort to find an escort; she was on her own. But she must have been a sensible girl, because she handed in her second ticket at the reception desk. How do I know? It had a number, and was sold at the door to a young man who had none—Evan Pugh. So in one sense he and Bianca substituted for the Dorleys, who one presumes had a lucky escape." She shivered, switched into high drama. "But why," she asked rhetorically, "didn't Mr. Norton fill his table with his own friends? None of them even attended!"

Experience with Delia had taught Carmine that she would re-count her doings in her own inimitable style, but that today's effort was a tour de force she had planned as meticulously as the Maxwell Foundation had its banquet. He just had to wait.

"Put succinctly, Mr. Norton was too terrified to invite his own friends," Delia continued, satisfied Carmine was on the edge of his chair. "Pride of place at the Fourth National table went to Mr. Desmond Skeps, who elected to sit at Mr. Norton's out of all the many tables he could choose from. With him as his lady companion he brought Dee-Dee Hall."

"*What?*"

"She's down in black and white on the master guest roster as ac-companying Mr. Desmond Skeps. See?" Delia thrust a sheet of paper at Carmine.

He grabbed it and read incredulously. "What the hell was he up to? Something nasty, I bet! Go on, go on!"

"That gave me four women—Cathy Cartwright, Bianca Tolano, Beatrice Egmont and Dee-Dee Hall—and four men—Desmond Skeps, Peter Norton, Evan Pugh and Dean John Denbigh. Eight people, all now dead. Which still left the Fourth National table rather lightly populated. Two of the ten chairs were unoccupied."

Carmine shook his head. "No wonder I haven't seen hide or hair of you for days! You didn't get all of this off a list."

"Well, no," she confessed. "I had to speak to a lot of people on the phone and visit the Maxwell Foundation several times. At one point I actually thought my precious lists had been thrown out or burned, but I should have known better. Even charities are riddled with bureaucrats, and bureaucrats won't discard anything that might imperil their parasitic existence."

"Why do you hate paper pushers so much, Delia? You're one yourself," Carmine said slyly.

She rose to the bait instantly. "I am not a parasite! My work bears fruit, I am a cog in the necessary machinery of the constabulary! And you give me an instance of one police unit that has even enough paper pushers!" she said indignantly.

"Calm down, calm down! I'm pulling your leg. And you have just processed more paper with positive results than an entire government department," he said. "Desmond Skeps! What was he doing arm in arm with a street whore? Not that she'd have looked like one. Dee-Dee could—could—"

"Tart herself up?" Delia suggested.

"Put on a nice dress and skate on the edge of respectability. She'd still have looked more street than home in the suburbs, but on Skeps's arm she'd have been forgiven a lot. People can't bear thinking that a man of Skeps's wealth and standing might be taking the mickey out of them." Carmine frowned. "Okay, that's eight out of the eleven. What about the black victims?"

"They were present too," said Delia. "The event was catered by Barnstaple Catering, a new name for affairs that size. It's a firm that has previously concentrated on smaller affairs, but there is a contract with Chubb coming up to cater its banquets, and the Maxwell function was a dummy run for Barnstaple. In view of this, at least according to their general manager, Barnstaple agreed to take a smaller profit than it will be asking in the future. Maxwell had some conditions of its own, apparently having had bad experiences in the past.

The thousand-dollar-table dinner dance was a new sort of venture, and they wanted the first one to be memorable, with the intention of having one each year. So Barnstaple had to provide a three-person wait team for each table. Cedric Ballantine, Morris Brown and Ludovica Bereson waited on the Fourth National table. The system worked a treat," Delia went on, the excitement dying out of her voice now that the last goody was revealed. "People got their meals piping hot and very quickly, the liquor flowed uninterruptedly, and no one sat staring at a dirty plate for longer than two or three minutes."

"Was there any method that assigned the three black victims to that table?" Carmine asked.

"No, beyond the fact that they all worked for Barnstaple at weekend functions, and had done for some time, including Cedric Ballantine, who put his age up to get the work. They didn't check ages very stringently, and Cedric looked older than his years. If it had been a weeknight, the two boys wouldn't have been able to work because of school. Mrs. Bereson probably wouldn't have been interested either, after a day housecleaning. But it was a Saturday night, ideal."

"If I were not a happily married man, Delia, I'd be waiting at your door determined to make you mine," Carmine said, smiling. "I also doubt that we three men would have found out half as much. You're a nit-picker, and if ever a job needed a nit-picker, this one was it. I can't thank you enough."

"Thanks are not necessary. I loved every minute of it." She got up, but didn't move to take her papers. "These should stay with you. Now, if you'll excuse me, I'll choofle off."

As soon as she disappeared, Carmine was calling Desdemona. "What kind of flowers can I give Delia for some terrific work?"

"Brightly colored orchids," said Desdemona instantly. "In a pot, not as a corsage. Cattleyas."

"The big question is, why did Desmond Skeps sit at Peter Norton's table?" Carmine asked Corey and Abe.

"I don't see how we'll ever know," Corey said gloomily. "Everyone attached to the table is dead."

"What I want to know," said Abe, "is why did four months elapse between this banquet and the murders?"

"I don't think we're going to find that out, so I propose we shelve it for the moment," Carmine said.

"But we can find out the names of plenty of people who went and didn't die," Corey said. "We need to get a feel for the kind of function it was."

"Silvestri!" Carmine exclaimed. "He was there, so were Danny and Larry." He was halfway to the door in seconds. "I'll talk to him, so don't mention it to the others. For the time being, we sit on this."

John Silvestri listened raptly, intensely proud of his niece and in a lightning moment resolving to write to his uppity Oxford brother-in-law to the effect that Delia would leave more of a mark on history than her father would. Then reality crunched down and he concentrated on Delia's actual revelations. "Jesus H. Christ!" he said at the end of it. "What was that tricky bastard doing? There's no use asking me, Carmine, I'm as much in the dark as you are."

"Yes, John, but you were present," Carmine said. "We'd just had Julian, and weren't. Tell me what it was like, what went on. I need to get a picture of things."

Silvestri closed his eyes, the better to remember. "I guess it stayed in my mind better than these charity functions usually do because, to pinch a phrase from Stan Freberg, it ran on mink wheels. Smooth! We got three courses in an hour, so there was plenty of time for dancing and socializing without our needing to be there until after midnight. The food was good, and it was served without a hitch because of the sheer number of waiters and waitresses. Once the dessert plates were cleared, they kept the coffee and after-dinner drinks coming as fast as we wanted them. The coffee was good and kept hot, there was tea for those who wanted it. I remember we all agreed you couldn't find a thing to complain about."

Carmine listened intently, then zeroed in on one word. "You said there was time for socializing, John. What did you mean?"

"If you went to more big events instead of dodging them, Carmine, you'd know," the Commissioner said, deftly inserting a tiny shaft of reproach. "New York City this ain't. A lot of the people who go don't meet much anywhere else, so as soon as the coffee's on the table, they start table hopping to catch up. Like Elder Jesse Bateman of Busquash—I hardly ever see him, so when a couple at his table got up and went somewhere else, the wife and I joined them. It was a big dance floor and the band was playing Glenn Miller, but not everybody wants to dance. Table hopping is probably more popular than dancing."

"And there were two vacant chairs at the Fourth National table," Carmine said. "That means other people must have joined Norton and his guests." He let out an explosive sigh. "Somewhere in Holloman are a bunch of people who included Norton's table in their hopping. All I have to do is find them."

"Well, don't count on me," Silvestri said quickly. "I took one look at Desmond Skeps sitting there and steered a wide berth around the Fourth National. So did a lot of others, including the Mayor and his ass-kissers."

"Why?" Carmine asked, astonished at the Mayor's omission.

"Even long distance, anyone could see Skeps was as drunk as a skunk."

"Wow! So much for the temperance myth. A million thanks, sir. You've helped immeasurably."

He returned to his office in a very thoughtful mood, to find Corey and Abe leaning over the Maxwell Foundation plan of fifty round tables, each one labeled with its sponsor and number. The Fourth National table was number 17, with 16 to its left and 18 to its right. There were ten rows of five tables, number 17 near the north end and well away from any important Cornucopia table. Phil Smith's was number 43, Wal Grierson's 39, Fred Collins's 40. Everywhere around number 17 were tables of relative nonentities. So why did Desmond

Skeps sit there? Because he knew he'd be on the sauce? Or because, squiring Dee-Dee, he had to walk almost the length of the hall to reach number 17?

"So why with Peter Norton?" Carmine asked yet again.

"And why with Dee-Dee?" Corey asked yet again.

"Erica Davenport would have been his logical choice," Abe said.

"No way! He'd just dumped her as his mistress," Corey said, "and she was with her usual date, Gus Purvey."

"He was throwing dust in someone's eyes," Abe said positively. "For sure he invited himself to sit with Norton, who must have been over the moon at being noticed by the King of Kings."

"Who was blind drunk, apparently," Corey said.

"Yeah, but Norton wasn't to know that would happen when Skeps told him to reserve two places at his table," Abe countered.

"I wonder," Carmine asked dreamily, "how did women like Bianca and Cathy and the old lady see Dee-Dee? Especially if Skeps was as pissed as a newt. Even if they hadn't recognized Skeps, Norton or Denbigh would have enlightened them, but I doubt they were impressed. Evan Pugh would have known, but it wasn't in him to be impressed by anyone except himself. So I'd say the vacant chairs were on either side of Skeps and Dee-Dee. Beatrice, Cathy and Bianca must have been on tenterhooks—women tend to think that drunks are going to throw up all over the place."

"We should get a few answers from Gerald Cartwright," Corey said. "I'm sure Cathy would have told him about Skeps the drunk."

"Any bets she didn't?" Abe asked. "Whichever way we turn, it's the same old blank wall. Norton's wife is crazy, Cathy Cartwright was overworked and coping with Jimmy, Bianca and the poor old lady came alone and lived alone, the blacks lived in a world where Skeps didn't matter, and I doubt Denbigh and his wife engaged in pillow talk. Though it's weird that Marty Fane didn't say anything about Dee-Dee's date with Skeps. He was willing to do anything to help us track her killer down."

"I don't think Marty even knew," Carmine said. "Dee-Dee was loyal to him in her way, but if Skeps slipped her a couple of big ones, she'd have buttoned her mouth. She probably pretended to have the bug that was going around."

"We never get a break," Corey said.

"Yes, we do! Delia's given us the Maxwell banquet, and I call that a break." Carmine put his elbows on his desk and his chin on his hands. "Erica Davenport told me Skeps never had more than one drink a day. She even gave me a reason for it. But the longer I know them, the harder I find it to believe anything a Cornucopia Board member tells me. Add to them Philomena Skeps, Anthony Bera and Pauline Denbigh. The other thing eating at me is the certainty that our mastermind has an assistant here in Holloman, probably someone we don't even know. Definitely not someone who hangs around County Services or Malvolio's with his ears cocked for information. He doesn't need to."

"What makes you think there's an assistant rather than a series of hirelings?" Abe asked.

"Oh, there was that, but every master has an apprentice." Carmine straightened and gazed at them sternly. "One thing is for sure. Those eleven people died because of something that went down at Peter Norton's table. What we have to do is find out what it was."

"Locate any table hoppers who sat there?" Corey asked.

"Of course. Beatrice Egmont was popular, she must have had visitors. Abe, you have a list of her friends. Go ask all of them what happened at Norton's table. Some of them were bound to be at the banquet."

Carmine switched his attention to Corey. "You get to grill Gerald Cartwright. If his wife was too harassed to tell him about what happened, the fact that he insisted she go unaccompanied says he knew there would be plenty of friends there. Get their names and talk to them as well as Cartwright, Corey."

"While you," Abe said, "tackle Erica Davenport."

* * *

With Myron's departure Dr. Erica Davenport had diminished, though the hair, makeup and apparel could not be faulted. Today she wore a softly draped dress of lavender-blue, with matching eyes. Her walk had lost its imperiousness, and when she sat behind her lacquered desk she couldn't keep her hands still, had to fiddle with a pen, a file, her own perfectly manicured nails. She was near some kind of breaking point, but what kind eluded Carmine, for he knew she wasn't the mastermind any more than she was Ulysses. It was more, he decided, as if she had suddenly realized that she was far less important than she ought to be, and harbored a colossal sense of betrayal.

Why had four months elapsed between the Maxwell affair and the murders? Sitting facing the nominal Managing Director of Cornucopia Central, Carmine felt that if anybody knew the answer to that question, she did.

It took him a full ten seconds to force her to meet his stare; when she yielded and looked, he was staggered by the craze of fear, worry and sick desperation in her eyes. Jesus, what exactly did she know? How could he pry it out of her? She was near the breaking point, yes, but he wasn't capable of giving the blow necessary to make her fly apart. Suddenly he longed for Myron, understanding that Myron might be the only one who could. If ever a woman needed exquisite tenderness to break, she was Erica Davenport.

"Missing Myron?" he asked.

"Very much," she answered. "But I'm sure you're not here to pay condolences, Captain. What do you want?"

"All eleven of the people whose murders I am investigating were closely attached to the table sponsored by the Fourth National Bank at a function held more than four months ago," he said, watching her so intently that he hated needing to blink. "December third of last year, a Saturday night. It was a banquet held by the Maxwell Foundation."

"Yes, I remember it," she said, composed now. "I went with Gus Purvey and we sat at Phil Smith's table."

"Do you know where Desmond Skeps sat?"

Her smooth brow creased, her lids fell. "He was in an odd mood, I remember that. Not that it was unexpected. I had been informed that my amorous services were no longer wanted. His table was at the other end of the hall, and the people at it were unknown to me."

"Yet you visited the table." Say yes, Erica, say yes!

"Yes, as a matter of fact I did." She grimaced. "It was unpleasant, but I should have known it would be."

"How, unpleasant?"

"Des was drunk."

"Yet according to your own statement, Mr. Skeps had limited himself to one drink a day for many years. At the time you gave that statement, you didn't mention his lapse from grace at the Maxwell banquet."

"It only happened the once, Captain."

"Why?"

"Why the lapse from grace, you mean?"

"Yes."

"I have no idea, but if you think it was because he had done with me, you're mistaken, Captain. There was no love lost between us." She thought a moment, then said, "Nor liking."

"What about the woman with him at the table?"

She looked genuinely puzzled. "What woman? He was alone."

"A woman who stood six feet tall, and would have seemed tall even seated. To your eyes, very common. Some black blood, handsome face, bottle-blonde hair, a lot of makeup, busty. I think she probably wore a tight satin dress in a bright color—emerald green or shocking pink. Not scarlet. There may have been a white mink stole, the real thing."

Her face had cleared. "Oh! She was at the table, but she was sitting between an attractive young woman and an old lady with white hair who had trouble breathing. She didn't pay Des any attention, and he ignored her. Well, he was too drunk to see across the table—sloppy drunk. I couldn't understand a word he said, so I didn't stay long."

"If you sat next to Desmond Skeps, was there anyone on his other side?"

"Yes, a very fat man who overflowed his chair."

"And beyond him?"

"I couldn't see. The fat man blocked my view."

"Who sat next to you besides Skeps?"

"A rather repulsive young man who tried to put his hand on my leg. The women were all bunched together, and I didn't blame them. Even Dean Denbigh was unpleasant."

Carmine kept at her for some time, but learned nothing new. When he left, it was with a sense of failure.

Before the elevator arrived, he was joined by the male secretary, Richard Oakes, in the company of a man at least ten years his senior. When they all got in and wanted the first floor, Oakes shivered and drew as far away from Carmine as he could.

"Who's your companion, Mr. Oakes?" Carmine asked.

When Oakes proved too petrified to reply, the stranger did. "I'm not Mr. Oakes's companion," he said, sticking his jaw out. "I'm Lancelot Sterling of Accounting."

"Oh, the lovely boss! A tormentor as well as a gossip."

"Excuse me?"

"Forget it," Carmine said, and rode down the rest of the way in silence. Sterling gave him several nasty glances, but the look on Richard Oakes's face said aggression would be a mistake. No one at Cornucopia had talked, least of all Special Agent Ted Kelly, but somehow the story of the fisticuffs outside Malvolio's had reached the executive floors. No doubt Accounting would be next, if Oakes's expression was anything to go by.

On the first floor Oakes and Sterling, heads together, went to wait for an elevator down to the parking levels. Carmine walked outside to his Fairlane, which no traffic cop would have dreamed of ticketing.

Several days passed, during which Carmine, Abe, Corey and Delia strove to find a table hopper who had visited table 17.

Coming up with nothing, Carmine went back to Silvestri.

"I need one of your television news bulletins," he said to the Commissioner. "Something to the effect that anyone who had contact with Mr. Desmond Skeps at the Maxwell Foundation banquet four months ago should come forward, as vital information might be forthcoming."

"Thank God it hasn't leaked that everyone sitting there is dead. Don't worry, Carmine, I'll make it sound routine as well as vital," Silvestri promised.

He was as good as his word, but no one emerged from the woodwork, as he put it himself.

"Thwarted," said Delia.

"Stymied," said Abe.

"Fucked," said Corey.

None of which made Carmine any easier to live with, Desdemona reflected as the fourth week of investigations wore on. So she tried to cheer him with tasty meals and as much exposure to Julian as possible. This latter was helped by the case's inertia, as a thwarted, stymied, fucked Carmine was home much earlier than a busy, productive one.

Though Julian was not yet six months old, she wanted another baby as soon as possible, believing that siblings closest in age stood a better chance of getting on together. It was a fallacy, her mother-in-law kept telling her, but Desdemona could be very stubborn, and in this case, she was. So the arrival of her period cast her into a bleak mood that exasperated Emilia Delmonico into a rare burst of temper.

"Stop feeling sorry for yourself!" Emilia snapped. "Take the baby for a walk and soak up some sun. He's a Thanksgiving Day baby, he's never felt a warm sun. Now it's high spring, and a beautiful day outside. Enjoy it!"

"But I want to make a bearnaise sauce," Desdemona objected.

"Carmine would eat steak with no sauce at all. Now go!"

"I feel like an afternoon in my kitchen."

"You need to get out of your kitchen more often! What do you want, a fat Carmine with heart disease?"

"No, of course not, but—"

"But me no buts! Put Julian in the stroller and go for a walk, Desdemona."

"He's too young for the stroller."

"Hogwash! He sits up straight and holds his head up fine. It's good exercise for both of you. Now go! Go!"

Since Carmine had fitted the stroller with straps, Desdemona ran out of arguments. Taking care that Julian was able to lie back if he felt sleepy, his mother set off. Truth to tell, she admitted, their land was too steep for the buggy, and Julian in the stroller sat up looking around, alert and interested.

After a tour of East Circle her despondency began to lift; she even felt kindly toward her know-it-all mother-in-law. It was indeed a beautiful day of cloudless sky and zephyr breeze; May would come in perfect. At the top of the long, snaky path that led from the street down to the house, Desdemona decided that today Julian should have his first cognizant sight of an expanse of blue water: the harbor, never busy enough to be foul with detritus.

Feeling her lungs open up, she pushed the stroller down past the house in the direction of their jetty and boat shed, rejoicing in the lush greenery all around her. The forsythia had done with blooming and now formed dense hedges, replaced along the water's edge by salt-loving bushes. The property sat in a lee, and Connecticut was not usually hurricane country.

Where the wife of the previous owner had put a park bench, the view from the path to the water had been cleared. Desdemona sat and gazed down at her baby to see how he was faring. He was drinking it all in, eyes wide between their lush lashes, silent witness to Emilia's wisdom. Yes, less time in the kitchen, more walking with Julian. She undid his straps and lifted him out to sit on her lap, her cheek against his curls, inhaling his sweet clean smell. My baby, my Julian!

The path here was sandy, and, true of many big people, Desdemona was light on her feet. Even after she and Julian sat, she made no sound, while he, a quiet child by nature, absorbed this new, wonderful experience. He will be a man of few words, she thought.

Perhaps two minutes went by before Desdemona realized that there was someone in the boat shed, moving things around; the water slapped and sloshed suddenly, as if greatly disturbed. As she turned her head to look, the door opened and a man came out. He was clad in woodsy camouflage and had pulled what she called a balaclava over his head, concealing all save his eyes and mouth under its khaki wool. In his right hand he held an automatic pistol, his demeanor that of someone who didn't expect to be discovered, but was prepared.

With the baby, she would never make it up the hill, that was her immediate reaction. Even as she saw him, he saw her, and the gun came up. Sure of her, he took his time; he meant to get her with his first shot. Her wide blue eyes sought the apertures in the balaclava, gaze pleading for her child; she even extended the baby a little toward him, as if to show him the enormity of the crime he was about to commit. The gesture didn't deflect him from his purpose, but moving the baby had spoiled his aim. He leveled the weapon again, going now for a head shot. That told the policeman's wife all she needed to know: the man was an expert shot, he wouldn't miss.

In the same instant Desdemona slapped one big hand over Julian's mouth and nose, and dived for the water twenty feet away in a vast double leap. She hit it holding the baby to one side, her big feet using the bank to push off before she dived again as deeply as she dared given the tidal slope. Her mind was racing—where to go? Julian was hugged against her now, but fighting her more strongly than she had expected; he couldn't breathe, but he was determined to.

The dive had taken her sideways in the opposite direction from the jetty, and she came up where salt-loving bushes grew thickly between the path and the water. When her hand released Julian's face he sucked in a lungful of air preparing to bellow, but she clamped her hand down again as she sucked in her own air, and dived once more.

The water was freezing. She knew she didn't have much time before it slowed her down too much to resurface, but Julian was her baby, hers and Carmine's, and she wasn't about to let him die. Icy water or not, she had to get off their property and onto the Silberfeins'. These neighbors had built on a narrow lot too near the water, the old fogeys said. For Desdemona, salvation.

By her fifth dive Julian was getting the hang of it, or at least that was what his mother thought; he would suck in the air, then push himself against her body without trying to fight her. But seven dives were as many as she could manage. If her enemy was waiting on the shore, she was done. She put the baby down on dry bank and crawled up beside him, exhausted. If the tide had not been in, the exposed bank would have been far wider, barnacled, slippery. No shot came. She hugged Julian to her again and dragged herself up the Silberfeins' yard, calling for help. Over, it was over!

Once he had assured himself that his wife and son were safe and relatively unscathed, Carmine banished the awful helplessness, the unmanning knowledge that Desdemona had had to save herself. Shock and horror insisted that he should have been there to defend her and Julian, but a wealth of experience and sheer common sense said that would be impossible nine times out of every ten. This was not the first time Desdemona had had to save herself; what he prayed was that it would be the last. Inside himself he would shake for days, weep the wakeful nights away, but that Carmine was not the Carmine he could show either to his world or to his wife. It was not a machismo issue; it was his heritage, his nature and his duty. Maybe, he thought, I have been blessed. I have been split open to the very firmament of my being by the knowledge that today I nearly lost my family. At last I realize exactly what they mean to me. Literally everything.

His mother was in worse shape than Desdemona and Julian; she blamed herself for making them go walking. The house was milling with sisters, aunts and female cousins, so he turned her over to them and Doc Santini. Only time and a lot of arguments would eventually see her mend. Julian had come through his ordeal with his psyche apparently unscarred; that, at least, was what Doc Santini thought after the baby, his stomach full, went to sleep in his crib looking and acting not a scrap differently than always. Warm from a bath and wrapped in a thick robe, Desdemona seated herself in an easy chair beside Julian's crib and refused to budge.

Later, thought Carmine, walking down the same path to the jetty. Right now she's hardly aware of me, and I'm not intruding my police presence between her and the sight of Julian.

Patrick and his team were outside the boat shed, talking to Abe and Corey. Near them on a fairly flat piece of ground was a canvas enclosure.

Erica Davenport's twisted body had been pulled out of the water and lay inside the enclosure. The slope was too steep for a gurney; she would have to be stretchered up to the road.

"Her legs and arms were broken a considerable time before she died," Patrick said to Carmine, "and each in two places—tib-fib and femur for the legs, ulna-radius and humerus for the arms. Death was due to strangulation by what I guess was thin rope."

"Different again," Carmine said.

"How are the folks?" Patsy asked.

"Unharmed, according to Doc Santini. Mom's the basket case. She blames herself."

"You have a wife in a billion."

"I know it. I'll be in to Cedar Street soon."

"We can manage," Abe said.

"That's not an issue, it never would be. The fact is that I'm in the way here—my home has been taken over by two dozen women, all likely to tear Holloman apart if we don't find who tried to kill a woman holding a baby," Carmine said, meaning it. "I feel the same way myself. First my daughter, now my wife and son. We must be closer to the fucker than we know."

*　　*　　*

The entire police segment of County Services was boiling; as Carmine came in, cops clustered around him, offering to do anything they could. Getting through the crush took time, but it gladdened his heart too. Despite the empty pit that yawned within him, he suddenly knew that the mastermind's days were numbered. The man had lost his cool, gotten too arrogant. Of course he hadn't planned on killing Desdemona and the baby, but he had decided to send Carmine a warning by stranding Erica Davenport under the water of his boat shed. In broad daylight! *Something* had happened at the Maxwell banquet, and for four months all had seemed well. Then Evan Pugh sent a blackmailing letter, and within four days every witness of the *something* was dead. So around about March twenty-ninth another something had happened—something that the killer was afraid would expose him for all the world to see.

"We need a living witness," he said to Abe and Corey when he made it in to his office.

"To what went on at Peter Norton's table?" Corey asked.

"Yes, but we also need a living witness to whatever incident or event triggered Evan Pugh's blackmail attempt. I think Erica Davenport knew, and now she's dead. I could kick myself for not talking Myron out of flying home! When I saw her, I realized that she was laboring under some burden she couldn't keep on carrying, and I wished for Myron. If he'd been here, it might have come out." Carmine passed a hand across his face. "Now I have to tell him she's dead."

"We'll get out of your way," said Abe.

It was a long call. Though he wept, Myron wasn't wounded to the core.

"I guess I've been expecting something like this," he said. "Maybe because I think *she* was expecting something like it. I can't say her own death, but definitely something awful. She was so glad to see me go! Not like she was sick of the sight of me, more as if I was just another worry. The trouble was, I couldn't get her to tell me what was making her afraid."

Carmine let him wander on, hating to make his suffering worse, but he had to be told how she died in case some fool in the know let it slip. Fools like Phil Smith or Fred Collins, constantly met in New York boardrooms.

And finally, after all that, Carmine had to tell him about Desdemona and Julian.

"Carmine, you've got to get them away!" he cried, real terror in his voice. "Listen, I was planning to ask if I could have Sophia for a while—she can finish her school year in L.A., it won't set her back—"

"You can have her, Myron," Carmine said. "I'd rest easier if she weren't here, I confess."

"Okay, okay, great, that's great, but that's not what I was going to say!" Myron yelled so loudly that Carmine had to hold the receiver away from his ear. "I'm sending some money to Desdemona, and you're going to take her and Julian to London. And shut up, Carmine! I won't take no for an answer!"

"The answer has to be no, Myron. Number one, I'm a public servant and can't take money from millionaires—nor can my wife, that's implicit. Number two, I'm in the middle of a case I can't leave," Carmine said patiently, ignoring the squawks in his ear. "And why London, of all places?"

"Because Desdemona wanted to live there before she married you, and because it's the other side of the Atlantic from this killer," Myron said.

"I appreciate the gesture more than I can say, you old fart, but it's impossible. Leave it there, please."

But it was a long call. By the time Carmine hung up, he was tired. Arguments were at the top of his pet hate list, whereas to Myron they were the food and drink of existence.

Abe and Corey weren't in their office. Carmine went to see Patrick, hankering for a friendly face.

"You've told Myron?"

"Yes. He took it well, all considered. The best part of it is that he's taking Sophia for a while. She'll be very happy to go, they'll spoil each other rotten, and I won't need to worry about her. I don't think this motherfucking killer will bother hiring someone to murder her in L.A."

"Me neither. And, if it's any consolation, I don't think he would have tried to kill Desdemona if she hadn't caught him in the boat shed. A pity, though, that she's not from Montana or New Mexico—it would be good to have a place to send her."

"That's what Myron says, except that his solution is for me to accept a large sum of money and take Desdemona and Julian to London for the duration."

Patrick laughed, then turned to his autopsy table. It was draped with a sheet. When he removed it, Carmine was forced to look at Erica Davenport's naked body, its arms and legs grossly swollen, misshapen and discolored, its face blue-black with tongue protruding, its trunk so unmarred and proper that it did not look as if it belonged to the extremities.

"Poor woman," Carmine said.

"Poor indeed," Patrick said, voice grim.

"What, Patsy?"

"At some time in her late teens or early twenties she was brutally raped, how many times I don't know, but multiple. Anal as well as vaginal, devices as well as penises. The scar tissue would have prevented much cavorting in a bed—she must have been terrified that a lover would notice. Skeps must have, if his relationship with her was as long-term as Philomena Skeps says. I found out when I was washing her."

Carmine leaned against the tiled wall. "That answers so much, Patsy."

"I thought it would."

"When's the full autopsy?"

"I was going to do it now, but this discovery will make it a longer business, so first thing tomorrow morning." Patrick's vivid blue eyes had dimmed; he loathed posting rape victims. "Who will bury her, Carmine?"

"Myron. He wasn't as surprised as he ought have been, because she gave him her will before he left. He's appointed executor. Her estate—I have no idea what it's worth—goes to Women Against Rape. I add that she fooled Myron, he didn't know she was a rape victim herself. Something else I have to tell him! As to Cornucopia, her guardianship of Desmond Skeps the Third, she made no mention. She must have known that if anything were to happen to her, Philomena Skeps's case for total custody of her son would be much stronger. The mastermind must have known that too, which suggests that, whatever he's all about, it's not control of Cornucopia. My, won't the dogs be snarling there!"

"Go home, Carmine" was Patsy's reply.

Carmine went home.

His house had emptied of the women, including his mother, but there were police patrolling the grounds and an air of urgency. News of what had happened had spread throughout East Holloman with even greater speed than usual. The Silberfeins, his closest neighbors, had risen to the emergency splendidly from the moment Sam Silberfein found Desdemona in their yard. Ordinarily he would have been at his dry cleaning business, but Sylvia hadn't been well that morning, and he had stayed home. By the time Carmine arrived, an ambulance with a physician's assistant on board had dealt with Julian, chilled to the bone but otherwise little the worse for wear. The problem had been Desdemona, who wouldn't leave Julian even to get out of her wet clothes, and was blue with cold. It was Carmine who persuaded her to go home complete with Julian and the medic, Carmine who thanked the Silberfeins ardently, fervently, Carmine who peeled off Desdemona's clothes and gave Julian a bottle of breast milk from his mother's refrigerated reserves while she warmed up in a bath of tepid water.

When he came into the bedroom she was still sitting near the crib, which normally stood in the nursery next door. She had managed to get her feet under her and sat hunched over, eyes on the sleeping baby.

Carmine didn't try to lure her away. He found another chair and put it down opposite hers, but not where it impeded her view of Julian. Her face was dry, though because of her huddled posture he couldn't tell if she was shaking. Her expression was of flintlike hardness, but her eyes held absolute love.

"It's time to give me some details," he said, matter-of-fact.

"Ask away."

"Can you describe the guy?"

"His size, yes. About average—not tall, not short. I think he was a fit man. His reflexes were quick. His pistol was an automatic, but I imagine a .22. There was no silencer, so a big round would have sounded loud. I certainly didn't hear a shot, and I presume he shot that poor woman in the boat shed?"

"No, she was strangled," Carmine said quietly. "The handgun must have been for emergencies. You were an emergency."

"What I have to sort out in my mind, dear love, is my fear," she said steadily. "I can do that better if I can see Julian. It wouldn't be logical or sensible to skulk about for the next however-many years expecting something like that to happen again, but that's what I want to do. Somehow I have to put today behind me, and Julian says I can do that. Look at him! He went for his first swim and his first underwater dive, he didn't have a clue what was happening to him, but he had Mummy."

"He's also not old enough to remember," his father said.

"We won't know that until he sees the Harbor again, or perhaps is taken into a swimming pool, or has a paddle at Busquash Beach. If there are buried memories, they'll surface."

"No one knows that for sure. Look at him, Desdemona! Our son is peacefully asleep. Has he woken in distress? Thrashed around in his crib?"

"No," she said.

"I'm not worried about him—half of him is me," Carmine said with a smile. "You're doing the English thing, bottling it all up, using logic to repress it. You wouldn't be human if you didn't carry some scars out of this, and the most prominent will be fear that it might happen again. My mother—who blames herself terribly, I should tell you—will certainly be a basket case for months. If you really want that little brother or sister for Julian, you can't let today rule your life. But not by doing mental gymnastics, my lovely lady. Just by keeping busy and enjoying what you've got—what *we've* got. You can't let that bastard ruin us, ruin our family. Stop thinking so much about how to forget it. Time will do that for you, it always does." He played his trump card. "After all, Desdemona, you came out on top! Nothing worse than a freezing swim happened to you and Julian. You're a heroine, just like that vaulting exercise on the outside of the Nutmeg building. Today should reinforce your confidence in yourself, not destroy it."

Finally she smiled and turned her gaze from son to husband. "Yes, I do see that." She unwound, shivering. "Oh, but I was terrified! For what seemed an eternity I didn't know how I could get away, then I looked at the water—*really* looked—and saw that the tide was right in. It's a steep slope underwater there, I knew it was deep enough for me to disappear. Once I had my plan, I was all right. Poor little Julian!" Her eyes filled with wonder. "Oh, Carmine, do you realize that on both occasions I would have died if I weren't so big? When I did all that vaulting on the Nutmeg, I was fit from lots of hiking, but today has made me realize that I need to get my fitness back. I've been lazy for over twelve months, and it showed today. It's lucky the man gave up, because I was done when I crawled out. If Sam hadn't been in his garden, we might have died."

"Hiking is no longer an option," he said, pulling her into his chair and holding her across his knees. "How about joining a gym? One of these new fitness clubs?"

"No, I'll exercise in my own home, thank you very much. I know it's silly, but I want to keep Julian with me," she said.

"As long as you don't smother him when he gets a bit older. Over-protective mothers don't do their children any service," Carmine said.

"I promise I won't smother him later. Mind you, I probably couldn't," she said. "Half of him *is* you. And thank you for your kindness, dear heart. I feel much better. What else do you need to know?"

"More about the man's appearance."

"His face was hidden by a khaki balaclava."

"A what?"

"A balaclava. A knitted thing that's pulled over the head and has two holes for the eyes and one hole for the mouth. I never got very close to him—I was on the seat, and he came out of the little door on the side of the boat shed. What's that, forty or fifty feet? I could see the flash of his eyes, but not their color or shape, and his brows were covered. He wore gloves."

"A ski mask," said Carmine.

"Yes, exactly! He was wearing camouflage—khaki, green, olive, dark green in patches like a Frisian cow—a closed jacket and rather baggy trousers stuffed into army boots. While I've been sitting watching Julian, I realized that his garb meant he'd come along the shore. He would have been hard to see if he was among the bushes."

"How quickly did you see the gun?"

"At once. He was vigilant but quite relaxed, but the moment he saw me he lifted the gun. One thing I know, Carmine. He was an expert marksman. When I spoiled his aim by moving, he chose to aim for my head. At that distance and with a light weapon, he couldn't afford to miss. You see?" she asked proudly. "I'm married to a policeman, I know the ropes."

"He must have been watching our house for long enough to think he knew our movements. That goddamn telescope in Skeps's penthouse! It was focused on the East Holloman shore. After I found it, it disappeared. But someone kept right on using it." Carmine hugged her, kissed her face. "I thought it was just a prurient interest—and it may have been, for Skeps. But someone else had a more practical use for a telescope."

"And whoever it was," she said excitedly, "would never have seen anyone in our front garden! I'd been too pregnant for the slope, then I had Julian, and it was winter. Today was my first trip down to the water's edge in yonks and yonks!" Suddenly she began to tremble. "Oh, Carmine, what if Julian had still been strapped into his stroller? We would have died!"

He rocked her back and forth; he'd already been in this place himself. "Julian wasn't, Desdemona! He was sitting on your knee. I guess that means that somebody up there likes you."

A good howl and a fit of the shakes helped get the shock out of her system. By the time it passed, she was beginning to return to the ordinary world.

"I've got nothing for your dinner!" she said.

"I brought pizza."

"Sophia! How could I forget Sophia?"

"Patsy's taking her to JFK. Myron wants her."

Whereupon Julian woke, hungry but otherwise himself.

Carmine sat and watched his wife feed his son, battling to banish the demons. The trouble, he thought, was that Desdemona mistook her importance in his police scheme of things. Holloman was small enough for his wife to have her own presence, and she drew enmity to herself like a magnet drew iron filings. It was her size, the dignity that went with it, her air of invulnerability. If his enemies hated him, they also hated her, but in her own right. Desdemona was not a princess: she was sovereign.

May 1967

The death of Erica Davenport was the epi-center of a human earthquake; it shook people and their constructions to their foundations, from the chief executives of Cornucopia, through Carmine Delmonico and his family, all the way to the FBI.

"But she's Ulysses!" Ted Kelly insisted, seeking out Carmine in his office at County Services. "We've known that for two years!"

"Then why didn't you arrest her?"

"Evidence! It's called evidence? No matter where we went, no matter what we unearthed, we could never find a shred of evidence against her that would stand up in court. If we'd tried her, she would have walked, and in a blaze of publicity that would have harmed our image as much as it enhanced hers."

"That's because she wasn't Ulysses," Carmine said. "I have actually heard of evidence, Ted, and it wasn't there for the simple reason that Erica Davenport wasn't Ulysses. I think she knew who Ulysses is, but that's a far cry from being him. And you know what, Special Agent Kelly? I don't like your attitude any more today than I did when I put your big ass on the ground. You're as thick as two planks."

"She was Ulysses, I tell you!" Kelly smacked his fists on his thighs, beat them up and down in frustration. "We'd just finished planning the neatest sting operation in espionage history—she couldn't have resisted the bait, she'd have gone to her drop and we'd have been waiting. Now—*Fuck!*"

"You found out where her drop is?" Carmine asked, looking astonished and ingenuous.

"This one," Special Agent Kelly said in goaded tones, then embarked on a tutorial. "Spies have a list of drop sites, they never use the same one twice. Their list is coded and they work through it. They have signals to alert their contact that something is going to be dropped, usually in a deserted spot like woods or an abandoned factory—"

"Or identical briefcases, or a package taped under a seat on a bus, or the fourth brick from the right seventeen rows from the top," Carmine finished with a grin. "Come on, Kelly! All that's horseshit, and you know it. The wad of money—the spy who can't name his contact because he doesn't know who his contact is—what a load of crap. First off, whoever's doing this isn't in it for the money or the intellectual thrill. He's an ideologue, in it for the greater glory of Mother Russia, or Marx and Lenin—a Communist ideology, anyway. Secondly, the stolen item is passed openly, after a phone call or a fax from a number no one could know about. You can't tap every phone in the country, or intercept every telex. No matter how fanatically you watch any individual, if he's as smart as Ulysses he'll pass his information right under your noses and you'll never see or smell it. You can't seriously expect me to believe that you and the FBI don't know how important in himself Ulysses is! Which means he rides around big cities in a limo, uses private facilities when he has to go, has the run of five-star hotels, eats in places where you and I couldn't afford the water in the finger bowls—how am I doing, Ted?"

"Ulysses was Erica Davenport," Kelly said stubbornly.

"Ulysses is alive and well and slipped a noose around that poor woman's neck," Carmine said harshly. "Not, however, before he broke her arms and legs in two places each, to be sure how much she knew and whom she might have told."

The mask fell completely. In a second the clumsy, slightly dense, distinctly lower-grade FBI agent disappeared, to be replaced by a highly trained, highly professional, intelligent and capable man.

"I give in," Ted Kelly said ruefully. "They warned me you were hard to dupe, but I had to try. The last thing I need or want is anyone at Cornucopia thinking I might be in your league at sniffing out wrongdoers. I want Ulysses to think I'm a dumb official of a dumb institution, and so do my bosses. It's okay for you, you're hunting a murderer. You can get farther by spreading your tail and peacocking your skill, but my quarry's different. I have to pretend I haven't got to first base even when I'm stealing home. My man doesn't make mistakes."

"He is these days," Carmine said, leaning forward in his chair. "All of a sudden, Mr. Kelly, you and I are hunting the selfsame predator. I've known for some time that my killer is your Ulysses. No, it's not a guess. It's fact." He glanced at his railroad clock. "Got a spare half hour?"

"Sure."

"Then I'll hang out the Do Not Disturb signs."

This consisted in closing his doors and routing all his calls through Delia. Then Carmine returned to his desk and told Ted Kelly why he knew that Ulysses had murdered eleven people who sat down to enjoy a charity banquet five months ago.

"So you see," he concluded, "it may end in our getting hard evidence not of espionage but of murder. Is that going to be a problem for the FBI?"

"Anything but," Special Agent Ted Kelly said. "Learning there are spies inside the city gates is very alarming for the general populace. You're welcome to the glory. I'll slink back to Washington happily looking like a fool. That way, I'm in good shape for the next traitor."

"I'm not after glory!" Carmine snapped.

"I know, but if we catch the fucker, someone has to shine and it can't be me. All I can say is, if you do catch him—no, *when* you catch him!—he can't ever be let out of prison."

"He won't have done anything to warrant a federal trial or a federal prison," Carmine said, "and Connecticut is a liberal-minded state. None of us can predict what some fool parole board of the future might decide. They're always stacked with idealists."

243

Kelly rose to his immense height and held out his hand to shake Carmine's warmly. "I wouldn't worry," he said cheerfully. "His parole board will be stacked with believers in recidivism. I forgive you for calling me a cunt. I behaved atrociously."

"In public," Carmine said, steering him toward the outer door, "we continue the pretense—flattened ears, bared teeth and snarls every time we meet. What, by the way, was on the film you took from the telescope camera?"

"Nothing worth reporting on," Kelly said. "Just Holloman Harbor's shoreline from the Long Island ferry wharf clear to the point beyond East Holloman. Tide in, tide out. We figured it might have had something to do with a meeting or a drop."

There was no one in the hall; Special Agent Ted Kelly went down it in three long strides and vanished into the stairwell. As soon as he had gone, Carmine went to see Delia.

"Our federal turkey is no turkey," he said, grinning. "He's an eagle, but if you catch sight of his wingspan while he's in turkey mode, he'll convince you he's really a buzzard."

"A very strange bird," said Delia solemnly.

"Any news?" he asked.

"Not a sausage. Abe and Corey have exhausted their lists of those who might have sat at Peter Norton's table, without any responses. I daresay people simply forget. No, don't go! The Commissioner wants to see you. Now, he shouted. I fear Uncle John is not in a good mood."

If the expression on Commissioner Silvestri's face was an indication, "not in a good mood" was putting it mildly. Carmine stood to take his medicine.

"What's the bastard going to do next?" Silvestri asked.

An innocuous question; he was going to be oblique. "That depends on whether he was in my boat shed himself or not."

"Why?"

"The assistant is extremely valuable, yes, sir, but expendable nonetheless. My feeling is that he stayed in the Bat Cave and sent Robin to my boat shed."

"Slimy rodent! How's Desdemona?"

"No different than she was the last time you asked, sir." Carmine looked at his watch. "That was an hour ago."

"And your mother?" Silvestri asked, squirming in his seat.

"Ditto."

"I hear Myron's managed to get Erica Davenport's body out of police custody and is flying her to L.A. for burial."

Carmine eyed his boss curiously. "Where did you hear that?"

A look of discomfort came over the Commissioner's face. "I—uh—I was talking to him."

"Phone or flesh?" Carmine asked warily.

"Phone. Sit down, man, sit down!"

His wariness growing, Carmine sat. "Spit it out, John!"

"That's no way to speak to your superior."

"My patience is finite, *sir.*"

"I guess you know how important Myron is?"

"I do," said Carmine, waiting for it.

"The thing is, he's buzzing around in Hartford like a wasp inside a pair of shorts."

"Angry, pushy and trapped."

"Those, plus a lot else. He wants Erica Davenport's murder put as our number one priority, and the Governor thinks that's appropriate, given the publicity."

"Myron leaked the story himself," Carmine said.

"Yeah, well, we all know that. But the Governor wants him buzzing somewhere far away from Hartford. He's got this bee in his bonnet—"

"Wasps, now bees. Just tell me!"

"I'm sending you to London to investigate Dr. Davenport's time there as a student." Silvestri coughed. "An anonymous benefactor has donated funds to send your wife and baby with you because of the recent attempt on their lives. Hartford has made a special grant to fund your own trip," Silvestri ended, shutting his eyes on the gathering storm.

There were only two ways to go. One would ruin his entire day, the other would at least allow him to vent some kind of emotion. Carmine chose the other, and laughed until he cried.

"Fuck a duck!" He gasped, clutching his sides. "I can't go to London, I just can't! The minute I'm away, all hell will break loose. Surely you can see that, John?"

"Of course I can! And I said so! But I may as well have saved my breath. This investigation is being run as a political football, thanks to Myron Mandelbaum."

"He means well, but he should butt out of what he doesn't understand. His trouble is that he tends to see life as a movie—everything happens at the speed of light and no one pauses to think. An odyssey to London won't help me find a killer or a spy, but it might let him get away." Carmine groaned.

"I know, I know."

"Did Hartford lay down any conditions? Like, how long I have to stay away?"

"Considering strains on the budget, I'd think the quicker you're back, the better. The anonymous benefactor can't bankroll a public servant."

"Any bets?"

"How can I help?" Silvestri asked.

"Run interference with Hartford for me. It's Desdemona and Julian preying on Myron's mind, so if I come back in a couple of days, I'll have to leave them in London for a few days more. If I can find the name of someone who can tell me about Erica's time there before I leave Holloman, it will help. I can fly back as soon as I've milked the thing dry," Carmine said.

"Delia! Put her on finding that name, Carmine."

"She's the one should be going to England."

"Yeah, yeah, I agree, but Myron wouldn't. However," said the Commissioner, looking conspiratorial, "we might be able to throw some dust in everybody's eyes. Don't tell a soul where you're going, just give it out that you're moving your family out of Holloman for a while, and drive off to JFK as if you're going to L.A. I'll talk to Myron and put the fear of a Catholic Hell in his Jewish soul. He's to tell everyone that Desdemona and Julian are going to stay with him. It makes sense, so I doubt you'll be tailed to the airport, at least as far as the departure gates. That way, if you can finish London in two or three days, no one will get too cocky at your absence."

In the end only Delia and John Silvestri knew where Carmine took his wife and son two days later. After some thought he also decided to confide in Ted Kelly, who could bumble around Cornucopia telling all and sundry that Carmine had gone to L.A. and could arrive back on the next plane if things got out of hand.

Desdemona was relieved and excited, explaining to the women of Carmine's family that she was looking forward to revisiting the place where she had honeymooned: Myron's Hampton Court Palace. That gentleman's lavish hand was everywhere, Carmine discovered; they were picked up at their house by a limousine that had enough space in its nether regions to hold a small party, and whisked onto their 707 aircraft without joining the crush of people waiting to board. Though Carmine objected that his own ticket was economy even if his wife and son were traveling first class, he was put next to them in first class because, the chief hostess said smoothly, he had been upgraded. It didn't escape his notice that the rest of the first-class passengers shuddered to see an infant and popped extra pills to ensure that they slept through a wailing baby. They needn't have bothered, he thought with an inward grin; Julian enjoyed the experience, wincing as ascent and descent altered the pressure on his eardrums, but not howling. To him it must be small potatoes after Holloman Harbor.

"I prefer a train," said Desdemona, thoroughly bored.

Myron had put them in the Hilton, clever enough to know that London's luxury hotels were not well endowed with big elevators, level floors, high doorways and vast beds; Desdemona needed room, especially in an elevator with a baby buggy. Thus, the Hilton.

It wasn't his first visit to London by any means, and Delia had given Carmine a name: Professor Hugh Lefevre. She had even arranged an appointment for him: eleven the next morning, at the professor's residence in St. John's Wood. Apparently Dr. Lefevre didn't care to eat out at a restaurant, even an expensive one; Carmine could have a cup of tea, he told Delia.

Expecting some degree of affluence, Carmine trod a street of conjoined houses, rather dilapidated, faintly Georgian, each with a flight of dirty steps leading up to a front door alongside which was a panel of handwritten names. He found his house, went up its steps and discovered that H. Lefevre lived in 105, up a dingy staircase in a dingy hall. There was no bell connection, and 105 of course was not the ground floor. A glance at his watch informed him that he was on time, so he bounded up the dark stairs onto a landing with five doors. His was the back one, would look down on whatever passed for a yard behind the house. He knocked.

"Enter!" said a voice.

Sure enough, the knob turned and the door opened. Carmine stepped into a large room lit only by two windows and the grace of a heavily overcast day. Like the whole house, it was dingy. The wallpaper had faded and peeled, the thick velvet curtains were stained, and the furniture, a mixture of styles, was chipped and battered if wooden or oozing stuffing if upholstered. Books lay everywhere, including a wall of shelves. The desk was piled with papers, and a small manual typewriter sat on a low table to one side of the desk chair, which rotated to face it or the desk.

A man standing by one window turned to face Carmine as he advanced with hand extended to his host, who shook it.

"Professor Lefevre?"

"That is I. Be seated, Captain Delmonico."

"Whereabouts, sir?"

"There will do. Where the light falls on your face. Hmm! Women must make utter fools of themselves over you. It's a New World look—America, Australia, South Africa—makes no difference. The Old World look is softer, less blatantly masculine."

"I haven't noticed any women making utter fools of themselves over me," Carmine said, smiling easily. It was a good technique, flattering him yet making him uncomfortable. Well, two can play at that game, Professor. He gazed about, seeming puzzled. "Is this the best England can do for a full professor?" he asked.

"I am a Communist, Captain. It is not a part of my ethic to submerge myself in comfort when so many people know none."

"But your private way of life can't benefit them, sir."

"That is not the point! The point is that I *choose* to live in a spartan fashion to display my ethic to people like you, who do live in comfort. I imagine your house has every luxury."

Carmine laughed. "I wouldn't say every luxury, just those that mean my wife doesn't have to drudge nor my child know the horror of monotony."

Ah, a hit! Professor Hugh Lefevre stiffened in his chair, no easy feat for one being devoured by arthritis. Twenty years ago when Erica Davenport had been his student, he must have had a certain attraction for women, been tall, probably moved with languid grace and enjoyed his handsomeness, a thing of straight thin nose, black brows and lashes, a wealth of black hair worn long, and cornflower blue eyes. The remnants of it still showed, but pain and an unnecessary degree of hardship had chewed away at him, outside as well as inside. Warm air, decent food and some help keeping house would have held his diseases at bay. But no, Carmine thought, he had an ethic, and now, when I said "the horror of monotony" to him, he reacted like a steer to a goad.

"What do you do with your money?" Carmine asked, curious.

"Donate it to the Communist Party."

"Where, in all likelihood, some lip-service member uses it to live in comfort."

"It is not so! We are all believers."

Time to stop annoying him. Carmine leaned forward. "I'm sorry, Professor, I don't mean to denigrate you or your ideals. My secretary told you—I'm glad you have a phone, by the way—that I need some background on Dr. Erica Davenport, who was one of your students, as I understand it."

"Ah, Erica!" the old man said, smiling to reveal bad teeth. "Why should I answer your questions? Is there a new McCarthy in the Senate? Is she being persecuted by your capitalist government? You've had a wasted trip, Captain."

"Erica Davenport is dead. She was murdered in a particularly brutal way, after a torture that consisted of breaking all the bones in her arms and legs," Carmine said steadily. "I'm not a capitalist tool, I'm simply the homicide detective assigned to investigate her death. Her political views are not my concern. Her murder is."

Lefevre wept a little in the easy way of the old; too many cracks develop in the emotional dam wall as the years go by, Carmine thought. And the old man had felt something for her.

"Just tell me what she was like twenty years ago, sir."

"Like?" The faded blue eyes widened. "Like the sun, the stars! Ablaze with life and enthusiasm, champing at the bit to change the world. We were all very left at the L.S.E.—in fact, we were famous for it. She arrived already indoctrinated to some extent, so to finish the process was easy. When I discovered that she spoke fluent Russian, I understood her future importance. I allowed her to think she had seduced me, then I went to work to—I believe the phrase is, 'turn her.' Naturally Moscow was interested, especially after I learned how able and intelligent she was. The chance to insert a sleeper in some huge American business enterprise was too good to miss. But she began to dither—demur, even."

"Why so frank, Professor? Aren't you talking to me about your treason as well as hers?"

"What treason? I've never done a thing," Lefevre said smugly. "There's nothing at the L.S.E. would interest Moscow apart from persons." He stopped suddenly and looked at Carmine in confusion. "Tea! You're here for a cup of tea," he said.

"Thanks, I don't need one. Go on about Erica."

"My superiors in the Party took over and arranged for Erica to go to Moscow and meet all the most important people. It was done on a special passport the KGB prepared for her, while her own passport was stamped to show a pilgrimage to the classical world, and she was equipped with souvenirs. Considering that the cold war was just commencing, Moscow was very careful with Erica, who might have to wait a very long time before she was activated."

Lefevre got up and went to the window, staring down into a yard filled with unkempt long grass and rusting pieces of junk—old kerosene heaters, chamber pots, tin trunks. No discarded washing machines here, Carmine thought, coming to gaze over the old man's shoulder. The tenants must all belong to the Communist Party.

"So Erica went off to Moscow in the summer of 1948?"

"Yes." Lefevre stopped again, frowning and pulling at his lower lip. Sighing, he returned to his chair.

"What happened in Moscow?"

"The first trip—three weeks—went splendidly. Erica returned in alt—over the moon. She had met all the members of the Central Committee, and held Josef Stalin's hand. He wasn't terribly well, you know. Then she had to return to Moscow for her training, and Moscow wanted to be absolutely sure of her loyalty. It was a nine-week sojourn. For anyone else it would have been longer, but she was an apt pupil, on fire with zeal. Also capable of significantly contributing to her story."

He stopped again, clearly distressed. Had it not been for the news of her horrifying death, Carmine knew, he would have fished in vain for any of this. No doubt FBI and CIA agents had encountered him in their own enquiries when Ulysses first came on the scene, and he had stuck to Erica's "pilgrimage" to the classical world. Luck travels with the harbinger of death, Carmine thought. He's old, lonely and by-passed. Now he can talk about her without endangering her.

"You've already told me she was a traitor, Professor. What else is there to know?"

He finally took the plunge. "On her last night in Moscow, Erica was raped. From what she told me, it was at a drunken dinner attended by Party officials and KGB officers just below the top ranks. Why they picked on her I don't know, save that she had been highly favored by their superiors, she was American, very beautiful, and not sexually generous."

"It was a terrible rape," Carmine said softly. "On autopsy twenty years later, she still bore the physical scars. How did she survive, sir?"

"Bound herself up and came back to London as arranged. To me. I sent her to Guy's Hospital, where I had a friend. It was manic in those days, battling with the teething troubles of the National Health. We arranged that her medical records should get lost in the system. London was a very different place then. The country was still on ration books for food, it was difficult to get decent clothes—a fruitful situation for us teaching in institutions of higher learning. Some very promising students fell into our hands like ripe peaches."

"What about Erica? She must have returned from Moscow that second time changed out of all recognition," Carmine said.

"In one way, yes. In another, no. The fire had gone, but an icy determination took its place. She abjured all sexual activity until someone in high authority made her understand that sex is a beautiful woman's best tool. She was instructed in the art of fellatio. A large amount of money was placed in a Boston bank in her name, and, as far as I know, she began her upwards climb. After a few mawkish letters, I lost contact with her."

"Then you don't know that she rose to be the highest executive in a very large American company that manufactures weapons of war?" Carmine asked.

"No, really?" Hugh Lefevre looked delighted. "How truly marvelous!"

"But she didn't spy for Moscow."

"You can't possibly know that. After her training, she would be able to dupe anybody."

"Erica was a blind for someone else. She must have had a controller—someone who guided her actions and told her what to do. She never behaved like a master spy because she wasn't a master spy. She was just a blind."

"I hope you're correct, Captain. If you are, then Erica's company is still penetrated. Splendid, splendid!"

When Carmine left, he walked all the way back to the Hilton, as much of his way as possible through Regent's Park, among azaleas and rhododendrons, blossoming trees and rich carpets of impossibly green grass. Hyde Park it wasn't, but it had its charms. Only when he found a refreshment pavilion and had that cup of tea did he lose the last of the sour taste in his mouth that was Professor Hugh Lefevre. Old, crippled, fueled by an ideology. There were plenty of people like him; differing ideologies, perhaps, but the same end result.

He joined Desdemona for lunch in the coffee shop, as she had just come in from a long walk through Hyde Park pushing Julian in what she now called a "pram"—less than a day, and his wife's Englishness was back with a vengeance. But she looked rested and relaxed despite her hike. Myron might be a pain in the ass, but occasionally he got some things right.

How to tell her that he was going home? Directly, no apologies and no prevarication.

"I got everything I needed from Professor Lefevre," he said, reaching to take her hand. "That means I have to go home."

The light died in her eyes, but she mustered all her resources and managed to look merely disappointed. "I know you'd stay if you could," she said steadily, "so it must be very urgent. I imagine all policemen's wives go through this sort of thing—the divorce rate is so high." She stretched her mouth into a smile. "Well, Captain Del-

253

monico, you're not going to get rid of me as easily as that! Yes, I'm disgruntled, but I knew when I married you what sort of person you are. And you do have a fatal attraction for nasty cases! It rubbed off on me straight away, so I must have the same quality. My bed will be cold, but not as cold as yours—I have Julian. Just promise me that when it's all over, you'll bring me back here. Not in Myron's luxury! Some smelly private hotel out on the Gloucester Road will do—I can bear the curry and the cabbage. And we won't need to hire a pram because Julian seems to prefer a stroller. He's inherited your curiosity, my love, and likes to see where he's going."

"It's a deal," said Carmine, kissing her hand. "I'll worry just the same. London's a big place."

"Oh, we won't be in London," Desdemona said blandly. "I arranged it with Delia. We both knew you'd go home quickly, so Julian and I are going to stay with Delia's parents in the Cotswolds. No one will find out where we've gone. Myron's generosity can get us there—I confess I quail at the thought of battling with a baby, a pram and luggage on a train. We'll travel in a Rolls."

"It will be trains, buses and taxis next time," he warned.

"Yes, but you'll be there to help. I am a very large person, Carmine, but I have only one pair of hands."

Light was dawning on Carmine. "You are pissed off at me! What a relief!"

"Yes, of course I'm pissed off!" she said crossly. "It's no fun trying to be a perfect policeman's wife, I can tell you! I didn't expect you to find what you were looking for quite so quickly. I thought Julian and I would have you for at least three days. I've never seen the crown jewels!"

"That's good, neither have I."

"How long have I got?" she asked.

"I was going to see if there's a plane tonight, but I'll try for one tomorrow morning. Is that a lynching party?"

"No, at least we can cuddle in a king-sized bed tonight. I'll call Mrs. Carstairs to tell her we're coming, then we'll check out together tomorrow morning and set off in Myron's Rolls. Our route is west, and so is Heathrow. We can drop you off," said Desdemona.

"That's very smart, lovely lady. I don't think you're in any danger here, but it won't do any harm to behave covertly, to use spy terminology. No one knows Delia has parents here."

"This *is* a spy thing, isn't it?"

"My interest is purely murder," Carmine said.

At last, thought Carmine complacently as the car set him down at the bedlam of Heathrow, I am free of Myron Mendel Mandelbaum! I can use my economy class ticket and suffer the proper indignities of air travel for nine hours. But Myron had the last laugh. No sooner was Carmine on board the 707 than the chief hostess came swanning into the tail of the plane and upgraded him to first class. Accepting a bourbon and soda in a crystal tumbler, Carmine surrendered to the fleshpots.

"You have all the luck," Ted Kelly said when Carmine ended his story. "We had several tries at Professor Lefevre, but he swore that Erica Davenport was just one more bright American student availing herself of the economic wisdom of the L.S.E. The lying old goat! He fooled us, all the time prating about his membership in the Communist Party. England's riddled with open Communists, while our really dangerous ones dived underground with the coming of Joe McCarthy. He did more harm than good."

"Witch hunts always do," Carmine said.

"We're no farther ahead for knowing about Erica."

"I disagree. Ulysses has lost his blind. Have you ever established when exactly Cornucopia began losing secrets?"

"When our blind arrived ten years ago. The rocket fuel governor two years ago brought the thefts into the open when too many people got to know of it," Kelly said.

"Has Cornucopia lost anything more since Erica began to get cold feet?"

"You think that happened after the Maxwell banquet, right?"

"Sure."

"We don't know," Kelly said gloomily. "There haven't been any leaps-and-bounds advances in Red designs, though we've made real big ones. Our own espionage network can't find anything."

"Well, my guess is that Ulysses is lying low. He's got a cache of secrets waiting to go, but he's not sure if the storm's blown over. With Erica silenced, he's probably relaxing, though that depends on what she told him when he tortured her."

"What could she have told him?" Kelly demanded.

"Whatever passed between her and Skeps at the Maxwell event, first off," Carmine said. "Ulysses may not have been there that night, but deputed Erica to quiz Skeps about something—maybe what Skeps knew about him? But she sidestepped until the Pugh black-mail letter. What we don't know is whether it was addressed to her and she passed it on to Ulysses, or whether it was directly addressed to Ulysses." Carmine growled in the back of his throat. "Like it or not—and I don't like it!—I have to make that god-awful drive to Orleans to see Philomena Skeps again. Now that Erica's dead, the lady might be more forthcoming about her relationship with Erica."

"Why don't you fly up?"

Carmine sneered. "Oh, sure! There's no air service, and I can just see the Commissioner authorizing the hire of a plane."

"Jesus, Carmine, sometimes you're dumb! I'll get you there and back in an FBI helicopter."

"And that," said Carmine grimly, "is why we small-time cops hate the FBI! Money to burn. Which is not going to stop me taking you up on the offer."

"Tomorrow?"

"The sooner the better."

"How's your family doing in London?"

"Gallivanting all over the shop," said Carmine, not about to tell this new ally that Desdemona and Julian were actually staying in a house outside a pair of villages called Upper Slaughter and Lower Slaughter. In fact, so paranoid had he become that he had fitted his home phone with a scrambler and conversed with Delia about his family in whispers. In some corner of his mind he wondered what the Carstairses thought when their phone was fitted with a scrambler too, but he didn't care; no one was going to get at Desdemona and Julian again if he could help it.

"Pity you couldn't stay with them a little longer."

"Yes, but they're safe, and having a great time seeing all the sights."

"I've realized," Ted Kelly said slowly, "the significance of the shots on that telescopic camera. Ulysses wanted to see how to get to your house by sneaking along the water's edge. There's no public access, all the properties go clear down to the water."

"My interpretation too, Ted. Though he sent his assistant, who's either fitter or younger or both. If he thinks we don't know he has an assistant, sending him would let Ulysses establish an alibi." Carmine gave a wry smile. "The odd thing is that hers isn't the first body to wind up on that piece of land. A poor murdered teenaged girl was dumped there during the tenancy of the previous owner. That body was moved by a rowboat, whereas Erica was carried or dragged along the shore."

Kelly was staring, astonished. "Jesus! Lightning does strike twice!" he exclaimed. "That was the Ghost case, right?"

"Yes. She was artistically arranged on the edge of the path, not anchored underwater."

The FBI agent got to his feet. "Call me when you have a time set up for Philomena Skeps. I'll have a chopper waiting at what Holloman calls an airport."

Carmine grinned. "We do have weekday flights to New York and Boston," he said. "Have you forgotten Chubb has a law school and a medical school that grow experts like a vacant lot grows weeds? There's always a bunch of Chubb experts testifying in some court."

What a difference flying made! Carmine was on the ground at a tiny airport for private planes in Chatham twenty-five minutes after rising precariously off the ground in Holloman. It was a curious sensation, especially staring down at the scene—often water—between his feet; the chopper was like a glass bowl inside and a mosquito outside. His pilot was a silent guy who concentrated on keeping the insect flying, though he did speak as Carmine alighted.

"I'll be waiting here" was all he said.

A Ford Fairlane lookalike was parked by the fence, the keys in its ignition but not a soul in sight. Well, well, Carmine thought, the FBI wants Mrs. Skeps and Mr. Tony Bera to think I drove here in my cop car, ass sore and temper ruffled.

Between his first visit and this one, the Cape Cod villages had greened up and produced some May flowers; the day was fine and the sky blue, the Atlantic placidly calm. I still want a summer cottage here, Carmine said to himself. It would be so great to take my children paddling, teach them to swim, help them build sand castles, have peanut butter and jelly picnics. My son's experience in Holloman Harbor won't turn him off. Julian is not timid or shy; he's too like his mother.

He thought about them as he drove the short distance to the Skeps house. People like Corey's wife deemed their overt happiness a front, but then, that was Maureen; she could never believe that other women weren't filled with her own discontent. And of course what almost everyone—even Patrick—failed to take into account was the age factor. Most people had been married at least ten years by the time he and Desdemona tied their knot, and the events that had drawn them together were as perilous as exhausting. Desdemona had never been married, and his own first marriage had been a brief thing of lust rather than love. Age, he reflected, brought wisdom, but it also brought a genuine gratitude for the happiness of sharing life with someone as much liked as loved.

Philomena Skeps was in her front garden watching for him, clad in cutoff jeans, sneakers and a plain white T-shirt. The flesh of her smooth brown legs was firm, and it was evident that her breasts did not need a bra to enhance them; her mop of black hair was carelessly bunched on top of her head. If she was aiming for a gamine look, however, she missed the mark; her beauty belonged in a French salon, not a street market.

"Captain," she said, shaking his hand firmly. "If we sit behind the house, we can enjoy the fresh air without getting cold. I do so much love fresh air."

"Where's Mr. Bera?" he asked, following her down the far side of the house and around the back to a flagged patio.

"He'll be here when he makes it," she said, indicating a white, woven cane chair. "Lemonade?"

"Thanks."

He let her settle, let her chat about the joys of spring and fresh air, watching her as he sipped an excellent proprietary concoction. Her eyes in the sunlight were the same green as water full of ribboned weed, dense and changeful.

"You weren't tempted to go to L.A. for Erica's funeral?" he asked, holding out his glass for more S. S. Pierce lemonade.

"No, I wasn't." The eyes filled with tears, blinked away. "No one would tell me how she died, Captain, beyond saying she was murdered." Now the eyes were direct, resolute. "However, I take you for a kind but hard man, and ask you. How did she die? Was it very bad?"

"Yes, it was very bad. She was tortured first. Every long bone in her arms and legs was broken. Then she was strangled with a rope noose."

"A hanging?"

"No. Simple strangulation, if I may be excused for saying that. It probably came as a relief."

No tears now, but the creature behind the eyes had retreated to some place he couldn't reach. "I see," she said. "That is an odd kind of torture, surely? There was no sexual element."

"From my experience, it was not a sexual murder. She was tortured to obtain information, I think. Certainly the textbooks would argue no sex was involved, though sometimes I wonder how much— or how little—we know about sexual murder. Did it ever occur to you that she might be in danger?"

"Not of murder. Rape I could understand, because she invited it—so cold, so sexually uninterested. There is a kind of man who regards women like Erica as needing to be brought down a peg or two, and what more effective way than rape?"

God, this is an intelligent woman! he thought. "Did you know that she had been gang-raped as a young woman?"

"No, but it makes perfect sense."

"She didn't confide in you?"

"I told you, Captain. We were not on good terms."

"Recently, yes, but at one time you were. There's no point in denying it, Mrs. Skeps."

"Yes, at one time we were great friends. It's because of me that she became Desmond's mistress—I begged her. Of course that altered our friendship, though we remained close for a long time after. Had I known of the rape, I would never have asked. I was very selfish, Captain. While Erica kept him sexually sated, Desmond left me alone. It surprised me when she said that they engaged in nothing but fellatio, but of course men love it."

"Why did it surprise you?" Carmine asked.

"Because she was so uninterested in sex. Not disinterested, uninterested." Philomena Skeps struck her hands together. "Oh, please! Let's leave this sordid subject!"

"Why were you such great friends?"

"A marriage of minds. Our intellects meshed perfectly. We loved to read, we liked to discuss what we'd read—all the myriad activities, phenomena and creatures of the world fascinated us. We loved beauty in all its guises—a moth's antennae, the iridescence of a beetle's carapace, fish—you name it, we loved it. Neither of us had ever known such a wonderful friendship. So when it ended, I was devastated."

"Why did it end? How did it end?"

"I still don't know. Erica ended it out of the blue. In November of 1964, Thanksgiving Day. She was coming here to dinner with me, Tony, young Desmond. But she arrived far too early. I was in the kitchen," Philomena Skeps said in a desolate voice, "at the counter, making the turkey stuffing. Erica came in, stood about six feet from me, and said our friendship was over. She disliked me, she said, and was sick of pretending otherwise. Desmond was making it hard for her, she said. Young Desmond detested her, and she was sick of that too. There were a dozen more reasons, all much the same as those. I was too astounded to argue, I just stood with my hands full of bread and listened. Then she turned on her heel and left. Just like that! I never really saw her again, except at functions and meetings we couldn't avoid."

"It must have been a sorrow for you, Mrs. Skeps."

"No, a tragedy! Life has never been the same since."

"How did you cope with the fact that your ex-husband gave Erica control over your son's inheritance?"

"I was crushed, but I wasn't surprised. Desmond would have done anything to make life difficult for me. It affected Tony worse. He couldn't find anything in the will that would enable him to challenge it legally. Of course now that Erica is dead, things will be different." She couldn't keep the satisfaction out of her voice.

"Why did your son detest Erica?" Carmine asked.

Her smile was twisted. "Jealousy, of course! He felt that Erica was more important to me than he was, and in one way he was right. An intellect craves equal company, and no matter how great the love, children can never compete on an intellectual level. It is a wise child who understands that. Young Desmond isn't wise. So he loathed Erica, who stole me from him. When the friendship ended, my son rejoiced. Which reminds me, I must stop calling him 'young' Desmond. He's simply Desmond now."

How he managed to keep his face expressionless, Carmine never after understood, only that somehow he had, while this very strange woman produced a mixture of Oedipus, Clytemnestra, Medea and about a dozen other Greeks who'd wormed their way into the psychology textbooks. I fervently hope, he thought, that by the time this terrifying amalgam explodes, I'll be safely retired. Jesus, what a mess!

"Mother?" came a voice.

Speak of the devil!

With two dark parents he couldn't help but be dark, though face and body were more Philomena than his father. Having come into puberty, he had embarked upon his first growth spurt, and was taller now than his mother. He wore nothing save a pair of cutoff jeans, revealing a wide-shouldered, narrow-hipped physique that ended in beautiful hands and feet. When he moved the hands, they were graceful. His face was as much feminine as masculine, of that kind called epicene, and Carmine doubted that the double-sexed look would vanish as he grew older. Chiseled features in a northern European mold, and large, bright green eyes smudged with thick black lashes. Nor would he develop acne; his brown skin was flawless, innocent of pustules.

Carmine felt his hackles rise. Here was *trouble.*

The boy came to lean against his mother, standing to one side of her chair, and she turned her head to kiss his arm, smiling.

"Captain Delmonico, this is my son, Desmond."

"Hi," said Carmine, rising and extending his hand.

The boy took it, but fastidiously, with a faint moue of distaste around his red-lipped mouth. "Hi," he said. Then, to his mother, "Is this about the Wicked Witch of Cornucopia?"

"About Erica Davenport, yes, dear. Some lemonade?"

"No." He stood posed like a Praxiteles statue, oblivious to the fact that the visitor's foot itched to kick some manners into the conceited little shit. "I'm bored," he said.

"With all that schoolwork still to do?" she ventured.

"Since my I.Q. is two hundred, Mother, it's scarcely a problem!" he said tartly. "I need a bigger library."

"Yes, he does," she said to Carmine ruefully. "I'm afraid that we're going to have to move to Boston. The Cape suits me, but it retards Desmond." Her head went back to her son. "As soon as the legal ramifications are disentangled, dearest, we'll go to Boston. Just a few more weeks, Tony says."

"I take it you've fully recovered from the chicken pox?" Carmine asked the boy.

He didn't like the reference to a pedestrian childhood ailment, so he ignored the question. "Where's Tony?" he asked, fretful and peevish.

"Here!" said Anthony Bera's voice from the back door.

The change in young Desmond was both sudden and dramatic; he lit up, bounded to Bera and hugged him. "Tony, thank God!" he cried. "Let's take the boat out, I'm bored."

"Good idea," Bera said, "but I have to talk to the Captain first. Why don't you get things ready? We need bait."

The boy went off, but not before a little more talk passed between him and Bera. Carmine smothered a sigh of mingled sorrow and disgust. Young Desmond had already been sexually initiated, but not by a woman. Bera was mentor in this area too. A few more Greeks flitted through Carmine's mind.

"Did young Desmond exaggerate his I.Q.?" Carmine asked as soon as the boy was out of earshot.

"Some," Bera said, laughing, "but it's right up there in the genius range." He frowned. "It's rather narrow, however. His gifts are mathematical, not artistic, and he lacks curiosity."

"A detached reading of someone devoted to you, surely."

"There's no point in being anything else," Bera said, not perturbed by the fact that Carmine had realized what was going on between him and the boy.

"I presume you'll contest the will now?" Carmine asked.

"I'm not sure it's even necessary. Skeps's will didn't make any provision for Erica's death. If a board of trustees is appointed and it's impeccable enough to satisfy the children's courts of New York State, I think things can be arranged minus any legal fuss," Bera said easily. "The boy's mother is a good guardian unfairly dealt with by a vengeful ex-husband. Can you see Phil Smith or the other Cornucopia Board members making life hard for Philomena now? As long as they're among the trustees, things will be hunky-dory."

A very superficial summary for someone he deems a legal ignoramus, thought Carmine, but it will probably work out that way in the end. And it answers my questions. Cornucopia will go on under the same management for at least another three or four years. After that, given young Desmond—who knows? He'll probably have graduated from Harvard by then, and be a player. The kid's homosexuality doesn't worry me. What does is his patriotism. Is Ted Kelly certain of Anthony Bera's loyalties in that respect? I'm sure going to ask him!

Rising to his feet, Carmine said his farewells. Philomena didn't escort him to the Fairlane, Bera did, eyeing the car.

"You've put some miles on it coming here three times," he said, holding the driver's door open.

"Yeah, well, shit happens," said Carmine, got in, and drove off with a wave.

A few minutes later he was in the air heading across Nantucket Sound.

"Is that Nantucket or Martha's Vineyard?" he asked as the water became a patchwork quilt land.

"Martha's Vineyard," said the pilot.

And so, after flying down I-95 on the Connecticut shore, he reached Holloman while the Fairlane would still have been negotiating the Cape itself. Ducking down as he left the chopper, Carmine resolved to buy Special Agent Ted Kelly a bottle of his favorite tipple. What a difference! Home again in time for a Malvolio's lunch. The whole trip had taken less than three hours.

For want of something better to do, he went back to his least loved destination, Cornucopia, that afternoon.

Phil Smith had moved into Desmond Skeps's offices but had not availed himself of Richard Oakes the male secretary, Carmine noted as he waited for Smith's exquisitely turned out elderly dragon to announce him.

Erica's decor was still in place, but subtly defeminized; the vases of flowers were gone, the pictures of dreamy country lanes had been replaced by starkly grim Hogarth etchings, and red kid had replaced sage green kid on the padded furniture.

"You need a few swastika flags," Carmine said.

"Excuse me?"

"A lot of black, white and red in here. Very Nazi."

"You, Captain, are fond of making incendiary remarks, but I am not rising to the bait today," Smith said. "I'm too happy."

"Didn't like a woman boss, huh?"

"What man genuinely does? I could have stomached her sex, however. What made my gorge rise was her indecision."

Perhaps aping mourning, Smith was in a black silk suit with a black tie closely covered in white spots; his cuff links were black onyx and yellow gold, his shoes the finest black kid. A sartorial wonder, thought Carmine, sitting down. In fact, Smith looked younger, even handsomer. Being el supremo of Cornucopia obviously pleased him mightily, just as he said.

"Where's Richard Oakes?" Carmine asked.

Smith looked contemptuous. "He's a homosexual, Captain, and I don't like homosexuals. I banished him to Outer Mongolia."

"And where's that, in Cornucopia's version of the globe?"

"Accounting."

"It would be my Outer Mongolia too, I confess. The arctic wastes of numbers . . . However, I can't agree with you about homosexuals. For some men, it's a natural state of being, not to be confused with some of the sexual criminals I encounter." To himself he wondered how long it was since Smith had set eyes on Desmond Skeps III— what a shock that was going to be!

The pretense of bonhomie disappeared; Phil Smith reverted to type. "What do you want?" he asked rudely. "I'm a busy man."

"I want to know your whereabouts all day on the day that Erica Davenport's body was put in my boat shed."

"I was here, and I can produce witnesses to vouch for that from eight in the morning until six that evening," Smith said. "Go and look somewhere else, for God's sake! The only kind of murder I do is

Outer Mongolian. And yes, I would have dealt with Dr. Erica Davenport, but not by extinguishing her life. What kind of punishment is that? By the time I finished with her, she'd have been in a straitjacket."

"I accept that, Mr. Smith. When you called her indecisive, what did you mean?"

"Exactly what the word suggests. Having a homosexual for a secretary was indicative, believe me. One of the ways Cornucopia stays on top is by absorbing smaller, independent companies, especially if they have clever ideas or find a niche in the market for a new product. Takeover negotiations have a form and a time span that Erica was ignorant of. We missed taking over four companies in fewer than four days, thanks to her. Three belonged to Fred Collins, one to me. We'd been performing the ritual mating dance for months or weeks, depending. But she dithered, the shortsighted fool, then ran to Wallace Grierson."

"Couldn't you override her?" Carmine asked curiously.

"Not the way Desmond structured his will—she had the yea or nay, holding Desmond Three's majority," Smith said sourly.

"Hmm. So there were advantages in being rid of her, even if your technique would not have involved murder."

"Are you a fool too, Captain? Haven't I said that?"

"No, Mr. Smith, I am not a fool," Carmine said coolly. "I just like to be absolutely sure." He got up and wandered over to the long wall, where the Hogarth etchings were hanging in mathematical precision. Depictions of a London long gone, a place of horrific suffering, starvation, dissipation, glaringly unwanted humanity. Smith watched him, puzzled.

"These are amazing," Carmine said, turning to look at the seated figure behind the black lacquer desk. "Human misery at its most acute, and the artist walked through it every day. It doesn't say much for the government of the time, does it?"

"No, it doesn't, I suppose." Smith shrugged. "Still, I don't walk through it. Why the interest?"

"No reason, really. It just seems a strange theme for the office of a company director, particularly when the products are aimed at creating more human misery."

"Oh, puh-lease!" Smith exclaimed. "Don't blame me, blame my wife! I put her in charge of the decorating."

"That would account for it," Carmine said, smiled, and left.

From there he went to see Gus Purvey, Fred Collins and Wal Grierson, in that order.

Purvey was genuinely upset, and had flown to L.A. for the funeral. Like Phil Smith, his alibi for the day of Erica's death was iron-clad.

"Mr. Smith says Dr. Davenport was indecisive," Carmine said to him, wondering if this was old news or new. Old, it seemed.

"I don't agree," Purvey said, wiping his eyes. "Phil and Fred are a pair of sharks, they bite everything in their path without stopping to think whether it would go down well or give them indigestion. Erica thought all four companies would wind up a liability rather than an asset."

Collins repeated Phil Smith's views, but Grierson came down on Purvey's side.

"She had a natural caution," he said, "that I think was why Des picked her to head Cornucopia. I do know, however, that she was in favor of Dormus buying out a small company with good ideas about solar power. That's decades off, but I'm interested. So was Erica. I want to let the firm alone, just infuse some much needed capital into their infrastructure, and reap the benefits down the track. The same with distillation of fresh water from salt. You have to browse through the world of small companies, Captain, not gobble," Grierson said, unconsciously echoing Purvey's shark metaphor. "In that respect Erica's indecision was great. Unfortunately, in most respects it was disastrous."

"What's going to happen now that Dr. Davenport is gone?"

"Phil Smith is bound to take over. Funny, that. For the last fifteen years he's been inert, now all of a sudden he's woken up and is behaving like a chief executive." Grierson frowned. "Trouble is, I'm not sure his burst of energy will last. I hope it does. There's no way I want the job."

"What's Smith's wife like?" Carmine asked, thinking of the brown pancake hat.

"Natalie?" Grierson laughed. "She's a Lapp—calls herself a Sami. Hard to believe she's an Eskimo, isn't it? Weird blue eyes, blonde hair. The Sami are fair, I'm told. Her English is awful. I like her, she's—uh—jovial. The kids are real lookers, all blonde. A girl, then two boys. None of them wanted to follow Pop into the firm—amazing how often that happens. No matter how rich people are, their kids do their own thing."

"No clotheshorses among them?"

"Just good workhorses, Natalie saw to that. She has some bug in her head about the homeland, so the minute each kid got through with college, off they went to the land of the midnight sun. They didn't stay, of course. Scattered around the world."

"The Smiths sound like an odd couple."

This is fascinating, Carmine was thinking; I would never have suspected Wal Grierson of this kind of cozy gossip. Just goes to show. He's best friends with a woman—his wife.

"The Smiths are absolutely orthodox compared to what the Collinses used to be like when his first wife was alive. Aki was Turkish—another blonde. Gorgeous in a weird way. Came from somewhere near Armenia or the Caucasus. Their sons are the best-looking kids—young men now, of course. One's a Marine officer stationed in West Germany, the other's a NASA scientist trying to put a man on the moon."

"What happened to her? Divorce?"

Wal Grierson's face sobered. "No. She died in a shooting accident at their cabin in Maine. Some fucking gun-crazy idiot mistook her for a deer and blew her face away. That's why we put up with Fred's bimbos. When Aki was alive, he was different."

"That's a real tragedy," Carmine said.

"Yeah, poor old Fred."

Strange pictures were forming in Carmine's mind, but they wavered and quivered on the fringes of actual thought, like moving objects some sadistic ophthalmologist deliberately kept right on the margins of peripheral vision. They were there, but they were not there. Swing your head to focus on them, and they vanished—poof!

"Or am I going crazy?" he asked Desdemona, the scrambler on the phone engaged.

"No, dear heart, you're stone cold sane," she said. "I know the feeling. Oh, I miss you!" She paused, then added in a master stroke of guile, "So does Julian. He does, Carmine! Every time a man approaches with something like your gait, he starts jigging up and down—it's adorable!"

"That's an awful thing to say."

"You have an idea who it is, don't you?" she asked.

"No, that's just it—I don't. I should, yet I don't."

"Cheer up, it will come to you. Is the weather nice?"

He got his own back. "Perfect Connecticut spring days."

"Guess what it's doing here?"

"Raining. At fifty degrees of latitude, Desdemona, with a climate that mild, it has to rain a lot. It's the Gulf Stream."

When Simonetta Marciano barged into his office, Carmine was surprised at the intrusion, but not at the manner of it; Simonetta always barged, it was her nature. She had never grown out of the war-year 1940s, which had seen her greatest triumph, the marital catching of Major Danny Marciano, who had thus far escaped entrapment. Barely out of her teens, Simonetta had no use for the GIs in her own age group. She wanted a mature man who could keep her in good style from the beginning of their relationship. And, setting eyes on Major Marciano, Simonetta went after him with all the delicious ploys of youth, beauty, and high spirits. Now he was within a couple of years of retirement from the Holloman Police, while she was in her early forties.

Today she was clad in a button-down-the-front dress of pink with darker pink polka dots; it ended at her knees, displaying good legs in stockings with seams, and her shoes were pink kid with old-fashioned medium heels and bows on their fronts. Her dark hair was rolled back from her face in a continuous sausage, and on the back of her head she had pinned a huge pink satin bow. The fashion these days was for pink or brownish lipstick, but Simonetta wore brilliant red. All of which might have suggested to strangers that she was free with her favors, but they would have been mistaken. Simonetta was passionately devoted to her Danny and their four children; her baser qualities were all channeled into gossip, and there was nothing she didn't know. She had feelers into the Mayor's offices, Chubb, the clutter of departments that made up County Services, the Chamber of Commerce, the Knights of Columbus, Rotary, the Shriners, and many more places that might yield some juicy tidbit. Having Simonetta on your side, her husband joked, was like enjoying all the benefits of the Library of Congress without the hassle of borrowing.

"Hi," said Carmine, coming to peck her rouged cheek and put her into a chair. "You look great, Netty."

She preened. "Coming from you, that's a compliment."

"Coffee?"

"No, thanks, I can't stay, I'm on my way to a women's lib meeting in Buffo's wine cellar." She giggled. "Lunch and a good Italian red as well as lots of dirt."

"I didn't know you were a feminist, Netty."

"I'm not," she said, and snorted. "What I am into is equal pay for equal work."

"How can I help?" Carmine asked, genuinely baffled.

"Oh, you can't! I'm not here for *that*. I'm here because I remembered hearing Danny say you and yours were looking for people who attended the Maxwell Foundation banquet."

"You were there yourself, Netty."

"I was, at John's table. None of us knew a thing about what you were looking for, I remember that." She plunged off on an apparent tangent. "You know the Lovely Peace funeral home?"

"Who doesn't? Bart must have buried half of East Holloman."

"The half that matters, anyway."

He was intrigued; this was typical Simonetta, a perfectionist at the art of gossip. Drop crumbs on the water and gather all the ducks, then produce your shotgun, that was Simonetta.

"He hasn't been the same since Cora died," Netty said.

"They were a devoted couple," Carmine said gravely.

"Such a pity he didn't have a son to take over the business! Daughters are well and good, but they never seem to want to follow in Pop's footsteps."

"Except, as I recollect, Netty, the older one's husband is a morti-cian who has taken over Bart's business."

"Don't let Bart hear you call him a mortician! He likes the old description—undertaker."

Carmine had had enough. "Netty, where are you going?"

"I'm getting there, I'm getting there! It's eighteen months since Cora died, and Bart's daughters worry about him," Netty said, deter-mined to pursue her own convoluted course. "They let him alone for the first six months, but when he didn't start to get out and around, they pushed him. He got nagged into going to the Schumann when-ever there was a new show in town, to the Chubb Rep season, the movies, public meetings—the poor old guy got no peace."

"Are you leading up to informing me that he was at the Maxwell banquet?" Carmine asked.

She looked crestfallen. "Gosh, Carmine, you're impatient! But okay, Bart's daughters nagged him into buying a plate for the Max-well banquet." She cheered up. "I was talking to his younger daughter yesterday, and she said something about Bart's being at the banquet. Seems he didn't have a good time, at least when he sat down at some table he told Dolores was full of drunks and weirdos. We were sitting next to each other in Gloria's beauty parlor, and Dolores mentioned this after I asked how Bart was doing." She grinned. "I got a blow by blow description of Bart's progress, we had plenty of time waiting for the lotion to set." She got up, gathering her sweater, her car keys and her pink plastic pocketbook. "Gotta go, Carmine, gotta go! You go see Bart. Maybe he can help."

And off she went, almost colliding with Delia in the doorway.

"Goodness! Who was that?" Delia asked.

"Danny Marciano's wife, Simonetta. One of the most valuable resources the Holloman PD owns. In fact, if the FBI could tap into her, their worries would be over." Carmine consulted his watch. "Nearly lunchtime. Could you find me a number for Joseph Bartolo-meo, please, Delia? And an address."

As Carmine remembered the proprietor of the Lovely Peace funeral home, he had lived in a very nice house next to his place of business, both conveniently located a reasonable walk or a short hearse ride from St. Bernard's Catholic church. But after his wife's death he had handed the business over to his son-in-law and bought a condominium apartment in Carmine's old spot, the Nutmeg Insurance building just yards down Cedar Street from County Services.

After some thought, Carmine decided to have Delia make the call inviting the undertaker to lunch at Malvolio's. He was at home, and had no hesitation in accepting.

By the time Carmine walked into Malvolio's his guest was installed in a booth at the far end of the big diner, sipping at a mug of coffee Minnie had already produced. Though his name was Joseph Bartolomeo, everyone who knew him called him Bart, and it suited him, having few connotations of ethnic background or physical type. The world was full of Joes, from Stalin to McCarthy, Carmine reflected, but of Barts there were far fewer. Now approaching seventy, Bart looked any age from fifty to eighty, for he had an Alec Guinness quality of anonymity that meant people failed to remember what he looked like or how he behaved. His physique was ordinary, his face was ordinary, his coloring was ordinary, his manner was ordinary. Which had been great assets for an undertaker, that self-effacing person who conscientiously cares for the beloved dead, organizes and supervises their obsequies, and leaves not a trace of himself behind to mar the last memories.

"Bart, how are you?" Carmine asked, sliding into his side of the booth and holding out a hand.

Yes, even his grip was ordinary: neither too limp nor too firm, neither too dry nor too moist.

"I'm well, Carmine," Bart said with a smile.

It wasn't necessary to offer him condolences a year and a half old; Carmine had been at Cora's funeral. "Let's have our lunch, then we'll talk," he said. "What's your fancy?"

"Minnie says the special's good—brisket. I think I'll have that, and rice pudding to follow," Bart said.

Carmine ordered a Luigi Special salad with Thousand Island dressing. With no Desdemona at home to cook ruinous dinners, he could revert to his bachelor meals.

They ate with enjoyment, passing the time as old East Holloman-ites did. Only after Minnie had cleared the pudding bowls away did Carmine become serious.

"I had a visit from Netty Marciano this morning," he said, "and she told me that you were at the Maxwell banquet. Is that right, Bart?"

"Yes, I bought a plate. It was real well organized, but I didn't enjoy it much, at least at first," Bart said.

"Take me through it, I need to know."

"Well, I was supposed to be at a table of friends, but when I got there I found out the rest had canceled—the gastric bug. So they sat me with five dentists and four wives—the odd dentist was a woman who turned her back on me. I didn't know one of them. They had a great time, I had a lousy time." Bart sighed. "That's the trouble with going anywhere on your own. And with being an undertaker. The minute people ask you what you do for a crust, they look at you as if you're Boris Karloff."

"I'm sorry," Carmine said gently.

"When the dessert was cleared, I decided to look for a better place to sit," Bart went on in his soft, anything but ordinary voice. "My first try was a flop—Dubrowski the lawyer and some lawyer pals from out of town. They all talked about business, whether the clients would tolerate a raise in fees, that kind of thing. I didn't stay past telling them I was an undertaker and getting the Boris Karloff treatment."

"Lawyers are the pits," Carmine said with feeling.

"Tell me something I don't know." Bart paused, furrowing an already furrowed brow.

"Where did you go next?"

"To a weird table—really, really weird! Four women and four men, but it was hard to believe that any of them were friends. One guy was a Chubber who looked down his nose at all the others—I remember he called them Philistines. One guy was so fat—I thought it wouldn't be long before he needed a funeral home. The same for an old lady who had breathing problems and a blue tinge under her nails. A few of them were drunk, I mean really drunk, especially a tall, thin, dark guy who sat with his nose in a glass of strong booze, drinking away. There was a pretty girl who looked out of her depth, and a woman who looked so tired I thought she was going to go to sleep with her head on the table. I don't think she was drunk, just tired. I knew the fourth woman because everyone knows her—Dee-Dee the whore. What she was doing there, I can't even imagine."

Carmine listened enthralled, wondering whether to interrupt Bart's narrative flow or hold his questions until Bart was done. No, let him continue, Carmine decided.

"The other man was very young, student age. He reminded me of the Chubber except that he was very plain in the face and the Chubber was handsome. I sat down between the fat guy and the Chubber in one of the two vacant chairs. The other one was on the far side of Mister Drunk, between him and the snooty kid. Just after I sat down, this woman came along and sat between the kid and Mister Drunk. She was drunk too, none too steady on her feet, and she looked as if she had a bone to pick with Mister Drunk."

Time to interrupt. "How come, after five months, Bart, you remember every little detail?" Carmine asked. If he didn't ask, some hotshot defense attorney sure would. Best to know now what answer Bart would give.

"It's my job to remember every little detail," Bart said with dignity, a trifle wounded. "Who's sitting where, who's not speaking to whom, what color the Mascetti family hates or what color the Castelanos hate—undertaking is a very delicate job. And I can't forget everything the next day either. Death picks and chooses, no one can be sure when the same people will be back to bury the next family member."

"How right you are, Bart! Can you describe the drunken new arrival at the table?" Carmine asked.

"Oh, sure. She was a really beautiful woman, much higher class than the four women sitting down. Blonde, with very short hair. Wonderful clothes, very pale blue. When the fat guy tried to act like a host, she cut him dead. In fact, I don't think she even noticed the others, she was too intent on Mister Drunk. I guess he was someone important, from the way the fat guy and the Chubber and the young guy treated him—as if they were afraid of him but needed him. No, not the young guy. He was like Netty Marciano—ears flapping to get all the gossip."

"Did he get any?" Carmine asked.

"Well, the beauty and Mister Drunk were lovers who'd just split up—that was what she was displeased about, if that's the right word." Bart smiled apologetically. "It's not necessary now, but I've spent most of my life speaking in euphemisms. But I'll say to you now, Carmine, she was pissed as well as pissed! Mister Drunk hardly noticed—he was too far gone, I think. She didn't understand that."

"Do you remember what they talked about? Was it all to do with the ending of their affair? Did she mention any names?"

Bart frowned. "She did, but I don't remember any of them. They weren't the names of people I knew. Except for one that caught my attention because it's the name of a saint, Philomena, and I've never heard of a real woman called it. The people waiting on the table were really attentive, I think due to Mister Drunk's importance. Their supervisor whispered in their ears, at any rate, and they hopped to refill glasses, keep the table neat, hand out clean ashtrays. So the beauty got drunker, and she started to ramble. Weird stuff! All about Russia and holding Stalin's hand, kissing Khrushchev's bald head—there was a lot of it. She started hissing in Mister Drunk's ear about if only he knew what was going on inside his own company, and how someone was his enemy. She kept it up, a kind of hiss—it sounded real mean, vindictive. He'd all but passed out, so I don't think he heard any of it.

The fat guy was trying to persuade both of them to have some coffee, and all three of the waiters were hovering."

For the first time since the Ghost, Carmine felt the icy needles crawling through his jaw. He gazed at Joseph Bartolomeo in awe, wondering at his luck. "What happened next?" he asked.

Bart shrugged. "I don't know, Carmine. I saw a table full of people I knew right against the back wall, and I got out of there. Brr!" He shivered. "I was never gladder than when I sat down among friends and started to have a good time."

"Later on, Bart, you might have to testify to this in a court of law," Carmine said, "so don't forget any of it."

The nondescript grey eyes opened wide. "Why should I?"

Carmine walked him back down the block to the Nutmeg Insurance building, shook him fervently by the hand, and then went in search of Abe and Corey.

His allusions to the espionage element in the case had been inadvertent or need-to-know, limited only because his team didn't have security clearances.

"Well, fuck that," he said in his new, much quieter office. "If either of you breathes a word, even to a wife, I'll shell out your balls, so make sure you don't. It's my career on the line as well as yours. I trust you, guys, and that's more than I can say for Ted Kelly."

At the end of Carmine's narrative, Corey and Abe exchanged glances of mingled relief and triumph; at long last they knew the ins and outs of this god-awful mess of a case.

"As soon as she was sober," Carmine said, "Erica confessed what she'd done to her controller, who is Ulysses. That surprises you? You think that was a stupid thing to do? Catholics confess to a priest, right? Erica was as indoctrinated as anyone is to any religion. She didn't fart without permission from Ulysses. As I see it, she told Ulysses exactly what had happened, and gave it as her opinion that no one had noticed, least of all Skeps. Ulysses will have known she was speaking the truth. She was utterly dependent on him, and he terrified her."

"So okay, Erica broke her cover, and Ulysses knew it on, say, December fourth, the day after," Corey said, struggling with behavior he found hard to understand. "But, Carmine, four months go by! *Then* everybody who was connected to table seventeen was murdered. Why did Ulysses wait so long?"

"Think about it, Corey—think!" Carmine said patiently. "The murder of eleven people is a massive undertaking. Even Ulysses needed time to plan it."

"And time for the world to forget there ever had been a charity banquet," Abe said, understanding. "Ulysses is a smart cookie— smart enough to know that murder produces different consequences from espionage. I don't say spies don't murder, but they do it covertly. The murder of civilians is overt. If what he planned was multiple murder, he must have known there would be cops crawling everywhere, and that some of them might be smart cookies too. Homicide cops are in-your-face guys."

"I get it!" Corey said. "Ulysses didn't want any murders, but if he had to, he would have preferred to kill his victims one at a time, spaced out. In a big city, no sweat. In Holloman? Impossible. Quite a few of his victims were pretty important, their deaths would have made the *Post*. He couldn't be sure that a potential victim wouldn't wake up to what was going down. *They* all knew where they were sitting on a certain night. He just couldn't risk so many deaths strung out. If he had to kill them, he had to kill them all at once."

"You're both right," Carmine said, smiling. "If they had to die, they had to die all at once, even the waiters. Not on the tail of the function, but maybe two months later, or three. So he waited for any consequences of Erica's indiscretion, and he waited in vain. Nothing happened, nothing at all. I see Ulysses sitting back with a sigh of relief as the fourth month ended. He was safe, and he wouldn't need to invite homicide cops into his little corner of the world. Then he got Evan Pugh's letter on March twenty-ninth. In a way, Evan's identity was manna from heaven. The one who'd woken up was another evil bastard."

"Pugh didn't send his letter to Erica?" Corey asked.

"No. Her drunken ramblings didn't really matter, even the garbage about holding Joe Stalin's hand and playing kissies with the Central Committee. If anyone had accused her, she would have laughed in their face and called it a fairy tale. It must have been something she hissed in Desmond Skeps's ear later on. When she was talking about a traitor inside the Cornucopia gates. I think she spoke his name," Carmine said.

"But if she did, why did Evan Pugh wait four months to act? I can see the logic of letting time go by," Abe said, "but I can't get my head around Evan Pugh's four-month wait."

On the far wall opposite Carmine's desk hung Mickey McCosker's only attempt at decoration: a cheap cardboard reproduction of a wilted arum lily in a vase. Suddenly it was too much to bear. Carmine got up, walked across, yanked at the picture, and pulled it down. He perched it on top of an empty wastebasket and brushed his hands together in satisfaction.

"I hate it," he said to his stunned team. "Mickey said it reminded him of his wife on their wedding night, though he never said which one."

He sat down again. "I believe the answer lies in Evan Pugh's character," he said. "Because it was sadistic, he got a kick out of the nasty vibes flying around after Erica arrived. But at the end of the evening he went back to Paracelsus and embarked on some other creepy mischief. He forgot about the events at table seventeen until he was reminded by one of those quirks of fate no one can predict. An issue of *News* magazine at the end of March featured a special article on the Communist leaders since the great purges of the late Thirties. It went on sale about March twenty-sixth, and Myron was carrying a copy when he came to Holloman to introduce us to his lady love, Erica Davenport. He was raving about the article, and begging me to read it. I didn't have the time because we'd just had twelve murders."

"My God!" Corey exclaimed. "Evan Pugh read it!"

"Yes, and whatever the journalist said about some of the Central Committee members tallied exactly with what Erica had said. After that, he must have remembered the things she hissed—a significant word from Bart Bartolomeo. Plenty of esses in her speech, I'm guessing. And think of our luck! We found Bart five months after the Maxwell banquet, and he's the perfect witness! His profession disciplined him to notice things and remember them."

"Erica told Skeps who Ulysses was," Abe said. "Wow!"

"Yes, and Evan Pugh remembered."

"Pugh recognized his name?" Corey asked.

"I doubt it," Carmine said. "All he needed was the name. He was a pre-med who got straight As—he knew how to research. After *News* came out, he must have decided all his Christmases had come at once. A chance to tease and torment someone with far more to lose than mere money. He didn't need money himself. That's one of the strangest things about this case—no one needs the money."

"He sent off his letter," Abe said.

"And Ulysses was forced to kill everyone connected to table seventeen," Corey added.

"Answer me this, Carmine," Abe said, frowning. "Why didn't Ulysses just hire an out-of-state gunman and mow each of them down? Why all the histrionics? Poison, injection, shootings, rape, knife, pillows. Is he laughing at us?"

"No, I think it was an attempt to make the killings seem unrelated," Carmine said. "Yes, he's got an ego the size of Tokyo, but it doesn't rule him. This guy probably has colonel's or even general's rank within the KGB—he's as cold as ice, he doesn't posture like a politician. All he's been trying to do since December third is patch up Erica Davenport's mistakes. We have to assume that he's never made a mistake himself, and it may be that Erica wasn't his choice—more that she was the only sleeper Moscow had to front for Ulysses. Women have a weakness, guys. They fall in love differently from men, which makes them hard for men to control."

"So Ulysses tried to vary his murders, hoping we'd be as confused as we were snowed under," Abe said thoughtfully.

"Exactly."

A pause ensued; Corey terminated it. "There's another thing puzzles me, Carmine," he said.

"What's that?"

"Why wasn't Bart murdered?"

Carmine looked uncertain. "The best I can come up with is that it's possible Erica never even knew he was there. He was a silent man on the far side of a very fat guy, and he would have been invisible to her if she didn't give the table her attention when she sat down. We know she didn't, because she was drunk, and focused on Desmond Skeps. If she never realized Bart was there, Ulysses wouldn't have been told. The other possibility is that she kind of noticed him, but he's such an anonymous type that she forgot him a moment later. One thing I do know, guys—if Bart's still alive, Ulysses either doesn't know he exists, or he hasn't been able to find out who he is."

"We have to put a watch on Bart," Corey said.

"And give his importance away? That's why I had lunch with him openly, even walked him back to the Nutmeg Insurance building. We didn't look like a detective and a witness, we looked like two old pals catching up. I used to live in the Nutmeg Insurance, and Ulysses will know that. So I must have friends there, right?"

"No watch," said Corey, mentally deducting lieutenant's points.

"What about Netty?" Abe asked hollowly.

They gazed at each other in dismay. Then Carmine shrugged.

"We'll just have to hope that she heard something really tasty at Buffo's wine cellar. There's a good chance. It was a women's lunch with plenty of libbers present. Pauline Denbigh on the menu?"

"One thing we *never* do," said Corey. "Whoever sees Netty doesn't so much as breathe Bart's name."

On the morrow Carmine, Danny Marciano and John Silvestri had to attend one of the Mayor's "ceremonials," as the Commissioner had named them. Ethan Winthrop was a true Connecticut Yankee by birth, but he owned the temperament of a P. T. Barnum. His much loved mayoralty was as stuffed with pomp and circumstance as he could persuade his councilors to condone, which meant there was plenty; his councilors were thoroughly cowed and didn't honestly care, so long as they could enjoy councilors' perks. Thus Taft and Travis High Schools received fat subsidies for their bands, a benefit all around: Taft or Travis marched off with all the band trophies far and wide, while the Mayor could fill Holloman's air with the sounds of brilliant brass during his ceremonials.

Having to attend these events irked the police chiefs, and was one of the few disadvantages Carmine suffered after his promotion to captain—lieutenants didn't need to go, captains did. Worse than that, it meant digging out his uniform. Under normal circumstances only Danny Marciano was in uniform, as he headed the uniformed cops. Silvestri, a law unto himself, was prone to wear a black suit and a black polo-necked sweater. Carmine stuck to chinos, shirts without a tie, a tweed jacket with a Chubb tie in one pocket, and loafers. Neat and comfortable.

Since the police dress uniform for such senior cops was encrusted with silver braid and detail, it was navy blue rather than black, to avoid any Gestapo connotations. Women like Delia Carstairs, Desdemona Delmonico and Simonetta Marciano privately thought that the three senior officers looked terrific in dress uniform; all were trim-waisted, broad-shouldered and handsome. Netty had a full wall of photographs of her Danny in full dress uniform, with a few of Silvestri and Carmine to round them off. This view was not shared by the martyrs encased in the uniforms, which had high Chinese-style collars that Carmine, for one, swore had been sharpened on a wheel.

However, needs must. Carmine, Danny and Silvestri attended on the Green while both high school bands played and marched, and the Mayor did his thing alongside M.M. of Chubb in all the glory of his President's gown and cap. It was Town's tribute to Gown as the academic year drew to a close. Luckily the day was fine and calm; the Green was in bloom, the grass springy and still lush. Best of all were the copper beeches, back in leaf and towering over Mayor Winthrop's celebration of an amity that sometimes had its fragile side.

They were bunched on or around a dais swathed in purple and blue, purple being the color of Chubb, blue of Holloman. On top of the dais the really important people stood, with the Mayor and M.M. in pride of place. The three police chiefs were three steps lower, their capped heads level with the knees of the dignitaries on the dais; the Fire Commissioner and his deputy, in lighter blue uniforms, flanked them.

"Typical Ethan," said Silvestri to his opposite number, fire chief Bede Murphy, "posing us like fucking flowers in an arrangement."

Carmine paid scant attention; his collar was simultaneously cutting him and choking him. He craned his neck, shifted his head from side to side, then tipped his chin up as far as it would go. Something flashed in the high branches of the closest copper beech. He stopped moving and stared, his face suddenly expressionless, an old reflex that went back to the lawless days during the war, when soldiers cracked and started shooting up hated figures like officers and MPs. There! Another flash as someone lying on a branch adjusted his weapon; it was the glass end of a telescopic sight catching the sun.

"Down!" he roared. "Everybody down, down, down!"

His right hand had cleared his long-barreled .38 from its holster, and out of the corner of his eye he saw John Silvestri doing the same, with Danny a little behind. The speeches had begun and the two bands were silent, kids sitting demurely on the grass as if they'd never heard of a joint or a hubcap.

It was not Carmine's words that sent the dignitaries diving in a flutter of robes; it was the sight of three fancy-dress cops, weapons drawn, running like sprinters in the direction of the copper beech, Carmine in the lead. The kids were scattering wildly, girls shrieking, boys yelling, while the watching crowd vanished save for Channel

Six's news crew, gifted with the best footage since that memorable day the year before.

Danny Marciano was down, clutching at his left arm, but Carmine and Silvestri were already too near for a long rifle, clumsy at close distance.

The sniper got off one last shot, useless, but no one heard the rifle, drowned in the much louder report of two revolvers as Carmine and Silvestri fired together, and again, and a third time. The smaller branches heaved and crackled as a limp body hurtled through them to lie motionless on the ground.

Sirens were wailing, flashing lights showing eerily on South Green Street; someone with a walkie-talkie must have radioed in almost as soon as Carmine moved.

"He's dead," Carmine said. "That's a pity."

"We couldn't risk the kids," Silvestri panted.

"Jesus, the gall!" Carmine looked up at Silvestri from a crouch. "How's Danny? We need to cordon this off, John, right now, so get it done."

Off came the silver-encrusted jacket; Carmine flung it to one side and knelt to examine his quarry. A total stranger, which was a disappointment: in his early forties, fit and trim in a brown sweat suit, his face streaked with brown greasepaint that would have made him all but invisible high in a coppery tree.

Silvestri returned. "Danny's okay—winged, but the bullet missed anything vital. Who is the bastard?"

"No one we know."

"Who did he mean to kill?"

"My guess is M.M. ahead of the Mayor, but probably as many on the dais as he had time to take out." Carmine picked up the rifle, anchored by a lanyard to the assassin, who was too well versed in his job to let it accidentally fall. "A Remington .308 chambering five rounds. New firearm, I've never seen one."

"Marine issue this year." Silvestri followed such things. "How dare he?" The Commissioner swelled with a terrifying rage, his lips peeled back to bare his teeth. "How dare anyone do this in my town? *My* town! Our kids were here—*our* kids! Someone is shitting all over us, someone who can get hold of a new weapon!"

"Someone we have to stop," Carmine said. "One thing I can tell you, John—I'll never bitch about this uniform again. My collar was giving me hell, so I was moving my head around. A ray of sun sneaked through the leaves and hit the lens of his sight just as I stretched my neck. I saw a flash, then another. It reminded me of a situation I had once at Fort Bragg. Know what? Danny's always at me to switch to an automatic, but if I hadn't been packing a long-barreled revolver— and the same for you!—we'd never have gotten the motherfucker."

"Yeah, right, Carmine," Silvestri said, thumping him on the back in what looked to Channel Six like a congratulatory gesture. "But Danny's right, snipers aside, and we won't get another of them. Time to go automatic." He sighed regretfully.

"There's nothing more we can learn here," the Commissioner went on. "Let's check out the turkeys in this shoot and make sure no one's hurt."

Dignity was sorely wounded, but nothing else except Henry Howard's Tudor bonnet, which was used as a vomit bowl by several grateful men. The probable primary target, Mawson MacIntosh, was too enraged to think of his dignity or his skin. He stalked over to Silvestri and Carmine with the kind of look on his face that had congressional committees shivering well before his tongue cut them to ribbons. The only person he was known to be afraid of was God.

"What is the world coming to, gentlemen?" he demanded, his eyes snapping fury. "There were children here!"

"I'm sure you won't feel like saying yes, M.M., but have dinner with me tonight at Sea Foam and I'll tell you a long story," Silvestri said. "Seven o'clock, no wives, and I don't give a flying fuck about security clearances!"

The President of Chubb exchanged his furious look for a triumphant one. "I know enough to realize I don't know nearly enough," he said. "I'll be there, John. And I want it all."

"You'll get it all."

Carmine suppressed a sigh. Whatever Special Agent Ted Kelly and various heads of various departments in Washington might say, once Holloman felt itself invaded, the ranks closed against all outsiders. Even Hartford tended to leave Holloman alone.

And it was such a beautiful day, he thought as he walked back to Cedar Street and County Services, where the first thing he would have to do was lodge his sidearm with the duty sergeant. Just as well it hadn't been a prolonged shootout; he didn't carry spare rounds in a dress uniform. This hadn't been a nasty case in that respect, either. His wife and son had suffered, but no one had tried to gun him down, even including on the Green this morning. Too insignificant a target? Well, Mr. Ulysses, you keep on thinking that way.

"The Commissioner will be lodging his .38 as soon as he comes in," he said to Sergeant Tasco. "We don't know whose round nailed the sniper, so both weapons will have to go to Ballistics for a test fire."

"Sure thing, Carmine." Tasco looked a little stunned. "After all these years, the Commissioner finally used his old long-barreled .38! I didn't know you packed a long barrel too."

"Better aim at a longer distance," Carmine said. "Came in handy this morning."

"How close were you?"

"About thirty yards."

"But the sniper was farther away than that by far!"

"When under fire, Joey, run toward the guns, not away."

He went upstairs on foot, to find Delia had already put chairs out for the meeting sure to happen; she was composed and efficient, apparently taking the threat to her boss and her uncle in stride.

Abe and Corey came in with the Commissioner; Carmine's team were more rattled than Silvestri, who glanced at the wall where the wilted arum lily had hung.

"Thank God you got rid of it," he said to Carmine as he sat down. "Mickey has a weird sense of humor."

"I'm putting up pictures of Desdemona and Julian instead."

They were all seated, including Delia, but no one seemed to want to open proceedings.

Silvestri spoke: "Is this a campaign of terror?"

"Ulysses would like us to think so, sir," Carmine said.

"Are we any closer to catching the bastard? Do we even know who he is?"

"The who is still in the wind," Carmine said seriously. "I have vague ideas, but nothing strong enough to send my other suspects home yet. However, I do think we're closer. Why? Because the evidence is mounting. How's Danny?"

"He can go home from the hospital in three or four days. Poor Netty's the basket case."

Abe and Corey exchanged a glance not lost on Carmine; it said, as if spoken aloud, that Danny's winged arm would save Bart Bartolomeo's life. Simonetta had bigger things to discuss than Bart and a charity banquet.

"I'm going to fill in M.M.," the Commissioner said in his no-arguments voice. "His security clearances are probably higher than the other President's, but I don't care anyway. Chubb is more important than Cornucopia in my book. It's been around far longer and benefited the world one helluva lot more."

"Yes, sir, no one would deny that, or your decision to fill him in," Carmine said patiently. "Among other things, two of our murders were committed inside Chubb colleges. Chubb's under attack too. There is an element of terror involved, and that fact gladdens my heart. It says that Ulysses is very worried. He's trying to send us in a dozen different directions at once, like racked-up balls on a pool table. Imagine the chaos if the sniper had picked off M.M., the Mayor, Hank Howard and however many more he managed to get before someone found out where he was roosting. Shots echo, the leaves would disperse the sound, and a good marksman with a Remington .308 would have kept on plugging away. We'd have been inundated with Staties, Feds, you name it. The place would have boiled over, and in the confusion Ulysses would have had time to smooth out the tracks Erica made him leave."

"May I ask a question?" Delia ventured.

"Ask away," Carmine said.

"I gather you think the sniper was prepared to die. Does that mean he's a political assassin? A man prepared to die for an ideal? It does, doesn't it?"

"A question needing to be asked," Carmine said. "However, I don't believe the Reds are so swimming in assets that they can afford to sacrifice good men for relatively nothing. I think of them as pretty much like us—scratching to make ends meet. The USSR is rich, but the USA is richer. Cornucopia is yielding them secrets, admittedly, and items with military applications must be at the top of their wish list. But it's my opinion that the whole operation is entirely at the discretion of Ulysses—that Moscow's interest is insulated from the realities Ulysses is facing. Erica Davenport had to be Moscow's mistake rather than the KGB's, so you can bet those in Moscow responsible are busy covering their asses. It's up to Ulysses to remedy Moscow's blunder, he's aware of that. From what I know about him, he'd use his black arts to search the market for a professional assassin, a man without political ideals of any kind."

"But to *die*?" Delia's face paled under its makeup. "A professional assassin would want to live to enjoy spending his fee, which I imagine would be very large indeed."

"Delia's right," said Abe.

"What if this is his dream job?" Silvestri asked. "What if he's got a family somewhere, and Ulysses offered him so much money that they'd be comfortable for the rest of their lives? Like, multimillions? If he's not a political idealist, then that's the only other reason I can think of that would tempt him to burn his boats and take the job. It must be part of his pact with Ulysses not to be taken alive, otherwise the whole fee wouldn't be paid."

"That's brilliant, sir!" Corey cried, the lieutenancy rising to the forefront of his mind. Not that his compliment was meant insincerely, just that under ordinary circumstances he would have said nothing. "A man might do it for his family."

"Snipers," said Carmine, "are in a special category. They don't see their prey close up after they've made a kill. All they see is a two-dimensional effigy in their sights, then a heap on the ground. Like a fighter pilot. It's clean killing, in that you shouldn't ever see the mess you've made. So I can understand how a man might become a professional sniper, yet still retain a part at least of his humanity."

"Well, the chaos never happened beyond whatever Channel Six can make of it," Silvestri said, sighing. "Between now and two this afternoon I have to fabricate a convincing story for my interview with dear old Di of the *Post* and whatever lady shark is anchoring Six's *News at Six on Six*. After Di, I have to face the out-of-town journalists. A crazy, huh?"

"Someone with a grudge against Town *and* Gown," Carmine said with a grin. "We'll have to hope that we can put a name to him from his prints, but somehow I doubt his prints are on file with anyone. He's a foreign national, probably from East Germany via Brazil or Argentina. I'd pull all the stops out, sir, give him any background you like, and say we're not releasing his actual identity to protect the innocent."

The Commissioner got up, wincing. "I'm getting too old to play chasings across the Green," he said with a grimace. "And I fired my sidearm at last! What a bummer."

"What happens now, Carmine?" Abe asked.

"We go to Judge Thwaites and we ask for search warrants for the homes, other properties, and offices of Mr. Philip Smith, Mr. Gus Purvey, Mr. Fred Collins, Mr. Wal Grierson, and Mr. Lancelot Sterling," Carmine said. "They have the money to pay five or ten million to a sniper. In one respect this morning's fracas was a godsend— Doubting Doug will be so fired up he'd give us warrants for anyone except M.M. and Delia's Uncle John."

"We don't have the manpower," Corey said, frowning. "If it's to work, we have to hit them all at once. Why chickenfeed like Sterling, Carmine? He's not a billionaire or anything like."

"By the pricking of my thumbs," Carmine said. "He's a sadist, which makes him interesting. As to the manpower, name me a better time to pull cops off ordinary duty than in the aftermath of a sniper attack. Various substances are being flushed down toilets, arsenals buried inside mattresses and walls, and every hood in Holloman has his head in the sand. That will go for Mohammed el Nesr and the Black Brigade too. We'll fill the air with the sound of sirens, and everyone will think we're on the trail of assassins."

"Offices first?" Abe asked.

"No, homes first."

Face downcast, Delia started clearing the chairs away.

"Delia, you get Wallace Grierson," Carmine said. "You've already taken the Oath, now I hereby depute you as a detective sergeant in the Holloman Police Department. Grierson's a waste of time, so you'll be safe even if I can't issue you with a sidearm. But the search has to be thorough. I don't want any of the Cornucopia Board imagining that I've played favorites. Most of them have cabins in Maine—the Maine Staties can deal with them, with particular attention to barns, sheds and bear traps. I'll call them while Tasco assembles the troops, who don't have to know ahead of time what we're up to."

Delia was in ecstasy, so much so that she didn't even mind being palmed off on Wallace Grierson. "What do we look for, Carmine?" she asked, brown eyes as bright as a bird dog's at the sight of the master's shotgun.

"Hobbies that don't fit," Carmine said instantly. "Most important, home darkrooms capable of color film development, enlarging, diminishing. A peculiar taste in books, such as Nazi Germany, Communism, Russia in all ideological guises, Mainland China. Also sciences at a higher level than we might expect. Abe, you get Lancelot Sterling because you have a knack for finding secret doors and compartments. I'm putting Larry Pisano on Gus Purvey. And you, Corey, get Fred Collins."

"Which leaves you with Phil Smith," Abe said thoughtfully. "Any reason for that, Carmine?"

"No, not really. Fred Collins smells the skunkiest, but I don't want him spooked by getting our biggest cannon. As chief executive, Phil Smith will expect to get me."

"His wife is a seed," Delia said, wrinkling her nose.

"How do you mean, Delia?"

"She says she's a Sami Lapp, but I doubt it. Too much Tartar in her features. Her accent's unusually thick for someone who's spent most of her life in an English-speaking country. More the way a Chinese speaks English, if you know what I mean—the syntax and sounds of her native tongue are just too far from those of any Indo-Aryan language," said Delia.

"That's right, you talked to her at Myron's party," Carmine said. "What did you think of her as a person?"

"Oh, I liked her. I told you, she's a seed."

Judge Thwaites having been very willing to issue warrants, Carmine began his searches at two in the afternoon. It was a coordinated operation, each team in place before all the homes were invaded simultaneously. Opposition was principally on account of each family's ejection from their premises while the search went on, with the single exception of the head of the household. All the men were at home thanks to the sniper, who had frightened every woman in Holloman and its surrounds.

Phil Smith lived quite a long way out, on a beautiful property nestled in the flank of North Rock where the basaltic outcrop had flung out a small canyon whose walls, decreasing in height, enclosed a large, classically Georgian house built of limestone. It stood in quite English gardens, replete with beds of flowers in full bloom and having a planned, Inigo Jones look to them from the placement of trees and bushes to fountains and statues. There was even a folly, Carmine discovered, a round, open temple of Ionic columns that held a table and chairs. It overlooked a small artificial lake on which white swans cruised gracefully and weeping willows fringed the far bank. No surprise then to see peacocks wandering, tails folded, to pick amid the grass for grubs and worms.

Philip Smith was not amused, but, after perusing the warrant thoroughly, he asked his wife to wait in the folly while he escorted Carmine and his cops on their search. The servants—all Puerto Ricans, Carmine noted, who seemed inured to Smith's arrogant treatment—were banished to their cars.

Smith was clad in camelhair trousers, a fawn silk shirt and a fawn cashmere sweater: what the lord of the manor wears when he is at home, Carmine thought. His superbly barbered iron grey hair was swept back from his face without a parting, and his freshly shaven cheeks smelled faintly of some expensive cologne.

"This is an unpardonable imposition," he said, following Carmine into the house.

"Under ordinary circumstances I'd agree with you, Mr. Smith, but after what happened on the Green this morning, I'm afraid the gloves are off," Carmine said, gazing around a foyer that rose three storeys and was capped by a stained glass ceiling of blues, greens and whites—no red spectrum colors to conflict with the sky. The floor was filled travertine, the walls pale beige, and the art stunning. Whoever had done the decorating had not attempted to impart a baronial look—no suits of armor or crossed pikes. The staircase flared to the second floor, and repeated the pattern up to the third. A balustrade ran around the second and third floors where they abutted the soaring foyer. The Smiths' taste in art was eclectic: old, Impressionist, modern, ultramodern, photography of a high order.

"Okay, here we go," he said to Smith. "Every painting has to come down, sir. Its back has to be inspected as well as the wall behind it. My men know to be careful, but do you want to stay and supervise, or would you prefer to go on with me?"

"I'll go on with you, Captain," Smith said, lips thin.

Carmine paid due attention to the various living rooms, but if Smith were Ulysses, he'd not use them for nefarious purposes apart from concealing something behind a painting. Each of them would have to be examined.

The library was a room to strike envy into the heart of any reader, though Carmine decided that its owner was not a scholar by inclination. Many of the volumes were there for gilt-edged, leather-bound show: beautiful Victorian editions of sermons, outmoded scientific theories, classical literature from Greece and Rome. The shelves bearing colorful dust jackets of novels and nonfiction works were those Smith frequented. Innocuous stuff, from Zane Grey to movie star biographies. The safe, he soon discovered, was behind a section of assorted editions of the *Britannica*; the beaded walnut trim had worn where Smith's hand triggered the lever.

"Open it, Mr. Smith," Carmine said.

Smith obeyed, smiling sourly; he wasn't worried.

It held $10,000 in cash, some securities and shares, and three locks of flaxen hair, two tied with blue ribbon, one pink.

"My children's hair," Smith said. "Have you done that?"

"No," Carmine said. "Why keep them in here?"

"In case of burglary or simple vandalism. The art doesn't really matter, but my children do."

"They're all away, aren't they?"

"Yes. I miss them, but one cannot impede the progress of one's children for the sake of having them nearby," Smith said a little sadly.

"Whereabouts are they?"

"Anna is in Africa—Peace Corps. Her mother worries about her constantly. She's already infected with malaria."

"Yeah, it's a slapdash program," Carmine said. "They never really prepare these kids for what's in store. And the boys?"

"Peter is in Iran—he's a petroleum geologist. Stephen is a marine biologist attached to Woods Hole. At present he's somewhere in the Red Sea."

The safe closed, they moved on. The bedrooms underwent scrutiny—Smith and his wife still slept together—and they moved to the top floor.

"Mostly junk," Smith said, "but Natalie likes everything kept tidy, so it's not difficult to search." He was relaxed and more affable than at the beginning of his home's inspection; it was hard to sustain outrage when its object was so patently indifferent to it.

"You have no live-in servants?" Carmine asked.

"No. We like our privacy as much as the next one."

"What's this?" Carmine asked, looking at a tightly sealed door. He pushed it, but it refused to open.

"My darkroom," Smith said curtly, and produced a key.

"You mean yours is the eye behind all those great photographs in the family room and the television den?"

"Yes. Also the little movie theater upon occasion. Natalie calls me Cecil B. de Smith."

Carmine chuckled dutifully and entered the best-equipped darkroom he had ever seen. There was nothing it didn't have, and everything was automated. Even Myron didn't have facilities like these—though why should he, owning a studio? Philip Smith could take a set of blueprints all the way down to a microdot if he felt so inclined. But was he so inclined? There was one way to find out.

"Given the nature of this case, Mr. Smith, I'm afraid I'm going to have to impound the contents of your darkroom," he said without apology. "That includes all your film, developed and undeveloped, these books on photography, your photographic paper and cameras. It will all be returned to you later."

The tension in the big facility was palpable; at long last he had gotten under Philip Smith's skin. But why?

"Close your ears," he said, and blew the whistle on a cord around his neck. "Clean cases, guys," he said to the cops who rapidly appeared. "Everything has to be packed as if it were made of tissue paper, and handle every item as little as humanly possible—around the edges if you can. I want nothing dislodged or smeared, from a print to a fly speck. Malloy and Carter, you stay here while the others go for boxes and cases."

"I'm going to lose pictures I would treasure," Smith said.

"Not necessarily, Mr. Smith. Anything undeveloped will be processed in our own darkrooms, and we'll try to keep your unused film unspoiled. What's on the roof?" he asked, already on his way through the door.

Smith was seething, but clearly felt it was better to stick with Carmine than protect his darkroom. "Nothing!" he snapped.

"That's as may be, but the paint on the midsection of these steps looks well worn." Carmine climbed them and pushed at an angled door that opened sideways.

He emerged onto a large, flat roof faced with asphalt, and stood staring at what from the ground had seemed to be a cupola. In the days when a building of this kind was what wealthy people aspired to, it would have contained a water tank; gravity feed would have enabled water to be piped throughout the house, a rare luxury. Above the cupola was a thin, whippy antenna he hadn't noticed from the ground, and in its straight side, hidden by the roof parapet, sat a door.

"What's this?" Carmine asked, walking across.

"My ham radio setup," Smith said. "No doubt, thinking me Ulysses, you'll want to impound its contents too?"

"Yes, I will," Carmine said cheerfully, waiting as Smith opened the door with another key. "State of the art," he said inside, gazing about. "You could talk to Moscow from here."

"With North Rock hemming me in? Possible, Captain, but not likely," Smith said, sneering. "In this Year of Our Lord 1967, I very much doubt that spies communicate directly with their masters. The world grows more sophisticated at an ever-increasing rate, haven't you noticed? You can look until the cows come home, but you won't find one single thing to suggest such a puerile activity! I've had no opportunity to alter my bandwidths or otherwise tamper with my ham setup, but confiscate away. As soon as my lawyers swing into action, I'll have it back—and it had better be undamaged."

"I'm sorry, Mr. Smith," Carmine said nicely, "but if it's any consolation, exactly the same thing is happening to your fellow Board members."

"Answer me one thing, Captain! Your business is murder, not espionage. Espionage is a federal crime, out of your legal sphere. I take it you've impounded the contents of my darkroom and my radio shack with a view to searching for evidence of espionage. I can sue you," Smith said.

"Sir!" Carmine exclaimed, looking thunderstruck. "Judge Thwaites's warrant clearly says 'pursuant to murder,' and I am pursuing murder. Poison can be concealed in bottles of developer, syringes and hypodermic needles inside all kinds of equipment, cutthroat razors in a bathroom cabinet or on a tiny guillotine—you had several guillotines in your darkroom—pistols in the weirdest places. Need I go on? The contents of your kitchen also suffered." He spread his hands in a very Italian gesture. "Until everything I confiscated has been examined, Mr. Smith, I cannot be sure it isn't part of a murder kit."

"Slippery," Smith said, nostrils pinched.

"As any other greased pig, sir," Carmine said. "Espionage is not my affair, as you so rightly point out. Apart from any other consideration, I'm not trained to look for evidence of it. Nor is anyone else in the Holloman Police Department. If Mr. Kelly of the FBI were interested in your darkroom or your radio shack, I'm sure he'd be obtaining his own warrants. What he does is his business. Mine is very definitely murder, and this morning saw what could have been yet another mass murder."

Smith stood on his roof listening, his anger dying. "Yes, I see why this sudden spurt of activity," he said, trying to sound reasonable, "but I resent the emphasis on Cornucopia."

Carmine looked conspiratorial. "I'll let you in on one sequestered piece of evidence, Mr. Smith, that might help you understand," he said. "The sniper wasn't a lunatic. He was a professional assassin, sufficiently skilled to hire himself out for big dollars. Which makes anyone in possession of big dollars a prime suspect in his hire. There are few multimillionaires in Holloman, apart from members of the Cornucopia Board."

"I see," Smith said, turned on his heel, walked to the door in the roof, and disappeared.

Carmine followed more slowly.

As it turned out, both Wal Grierson and Gus Purvey owned fully equipped darkrooms, though Smith was the only ham radio operator.

"The quality of their photography is very high," Carmine said the next morning, "so, taking into account the fact that they could all buy and sell J. P. Morgan, we can't impugn their patriotism because of their plush darkrooms. All we've done is what we set out to do—rob them of the chance to turn Cornucopia secrets into something small enough to smuggle out of the country. Though I think it's more likely that Ulysses has already performed his darkroom magic on at least some of what he hasn't yet passed. And I agree with Phil Smith—espionage is not our business. Our other objective was to rattle a few cages, and I think we've done that. Through Smith, they'll all soon know about our assassin theory." He looked enquiring. "Anyone got anything interesting to report?"

"I do," Abe said, but not triumphantly. "You were right about Lancelot Sterling, Carmine—he's a sadist. He lives on his own in a very nice condo just beyond Science Hill—no wife or kids on his horizon ever. The pictures on his walls were all photographs of muscular young men, emphasis on butt shots. He had a concealed closet full of leather, chains, handcuffs, fetters, and some pretty weird dildoes. I think he hoped I'd be content at finding that, but something about his attitude told me there were other goodies better hidden. So I kept on poking and pressing. Under a fancy chopping-block island in his kitchen I found the kind of whips that would shred flesh. They stank of blood, so I confiscated them. But the thing that turned my stomach was carried openly in his pants pocket— a change purse with a drawstring. It looked like leather, but finer than kid or chamois, light brown in color. The minute I focused on it, he started to yell about his civil rights and how dare I, and when I picked it up he went bananas. So I brought it in and gave it to Patrick."

"What's your considered opinion, Abe?" Carmine asked.

"That we've stumbled on another murderer unconnected to our case, Carmine. I've cordoned off the apartment—it's on the first floor with its own section of basement—and I need to go back with two good men and maybe a jackhammer. He's killed, I'd swear to that, but I don't know whether he's put the body in his walled-up basement or somewhere else. I checked him into Major Minor's motel for tonight, but he's looking for a lawyer."

"Then get a fresh warrant from Judge Thwaites now, Abe. Produce one of the bloody whips," Carmine said. "Anyone else?"

His answer was a general shaking of heads; his team was tired, not in a mood for discussions.

Carmine went to find Patrick.

A very enterprising man, Dr. Patrick O'Donnell had seized upon the landslide of murders to augment his Medical Examiner's department. Several new pieces of equipment had been approved by the Mayor and Hartford, and he had expanded his empire to embrace ballistics, documents, and other disciplines not usually under the sway of the coroner. What made it easier—and more sensible—was the small size of the Holloman PD and his own persuasive, loquacious, charming personality. His latest coup came as a great relief to his deputy coroner, Gustavus Fennel, namely the addition of a third coroner, Chang Po. Gus Fennel was happiest on autopsies, but Chang was a forensics man.

"How goes it, cuz?" Carmine asked, pouring coffee.

Patrick propped his booteed feet on the desk and grinned. "I've had a great morning," he said. "Look at this, cuz."

He reached into an evidence box that would have been a snug fit for a pair of light bulbs and withdrew a small, pale brown drawstring bag.

"Careful," he warned as Carmine took it. "Abe thought it held change, but the change was actually inside a rubber liner."

Carmine turned it over in his hand curiously, noting its peculiar construction and marveling at the patience that must have gone into fashioning something that puffed out on either side of a complex central seam.

"Any ideas?" Patsy asked, eyes bright.

"Maybe," his cousin said slowly, "but enlighten me, Patsy."

"It's a human scrotum."

Only iron self-control prevented Carmine from dropping the thing in sheer revulsion. "Jesus!"

"There are some indigenous populaces that cure the scrotums of large animals," Patrick said, "and in Victorian times it was a fad among some pukkah hunters to take an elephant's or a lion's scrotum as a trophy, have the taxidermist turn it into a water bag or a tobacco pouch. But such," he continued blithely, "is the human male's horror of castration that it's a rare man indeed who would take a human scrotum as a trophy. This suspect of Abe's certainly has."

"Are you sure it's human?"

"He left a few pubic hairs, and the shape and size are exactly right if the victim was possessed of a loose rather than a tight scrotal sac. The testes don't vary much, but the scrotum does. Whoever did this is a real sicko."

"I'd better tell Abe before he goes to Doubting Doug."

One brisk phone call later and Carmine was free to quiz Patrick on other things. "Whose bullet killed our assassin?"

"Silvestri's. No wonder he could take out whole Nazi machine-gun nests! The man's a wonder with that old .38 he won't be parted from. I bet he never even goes to the range to practice, either," Patsy said. "Head shot—well, you know that. But you didn't do too badly yourself, Carmine. Two of your three rounds plugged him in the right shoulder. Your third round lodged in the tree branch. Silvestri's other two were in the chest."

"I never claimed to be Dead Eye Dick, especially at thirty yards or more."

"I know you—you were hoping to immobilize his shooting arm and keep him alive for questioning," Patsy said shrewdly.

"True, but John was right—we couldn't risk the kids. I was in error. Do me a favor, Patsy?"

"Sure, anything."

"Send the guy's prints to Interpol and our military. He's not from these parts, I know it in my bones, but he just might have come to someone else's attention. I'm thinking East Germany as state of origin, but he's no ideologue. He was in it for the money, which means he has family somewhere."

"Faint hope, but I'll do it, of course. One last thing, cuz, before you vanish?"

"Speak."

"What am I supposed to do with a whole room crammed with cases of photographic and broadcasting apparatus?"

"Since we don't have the manpower to mount that kind of examination, Patsy, I'm donating it to Special Agent Ted Kelly. Let the FBI find any microdots or snapshots of Granny holding up a set of blueprints," Carmine said with a grin. "I'll have Delia inform the Cornucopia Board that our evidence has been subpoenaed by the FBI. They'll get it back, but not for weeks."

"How can that really help? They're all so rich they can buy new gear and get going again within days."

"They could, but buying new gear would be noticed, and even rich people hesitate to spend their money on stuff they've already got. They know they'll get it back, so what's the hurry? There are reasons why none of them wants to draw attention to himself."

"You mean Ulysses?"

"How do you know that name?"

"Carmine, honestly! Ted Kelly has a mouth as big as his feet, and he has a habit of using Malvolio's as his meeting place whenever another FBI agent comes to town. I mean, we're hicks, the next best thing to Ozark hillbillies on his map of the nation," Patrick said. "Besides, Holloman is Holloman. It has no secrets."

"*Please* tell me Netty Marciano doesn't know!"

"Of course she doesn't! This is men's business."

So Carmine left in a pall of gloom; the whole of his world knew about Ulysses, which was the penalty for a rather strident independence, he reflected. He was as guilty as the next man; so was John Silvestri. It reminded him of the time a more zealous mayor than Ethan Winthrop had tried to introduce a one-way traffic system to Holloman, where streets had gone both ways since the horse and cart. Holloman didn't like it, and Holloman refused to obey. Years went by before sheer automobile pressure finally brought one-way streets. It's a fool politician who tries to create Utopia, he thought. I bet the Reds know that.

Lancelot Sterling didn't move back into his condominium, which became permanently cordoned off when Abe discovered the well-preserved remains of a man carefully laid out beneath the false bottom of a very long, capacious storage bin attached to the wall of his basement. When its lid was lifted it was found to contain someone's property: clothes, books, a set of weights, geographical magazines, maps, a tent, a sleeping bag, and other items that suggested an up-front, hiking itinerant.

The body was nude and, externally, missing its scrotum, though the penis was intact. A midline incision, meticulously sutured, ran from his throat to just above the pubes, but the contours of the trunk were perfect. Very little decomposition had occurred, Patrick thought because the compartment under the body was full of hygroscopic crystals. Someone, presumably Sterling, was reactivating them a bucket at a time, which made them a pink or colorless patchwork.

"He heats them in an oven to drive out the moisture they soak up," Patrick explained, "which accounts for the change in color. It must have cost Sterling a bundle to accumulate this much. He's put pans of sodium bicarbonate around to remove any smell, but I doubt the smell's as bad as a freshman dissecting lab." He pointed at the incision. "I'll have to get him on my table to find out, but I predict that Sterling has removed the entrails—alimentary canal, liver, lungs, kidneys, bladder. Probably left the heart in situ. This is a mummy. With the false bottom in place, I imagine the humidity inside his secret compartment is very near zero. I'll test it with a hygrometer."

He was talking to Abe; Carmine had handed the case over to him to see how he fared, very glad that his decision seemed the logical one. Abe was the original investigating officer. Corey had no valid grounds to assume either that Abe had been favored or that he had been excluded for any reason having to do with Larry Pisano's lieutenancy. Now Carmine hoped for a case to give to Corey. The day when the panel met to decide which man got the job was looming, and there were four people—two detectives and two wives—who would be examining their treatment with a microscope. The closer the day drew, the greater Carmine's grief. Why did Lancelot Sterling have to be such a meaty murder, and how could he equilibrate Corey?

Abe was glowing when Carmine walked into the autopsy suite, despite the grisly nature of the crime; it was his talent for finding concealed compartments that had broken the case open, and he felt all the thrill of a job done better than others could have. He was not by nature overambitious, nor was he a selfish man, but he had his share of pride, both in his work and in himself.

"There was a wallet in the storage bin," Abe said to Carmine. "The victim's name is Mark Schmidt, according to his driver's license, issued in Wisconsin two years ago on his eighteenth birthday. Whatever money he had is gone, but his MasterCard is there. The last receipt is dated October of 1966—seven months ago. No photos or letters."

"The thoracic and abdominal cavities have been stuffed with a plastic mattress foam," Patrick said, "as well as sticks of incense and spices. This is a serious attempt at mummification without the natron Herodotus describes. Sterling's brought the Egyptians up to date—better tools, better techniques. As you can see, Mark is very good-looking, with a head of hair like M.M.'s, kind of apricot-colored. That may be why Sterling made no attempt to remove the brain—didn't want to risk ruining it. The kid was in the pink of health when he was asphyxiated, probably with a plastic bag during a drug-induced sleep. Strangulation would have marred him. I can't establish a time frame for the anal sex, so I can't tell you whether he was by inclination homosexual. There's been a lot of anal insult over the past year, certainly. The ligature tying off the rectum—the one that severed the colon—is a good ten inches in from the anus, which suggests that Sterling has been engaging in necrophilia."

All Abe's pleasure fled in an instant; he stared at Patsy in horror. "No!" he whispered.

"Definitely yes, Abe," Patsy said gently.

"Any idea when he died?" Abe asked, valiantly recovering.

"I think that receipt tells you more than autopsy can. Put down seven months ago, Abe." Patrick looked at Carmine. "Where is Mr. Lancelot Sterling?"

"Downstairs in a holding cell."

From which he was brought to an interrogation room. Abe did the questioning, while Carmine watched on the far side of the one-way window.

He appears so inoffensive, Carmine thought. Just one of literally millions of men who spend their working hours pushing paper in offices, have never done any other kind of job, and never will. Living unexciting lives, looking forward to putting their feet up with a few cans of beer to watch football.

Sterling was on the tall side of average, had a good head of nut-brown hair, and regular features that should have made him handsome, yet didn't. A part of that was his expression—haughty, conceited, humorless. The other contributing factor was his eyes, which lacked all animation. He would never pull the wings off butterflies, Carmine thought, because he wouldn't even notice their existence. Whatever world he lives in has no color, no vitality, no joy, no sorrow. All it consists of is a single appalling drive. In all truth he is a monster. Being caught hardly impinges on him; all that matters is that he's lost Mark Schmidt and his little change purse.

"Do you think he's killed others?" Abe asked later, seeking the respected opinion he'd leaned on for years.

"You know more about this case than I do, Abe. What do you think?" Carmine countered.

"Then, no," Abe said. "He's paid to flog youths, but Mark Schmidt is his first murder. It's taken him years to assemble his tools and things like seventy pounds of hygroscopic crystals."

"Do you think he'd kill again?"

Abe thought for a while, then shook his head. "Probably not, at least while Mark Schmidt fascinated him. If the attraction faded or the body decomposed too much, he'd wait until he found the right person, even if it took a long time. He made no secret of the fact that they lived together for six months. Well, he made no secret of any of it. He maintains that Mark died from natural causes and he couldn't bear to part with him." Abe flailed his hands around, frustrated. "It's a good thing he's mad—really, really mad. No one will want to try him, too much publicity."

"And there you have it, Abe. If it's any consolation, you worked the case exactly as it needed to be worked." Carmine looked into his eyes. "Will you sleep tonight?"

"Most likely not, but all things fade. I'd rather lose my sleep than my humanity."

And home to an empty house. Carmine went up to his bedroom and stood staring at the big bed, properly made because he was a tidy man who disliked all kinds of disorder. Born and raised a Catholic, he had long left organized religion in the past; his job and his intellect rebelled against the astronomical conundrums lumped together under the single word "faith," something he couldn't see or feel. Of course Julian would go to St. Bernard's Boys together with however many male siblings he might end up owning, but that had a certain logic.

Kids needed ethics, principles and morals instilled in them at school as well as at home. As to what Julian and his potential brothers made of "faith" once they were grown, that was their business.

Even so, gazing at the bed, Carmine was conscious that his house was filled with presences, the intangible spiritual relics of his wife, his son, all the others who had lived here. It made his loneliness worse, not better. Oh, the time and thought he'd put into this room, once he was entrusted with the decorating! A very plain room, Desdemona had said, but sumptuous in color; she had been awestruck at his instinct for color. He'd had an antique Chinese three-leafed screen in storage, trimmed in black and silver brocade, painted in black upon a white background, of rounded mountains poking their heads through mist, wind-warped conifers, a small pagoda up a tortuous flight of a thousand steps. He'd hung it above the bed, and done the room in lavender blue and peach so that neither sex triumphed. Desdemona loved the room and when heavy with Julian had embarked upon embroidering a bedspread in black and white, an echo of the screen. His birth had interrupted it, and it lay inside a cedar chest awaiting, she joked, her next pregnancy. If they had enough children, one day it would be finished. In the meantime, the spread was lavender blue with a little peach detail.

Missing her unbearably, he turned away and went down to the kitchen, where his aunt had left a clam sauce for pasta. His mother was still too busy blaming herself for Desdemona's peril to bother about cooking, but his sisters, aunts and cousins were making sure he didn't starve. The door to Sophia's tower led off the family sitting room, and was firmly shut; the owner of the eyrie was having a hard time of it in L.A., she informed her true father over the phone, as Myron was hovering on the verge of a nervous breakdown. Justifiably annoyed, Carmine had called him, abused him roundly for worrying a teenaged girl, and told him to snap out of it. *Damn* Erica Davenport! he thought for the hundredth time as he tipped fine fettuccine into a pan of boiling, salted water. She had cut a swath through the people he loved.

Voices sounded at the front door; a key turned in the lock. Carmine stood stock-still by the stove, the last of the fettuccine falling into the water of its own accord. Desdemona! That was Desdemona's voice! But he couldn't move to go to her, shock had nailed his feet to the floor.

"I might have known he'd still be at Cedar Street," she was saying to someone, "and I'll bet he forgot to shop." Then, in a loud call, "Thank you, sir! I'll be fine." The taxi driver.

She forged into the kitchen like a battleship in full sail, Julian on her left arm, wearing slacks and a blouse creased from her journey, her face flushed, her eyes sparkling.

"Carmine!" she said, stopping in her own wake as she saw him. The wonderful smile transformed her plain face. "Dearest heart, you look like a fish in the bottom of a boat."

He closed his mouth and enveloped her and the baby in his arms, his lashes wet as he searched for her lips and found them. Only Julian, squawking at being squashed, recalled them to the time and place. Carmine took his son and kissed him all over his face, something Julian loved; Desdemona moved to the stove.

"Pasta and clam sauce," she said, peering into the bowl and the pan. "Aunt Maria, I'll bet. There's tons for two of us." Then she took Julian from his father. "If you'll excuse me, I intend to give him his dinner, then a bath, after which he goes sleepy-byes."

"What about jet lag, kid?" Carmine asked the baby.

"Don't worry about it," Desdemona said. "I've deliberately kept him awake for hours and hours. The rest of first class was not amused."

"How did you get from JFK?"

"Caught the Connecticut limousine. I wasn't game to tell Myron that I was coming home. He wouldn't understand."

And off she went with Julian, talking some nonsense in his ear. All the ghosts had vanished.

"We didn't find a thing in all that darkroom and radio gear," Ted Kelly said gloomily. "Not a god-damn thing!"

"Did you really think you would?" Carmine asked, still wrapped in the bliss of having Desdemona and Julian home.

"I guess not, but it's a disappointment all the same. I will admit, Carmine, that you and/or the Commissioner were pretty clever over the sniper on the Green," Kelly said, a trifle grudgingly. "We could never find an excuse to search the Cornucopia Board's homes. Though you're skating on thin ice. Those guys have the money to take the County of Holloman all the way to the Supreme Court."

"We've apologized for acting overhastily in the stress of the moment. Do you honestly think they will sue us, Ted?" Carmine asked, smiling.

"No. Too much public fuss. They're petrified that someone will tell Ed Murrow about Ulysses."

"So thought the Commissioner and/or I."

"You're a cunt, Delmonico."

"Step outside."

"I take it back. How come everybody knows about Ulysses?"

"Blame yourself. With your voice, you don't need a megaphone, yet you will persist in having your meetings right here in a cop diner. The ears flap like Dumbo."

"I hate small towns!"

"This is a small city, not a town."

"Same difference. You all know too much about each other."

"Switch from your turkey to your eagle hat for a moment. Is it true that the entire Cornucopia Board is flying to Zurich in an attempt to acquire some Swiss company that makes transistors?"

"Who's your source?" Kelly demanded suspiciously.

"Erica Davenport's ex-secretary, Richard Oakes, who is now demoted to working for Michael Donald Sykes, yet another unhappy victim of top management," Carmine said, toying with a plain salad. "Oakes and I went for a stroll this morning along the banks of the Pequot, where our words floated away on the breeze and our only witnesses were a flock of gulls. We must be in for a storm."

"Why are we in for a storm?" Kelly asked, sidetracked.

"The gulls, Ted! Inland a bit?"

"Oh! What exactly did Oakes tell you?"

"That it's more profitable these days to make transistors than cuckoo clocks, and that this Swiss company is onto something big. The word's out, so everyone's after the firm. Oakes said Cornucopia's howling for the moon. Neither he nor Sykes can understand why the Board is going to Zurich."

"But we know why," Kelly said grimly.

"That we do. The trip enables Ulysses to take his purloined secrets with him. Which tells me, Mr. Kelly, that Ulysses hasn't passed any to Moscow since sometime before April third. His briefcase must be full."

"Tell me about it! There's nothing we can do, Carmine! The bastard will depart the country smelling like a rose, safely hemmed in by his fellow Board members."

Carmine felt like pacing, but that would rivet all eyes on them as well as all ears. Instead, he threw his hands into the air wildly. "But how did he talk the others into making the trip? They're *businessmen!* If Sykes and Oakes know they're howling at the moon, so must they! How did he bring them around?"

"That's the easy part," Kelly said ruefully. "The Board's just taken delivery of a brand-new Lear jet—long-range fuel tanks, reclining seats, spare pilot—the works. I bet all of them are eager to see what color the sky is over Zurich. Even better, the wives will have to stay home. Not enough room with a three-man flight crew and a couple of hostesses."

"When is this jaunt happening?" Carmine asked.

"Tomorrow afternoon. The jet's on the tarmac here. Then they'll fly down to JFK to get international clearance," Kelly said, and sighed. "Yep, tomorrow afternoon all Cornucopia's secrets fly away, and there's nothing we can do about it."

Ulysses is going to get away with it, Carmine thought as he walked back up Cedar Street to County Services. The fact that I know who he is beyond a shadow of a doubt is irrelevant; I have absolutely no proof. Just a cop's instinct and the end result of myriad little facts and details coming together in my mind, some of those facts and details gotten with great pain and the calling in of favors.

Kelly doesn't know, and I'm not inclined to tell him. Fate pushed him into being here, a behemoth, and there's a message in that: he belongs to a behemoth. He's not the problem, it's his faceless bosses, the ones who'll push the buttons, the papers and the people in that ponderous sequence of steps protocol dictates before the big guns are ready for firing. By the time the sixteen-inchers roar, Ulysses will have performed his conjuring trick and look squeaky-clean. Ulysses is one guy; it doesn't take an army to catch him. In fact, an army can't. No one would notice him slink off in the clouds of dust. Let Ted Kelly go his way; I'll go mine because I know who and what I have to contend with, have known since the significance of Bart Bartolomeo's words sank into my mind and the lightbulb lit up.

What I have to do is get Ulysses for murder. It's neater and more final, if final can have a degree. My espionage facts and details paint a picture, but I don't have an atom of proof; when Ulysses paints the same picture it will be more convincing. Whereas the murders he's committed *must* leave a trail of hard evidence that I can find if I look in the right places.

He had long passed County Services and decided now to keep going for a while. The wind was whipping up a little, but it felt good snatching at his face. He glanced up at the sky to see mackerel cloud up there and found the time to file a resolution to make sure the shutters on his house were closed before he went to bed. Then it was back to Ulysses.

Think, Carmine, *think!* Who did Ulysses kill with his own hands? Desmond Skeps. Dee-Dee Hall, which flummoxes me. Why a whore who gives great blow jobs? No one else. His assistant killed Evan Pugh, Cathy Cartwright and Beatrice Egmont. Hired guns shot the three blacks—black hired guns, to blend into the neighborhood. The assistant impersonated a peddler of potions named Reuben to trick Peter Norton's wife, and probably egged on Joshua Butler. It may have taken Ulysses himself to pierce Pauline Denbigh's armor, but he didn't kill the Dean. I don't have the chance of a snowflake in hell to prove any of them. It has to be Skeps or Dee-Dee, or both.

What were his weapons?

Desmond Skeps . . . A hypodermic needle and several syringes, inexpertly wielded. Once upon a time he was shown how to use them, but the years have gone by since, and Skeps must have had tricky veins. Curare. An ammoniac household liquid. Drano. A tourniquet. Chloral hydrate in a glass of single malt Scotch. A safety razor. A midget soldering iron. Steel wire.

Dee-Dee . . . A cutthroat razor. Only a scalpel has that kind of edge apart from a razor, and even Patsy's autopsy blades couldn't inflict a wound like that on a standing woman by an assailant looking her in the face. It's the way forefinger and thumb hold the junction of the razor's shell and its—tang? Very close up, and very personal. Ulysses must have been drenched in Dee-Dee's blood like a man under a running tap. He didn't cut the carotid arteries until the jugular veins slowed to a trickle, then he got a second bath. *Hate!* This was done in absolute hatred fiercer by far than Desmond Skeps. Who escorted Dee-Dee to the banquet. That says Skeps knew why Ulysses hated Dee-Dee, even if Skeps didn't know Ulysses was Ulysses. And what was it with Dee-Dee? She stood and took her death without a protest, according to Patsy. So she knew why Ulysses hated her, and admitted her guilt.

I wonder if he kept those blood-saturated clothes? If his hatred burned that hot, maybe he needed a souvenir. The razor? That, he will definitely have. Enshrined somewhere. Not as a remembrance. As an instrument of execution.

An image rose behind Carmine's eyes so vividly that the hairs on his neck stood up. Jesus! I know where! I know where!

His steps slowed; he stopped, turned around and walked back to County Services at a steady pace, jubilation dying. Knowing was one thing; marshaling his forces to prove it was another. Doubting Doug would have reverted to normal; easier to get blood out of a stone than a warrant to search premises. Not that Ulysses would part with his mementos. In that respect there was no hurry. Strictly speaking, the urgency was not his affair, as it concerned the spy rather than the killer. Except that Carmine was an American patriot. It was his duty to foil the spy too.

By the time he gained his office his demeanor was as always. Delia, bursting on his gaze in green and orange paisley, gave him the kind of fright that only days ago would have provoked a smile. Today it was merely jarring.

"Abe's down with Lancelot Sterling," she said, "and Corey is skulking around the aerodrome. He said something about a new Lear jet, but I confess I was only half listening. I was on the phone to Desdemona."

"I might have known," he said, torn between an urge to tell Delia what was filling his mind and reluctance to burden her with his own frustrations.

"They're safe here," she said, smiling.

That decided him. "Sit down, Delia. I need to talk."

By the end of it she looked horrified. Then she did a very un-Delia thing: she stroked his arm. "My dear Carmine, I fully comprehend your dilemma. But if Ulysses hated Dee-Dee with such passion, it must relate to some sort of ruination, and she must have been the instrument of it. I think it might pay me to make exhaustive enquiries into Dee-Dee's background. That's the trouble with prostitutes. No one bothers to look at them with a magnifying glass. Am I still empowered to act as a detective?"

"I haven't rescinded the order, as you well know."

"Then I'm going to see Dee-Dee's pimp, her friends, enemies and acquaintances." She paused, brows lifted. "It would be a lot easier if I had a badge," she said.

"That far I won't go, Delia. Don't push your luck."

The storm blew into Holloman on gale-force winds halfway through the night. Curled in bed with his front shielding Desdemona's back, Carmine woke to the whipping roar of hard-driven rain on the windows, lifted his head to listen, then lay back with a sigh. No hope that this would last long enough to delay the Cornucopia expedition to Zurich. By afternoon the gale would be blown out.

"Mmf?" Desdemona asked.

Carmine cupped a breast. "Just the storm. Go back to sleep."

"No damage, but the garden's a mess," Desdemona said the next morning, removing her rubber boots in the laundry. "I had high hopes for a weeping cherry, but a flying branch clobbered it. Too exposed to the elements, our dream home."

"You can't have it all, lovely lady." Carmine shrugged his shoulders into his jacket and poked through the waterproofed coats hanging on pegs. "It's going to rain all day, so don't take Julian out. If you need groceries, call someone."

A rather cold rain beating in his face, Carmine plodded up the path to their big garage, which had to be on East Circle itself and thus had no sheltered communication with the house, a good fifty feet lower. Inside the garage he shed his raincoat before climbing into the Fairlane; he'd park under the building and keep dry. As soon as he keyed the ignition he turned on the police radio and sat listening. Nothing much, just terse talk larded with the abstruse numbers and letters designed to keep police business the business of the police. If only it did! he thought as he rolled out into the aftermath of the night's storm. Maybe I'll take a detour and look at the Cornucopia jet. But I won't announce my intention on the radio. Too many people make a hobby of tuning in, and they don't need a radio shack.

Holloman's little airport lay behind chain-link fencing on the west arm of the Harbor, which was part industrial wasteland and part working factories. Between it and the perpetually humming artery that was I-95 reared the clusters of tall cylindrical tanks holding every kind of petroleum-based fuel from aviation gasoline to diesel and heating oil.

Instead of using I-95 for such a short run, Carmine drove along the waterfront dockland, past the fuel farm, and so, finally, turned through the open airport gate onto a concrete apron used as a parking lot. He crossed it and swung around behind the upmarket shed that served Holloman's commuters as a terminal, his eyes absorbing their first sight of a Lear jet. Disappointingly small, it sat not far from the shed in the glory of flawless white paint, the Cornucopia horn-of-plenty logo emblazoned on its tail.

A rap on his passenger-side window made Carmine jump. Corey opened the door and slid in, coat streaming.

"You're wet, Corey!"

"*It's* wet, Carmine! Sorry, but I had to hide my wheels. No choice except to run through the rain. I figured you'd cruise by to take a look. What d'you think? Squeezing into that must be like going inside a tube of toothpaste. Doesn't look as if they'd be able to stand up, though I guess they can in a central aisle. Give me a train any day."

"It's a power thing, Corey. They can spit on the peasants being herded like cattle. Have you been here all night?"

"Didn't need to. They weren't going anywhere in that storm. They mightn't be going anywhere today if the rain doesn't stop."

"What do you hope to find?" Carmine asked curiously.

The long, dark, beaky face screwed up, the dark eyes narrowed. "I wish I knew! It's just a feeling I have, boss. Something's in the wind—or the rain, or the sea spray. I don't know."

"I'll send someone over with a bacon roll and a thermos of coffee. In an unmarked, over by that hangar," Carmine said. "Go with your hunches, Corey."

And what do you think about that? he asked himself as he drove away. Corey's found his own case. The fact that nothing's going to come of it is beside the point. It should have occurred to me that the Cornucopia bunch are sneaky enough to aim for an earlier departure.

Two bacon rolls and a thermos of coffee were most welcome. Warm and relatively dry, Corey Marshall settled to spend a few boring hours of waiting. The windows of his car were cranked down just enough to prevent his windshield fogging up, and he was cunningly situated where he couldn't be seen, yet could see in all directions. The rain had steadied, neither pouring down nor sprinkling, and it had been falling now for eight hours. The ground was hard even where it was exposed; between that, the big areas of concrete, and some patches of tar-seal, runoff was copious. On the road outside the airport gate a section of the bed had sagged and crumbled, plugging up a drain grating and causing the water to pool fairly deeply. Lovely weather for ducks, thought Corey, trying to find interest in everything. He had to stay awake, but more than that: he had to stay alert.

A great deal of his time was occupied in thinking about the lieutenancy and, he had come to realize with a sinking horror, a marriage that hadn't panned out the way he had envisioned. Oh, he *loved* Maureen and more than loved his two children, who seemed to suffer from Maureen's deficiencies even more than he did; he pitied them, an awful emotion for a father to feel. He understood that a person's nature was a given, but he wished with all his heart that Maureen's nature was less avaricious, less scratchy. His daughter, nine years old, had worked out how to keep out of trouble, mainly by effacing herself, whereas his son, now twelve, was beginning to inherit his mother's frustrations at the world of men. Always in trouble for untidiness, loudness, poor grades at school. It had come to a head a couple of weeks earlier, and he had hoped that, recalled to a sense of her own imperfections, Maureen would let up on the two males in her home. And she had—for a week. Now it was drifting back to where it usually was.

In his heart of hearts he knew that divorce was inevitable, for he knew that even if he did get Larry Pisano's job, Maureen would find something fresh to pick about. A clunky second car, an unsatisfactory kitchen, Gary's acne due to eating junk food—what the raise in pay wouldn't stretch to fix, she would nag about. Not for any other reason than that she was permanently discontented, and how could you fix that? If it weren't for the kids he would file for divorce tomorrow, but for the sake of the kids he couldn't do that, ever. No fool, he knew that they loved him as the bearable side of their home life, their coconspirator and ally. *In a war?*

Well, he decided as midday became early afternoon, the Marshall family just has to get through this. It won't end until Denise is at college and no one's left at home except Maureen and me. Then the shit can hit the fan in all directions, and I won't care.

His preoccupation vanished the moment a passenger van drove through the gates and crept across to the Lear. The crew, Corey decided as they got out, talking cheerfully among themselves, chiefly about the fact that the rain had stopped. A flight crew of three men in tailored navy uniforms, the captain with four rows of gold braid on his sleeves, the other two with three rows. Wow! The Cornucopia Board wasn't stinting on what they paid the guys responsible for keeping them safely in the air. Two slender, very pretty women in navy uniforms Corey put down as the cabin crew. No stinting here either. The steps were let down, and the men entered the cockpit, one armed with a clipboard; the two girls went to the back of the van and dealt with foil-wrapped containers, a big styrofoam chest for cold food, and various towels and linens. Amazed, Corey watched the girls work for some time. Even several small flower arrangements were unearthed.

The ground crew turned up; one of them connected the Lear to a fuel source, taking exquisite care that not a drop spilled onto the concrete. Hoses were hooked up, tires checked, a dozen and one tasks performed. In the cockpit Corey could see the heads of pilot and copilot, their hands fluttering over what he presumed were the toggles and switches of gear on the roof above the instrument panels.

Next to arrive was a Rolls-Royce Silver Ghost, two men seated in its front: Wal Grierson and Gus Purvey. They alighted and went into the shed, Corey guessed to use the rest room—a bigger facility than available on an airplane, even a private jet. Each was carrying a brief-case, but neither was dressed formally. Jeans, open-necked shirts, button-up sweaters, jackets over their arms. Laughing, they walked to the Lear and climbed the steps. As they disappeared inside, a small Ford drove up, two men aboard. One got out, went to the Rolls and got in. Then Ford and Rolls drove away. That's how you do it when you don't feel like a chauffeur, Corey thought. A peon picks up what you've discarded.

A fire engine from Station Two trundled in, the special truck fitted out for airport duty. No plane bigger than a joyriding specimen could take off or land without a fire truck's presence. Its crew looked pleased to be liberated from a rainy shift, and patently admired the neat little jet they were obliged to shepherd off the runway in as much safety as tanks full of avgas allowed.

Only Phil Smith and Fred Collins to come. Activity died down as the hostesses entered the plane for good. The van drove away, the fire truck went to its designated position.

Corey didn't huddle down again. Instead, he turned in his seat to look back up the road, idly noting that beyond the pool where the road had subsided a little, a four-inch steel pipe had risen through the asphalt and lay right across the road like a ship's cable or a filled fire hose. A silence had fallen with the cessation of the rain, and in the distance Corey heard the roar of a powerful sports car approaching. Going far too fast, it appeared in his vision on the heels of its grunty sound, a twelve-cylinder XKE Jaguar painted British racing green, Phil Smith behind its wheel, Fred Collins beside him. They too were laughing, "away at last!" written all over their faces.

The front wheels of the Jag hit the pipe, and the rest seemed to happen in slow motion. First the sensationally long hood of the sports car rose vertically into the air, followed by the remainder. The car actually did a somersault, Smith and Collins spilling out onto the road before the Jag crashed, top side down, and lay next to the pool with its front wheels spinning crazily.

"Ambulance! Ambulance to airport, road emergency!" Corey was barking into his radio before the Jag came down. "Medics! Need medics! Road emergency at airport! Road emergency!"

Almost before he had finished speaking, Corey was out of his car and running, suddenly aware that no one else had seen a thing. He went first to Fred Collins, closer, and bent to find a carotid pulse. Yes! Strong, and there didn't seem to be a widening sheet of blood. One leg was twisted under him and he was groaning. He was probably all right unless he had internal injuries.

Now to Smith, who lay on his right side, eyes closed. Yes! A carotid pulse, and fairly strong. He wasn't moving.

The wind gusted; a sheet of paper blew into Corey's eyes, was brushed away impatiently. Then Corey saw Smith's briefcase, still in his hand. Had the fool tried to drive a stick-shift sports car hanging on to a briefcase? Or had he grabbed for it even as the accident happened? It was beautifully turned and crafted stainless steel with two combination locks, but the force of the impact had sprung them, and there were papers everywhere. Most had settled on the surface of the pool.

"Nothing I can do for you, buster," he said, "but I can pick up your papers before they blow away."

Working in a frenzy, he gathered every sheet he could find. Many were wet from immersion in the water, but Corey didn't care; he collected them as the sirens wailed in the distance, then ran for his car. The firemen were coming, but he had the excuse of needing to use his radio again, and who'd remember that he was carrying loads of papers? Their attention was on the accident.

The papers went into his trunk, just in case some nosy Cornucopia guy came looking. He picked up his mike and talked to Dispatch, who informed him that Captain Delmonico was on his way and that two ambulances should already be there.

"Thank God it stopped raining," he said to Carmine a minute later. "Want me to tell those turkeys on the jet that they're not going anywhere unless they want to leave two Board members behind in the hospital?"

"Abe's got that," Carmine said, eyeing Corey shrewdly. "I want to know why you look like the mutt that got to the pedigree bitch ahead of her designated mate."

For answer, Corey led him around to the back of his car and popped the trunk. "The contents of Phil Smith's briefcase," he said. "I wish I could say I'd gotten all four briefcases, but one is a start. The way I saw it, there the guy is, lying unconscious in the road, and his papers drowning in that pool there. So I did what any considerate citizen would do—I picked them up. Then I figured I could always say later that our police labs have great facilities for drying papers that would otherwise have disintegrated, so I saw it as my citizen's duty to save them if I could. He won't buy it, but he can't argue about it either."

"Great work, Corey," Carmine said sincerely. "Our luck that the accident happened, but your initiative and presence of mind that Smith's papers have fallen into our hands."

The two men walked back to the road, where both ambulances were loading up. Thanks to Corey's having demanded medics, two of the new physician's assistants had come with the standard crews.

They reached Fred Collins's medic first.

"I don't think he's suffered much internally," the woman said, folding up her stethoscope. "Blood pressure's okay. Comminuted fracture of his right femur—he won't be going skiing for a while. Grazes and bruises. That's about it."

"Head injury," said Smith's medic. "Broken right humerus, right scapula is suspect too. His skull impacted on the road, but the water cushioned it some. No left-sided weakness that I can find, but we'll know more when he's examined by neurosurgeons. His pupils are reacting. If you'll excuse me, I'll get him to where they can deal with any cerebral edema."

Wal Grierson and Gus Purvey were waiting anxiously, prevented from approaching by the customary police cordon. Sergeant Terry Monks and his team had just arrived, and would inspect the site of the accident to reconstruct it and apportion blame.

"Though," Terry Monks said to Carmine angrily, "what are two stupid old men doing in an E-type Jag with no roll bar and no seat belts?"

"A roll bar would spoil the car's looks, and seat belts are for people who drive Yank tanks. However, if you're fair, Terry, you'll have to admit that not wearing seat belts saved their lives," Carmine said, just to ruffle Terry.

"Yeah! But a roll bar *and* seat belts would have seen the stupid old geezers walk away."

Onward to Grierson and Purvey.

"This is terrible! Terrible!" Purvey said, face ashen. "I can't count the times I've told Phil to stop behaving like Stirling Moss! He drives like a bat out of hell!"

"A pity he's not conscious to hear himself described as a stupid old geezer," Carmine said. "That's the verdict of our traffic accident men."

"Stupid is right," Grierson said through his teeth, more angry than upset. "I guess we're not going to Zurich. Gus, you get to tell Natalie and Candy while I deal with things here." As if on cue, the little Ford and the Rolls appeared and parked just down the road.

"Take the car. It can come back for me as soon as you get home and get your own wheels."

Purvey, looking hangdog, set off along the airport's chain-link fence in the direction of the Rolls.

"I thought you were a Mustang man," Carmine said.

"The Rolls is the most comfortable car on the road," said Grierson, smiling slightly. "Jesus, what a mess!"

Carmine looked at Corey and Abe. "Corey, drive across the tarmac and out the far gate. Abe, you're still with me."

The Fairlane followed Corey's car closely. Only when they were out of the far gate and back on the road past the fuel farm did Carmine breathe a sigh of relief. He had used the time to fill Abe in on what resided in Corey's trunk, and Abe's hands were trembling in sheer excitement. He glanced at Carmine.

"One chance in four it's the right briefcase," he said.

"Where's Delia?"

"Out like a bloodhound on Dee-Dee's trail."

"There's a phone booth, and I do believe the phone is still connected," Carmine said, pulling in to the side of the road. "Abe, get on to Danny and ask him to send out search parties for Delia. This isn't something I want going out on our radio; it's too important for truckers and bored housewives. The one person we need most in this operation is Delia."

Who was waiting, eyes bright, when Carmine and Abe walked in. Two Plant Physical workmen had erected a setup consisting of as many trestle tables as the office would hold, their tops newly covered with butcher paper held down by thumbtacks. The limp and sodden contents of Philip Smith's briefcase were stacked haphazardly on a chair seat under Delia's martial eye. As soon as the last table was finished and the two handymen had left, she began distributing the papers, one sheet at a time, on the off-white surfaces at her disposal.

"Oh, the man is a treasure!" she exclaimed, bustling from one table to another with various sheets. "Meticulous in the extreme! *Not* his secretary's doing, I can assure you—apart from Yours Truly, no secretary would dream of such precision. See? Every follow-on page is labeled in the top left-hand corner with subject or person plus date of the missive, while the page number is in the right-hand corner. Wonderful, wonderful!"

In all, there were 139 pages of letters and reports, plus a bound 73-page dissertation on the advantages of maintaining a research facility. That seemed peculiar to Carmine; Cornucopia Research was at least five years old, so why carry a bulky book full of long-established facts well known to the whole industry?

"He's a paper snob," said Delia when every page had been laid out and the bound report sat wrapped in a clean towel to dry its outer leaves and edges. "Nothing but high rag content paper, even for his memo pads. No cheap pulp for Mr. Smith! Nor ordinary print for his captions and letterheads—hot-pressed print only. At the same time, he's not splashy. Plain white stationery, black print, not even a color horn-of-plenty logo. Yes, everything of the very best, yet understated."

"Then you and I are going to go to work reading, Delia," Carmine said. "Corey, you take the hospital watch. Report any change in Smith's condition to me the moment you hear. The chief neurosurgeon, Tom Dennis, is a friend of mine, so I'll make sure we know as soon as a change happens. Abe, you hold the fort with Dee-Dee, Sir Lancelot, Pauline Denbigh and anyone else of interest. If there's a new case, you take it."

"What are we looking for?" Delia asked as Abe and Corey left. "Naturally I have some idea, but I'd like detailed instructions."

"The trouble is that if it's a verbal code, I don't think we stand a hope of cracking it," Carmine said, frowning.

"You mean statements like 'the clouds are dark over dear old Leningrad'?"

"Yes. If 'the rifling commences two feet down the barrel' actually means 'don't expect more from me quickly,' we won't know. But I don't think that kind of information interests us. We're looking for plans and formulae, probably reduced to microdots."

"How big is a microdot?" Delia asked.

"According to Kelly, whatever size will look logical, from the dot over an i to a fly speck or the bull's-eye in a two-inch drawing of a target. They don't have to be round, anyway. Round is less likely to be detected, Nature being nonlinear."

Her face puckered in dismay. "Oh, Carmine! There must be literally a million dotted i's here! Even if Mr. Smith's comatose state lasts several days, we have no chance of finding anything."

There was a fresh carafe of coffee on the counter. Carmine poured himself a mug and sat down on the wheeled chair he had stolen from the typists' pool because he could move around with his chair still attached to his butt. "That's why I don't think microdots are above an i. Or at least, an i with an ordinary dot. We should be looking for dots that are too big. That look like typos or smears. Kelly's so cagey that I haven't got much useful out of him, so we're winging it, Delia. To the best of my knowledge, cameras have finite limits, so maybe the reduction process can only be taken so far before another shot has to be taken and the reduction process recommenced. Since the space race began, things have miniaturized fast, but . . . I'm in true ignorance as to how it's done or how small a reduction in size can go." Carmine shrugged. "The best advice I can offer you is to use your common sense, Delia. If it looks wrong, we should see if it comes off. If it comes off, we should examine it under fifty or a hundred power on one of Patsy's microscopes."

They started to read, Delia on the letters, Carmine on the reports. An hour went by in silent intensity.

"How extraordinary!" Delia said.

Carmine jumped. "Huh?"

"Hasn't Mr. Smith always had a reputation for doing nothing?"

"So my sources have led me to believe."

"Well, for someone who has coasted through the however-many years of his—er—emboardment—he's kept a close eye on all sorts of people. Nor, it seems, is he happy to leave some of his observations behind during his absence. I'm reading a letter Mr. Smith apparently means to send to an M. D. Sykes, who bears the title of general manager of Cornucopia Central. I gather this means Mr. Sykes orders the stationery, checks the salaries and wages, looks after cleaning contracts and all sorts. Though from time to time over the years Mr. Sykes has had to substitute for men more senior than he."

"Jumping Jehoshaphat!" Carmine exclaimed, careful of his expletives when ladies were present. "I wouldn't have thought that Smith so much as noticed Cornucopia Central employed a general manager, let alone noticed it's Sykes. But to notice what Sykes has done! Is the letter interesting?"

"Yes and no. It's quite long. Mr. Smith lays out the feats Mr. Sykes has accomplished over the years when substituting for more senior executives, and praises his diligence and experience. Mr. Smith informs Mr. Sykes that, in his capacity as Chairman of the Board, he is promoting Mr. Sykes to the position of managing director, immediately under the Board. Mr. Sykes will now be responsible for overseeing all the Cornucopia subsidiaries on an executive level, and will answer only to the Board."

"That's a real bombshell," Carmine said, grinning. "Michael Donald *will* be happy! I can understand why Smith wouldn't want it lying around on his desk while he's away, though I wonder why he didn't just ship it off as internal mail before he went? A minor mystery. He plays Napoleonic war games."

"Who, Mr. Smith?"

"No, Mr. Michael Donald Sykes. On his new salary, he'll be able to stage his hero's coronation in Notre Dame, complete with gold and jewels."

"How odd!" Delia exclaimed, still on the letter to Sykes.

"What's odd?"

"Mr. Smith's system of tabulation—to which, by the way, he is much addicted. I've always preferred the letters of the alphabet to numbers when I tabulate because, provided one does not need more than twenty-six items, the tabulation column remains the same width. With numbers, once the number ten arrives, the column is one character wider, and to the left side at that. Most annoying! Whereas Mr. Smith neither enumerates nor eletterates—he uses a big, round black spot to tabulate—" She drew a hissing breath. "A big, round black spot!" she squealed.

Carmine scooted around the table on his wheeled chair and looked. "Holy shit!" he cried, forgetting ladies.

"There's another thing, Carmine," Delia said, voice shaking. "What machines can make a spot this size? A typewriter can't, nor anything I can think of apart from a printing press setting type. These tabulation spots must have been applied by hand. If they're not microdots, then Mr. Smith has gone to the trouble of using Letraset, and a man as fanatically tidy as that would be insane, even if he did force his secretary to do it."

"One thing for sure, Delia, Mr. Smith is not insane," said Carmine in grim jubilation. "I've got the bastard!"

"You mean he's Ulysses?"

"Oh, I've known that for some time."

He propelled himself across to a little table on which he had assembled a box of glass microscope slides, another of glass cover slips, some fine tweezerlike forceps, and a thin, pointed scalpel. Picking up the tray holding them, he returned to Smith's letter to M. D. Sykes and, working very delicately, tried to get the tip of the scalpel under the edge of a spot. It slid in easily; the spot came away, balanced on the scalpel tip. Carmine transferred it to a slide and dropped a cover slip on top. He took a total of five of the eleven spots in the Sykes letter, chosen at random.

With five glass slides on a paper plate, he walked to the Medical Examiner's department, Delia at his side.

"Tell me these aren't Letraset spots," he said to Patrick, giving him the plate. "Tell me they have typing on them, or schematics, or anything that shouldn't be there."

"You have found yourself a genuine, one hundred percent,

twenty-four karat, first-water microdot," Patsy said after examining the first slide. "A hundred-power—man, what a camera! What reduction ratios! Even so, it must have taken a dozen separate shots to get this down so small. No resolution has been lost, the definition's perfect."

"So now we know why Smith didn't send M. D. Sykes's letter by internal mail before he left," Carmine said to Delia as they went back to his office. "It had to travel out of the country with him. In Zurich the microdots in it would have been removed and Letraset spots substituted. Once back in Holloman, he could personally hand Mr. Sykes his promotion."

"Oh, Carmine, I am so delighted for you!"

"Save your ecstasies, Delia. Now I have to call Ted Kelly and tell him what we've found. I'm afraid that our participation in the case of Ulysses the spy is at an end."

An accurate prophecy. The astounded Ted Kelly arrived in minutes, gasping at what he called Carmine's luck.

"No, it wasn't my luck!" Carmine snapped, temper flaring. "It was the initiative of Sergeant Corey Marshall that got you your proof of espionage, Special Agent Kelly, and I insist that he be properly credited! If his name and his feat don't appear in your report, I'll tear Washington down around your ears!"

"Okay, okay!" Kelly yelled, backing away with palms up. "It will be written into my report, I promise!"

"I wouldn't trust you as far as I could throw you, Kelly!" Carmine thrust two typewritten sheets of police paper at him. "This is Corey's report of what happened, and that's how your own report starts. Fuck the FBI, and fuck you! You've piggybacked on our work, and I want that acknowledged."

"I'm so happy I'd consent to anything," Kelly said. "Are Smith's papers here?"

Carmine handed him a Holloman Police Department cardboard box. "Every last one, minus five spots off the Sykes letter. Which, by the way, I photocopied to make sure Mr. Sykes gets it. There's probably a copy in Smith's office, but I wanted to make sure. M. D. Sykes has been screwed around enough."

Kelly took the box as if it contained the crown jewels, then looked enquiring. "Um—the five spots?" he asked.

"Are going, together with a microscope, with me to the chambers of Judge Thwaites. I need proof of wrongdoing to get a search warrant. As soon as I've done that, I'll send you the evidence," Carmine said.

"You can't do that!"

"Try and stop me. I told you, you'll get them back. I was not kidding when I said I don't trust you or the FBI, Special Agent Kelly. As far as I know, the contents of Smith's briefcase may never come to light, or his person be tried for treason. But he will be tried for at least one murder, and for that, he'll go to prison for a very long time. Now piss off and leave me to my own business."

"Do you think they will try Mr. Smith for treason?" Delia asked, looking at a room full of trestle tables.

"I have no idea. Get rid of the tables, Delia. I'm going up to see your Uncle John." In the doorway he stopped. "Delia?"

"Yes?" she asked, one hand on the phone.

"You did a brilliant job. I don't know what I'd do without you, and that's the truth."

His secretary made a sound like a squeezed kitten, went very bright red, and turned away.

"Once Doubting Doug gets a look at my microdots, John, I should get my warrant," Carmine said.

"The more so because it vindicates his issuance of warrants after the sniper," Silvestri said. "No egg on his face. I hope the proof of Dee-Dee's murder is where you think it is, Carmine, because I have a funny feeling the Feds don't want this guy tried for treason. The days of the Rosenbergs are over. Smith's a high-end Boston WASP."

"I don't think so," Carmine said thoughtfully. "There was a Philip

Smith, I'm sure, but at some time over the past twenty-five years, a KGB colonel assumed his identity. Sometimes Smith makes weird mistakes about American customs and traditions, and his wife, according to Delia, is not a Sami Lapp. Delia thinks she hails from one of those Stans that comprise Siberia or the Central Asian steppes. Her native language is not Indo-Aryan."

"Nor are Turkish and Hungarian, for that matter."

"True. Despite which, John, I'd bet my last buck Smith's a plant. There is no Anna Smith in the Peace Corps in Africa, and the Stephen Smith who's doing marine biology in the Red Sea—interesting color choice—isn't really attached to Woods Hole. He has a kind of honorary status there thanks to hefty donations to projects the Woods Hole people find difficult to fund. As for Peter Smith, petroleum engineer, he was in Iran working for BP, but went off wildcatting to Afghanistan, of all places."

"You suspect all three kids are in the USSR?"

"Between assignments, yes. Think how valuable they are! Totally bilingual, as American as apple pie."

"There's apple pie everywhere, Carmine."

"Yes, but not flavored with cinnamon. Flavored with cloves."

"What's really worrying you?" Silvestri asked.

"First off, the assistant. We still haven't found him, and he's even more resourceful when it comes to murder than Smith is. He's why I've had Danny put a guard on Smith's hospital room—the most vigilant men only, and in pairs."

"Any ideas at all about who he is?"

"Only that he's attached to Cornucopia. Lancelot Sterling was my pick, but I was wrong. It's not Richard Oakes the male secretary—he's too frail. So whoever it is hasn't been noticed as a suspect of anything. If he is caught, we may not even know his face, let alone his name."

"Don't Communists usually congregate in cells, Carmine?"

"The ideologues do, but does anyone know about the people who conduct active sabotage or espionage? That's where the Communist witch hunts failed. Ideology tended to be equated with damaging activity. It didn't always follow. But there might be a cell of damaging activists centered on Holloman and headed by Philip Smith. We know Erica Davenport was involved, and we know Smith has an assistant. That's three. How big is a cell? I don't feel like asking Ted Kelly, but that's my stubbornness. Say, four to six members? In which case, we're still in the dark about one to three of them."

"Pauline Denbigh?" Silvestri asked.

"I doubt it. She's an elitist and a feminist. The Reds may have loads of women doctors and dentists, but the Communist Party isn't stuffed with women at a high level, is it? No, I think she was tricked into killing her husband on the correct date, and is getting her kicks out of refusing to admit it."

"What about Philomena Skeps?"

"I can't imagine she's anything worse than an overprotective mother, but I intend to see her again," Carmine said. "For one thing, the ultimate control of Cornucopia is undecided, and that's not helped by this car accident. Can Philomena Skeps run the company? Or will she hand it over to her cat's-paw, Anthony Bera? Or leave it with the suddenly invigorated Phil Smith, given that she doesn't know he's a traitor and a killer?"

"Maybe Mr. Michael Donald Sykes will inherit the mantle," Silvestri said with a grin.

Carmine sighed, so loudly that the Commissioner blinked. "What's that for?" he asked.

"The FBI helicopter that made it so easy to get to Orleans on the Cape. I don't suppose County Services can afford one?"

"About as likely, Carmine, as a ticket to Mars."

"I hate that drive!"

"Then take Desdemona and make a day of it."

"I will, but not until Saturday," Carmine said.

"How's Smith?"

"Coming around, Tom Dennis says. No subdural hematoma or gross cerebral contusions, just a fractured skull and some swelling of the brain that's going down nicely. His right upper arm and shoulder blade are more painful. Collins needed surgery to fix his broken leg, and is swearing he'll never ride in an open car again. According to Corey, it was amazing to watch that machine flip in midair."

"Middle-aged teenyboppers!" Silvestri said. Suddenly he looked curious. "Carmine, what exactly tipped you off that Smith was Ulysses? I mean, it could have been any of them."

"No, I never suspected Grierson, John. What tipped me off was the verb Bart Bartolomeo used when he described what Erica Davenport said to Desmond Skeps at the Maxwell banquet. Not her words—those he didn't hear. But he said she kept hissing. It took a while for the lightbulb to go on, and I'm not sure when suspicion became certainty, but you can't hiss Collins or Purvey or Grierson. Smith, you can. Big time. Whatever else she said must have been full of esses too, but if she'd spoken a name that interrupted the sibilants, Bart would have noticed. Once I realized what Bart had actually said, I concentrated on Mr. Philip Smith."

"So it was all in a name," Silvestri said.

Warrant in hand, Carmine drove the next morning together with a squad car and Patsy's forensics van to the beautiful valley wherein Philip Smith had built his mansion.

Natalie Smith met him at the door, her profoundly blue eyes flashing fire, the anger distorting her smooth, yellowish face. "Can't you leave him alone?" she asked, her thick foreign accent making the words difficult to understand.

"Sorry, Mrs. Smith, I have to exercise this warrant."

"Must I sit in the folly? It's cold today," she said.

"No, ma'am. It's the folly we're searching, so you can stay in your house."

Carmine walked across the lush grass between the garden beds to where the little round temple stood, its Ionic columns, each fluted, supporting a tiled terra-cotta roof that sat on it like a Chinese coolie's hat. Only the English could have termed a garden adornment a folly, Carmine thought, treading up the steps. Steps and floor were both greenish terrazzo; the rest of the folly was constructed of pure white marble. Who in America had the skill to fashion this? he wondered. No one, he decided. The columns were probably imported from Italy, where sculptors abounded. American equivalents would be carving fancy tombstones.

A cursory inspection revealed no overt hiding place, but he had Abe Goldberg.

"Think you can find the secret compartment?" Carmine asked.

Abe's fair, freckled face broke into a smile, his blue eyes sparkled. "Does a fat baby fart?" he asked.

Carmine moved off the steps onto the grass and watched Abe work. First he had two cops remove the white table and chairs, then he stood at the center of the folly and rotated, his head tilted toward the roof. That over, he repeated the rotation, this time gazing at the floor. Then he walked each circular step all the way around, using Carmine as his marker. After which he lay flat out on the floor and started rapping it with his knuckles.

"Nothing," he said curtly.

The steps had been installed in sections of arc thirty degrees wide, which meant each full step had twelve sections. The edge of the highest step measured about three and three-quarter feet per section.

"Cumbersome to remove, but feasible," he said, picking up a crowbar and inserting it under the overlapping lip of the step.

He found the one that lifted on his fifth attempt. It was fitted as snugly as the others, but dislodged when levered and broke into jagged pieces.

"He doesn't open the compartment with a crowbar, Carmine. See? The section actually slides outward on runners like an expensive drawer. I've broken it," he ended with some regret. "Such nice work too." Up went his shoulders in a shrug. "No use regretting. Where's my camera?"

The Holloman PD used supermarket brown paper bags for large

items of evidence, small brown paper bags, and little brown paper envelopes. Abe's camera flashing blue under his eyes, Carmine flinched at the smell emanating from the compartment, then put both hands inside and withdrew a pair of coveralls akin to a boilersuit. Flash, flash from the camera. The garment was rigid with browned, dried blood, so much so that it took time to compress it into folds, reduce it to something that would slide into the bag. It had not been as carefully preserved as Lancelot Sterling's souvenir; mold and mildew fuzzed and whiskered its crevices, and insects scurried for shelter.

"There's nothing else inside," said Abe, disappointed.

"Well, we photographed it in situ, withdrawn, the step, the sliding mechanism and everything else we can think of," Carmine said, sitting back on his heels. "It's enough, but I want the razor. Where is it?"

"You said enshrined, but you don't enshrine anything you revere in the same space as you put your bloody clothes," Abe said. "The Ghost, Carmine! Think adoration."

"Then it's somewhere else in here, Abe. In one of these columns. There must be a column drum with a compartment in it at about . . . head height. So he can look without touching."

"Won't happen," Abe said pessimistically. "The marble will be too thick to sound hollow. There must be a spring that opens a door when pressed, but not manually. At the weight, given that the door will be the full length of one column drum, Smith must have electrically wired the spring. Wiring under the ground, under the steps and the floor, up inside the shrine column. All of them are probably hollow at their centers, but the shrine one much more so. I bet he triggers the door by an impulse from a wireless control he holds in his hand—he's a ham radio nut, he must know every trick there is. If he wasn't carrying the control to Zurich with him—and why would he?—then it's lying in the open among the other junk in his radio shack."

"Check the columns with a magnifier first, Abe. If there is a door, the joins must show."

"Look at a column closely, Carmine—any column will do."

"Shit!" said Carmine, peering. "A thin line runs down the middle of each flute."

"We have to find his control. Either that, or demolish the whole temple."

"Which would be a terrible shame," Carmine agreed. "Okay, Abe, go look in the radio shack. Our warrant doesn't extend to the house, but the shack's in the open on the roof. Find the control, and it won't matter—no, it does matter! Smith's too rich for us to bluff the lawyers he'll hire. Back I go to the Judge."

Two hours elapsed before Carmine returned with a warrant to look in the radio shack. Judge Thwaites, horrified at the news that evidence had already been recovered implicating Smith in murder, made it a sweeping one. If they needed, they could search the house as well.

They didn't need to. A search of the radio shack yielded three small switch panels of the kind people use to open their garage doors. The difference was that all three were homemade. The second opened the door hidden in one column.

Folded into its ivory shell, the razor was perched on two forked silver prongs arising from a stand worked in exquisite filigree; the whole cavity was lined with padded crimson satin.

"The stand isn't silver," Abe said. "It's not tarnished."

"My guess is chromium plating rather than platinum," said Carmine, peering closely.

Using his clean handkerchief, he removed the razor, taking care not to smudge its surfaces. It hadn't been washed, and dried blood coated it thickly, especially around the hinge. It went into a brown envelope, sealed and witnessed.

"I should have remembered to bring rubber gloves," Patsy's technician said regretfully. "Dr. O'Donnell is very keen to make them compulsory for gathering evidence."

"It's okay, we'll manage," Carmine said. "After all the fuss about this case dies down, the Commissioner and your boss are planning a think tank about evidence. It's a headache."

"If Smith's prints are on that razor," Abe said, packing up his camera, "we've got him cold."

"Provided the prints are either in the blood itself or over the top of the blood," Carmine said.

"They will be, Carmine, they will be!"

"What I'm wondering is what those other two garage door buttons open. Doubting Doug is going to murder *me*, but I think I have to have a warrant for this entire property, inside and out, and go around every room, statue, sundial, pillar and post until I open two other electrically controlled secret doors. I have a feeling it will pay me to do that," Carmine said.

"You've already got warrants up the wazoo," Abe objected.

"Yes, but the judicial climate is changing, Abe, and the cops who don't go with it are fools. I want my new warrant to specify that I'm looking for what these two controls open."

"Then make sure the batteries powering them are new."

On Saturday the Delmonico couple piled into the Fairlane and set off for Orleans. Even though she knew she would have to wait elsewhere while Carmine quizzed Philomena Skeps, Desdemona was delighted at the expedition. She had never been to Cape Cod, and the prospect of a rare day out with Carmine thrilled her. In Holloman he was at the mercy of his huge family, and so by extension was she, not to mention the demands of his job. Now she was almost one hundred percent sure she had him captive for eight or ten hours. No one was going to walk through the door, no phone was going to ring asking for his police presence. Into the bargain, it was a perfect day on the cusp of summer.

Julian had been left with Aunt Maria and a tribe of girl cousins who would spoil him rotten, and Desdemona was not so doting a mother that she fretted when he wasn't with her. This was a holiday, and she could see from the volume of traffic on I-95 that quite a number of other people had decided to take a drive Capeward on such a beautiful day. The only thing that blighted her mood was Carmine's wearing a .38 automatic on his belt together with his gold captain's shield. But when she opened the glove box to put a bag of candy inside and saw a second .38 nestled among spare ammunition clips, she gasped in horror.

"Oh, I don't believe it!" she cried. "Where are we going, to Dodge City?"

"You've been watching television," he accused, smiling.

"And you've been accumulating paranoia! Honestly, Carmine! Two guns? Extra ammunition? How can I be comfortable in the midst of an arsenal? Is Julian to see this sort of thing?"

"The spare is always in the glove box, Desdemona. You don't normally open it, is all. I'd forgotten it was there."

"Codswallop! You'd forget your own head first!"

"Well, maybe." He grinned. "Without my sidearm I feel naked, and that's the truth. When we go into a HoJo's for some breakfast, I'll be wearing my jacket and no one will know. John Silvestri suggested I take you, but don't make me regret it, Desdemona. I have to see two suspects today, and while I don't expect fireworks, it's a stupid cop that isn't prepared for them."

She sat in silence for a while, digesting the note of finality in his voice and not liking the fact that he had rebuked her as if it were she at fault. Her strength and independence rebelled, but her sense of justice said she had known when she married a cop what it entailed. What bothered her was the gap that yawned between the sexes when it came to guns. Women abominated them. Men esteemed them. And Julian would be on his father's side.

"I wonder," she said at last, "how do other women manage to sleep knowing their husbands have a gun under the pillow?"

"About like you, lovely lady. Out like a light for as many hours as the kids permit."

She laughed. "Touché!"

"If I pushed papers or machined metal for a living, there would be no need for me to carry a gun," Carmine said. "But cops are peacetime soldiers. There's a war going on, and soldiers have to be armed.

The worst of it is that the war involves civilians too. Look at you and Julian by the boat shed."

"Then perhaps," she said, swallowing, "I should learn to use a gun, even if I don't carry one."

"I think that's sensible," Carmine said warmly. "Shooting accidents happen through sheer ignorance. I'll arrange for you to learn at the police range. Better fire a .38 automatic, because I've switched to one, though Silvestri won't."

Yet one more battle lost, Desdemona thought. I wasn't able to make him see my side of it, but he worked me around to seeing his side. And what would I do if someone came after Julian? I would want to protect him.

They pottered through the incredible seaside mansions of Rhode Island, mostly converted now to institutions and rest homes, but still betraying their millionaire origins. After a good breakfast they entered the biceps of the Cape, and Desdemona marveled at the beauty.

"Better in July, when the roses are out," Carmine said.

"I never realized how many hauntingly beautiful, Old World spots this part of America has. I thought seaside villages like Essex in Connecticut were glorious, but the Cape Cod villages are more so—no, make that differently so," said Desdemona.

They reached Orleans in the early afternoon. Carmine set Desdemona down in the sand dunes beginning to run up the Atlantic side of the Cape's forearm, and drove off to see Philomena Skeps.

Who was waiting, placidity unruffled. Well, I'm here to spoil that, Carmine thought, seating himself in a white chair on the patio behind her house.

"When do you move to Boston?" he asked.

"Not before September," she said. "One last Cape summer."

"But you'll keep this house, surely?"

"Yes, though I doubt I'll manage much more than an occasional weekend visit. Desmond is keen to be somewhere that he can see movies, play pinball machines, mingle with friends."

She spoke in the same gentle, even voice, but the unhappiness ran beneath its timber like water in an underground stream. Ah! Carmine thought. She's beginning to realize her son's sexual inclinations.

In fact, she had subtly aged in a very few short weeks. Her eyes were starting to produce crow's-feet at their outer edges, and two faint lines ran down her cheeks to the corners of her mouth, which now turned down a little. The most amazing change of all was a broad ribbon of stark white hair through the black curls above her left forehead; it gave her an eldritch quality, as of a medieval sorceress.

"Have you established the future of Cornucopia yet?"

"I think so," she replied with a faint smile. "Phil Smith will continue as Chairman of the Board, the present members will all continue, and I will stay in the background as trustee of my son's controlling interest. Provided nothing untoward happens, I don't see why anything should change. Erica's death leaves a vacancy on the Board that I intend shall be filled by Tony Bera."

"It's in relation to the composition of the Cornucopia Board that I'm here, Mrs. Skeps," Carmine said in the same formal way. "Philip Smith will be leaving the Board permanently."

Her deep green eyes widened. "What do you mean?"

"He's been arrested for murder and espionage."

Her breast heaved; she clutched at her throat. "No! No, that's quite impossible! *Phil?* You are mistaken, Captain."

"I assure you, I am not. The evidence is overwhelming."

"*Espionage?*"

"Oh, yes. He's been passing secrets to Moscow for at least ten years," Carmine said.

"Is *that* why—?" She broke off.

"Why what, Mrs. Skeps?"

"Why he speaks Russian when he's alone with Natalie."

"If you'd told me that earlier, ma'am, it would have helped."

"I never thought anything of it until now. Natalie's not comfortable in English, and though Russian isn't her native tongue, she speaks it well. Phil said he'd done a Berlitz course when he married her. He used to laugh about it."

"Well, he's not laughing now."

She twisted in her chair, upset and distracted. "Tony! I need Tony!" she cried. "Where is he? He should be here!"

"Knowing Mr. Bera, I predict he's lurking outside waiting for the right moment." Carmine got up and went to the corner of the house. "Mr. Bera!" he bellowed. "You're needed!"

Bera appeared seconds later, took one look at Philomena, and glared at Carmine furiously. "What have you said to put her in such a state?" he demanded.

Carmine told him, which clearly astounded him as much as it had Philomena. The two of them huddled on a cast iron settee and stared at Carmine as if he bore their execution orders.

"*Two* places vacant on the Board!" Bera exclaimed.

Which gives me an idea of his priorities, Carmine thought. He doesn't give a rat's ass about espionage or murder, all he cares about is a pliant Board to protect young Desmond's—and his own— interests. Mr. Anthony Bera bears watching.

"If it's any consolation, Mr. Smith's last executive order was to appoint a new managing director for Cornucopia Central," he said briskly. "He fills Erica Davenport's non-Board shoes, though not her Board ones. His name is Mr. M. D. Sykes."

This news item didn't interest either of them, but Carmine hadn't thought it would. He'd thrown it in to provoke a reaction, and had he got one, he would have had to dig into the past of Mr. M. D. Sykes. A relief to know there was no necessity.

When he left, it was with the rooted conviction that Tony Bera would skim as much cream off young Desmond's milk pan as he could over the next eight years. But that was white-collar crime, not his concern.

"What an odd world it is," he said to Desdemona as they headed for a lobster restaurant. "Some guy pinches ten grand from his firm, and he goes to prison. Whereas some other guy pinches millions from a company's funds and doesn't even get prosecuted."

"Better to be at the top of the heap than the bottom," Desdemona said. "Oh, Carmine, thank you for today! I rolled in the sand, paddled, let the wind blow through my hair, feasted my eyes on these gorgeous villages—absolute heaven!"

"I only wish I'd accomplished more," he grumbled. "That pair may not be spies or killers, but they're guilty of a lot of things. Bera's got Philomena hooked, yet he's also seduced her son. The bastard swings both ways."

"Oh, that's disgusting!" she cried. "To make love to a woman *and* her son! Surely she doesn't know?"

"No, she doesn't know, though she's starting to suspect that young Desmond likes men too much. If you saw the kid, you'd know he's behind the eight ball anyway. *Too* beautiful. It probably began at school, and that's what she's blaming."

"You're saying it's inherent in the boy?"

"Definitely."

"Is he effeminate?"

"No! Tough as old leather, hard as nails."

At which moment the Fairlane entered the parking lot of the lobster restaurant.

Desdemona dismissed worries that were not her concern save as a mother. She was too happy to be cast down, she reflected, ordering a lobster roll. What had sent her in a hurry from London back to Holloman was the knowledge that the fertile segment of her monthly cycle was due, and that if she missed spending it with Carmine, she would have to wait another month to try again. Julian was about to turn six months old; if she conceived now, he would be fifteen or sixteen months old when the new baby arrived. That was long enough. If they were brothers, the younger stood a chance of physically catching up before Julian left home. And that, she thought in satisfaction, means that if they do detest each other, the older won't always be able to wallop the tar out of the younger.

Tummy full of lobster roll, Desdemona fell asleep before they got to Providence.

And so much for Silvestri's theory about companionship, Carmine thought, his right arm aching from the pressure of his wife's head. Still, it's been a great day, and with any luck I'll never have to go back to Orleans.

On Monday, Carmine was allowed to see Philip Smith, who occupied a private room high in the Chubb-Holloman Hospital. At Carmine's request it was the last room down a long corridor, and as far from the fire stairs as any room could be. The room opposite had been requisitioned by the County and served as a recreation area of sorts, enabling Smith's round-the-clock guards to use its bathroom, have a coffee carafe on permanent tap, and sit in comfortable chairs on their breaks. How the Commissioner had wangled it Carmine didn't want to know: the FBI was picking up the tab.

Smith's room was filled with flowers. That, together with the soft lilac of its walls and padded vinyl furniture, gave it an un-hospital look at first glance. Then, past such things, the eyes noticed the sterility of the bed, the ropes and pulleys, the incredible way any occupant of such an infernal rack was automatically shrunken in size, stripped of authority and power.

This Philip Smith looked older than his sixty years, his handsome face collapsed in on itself a little, his blue-grey eyes unutterably weary.

When Carmine entered, only those eyes moved. Smith probably had to be turned and adjusted by a nurse, given his arm and shoulder. Surprisingly, there wasn't a nurse in attendance.

"I've been expecting you for several days," Smith said.

"Where's your private nurse?"

"Fool of a woman! I told her to wait at the station until I buzzed.

I'm grateful for the attention when I need it, but I loathe gratuitous solicitude. Can I do this for you, can I do that for you? Pah! When I want something, I'm capable of asking."

Carmine sat in a padded lilac vinyl chair. "For what they charge, these should be covered in Italian kid," he said.

"So a visitor's toddler can wee on them? Have a heart!"

"True. Save Italian kid for boardrooms and executive offices. Where you're going, Mr. Smith, there won't even be vinyl. Just hard plastic, steel, mattress ticking and concrete."

"Rubbish! They'll never convict me."

"Holloman will. Have you been interviewed by the FBI?"

"Interminably. That's why I've hungered to see your face, Captain. It has a certain Romanesque nobility the FBI faces have lacked. I think the only person who hasn't made the journey from Washington to see me is J. Edgar Hoover himself, but I hear that he's a disappointment in the flesh—soft and rather chubby."

"Appearances can be deceiving. Have you been charged?"

"With espionage? Yes, but they won't follow through." Smith's lips drew back to reveal teeth yellowed by his hospital stay. "I lost my luck," he said simply. "It ran foul of yours."

"Men your age shouldn't drive twelve-cylinder sports cars, more like. It was wet, the road was a mess, you were going way too fast, and you weren't concentrating," Carmine said.

"Don't rub it in. I must have driven that road a hundred times to board a hired plane. I guess it was the thought that this time I'd be boarding my own plane."

"I'm charging you with the murder of Dee-Dee Hall, Mr. Smith. We found your coveralls and the razor."

The hatred blazed; his body stiffened, battling to shed its restraints until the pain struck. He groaned. "That unprintable, unmentionable whore! She deserved to die as all whores should—cut from ear to ear! The scarlet yawn for a scarlet woman!"

"I'm more interested in why Dee-Dee didn't flee or fight."

"I need the nurse," he said, groaning again.

Carmine pressed the buzzer.

"Now look at what you've done!" the woman chided, slotting a syringe into an outlet on his IV drip.

"Speak not in ignorance, you moron!" Smith whispered.

Bridling indignantly, she left.

"I'd like to know the why of Dee-Dee," Carmine said.

"Would you indeed? The thing is, do I feel like telling you?" Smith asked, settling into his pillows gratefully as the pain ebbed. "Are we alone? Are you recording what I say?"

"We are alone, and I am not recording us. A tape would not be valid evidence in a court of law without witnesses present and your consent. When I charge you formally, I'll have witnesses, and remind you of your rights under the Constitution."

"So much solicitude, and all for me!" Smith mocked. His eyes clouded a little. "Yes, why not? You're a cross between a mastiff and a bulldog, but there's cat in there too. Curiosity is your besetting sin, Erica said to me, very frightened."

His lids fell, he dozed. Carmine waited patiently.

"Dee-Dee—!" he said suddenly, eyes open. "I suppose you searched for my Peace Corps daughter?" he asked.

"Yes, but I couldn't find one."

"Anna wasn't interested in good works," Philip Smith said. "Her bent was purely destructive, and America suited her because here there are so few social brakes one can apply to headstrong children. She was the wrong age to make the move from West Germany to Boston and then Holloman—the bleakness of her old life was blown away on the gale of indulgence, promiscuity, infantile aspirations, undisciplined passions. The wrong age, the wrong place, the wrong child . . ." Smith stopped.

Carmine said nothing, did not move. It would come out at Smith's pace, and in chunks.

"School? What was school, except a place to avoid? Anna played hookey so much that Natalie and I were obliged to give it out that we were teaching her at home. We were utterly impotent, we couldn't control her. She laughed at us, she mocked us, she couldn't be trusted with socialist enlightenment. From her fourteenth year onward, it was like having an enemy in the house—she knew we were hiding something. So Natalie and I agreed that she should have whatever money she wanted, and do whatever she wanted." Came a sinister chuckle. "Since she hardly lived at home or acknowledged us, few people knew of her, isn't that odd? We were able to continue our socialist duties by giving up Anna as a lost cause."

Another pause. Smith dozed, Carmine watched.

"She acquired a boyfriend when she was fourteen. A twenty-year-old petty criminal named Ron David—*a black man!*" Smith shouted it; Carmine jumped. "Sex enthralled her, she couldn't get enough of it or him, would rut with him anywhere, anytime, anyhow. He had an apartment on the edge of the Argyle Avenue ghetto—disease-ridden, rat-infested. Full of whores, including Dee-Dee Hall, who was a good friend of his. Ron introduced Anna to Dee-Dee, and Dee-Dee introduced Anna to heroin. Does that appall you, Captain Delmonico? Don't let it! Save your horror for my next item of news: Anna and Dee-Dee became lovers. They were inseparable. Inseparable . . ."

Dear God, thought Carmine, I don't want to hear this. Take a break, Mr. Smith, sleep a while. Did you love your wayward daughter, or was she an embarrassing nuisance? I can't tell.

Smith continued. "There was no difference between Dee-Dee and the heroin. Both were vital necessities to Anna, who moved out of Ron's apartment and into Dee-Dee's." Another sinister chuckle. "But Ron refused to take his marching orders. The money Anna had lavished on him was now being lavished on Dee-Dee. You would think, Captain, wouldn't you, that my daughter would have accepted my offer to house her and Dee-Dee in the lap of luxury on the West Coast? No, that would have been too convenient for her parents! She and Dee-Dee *liked* living in squalor! The heroin was easy to obtain, and what else mattered?"

"How long were Anna and Dee-Dee together?" Carmine asked.

"Two years."

"And this was back in the very early 1950s?"

"Yes."

"Then Dee-Dee wasn't much older than Anna. Two kids."

"Don't you dare pity them! Or me!" Smith cried.

"I do pity them, but I don't pity you. What happened?"

"Ron invaded Dee-Dee's apartment with a cutthroat razor, intending to teach them a lesson. I am not conversant with the cant, but I gather that he was 'off his face' with drugs. So it was Anna used the razor. She cut his throat very efficiently. Dee-Dee called me at home and told me. I was obliged to deal with that nightmare just as my—my patriotic socialist duties at Cornucopia were commencing. Ron vanished—and don't hope to find his body, Captain! It lies very far from Connecticut."

"Where is Anna now?" Carmine asked.

"In a camp in Siberia where she has no access to heroin or sex or whores," her father said. "She's thirty-one years old."

"And all these years later you took out your spleen on a poor, defenseless whore?" Carmine asked incredulously. "Christ, has it never occurred to you that you yourself might be to blame for some of it?"

Smith chose not to hear the second part. "Defenseless, nothing! Poor, nothing!" he shouted. "Dee-Dee Hall is a symptom of the disease rotting America's stinking carcass! Women like her should be shot or put to hard labor! Whores—drugs—Jews—homosexuals—blacks—adolescent promiscuity!"

"You make me sick, Mr. Smith," Carmine said evenly. "I don't think you're a patriotic socialist, I think you're a Nazi. Marx and Engels were both Jews, and they'd spit on you! How long is it since you slid inside the original Philip Smith's shell? He was a full bird colonel in the U.S. Army, but a shadow. He answered to no one, he did what he pleased, he went where he pleased, and everybody on his West German base assumed he was someone big with one of the secret services. How do I know this when the FBI thought you were CIA and dropped their enquiries? Easy, Mr. Smith! I spent the war in the military police—there's nothing and no one I can't learn about. In 1946, when he went on a secret mission, one Philip Smith was kidnapped and shot, and another Philip Smith took his place. That Philip Smith—you—returned from Germany to Boston early in 1947, complete with foreign wife, like so many of those Occupation guys. The hardest thing to conceal was the age of your marriage and your kids. But you did it the best way—you just appeared, a discharged colonel and his family, in Boston."

Smith was listening impassively, his mouth shaped into a sneer. But the eyes, windows on a morphine-dulled brain, were confused and astounded.

"The aristocratic Boston millionaire adopted an aloof pose that enabled him to fill the shoes of someone never seen since 1940, when the original Smith, having no close relatives, joined the army way ahead of Pearl Harbor. You manufactured a blood kinship to the Skepses in the shrewdest way—simply say it to all and sundry, and sooner or later all and sundry will believe it. Including the Skepses. You joined the Board of Cornucopia in 1951, four years after your reappearance in Boston society. Having built that beautiful house, you moved to Holloman and became who you really are—a rude, arrogant, ruthless shit. People at Cornucopia, including the very young Desmond Skeps, accepted the fact that you adorned the Board but did no work. After all, what's unique about that? Most members of boards do nothing except take fat fees."

"Envious, Captain?" Smith asked with a purr in his voice.

"Of you? No way, Mr. Smith. I am consumed with admiration of the dedicated socialist agent doing his patriotic duty as he lives high off the hog among his ideological enemies. You've never lived in a cold-water walk-up flat on the sixth floor where the pipes freeze, and you never will. You, Mr. Smith, are far above ordinary people, and that won't change, whichever country you live in, will it, huh? The USSR or the USA, you'll still be in a limousine, still have servants to treat like dirt, still have all the perks of a rich and powerful party man. Here, it's a capitalist party. There, it's the Communist Party.

Makes no difference to you! Well, you've failed both masters. You're of no further use."

"What a romantic you are, Delmonico," Smith said, lips distorted in an anger he couldn't quite suppress.

"I've been accused of that before, but I don't find it an insult." Carmine leaned forward in his chair until his face loomed close to Smith's. "You know what's most romantic of all? That you were exposed for what you are by a capitalist toy like a sex-symbol sports car. You so nearly got away with it! That you didn't is entirely your own fault. Think about that when you sit on your stinking toilet in your prison cell, staring at the stains on your hand-me-down mattress! They'll have to isolate you because the most degenerate killer or child molester will deem you the pits—a traitor to your country. Oh, but you figure you'll be imprisoned for murder, not treason, right? Rich guy, bribing the warden for special privileges? It won't happen, Mr. Smith. Whichever prison is honored by your presence is going to know all about your treason. Your books will arrive covered in shit, your magazines will be torn to ribbons, your pens won't work—"

"Shut up! Shut up!" Smith screamed, his face the color of his bedsheet. "You wouldn't dare! The FBI and CIA won't let it happen! They need names, they think I can give them names! I will be very comfortably housed, wait and see!"

"Who's the romantic here?" Carmine asked with a grin. "They'll leave you to Connecticut's mercy until one of your names bears fruit, and none will. The only names you know belong to your own cell, all implicated in murder."

"You're wrong!"

"I'm right. You'll never come to trial for treason, it's too sensitive. Prison for murder suits everyone, Mr. Smith, and there won't be any comfort."

Smith's free left hand flailed. "All this for a whore?"

"You bet your life it is," Carmine said grimly. "Desmond Skeps found out about Dee-Dee and Anna, and brought Dee-Dee to the Maxwell banquet to flaunt her in your face. I'm guessing that he blamed you for the breakup of his marriage and then his affair with Erica—why, I suspect you don't know any more than I do. He was a paranoid kind of guy, and you represented a bunch of things he envied. You wore your clothes as easily as you did your persona, while he was behind the door when God handed out the gifts. Among his other deficiencies, he lacked courage, so he fortified himself with booze that night. What he didn't know was that you were Ulysses—but Erica did. She told him. Your good luck that he was too drunk to take it in. Yet that banquet was the start of your downfall."

"Nonsense, all nonsense," Smith said wearily.

"Not nonsense. Good sense. How you must have sweated! Though it looked as if you'd gotten away with it, you still made your plans in case you hadn't. Four months went by. Four whole months! Then Evan Pugh fronted up to your office, bold as brass, and handed you a letter. By the time you'd read it, he was gone. But you'd set eyes on him, and you knew what he was. It takes one to know one. The plan swung into action." Carmine stopped.

"I'm tired, and in pain," Smith said. "Go away."

"A bear trap!" Carmine said. "What was its significance?"

"It had none because I have no idea what you're talking about. It's because of people like him that you're persecuting me. Not because of a whore. Dee-Dee Hall doesn't matter."

"She does to me," Carmine said, and walked out.

"It was unreal, John," he said to the Commissioner later. "At first I thought Smith adored his daughter, but he couldn't have. No one who loves would incarcerate the object of his love in a Siberian concentration camp. He could so easily have shut her away in some plush asylum—places like L.A. and New York must abound in them! No, maybe that's an exaggeration, but you know what I mean."

"I do." Silvestri chewed on his cigar and grimaced, then threw it in his wastebasket. "Where did you find the time to do all the research?"

Carmine smiled. "A bit here, a bit there. It seemed so far out that I couldn't share it until I'd gotten it all straight. I think maybe Smith's people in Russia were czarist aristocrats who switched camps in time to ride the Communist parade. Lenin was short of educated helpers in 1917 and probably willing to overlook the antecedents of some eager volunteers. Smith himself would have grown up under the system from his tenth birthday. We tend to forget that it's only fifty years since the Red Revolution."

"A mere mote in history's eye," Silvestri said. "It runs so counter to human nature that I'm picking it only has another three or four decades to go before the greedies pull it down."

Carmine's eyes danced. "I love it when you philosophize," he said, grinning.

"Any more remarks like that, and you'll feel the toe of my regulation boot up your ass." He changed the subject. "I'd feel happier if I thought we were any closer to catching Smith's assistant, Carmine."

"Not a sign of the bastard," Carmine said. "He's lying low and waiting for orders. What I don't know is if his orders will come from Smith or Moscow."

"I'm fed up with wars, especially cold ones."

"Insane, isn't it? Smith's not in a position to issue any orders at the moment. The FBI or CIA or whoever are tapping his phone." Suddenly Carmine bounced in his chair. "Want to hear something weird, John?"

"Weird away."

"Smith can't bring himself to use the word 'spy.' When he came to a spot in his narrative where he had to say it, he went all melodramatic on me and called it his 'patriotic socialist duty.' I've never heard anything weirder than that, spoken by a sophisticated smoothie like him. For a minute I really felt as if I were in the pages of a Black Hawk comic book."

"In denial, I suppose," Silvestri said.

"Yeah, I suppose."

"When are you going back to Smith's property to play with your garage controls? It might pay off."

"I agree, but give me a day or two, sir! The Judge can be very exasperating," Carmine wheedled.

It got him nowhere. "Tomorrow, Captain, tomorrow." Then Silvestri relented. "I'll call the persnickety old terror and beg him to be nice. Once he hears the story, he'll play ball."

Abe and Corey were in their office, sufficiently bored to follow Carmine to his room with alacrity.

"We have two controls," Carmine said, "and five acres of landscaped gardens as well as a three-storey mansion to search."

"No, sir, three controls," Abe said. "The one that opened the column might open another door out of signal range."

"I don't know about that," Corey said dubiously. "I heard that a garage door control on Long Island was opening the missile silo doors on a base in Colorado."

"Yeah, and we can all get Kansas City on our television sets if the weather's right," Carmine said. "Well, on this exercise we're not going to worry about missile silo doors or Kansas City, okay? You're right, Abe, we should use all three controls. What I want to do today is work out a plan."

"Delia!" said Abe and Corey in chorus.

"Delia?" Carmine called.

She came in quickly, the only one of his little task force disappointed at the solution of the importance of Dee-Dee Hall; her mission of exploration had fizzled as soon as Smith explained about his daughter.

"Isn't it lucky," she said gleefully, "that I have aerial survey maps of Mr. Smith's property? I got maps of all four suspects' properties and had Patsy blow them up to poster size."

"One step ahead as always," said Carmine.

Though the picture was black-and-white, it displayed most features clearly, provided they were not under the canopies of trees. A border of tall conifers surrounded Smith's five acres. The house showed all its exterior features, from cornices to the radio shack, and the artificial lake proved to have a tiny isle in its middle joined to land by a Chinese bridge. The picture had been taken with the sun directly overhead—a necessity for a useful survey from the air.

"The white or grey dots must be statues, and the fountains are self-explanatory," Delia said. "The jumble behind the house must be garages, garden or equipment sheds, the usual appurtenances of a mansion on a fair-sized piece of land. See there? That's a patch of dead or dying grass, so you should check it for a slab of concrete underneath. My papa insisted on building an atomic bomb shelter in our back lawn, and the grass was never the same over it. He still keeps it stocked with food."

"Well, I don't think we should deal with the outside first," Corey said firmly. "If I were Smith, I wouldn't have my secret compartments anywhere I'd get wet. And what about a hard winter? *Feet* of snow!"

"You're right, Corey," said Carmine. "We do the house first. Also the outbuildings and the immediate vicinity of the house. He has an army of Puerto Rican servants to clear snow away."

"There's one more thing," Abe said.

"What's that?" Carmine asked, enjoying listening.

"The controls might trigger more than one door each."

"Depending on missile silo doors and Kansas City. What a bummer! Who can give us advice?" Carmine asked.

"The new guy working with Patrick," Corey said. "I had lunch with him the other day. He was the one told me about the missile silo doors—he used to be a master sergeant in the air force. This guy—his name is Ben Tucker—is a utility player. Photography, electronics, mechanics. I can ask him for tips."

"Do that, Corey."

"What about warrants?" Delia asked.

"The Commissioner assures me that Doubting Doug will play ball," Carmine said.

"Huh! I'll believe that when I see it," Abe muttered.

*   *   *

Whatever Silvestri had told Judge Thwaites worked. When Carmine appeared in chambers the next morning, his warrant was already waiting for him.

"Commie spies!" His Honor exclaimed, wearing the same face that saw him hand down a maximum prison term. "You nail this bastard to the wall, Carmine!"

Their plan had been worked out: they would start as far from each other as possible, Carmine upstairs on the roof working down, Abe on the bottom floor working up, and Corey in the outbuildings. Each had a control, understanding that, having done it all, they would have to exchange controls and do it again, and yet a third time. For that reason, a system was mandatory, and each man was doomed to the same territory three times over.

It took less time than they had originally envisioned. If the batteries powering the controls were kept fresh, one press on a button could last as long as the thumb or fingertip doing the pressing. They became expert at standing in the center of a space and pressing, rotating slowly as they did so. Provided the signal beamed out above occluding furniture or objects, it was powerful enough to work in situations where a garage control would not have. Carmine began to understand the Long Island garage and the missile silo doors. Wow! That must have sent people back to the drawing boards! But what genius to trace the offending control! Kansas City was more captious by far.

They discovered a total of seven concealed compartments, only one of which was triggered by the folly control. That one yielded a metal box similar to three others found elsewhere, all fitted with padlocks. Each compartment was photographed, contents in situ, then contents removed, and contents themselves.

"When are you going to tell the FBI?" Abe asked, back at Cedar Street.

"Only after I've filtered out evidence of eleven murders," Carmine said. "Once that's done, they can have the espionage data and the controls. Knowing Special Agent Kelly, they'll be there for months, and end in tearing the place apart stone by stone. Pity, but I can't think anyone would ever want to live there again."

Carmine kept Delia but liberated Abe and Corey to take new cases and go back over Smith's murders.

His trove consisted of four locked metal boxes the size of a shoe box, a stack of ten thin children's exercise books, five fatter leather-bound books, and a series of Holloman County property plans, including the Cornucopia Building, the County Services building, the Nutmeg Insurance building, and Carmine's house and grounds on East Circle.

"These, we keep," he said to Delia, putting the plans to one side. "None relates to his spying activities."

The leather-bound books were all to do with his spying: codes, ciphers, a journal written in Russian Cyrillic script.

"We hand these over to the FBI," he said. "If they need additional proof of espionage, here it is."

"The microdots were proof enough!" Delia snapped.

"Ah, but he's an embarrassment, you see. In the social pages of papers and magazines, object of articles in the *Wall Street Journal* and *News*—how terrible! What do we inspect next? The exercise books or the tin boxes?"

"The boxes," Delia said eagerly.

"Pandora at heart." Carmine picked up the one taken from the compartment triggered by the folly control. "If there's tangible evidence of murder, this is the one." He picked up a pair of double-action snips and broke the padlock's U.

"Ohhh!" sighed Delia.

The box held an ampoule and a vial of two curares, six 10cc glass Luer-Lok syringes, a hypodermic needle, steel wire, a tiny soldering iron, an ordinary safety razor, and two small bottles fitted with thick rubber caps.

"Bingo!" cried Carmine. "We've got him for the murder of Desmond Skeps."

"Why on earth did he keep all this?" Delia asked.

"Because it amused him. Or fascinated him. Or he couldn't bear to part with it," Carmine said. "Mr. Smith is a mixture."

Two of the three remaining boxes contained money, each to the sum of $100,000 in mixed denominations.

"But Carmine, he doesn't need money!"

"His cache for a fast getaway," Carmine explained. "Once he got to Canada, it's enough to hire a private jet to anywhere."

The last metal box contained a 9mm Luger automatic with spare clips and assorted travel documents; among the passports was a Canadian one for a Philippe d'Antry.

"There are none here for his wife," Delia said sorrowfully.

"Rats and sinking ships, I'm afraid. Just as I'll bet he's left her to fend for herself in this crisis. If she has any sense, she'll have a cache of her own, and disappear."

"Remain only the exercise books," Delia said, handing them to Carmine.

"Russian, Russian, Russian, Russian, Russian," he said as he tossed each of the top five onto the FBI pile. "Ah! We have English!" He read for a moment, then looked at Delia, his face puzzled. "It's as if he has two personae. The spy thought, wrote and worked in Russian. The killer thought, wrote and worked in English. His entire life is compartmentalized! If ever a man was made to be two different men, it's Mr. Philip Smith a.k.a. whatever his Russian name is." He reached for the phone. "I'd better tell Desdemona I won't be home early. With any luck, I'll find out who his assistant is, maybe even his hirelings." He held up five of the exercise books. "Straight down the middle. Five in Russian, five in English. And I can't leave until I've read my five and digested their contents."

He leaned over, took Delia's hand and lightly kissed it. "I can't thank you enough, Miss Carstairs, but your part in this is done. Go home and relax."

"It was my pleasure," Delia said gruffly, "but I'm not going home. First, I'm off to Malvolio's to get you a snack and one of Luigi's thermoses of decent coffee. A burger, a bacon roll or a roast beef sandwich?"

"A burger," he said, crumbling. Two dinners wouldn't hurt for one night, would they?

"Then," she continued, "I'm going around to see Desdemona and Julian. I've been so busy since they got back from England that I haven't had a chance to find out how my potty papa is."

"From what I've been told, potty," Carmine said.

The first exercise book contained the sketchy details of Smith's occasional forays into crime during the first fifteen years of his tenure on the Cornucopia Board. The first entry of all, however, predated his appointment.

"The first Skeps has to go," it said in part. "My orders are explicit, as the son will be much easier to fool. It will be perfect KGB—as much powder as will fit on the head of a thumbtack, made from the same plant my mother used as an aperient when I was a child. A smaller dose would do it, but the swifter the better. In the first teaspoonful of the caviar I buy him, old miser. He wonders at its quality."

And then, some entries later: "The old man died, and the clock stopped, never to go again. A good song, I like it. The second Desmond Skeps has inherited, and Phil is there. Phil is always there. But I have refused to sit on the Board."

Two more entries saw Smith on the Board, though the book made no mention of Dee-Dee and his daughter.

It was kept, Carmine was interested to see, as a kind of diary; each entry was dated as day, month, year, which was not the American way of month, day, year. Each entry spoke about the murder of someone who had gotten in Smith's way, always dispatched by a dose of the magic powder developed by the KGB—a vegetable alkaloid of some kind, probably, unbelievably potent. Which plant? And why did none of his eleven victims of April third, 1967, die of it? Apparently it caused a total breakdown of the body's systems akin to the death mushroom, and produced a diagnosis of nonspecific septicemia, etiology unknown.

There were no references to what secrets he stole, or when he stole them; these must be in the Russian diaries. What a feast the FBI was in for!

The second-to-last book contained the Maxwell Foundation banquet, but it also contained many ravings about the perfidies of Dr. Erica Davenport, whom Smith loathed.

"I curse the day Moscow foisted this idiot woman on me!" Smith said, his anger—rarely expressed until now—let loose. "A fool, a beautiful fool who has left a trail a kilometer wide for the Americans to trace. When she appeared ten years ago I inundated KGB with protests, only to be told that she had powerful Party friends out to bring KGB down. Said friends have put her here to report on my loyalty. She transmits my every move to Moscow! Ah, but she's afraid of me! It didn't take me long to establish ascendancy over her, to intimidate her, to make her cower and cringe. But fear of me does not prevent her reporting back to her Party friends in Moscow, I am perpetually aware of that. Of course I report on her to KGB: I complain of her, I criticize her stupidity. Her friends in the Party may defend her, but I have the ear of KGB, I hold high KGB rank, my power in Moscow is greater than hers."

Carmine leaned back in his chair, metaphorically winded. So that's it! Stupid of me, to assume they were a team working together to steal our secrets. They turn out to be opponents in a game of surveillance, constantly watching each other for evidence of ideological disloyalty. Her Party bosses were appalled at Smith's lifestyle, whereas his KGB bosses, pragmatists to the core, understood that his lifestyle was imperative for success. So Smith deemed Erica the spy, and Erica deemed Smith the spy. The mere smuggling of secrets was incidental to their political tussle. Only one of them could win in Moscow, and Erica knew she was losing. KGB rules, not the Communist Party.

He read on. The date was the fourth of December. "The crazy bitch! I *abominate* obscenities, but she is a bitch—a stringy, fawning female dog. Six days ago she came to me in hysterical tears to tell me that Desmond had finished with her services as a fellatrix—he's going back to Philomena. Oh, the tears! The grief! 'But I love him, Phil, I love him!' So what? was my answer. You continue to do your patriotic duty! You will be nice to him, you will feed him business inspirations that I have fed you, and he will be grateful, he will be impressed, he will advance you even higher. All that and more I told her while she shivered and howled, the stupid bitch.

"Now she was here again with a new confession, hard on the heels of my witnessing last night with my own eyes Desmond Skeps arm in arm with Dee-Dee Hall! He brought that whore to the banquet! No wonder he chose to sit far from me and the other executives! 'I know your secret, Phil,' he said to me as he passed by. 'I know what happened to your daughter. What would the world make of the pristine Phil Smith and a junkie girl?' I pondered the answer to that question as I watched him at the fat banker's table, Dee-Dee preening in skin-tight puce satin and white mink. It was she got him drunk, of course. Desmond can't take a second drink. If he does, he keeps on drinking.

"I saw Erica, drunk, weave her way to his table and sit there for a few minutes. Why can't people govern their passions? Desmond was drunk because he's missing Erica's fellatio and unsure of Philomena, Erica was drunk because she's in love with Desmond. Round and round they go, where they stop, only I will know . . .

"Today I learned what transpired when Erica sat down with Desmond. She has confessed to me that, in the throes of her drunken state, she told Desmond that I am Ulysses. Confessed to me in floods of terrified tears! It is the weapon I've needed to fire at her Party friends in Moscow for ten years, so I made her write it out in Russian, and had Stravinsky witness it. 'However,' I said to the stupid bitch, 'if you do as I order you, I won't send it to Moscow.'

"I am released from her! I have my lever! Desmond was too drunk to hear what she said. She swore it, and I believe her, having seen him with my own eyes. Now I have my lever, and I wait. I wait to see what will ensue. If the Ulysses story comes out, Erica has to deny it—convincingly. I have my lever!"

What a world you live in, Mr. Smith, Carmine thought, the book dropped as he poured himself another mug of coffee. What a world you live in! Dog-eat-dog is too kind. Snake-eat-snake, more like. It's Smith who is the financial genius, not Desmond Skeps, not Erica Davenport. They were his pawns, he used them to build that company ever upward. More and more secrets. And that's how come he could finally dispense with Erica—a written confession for Moscow, himself the head honcho of Cornucopia. He didn't fear her Moscow bosses anymore.

His plans were made with KGB thoroughness.

An entry on the tenth of December read: "Not a peep about Ulysses the master spy as yet, but I have been thinking, and thinking hard. If there is a peep, I must be ready to move as quickly as a bolt of lightning, and with the same devastation. It won't be Desmond who makes the accusation—I've spoken to him many times since the banquet, and he suspects nothing. All he feels for me is gratitude that I gave him my special hangover cure. He doesn't even seem to remember that he brought Dee-Dee Hall, and when I asked him why he had, he looked utterly blank. In the end he said it must have been a combination of booze and her ability to perform fellatio— he was missing Erica's attentions in that department, but Philomena had insisted that Erica must go, and he was desperate to get Philomena back. I believe him on that point; he showed me a suite of pink diamonds he had bought her—a million dollars! Coming from Desmond, that's desperation. He's an inveterate miser. It must have been Dee-Dee who told him about Anna, and asked him to take her to the banquet just to torment me, the whore gone sanctimonious.

"Erica won't say anything, that is a given. Therefore the accusation, if it comes, will be from someone else at the table—someone not too drunk to remember. I do not believe Erica's protestations that her voice was too low for anyone save Desmond to hear. However, were it to be made in a spirit of patriotic zeal, I think it would already have been made, and loudly. That it has not predisposes me to think it will come as blackmail, either to Erica or directly to me. I have alerted her, which terrified her anew, the silly bitch. All I do is clean up the messes she makes.

"Naturally I have observed all the people attached to the table, so I have a fairly good idea whence the blackmail will come, if come it does. Blackmail is a two-edged sword, and Stravinsky agrees with me there. We have concluded that, if a blackmail threat does arise, all eleven people will have to die.

"If I commenced now, I could kill them one by one over time. The local police are surprisingly good, but not of KGB excellence. On the other hand, I confess that I am intrigued at the prospect of killing all eleven en masse. Such a coup! It would do more than merely confuse the local police—it would bamboozle them. And the exercise in sheer logistics is very appealing. Stravinsky demurs, but Stravinsky will obey orders. All good tools do, and Stravinsky is a good tool. A dream project! I am so bored! I need the stimulus of a completely new and novel project to lift me out of my doldrums, and this particular project is feasible. Stravinsky is forced to concur. Who would ever suspect one hand at the back of eleven deaths, if the way each person dies is utterly different? Oh, what a challenge! I am wide awake at last!"

And there you have it, Carmine thought. Ulysses had his espionage work down to such a fine art that he was bored, needed a fresh stimulus. A nice backhanded compliment for the Holloman Police—

we're surprisingly good, though not the KGB. I thank whatever gods there are for that!

"I've discovered that two of the men at the table have wives who can be tricked," wrote Smith on the nineteenth of December. "Mrs. Barbara Norton is quite insane, but hides it well. Disguised as a bowler named Reuben, Stravinsky struck up a conversation with her. An empty gourd where her brain should be. Norton the fat banker terrorizes her, and she's ripe for murder.

"The same can be said of Dr. Pauline Denbigh, though I will appeal to her personally, as one snob to another. Her husband beats her sadistically—what scum! She showed me those of her wounds that can decently be exposed. A mind of her quality, scorned for adolescent sluts! I'll leave her a jar of cyanide. She'll do the rest without prompting, except that I'll force her to act on the date of my choice. She'd resist all bribes except a Rilke original. I'll let her see it, and arrange that she'll have it after she's acquitted. I'll pay Bera a fortune—anonymously—on condition that he gets her off. He will!"

That would do it, Carmine thought. I doubt anything Smith has said in here would alter the jury's verdict, either. It's the mention of her wounds that will matter, not the date. A Rilke original! Man, the guy must have some contacts! Not that the jury would ever see this diary. Bera would find some way to have it struck from evidence.

And the feminism aspect fizzled out with Pauline Denbigh. Carmine abandoned it without much regret. All his enquiries had produced nothing that helped the case against Dean Denbigh's wife, nor had it unearthed a lover. Perhaps she truly was a sexually frigid person. Perhaps all her energies were channeled into women's causes and her love of Rainer Maria Rilke.

Bianca Tolano tore at the heartstrings. "I noted her at the table next to Dee-Dee the whore, and couldn't tell the difference between them," Smith said on the twenty-second of December. "A pair of whores! One the brassy finished product, the other the demure, sweet whore-in-the-making. The one in the making reminds me of Erica, so I'll visit the death on her that I long to give Erica. I've seen my tool. A sycophantic crawler named Lancelot Sterling drew my attention to him when I paid a visit to the twentieth floor of Accounting. A crippled runt named Joshua Butler. I admit I went there thinking Sterling might be my tool, but he's a deviate, not a cripple. Scum! When Joshua Butler left work I loitered in my Maserati and offered him a ride home. He was enthralled! I ended by taking him out to my house—no one was home—and giving him dinner. Stravinsky waited on table and agreed he was perfect for our purposes. By the end of the evening he was so enchanted he would have done anything for me. Not that I mentioned what I wanted! I simply started peering into his more disgusting fantasies. He'll do beautifully, though Stravinsky, stronger-stomached, will have to do most of the psychic exploration."

Intermixed with Smith's cold-blooded planning were touches of— mercy? Carmine wasn't sure that was the right word. But he did seem to have compassion for two of the victims, Beatrice Egmont and Cathy Cartwright. Eventually Carmine concluded that Smith esteemed them as worthy matrons who did not deserve to die, so should die quickly, painlessly.

Evan Pugh, he was interested to see, was intended to get a dose of KGB powder and die of nonspecific septicemia. Not a pleasant death by any means, but not as payback as the death he did get. Nor as terrifying while the agony lasted. He would have been in the hospital, drugged to the limit and not really suffering the way the bear trap made him suffer.

The three black victims had their entry.

"The waiters will have to die too. Interesting, that for all their prating, white Americans still use black ones as their servants. And their whores, witness Dee-Dee. Stravinsky will procure out-of-state as-sassins—three, one for each. I like the idea of three different guns, all American-made. With silencers, as in the movies. Stravinsky thinks I go too far, but the decisions are not Stravinsky's. *I—am—so—bored!!!* These American fools can't catch me, so what does it matter?"

Jesus, you supercilious bastard! You're bored! Isn't that a shame?

The entry for the twenty-ninth of March was fascinating.

"And to think I was convinced the threat was over! Now I find it isn't. How stimulating! I am wide awake, alert and intelligent, as their advertisement says. Well, Mr. Evan Pugh, Motor Mouth is go-ing to kill you differently than originally planned. The bear trap will be used, with Stravinsky doing an impersonation of Joshua Butler. The preparatory work has already been done, just in case. I have sus-pected for a long time that the blackmailer would be Mr. Evan Pugh, so the beam has been located and the bolt holes reamed out one size too small, no threads. Stravinsky has the proper tools, a strong right arm and sufficient height. You shall have your wad of money—a drop in the ocean to me! And you shall have a most painful death. Motor Mouth. So American. The bear trap is made in America too."

The entry on the fourth of April concerned Desmond Skeps.

"Dead at last, Desmond Skeps, with your perpetual whinging about Philomena, your denial of your own guilt in driving her away. A very good woman, for an American.

"I did enjoy watching him die! I despise those men who obtain sexual pleasure from the suffering of others, but I confess that I was moved to an erection at the sight of Desmond Skeps trussed like a Thanksgiving turkey, eyes and brain alive, the rest of him as dead as a dodo. I played with him, I and my tiny soldering iron. How he tried to scream! But his vocal cords weren't up to it. Just hoarse yowls. The ammonia in his veins really hurt, but the Drano at the end was inspired. What a way to go! I loved every minute of it. From the moment he told me that he'd appointed Erica as young Desmond's guardian, he had no further use. He was so enamored of her business acumen, never knowing that the acumen was mine. Bye-bye, Desmond!"

Of Erica's murder he had nothing much to say; clearly it wasn't necessary for him to dwell on her agony.

"Stravinsky broke the bitch's arms and legs one bone at a time, but she gave nothing away except the names of her Party friends in Moscow. Had she had anything more to confess, she would have. Stravinsky especially enjoyed it. We agreed that it would have to be the hired assassin Manfred Mueller—as good a name as any—who got rid of her body. I wanted it put on Delmonico's property, Stravinsky thought that a mistake. Of course I won the argument, so Mueller took the body there. My luck that the gigantic wife appeared. Not that it made much difference. Mueller got away cleanly. So, unfortunately, did the wife. A grotesque."

The entry on the sniper in the copper beech was extremely interesting; Smith was very rattled.

"I have lost my luck," he wrote. "The great Julius Caesar believed implicitly in luck, and who am I to contradict him? But the trouble with luck is not that it runs out—it doesn't. Rather, it encounters another man's luck that is stronger, and fails. As mine has. I have encountered Delmonico's luck. Now all I can do is send him in a thousand different directions at once. Manfred Mueller is willing to kill as many of Holloman's illustrious citizens as he can, and lay down his own life in the process. His price? Ten million dollars in a Swiss bank account in his wife's name. I have done it. But Stravinsky says it will not answer, and I very much fear that Stravinsky is right."

Interesting, thought Carmine. He said something like that to my face. About losing his luck because mine is stronger.

That was the last entry in the fifth book. Tired and sick, Carmine gathered his evidence together and put it in an old box he marked

ODDMENTS—1967. Then he took it to the cage and saw it put among a dozen other equally grimy boxes. Even if the faithful Stravinsky donned the uniform of a Holloman cop and came asking, he would not get it.

Stravinsky . . . A code name, it had to be a code name. The exercise books had given absolutely no hint as to who Stravinsky was. The music? No, surely not! Any bets Stravinsky is Stravinsky because Stravinsky picked the name? Or the KGB bosses? He's like Smith, KGB. And here I thought Desdemona had seen him when Erica's body was dumped. Now I learn that the sniper dumped the body. Smith always spoke of Stravinsky as an almost-equal, as someone whose opinion he respected. Stravinsky was treasured, valued too much to confide his identity to the pages of these diaries of murder.

"I always feel let down at the end of a difficult case," Carmine said to Desdemona that evening. "As usual, the end of it depends on the courts—anticlimactic, not high drama. Smith can't escape conviction, but I strongly suspect Pauline Denbigh will, and as for Stravinsky, he won't even be identified."

"You don't think he might be Purvey or Collins?" she asked.

"No, that feels wrong. This is master and apprentice, not a hierarchy."

"What will happen to Cornucopia?"

"There's only one hand strong enough to take the helm, and it belongs to Wal Grierson, who won't like it one little bit. His heart's at Dormus with the turbines, not spread across thirty different companies." Carmine shrugged. "Still, he'll do his duty—pray note that I do not include the word 'patriotic' in that! Meaningless cant, when it's trotted out endlessly."

"Your mama will come out of her conniption fit the moment she hears the villains have been caught. Though what will she hear, Carmine? How much of it will make the news?"

"Precious little. Smith will be written off as a maniac found fit to stand trial. The information in the exercise books will never be used. He'll go down on physical evidence—the razor for Dee-Dee and the killing kit for Skeps. His motive? Control of Cornucopia," said Carmine without regret.

"How can that be stretched to encompass Dee-Dee?"

"The DA will allege that she tried to blackmail him as one of her customers."

"He'll hate that! He's a shocking Puritan."

"Then let him produce a better reason for killing her. One thing for sure, he won't admit to treason. He's convinced he won't stand trial for treason."

"Do you think he will?" Desdemona asked curiously.

"I have no idea," Carmine said.

"He must be a very vain man."

"Vain in every way," Carmine said with feeling, "from his custom-made clothes to his custom-made house."

"Not to mention his custom-made sports cars." She unwound her legs. "Dinner."

"What is it tonight?"

"Saltimbocca alla Romana."

"Wow!" Carmine slipped an arm about her waist and walked with her to the kitchen.

"Myron's bringing Sophia home," she said, setting out the dishes and checking her ziti in tomato sauce. The frying pan was already sitting on the stove, the veal and its prosciutto waiting alongside a small bowl of minced fresh sage. "Fancy a sear of marsala liquor in the pan afterward?"

"Why not? Has Myron gotten over his depression?"

"The moment, I gather, you ripped him a new arsehole for making Sophia's life hard." She lit the gas under her pan, wiped it with a smear of olive oil. "Fifteen minutes and we can eat."

"I can hardly wait."

* * *

"Have you decided which one gets the lieutenancy?" asked the Commissioner.

"Sir!" cried Carmine, looking thunderstruck. "That's not my decision to make!"

"If it's not yours, whose is it, for crying out loud?"

"Yours and Danny's!"

"Crap. It's yours. Danny and I will go along."

"Sir, I can't! I honestly can't! Just when I think one guy is it, the other one comes back stronger than ever! Look at their last two cases! Abe collars the mummy fruitcake in a brilliant piece of work. Right, he's got Larry's job. Then Corey collars Phil Smith's papers in a brilliant piece of work. John, they're both so good! It's a crying shame that I have to lose one of them to another police department when he doesn't get the job. Abe is intellectual, thoughtful, sensitive, calm and precise. Corey is clever, thinks on his feet, seizes the initiative, has enough logic to pass, and copes. Different qualities and different styles, but either of them would make a much better lieutenant than Larry Pisano, and you know it. So don't go passing the buck to me, Commissioner! You're the head of this department—*you* make the decision!"

Silvestri listened solemnly, temper unruffled. When Carmine ran down he smiled, nodded, and looked insufferably smug.

"Did I tell you that I had a call from J. Edgar Hoover this morning?" he asked. "He was mighty pleased at the solution to the Cornucopia mess, and very happy to have the FBI take the credit for what was Holloman Police Department work. Well, I played along all dipshit dopey local cop, then I struck a pretty neat deal with him. I wouldn't contradict a thing, provided that he took Mickey McCosker and his team onto the FBI payroll. J. Edgar was delighted to oblige." Silvestri huffed, immensely tickled by his own crafty thinking. "Therefore, Captain Delmonico, there are *two* lieutenant's jobs going begging. One for Abe, and one for Corey. And I'll have a proper number of detectives on my payroll at last."

"I could kiss you!"

"Don't even think about it."

"You can have the honor of telling them, John."

"Any idea who you want for your own team?"

"One certainty. Your niece Delia, if she's willing to go to police academy and qualify."

Silvestri gaped. "*Delia?* Honest?"

"Dead earnest. That woman is a brilliant detective, she's wasted as a secretary," Carmine said.

"She's too old and too fat."

"Depends on her, doesn't it? If she makes it through, she makes it through. I'm betting she will—she's got all of the Silvestri guile and brains. She doesn't need to be Hercules, just capable of giving chase and tackling. If she can't cross a foaming torrent hanging onto a rope by her arms, tough shit. She comes from the academy straight onto my team."

"What about Larry's men?"

"I'll split them up. One to Abe, one to Corey. That way, we each have one experienced detective, plus one new. We'll choose our second-stringers from the applicant pool."

"It might earn Delia some enemies."

"I doubt it. The most the pool will be hoping for are two men into detectives. Instead, there'll be three."

"No one will ever believe she's a cop!" Silvestri cried.

"Ain't that the truth?"

What fantastic news! Carmine left County Services in the Fairlane, a very happy man. Summer was almost here, though it rarely became hot until after Independence Day, six weeks away.

He picked up the winding, leafy domain of Route 133 and headed for Philip Smith's property. It bore the scars of much frantic digging, he noted after he passed through the imposing gates and followed the curves of the drive to the house.

"Though," Special Agent Ted Kelly had told him, "no one's found another secret compartment. You Holloman cops scooped us. Great stuff you found!"

One of the better outcomes, Carmine reflected as he pushed the bell, was the disappearance of the FBI back to their federal play-ground. No one would be more relieved than Wal Grierson.

Natalie Smith opened the door, then put her finger to her lips and led him back down the steps to an exposed position on the grass many yards away from the nearest FBI hole.

"They have put microphones inside," she said.

"How did you know that what I have to say is better said without federal eavesdroppers?" he asked.

The impossibly blue eyes narrowed as the face smiled. "I know because you are the only one who really understands," she said, her accent far less thick. "Philip found it impossible to believe that a local policeman could spoil his plans, but I knew differently."

"The faithful Stravinsky," he said.

Her eyes widened. "Stravinsky? Who is that? The composer?"

"You, Mrs. Smith. Stravinsky can't be anyone else."

"Are you arresting me?"

"No. I have no proof."

"Then why do you say I am this Stravinsky?"

"Because your husband is a very rigid, puritanical man. He has strong feelings about women, wives, whores, the whole feminine half of the human race. Yet on the surface he seems to have aban-doned you, his wife. That, Mrs. Smith, he would never do. Therefore he knows that his wife is capable of looking after herself. As would Stravinsky. Who else can the faithful Stravinsky be, except you? Who else shares Philip's days, nights, thoughts, ideas, aspirations, plans? Who else could impersonate Joshua Butler going up the sophomore stairs at Paracelsus? And why couldn't Stravinsky get rid of Erica's body? Because he didn't have the strength. Mounting a bear trap took every ounce of it. He could hold a pillow over an old woman's face, or slip a needle into a drugged woman's vein. His appearance can be so scary that he could walk the streets of Harlem looking for professional gunmen in complete safety. You, Mrs. Smith, you! Don't bother denying it. You're a master of true disguise. You alter your appearance from inside your mind."

She stared across the lawn, red lips compressed. "So what are you going to do with Stravinsky, my dear Captain?"

"Advise him to quit the country in a hurry. Not today, but certainly tomorrow. You must have your cache—money, a weapon, travel documents. Use them!"

"But if I choose to stay with Philip, what can you do?"

"Hound you, Mrs. Smith. Perpetually hound you. Do you think, because I can stand here talking to you as if you're a human being, that I've forgotten you tried to murder my daughter? I haven't. It burns my brain like a white-hot poker. I'd give a lot to kill you, but I prize my family too much."

"You won't stop my going?"

"I can't."

"I too am KGB," she said, staring at North Rock.

"Stravinsky would have to be. I trust that fact will make you welcome in Moscow?"

"I will survive."

"So will you go?"

Her shoulders hunched. "If I can say goodbye to Philip, I will go. He would want it."

"I'm sure you'll have plenty to tell them in Moscow when they debrief you."

"You would indeed hound me," she said slowly. "Yes, you would. I will go tomorrow."

"Tell me how. I want to be sure you do."

"I will send you a telegram from Montreal. It will say, 'Stravinsky sends greetings from Montreal.' Of course I could have someone else send it, but my patriotic duties in America are at an end. KGB will want me back."

"Thank you, the telegram will be fine."

*   *   *

A sorry conclusion, but the only one, Carmine thought as he drove away. Today Stravinsky will visit the hospital to see Smith, and say her farewells. He, good KGB agent that he is, will wish her well. Any federal tape recorders will inform those who listen that the grieving wife is simply telling her husband that her psychiatrist is putting her in a private hospital for a few days, and that it's on the outskirts of Boston. She'll catch the commuter plane from Holloman to Logan, but not to leave the airport. She'll switch to the Montreal plane and be away, the faithful Stravinsky. A murdering bitch, but indeed a faithful one. That squat figure, that shapeless body, that rather terrifying face. But most of all, those spooky blue eyes. A contradiction, that's Stravinsky.

There was still time to make his last call on this nasty case, a kind of valediction his so-called insatiable curiosity made imperative. Namely, a visit to some of the inhabitants of the Cornucopia Building.

He took an elevator to the thirty-ninth floor, and found Wallace Grierson occupying Desmond Skeps's old office.

"Look what you've done!" Grierson said angrily.

"You're in a suit and tie," Carmine said mildly.

"And you don't care, do you?"

"It's not my fault. Blame Philip Smith."

"Don't worry, I do." Grierson's spurt of temper died. "I may have found a way out of my predicament, however."

"May you? Who?"

"You're quick, I'll give you that. None other than Mr. Michael Sykes."

"Ah, Michael Donald himself!" Carmine said, grinning. "He was promoted, but as Smith did the promoting, I wasn't sure the rest of the Board would—er—come to the Party."

"Ha ha, very funny! Actually Phil may have done us a big favor. Mickey turns out to be amazing."

"Mickey?"

"That's his diminutive of choice."

"It fits." Carmine held out his hand. "This is goodbye, sir. I won't be haunting your corridors anymore."

"Thank God for that!"

And why not? Carmine asked himself when the elevator came. He pressed 38, wondering which floor M. D. Sykes was occupying. Floor 38, it turned out. Richard Oakes was in the outer office and went so white when Carmine filled his gaze that he seemed likely to faint.

"Is your boss in?" Carmine asked.

"Mr. Sykes?" It came out as a squeak.

"The very one. May I see him?"

Oakes nodded, throat working. It was probably a signal to proceed, Carmine decided, and proceeded.

He found Michael Donald Sykes sitting at Erica Davenport's lacquered desk, but it was hard to associate this person with the disgruntled denizen of a managerial limbo. Sykes actually seemed to have trimmed down in size yet grown in height, and wore a well-cut suit of Italian silk, a shirt with French cuffs and gold links, and a Chubb alumnus tie. No wonder he'd resented being passed over! He had the proper credentials. Carmine felt a rush of pleasure at the thought that Sykes had triumphed.

A cardboard box sat on the desk in front of him, spilling curly wood shavings, and about a dozen two-inch-high figures, exquisitely painted, stood freed from their packing: Napoleon Bonaparte and his marshals, all on horseback.

"Mr. Sykes, I'm very glad to see you here."

"Why, thank you!" the not-so-little man exclaimed. "What do you think of my new acquisitions? I can afford to add Jena and Ulm to my battles! Aren't these gorgeous? They're made in Paris by the best militaria model maker in the world." He picked up a splendid figure wearing a leopardskin hussar's pelisse. "See? Murat, the great cavalry commander."

"Wonderful," said Carmine. He held out his hand. "This is definitely goodbye, Mr. Michael Donald Sykes."

"Don't tempt fate, Captain! Still, Cornucopia is safe now, and in excellent hands," Sykes said.

He escorted Carmine to the elevators and saw him leave, then returned to his office and sat for a moment drinking in the sight of his new goodies. Inside his desk drawer was a powerful magnifying glass with a battery-operated light; Sykes switched it on and stared through it, his blue eye huge, its white shot with scarlet veins. Murat was close to hand; he lifted the figure and turned it over, looking for any impairment, any sign that Murat had been maimed. Then he sighed, smiled, and produced a dissecting needle. It went under the edge of the satchel Murat wore and pried a section of the paint away.

"Shostakovich will be pleased," he said.